Dark Redemption

Dark Redemption

ANGIE SANDRO

New York   Boston

Copyright © 2014 by Angie Sandro

Excerpt from *Dark Paradise* copyright © 2014 by Angie Sandro

Cover design by FaceOut

Cover copyright © 2014 by Hachette Book Group, Inc.

Forever Yours

Hachette Book Group

237 Park Avenue

New York, NY 10017

hachettebookgroup.com

twitter.com/foreverromance

First ebook and print on demand edition: September 2014

Forever Yours is an imprint of Grand Central Publishing.

The Forever Yours name and logo are trademarks of Hachette Book Group, Inc.

The publisher is not responsible for websites (or their content) that are not owned by the publisher.

The Hachette Speakers Bureau provides a wide range of authors for speaking events. To find out more, go to www.hachettespeakersbureau.com or call (866) 376-6591.

ISBN 978-1-4555-5490-4 (ebook edition)

ISBN 978-1-4555-5489-8 (print on demand edition)

For Nate, Kierstan, and Maxwell. I love you.

Dark Redemption

Chapter 1

Mala

Crazy Like a Rabid Raccoon

I glance at the clock. *Crap*. We're late. Again.

I stumble down the hall and push open the door to my old bedroom. When the Acker boys moved in, I moved into Mama's old room. They have their own twin beds, but both boys startle easily. They sleep together most nights.

I shake the larger blanket-covered lump at the foot of the bed. "Jonjovi." I hiss the last syllable through my teeth, careful not to wake Axle. "Wake up."

Jonjovi sits up, rubbing his blond head. He squints in my direction, then tries to lay back down. "Aw, Mala. Just five more minutes. Please."

"We're running late."

"Didn't you set the alarm?"

"No, I forgot. Hurry and get dressed. No time for a shower. I'll drive you to the bus stop."

Jonjovi scrambles off the bed. "What about the twins?"

"Landry promised to get them on the bus."

Jonjovi's lip pokes out. I've learned how to read his skeptical expression. I also know he's right to doubt Landry's ability to get the twins to do anything they don't want to do. And right now, they're on a finishing-high-school's-bullshit kick. Daryl and Carl's grand plan is to drop out and work odd jobs like gator wrangling or taking city folk on haunted-swamp tours.

No. Come to think of it, Landry came up with the haunted-swamp bit. He figured he'd put my swamp and his ghost-seeing ability to good use by starting his own business. I shot that plan down faster than the wild turkey we ate for Thanksgiving dinner. I'm not losing all the insurance money Mama left for me 'cause some sue-happy idiot gets his arm eaten by a gator.

I sigh. "We'll worry about the twins later. Go on."

Truth is, I understand the reasoning behind the twins' quest for fast money. They want to support themselves and their little brothers. The idea of living off my insurance money rubs them the wrong way. Makes them feel less than manly. Course I'd feel the same in their position—chock-full of raging testosterone—and prickly over being beholden to someone else. But no matter how uncomfortable I may be, I always pay my debts.

What the Acker boys don't realize, and for all our sakes I hope they stay oblivious to the truth forever, is that I owe them more than I can ever repay. I let their sister die. Or rather, I didn't bring Dena back from the dead when I had the chance.

At least not completely. I trapped her in limbo during a conjuring gone wrong. *Brain dead.*

I blink back tears that well up whenever I think of Dena and lean over to gently rub Axle's back. At twelve, Jonjovi's pretty good about controlling his temper, but three years age difference is huge when it comes to the baby of the family. If Axle wakes up on the wrong side of the bed, he's liable to flip out into a total meltdown, setting the tone for the rest of the day—his first day back to school after Thanksgiving break.

"Wake-y, wake-y, it's time for eggs and bac-y…" I sing. "Time to get ready for school."

The kid buries himself under blankets. "I'm not goin'…"

"Come on, Axle."

The blanket bundle rolls across the mattress. I catch his foot before he topples off the bed and lands on his head. His social worker would be royally pissed if the kid had bruises when she checks up on him. And I'd be declared unfit for guardianship before appealing to the court.

"Kids, breakfast!" a voice booms through my paper thin walls.

Axle throws the blanket off and scampers from the bed. "Coming, Rev."

I can't control my eye roll. All of the kids respect Reverend Prince. I'm the wicked stepmother—a place filler—until they need me. Every move I make with them is wrong. I can't replace Dena in their hearts or remove the pain in their eyes, no matter how guilty I feel. The only way for their lives to return to normal is to give them their sister back, even if it's at the expense of my soul.

I make it sound easy. As if raising the dead's like baking home-made bread. Just throw the correct ingredients into a bowl, add yeast, and let the dough rise. Only everyone in these parts knows that there are more steps involved in the process of raising a zombie. I just don't know what they are. And the one woman who does know, my aunt Magnolia LaCroix, Hoodoo Queen of New Orleans, is someone I've done my best to avoid.

I sniff the air, and my mouth waters. Bacon, even burned and extra-crispy, smells heavenly. If I want breakfast, I have to hurry. I check to be sure the boys are at the kitchen table, then grab a change of clothes and run into the bathroom. The bus will be at the crossroad in twenty minutes. After a two-minute shower to wash off the filmy sweaty layer coating my skin, I pull on clean panties and then try to stuff myself into my tight jeans. They won't button.

Freaking Reverend Prince and his homemade pie experiments. The man can't cook worth a damn because his wife took care of the kitchen duties for twenty-five years, but bless his heart, he takes his duties seriously. He promised to help me care for the Acker kids and do all the housework while he stayed with me. It makes for a crowded house. It's been almost impossible for Landry and me to find any private time. The rev takes offense to any impropriety or allusion to sex outside of marriage. He'd shit a brick and then stone us with it if he ever caught wind of our midnight trysts in the toolshed.

The image of a naked Landry going down on me flashes before my eyes, and my heart rate speeds. The muscles down low clench. Sweat breaks out. I fan myself, not wanting to get all hot and bothered right after freshening up, but that man sets me on fire with nothing but a smoldering glance or the quirk of his dimpled smile. Guess that's the inherent power of true love. Really steamy sex. Ha.

A firm knock on the bathroom door startles a high-pitched, guilty squeak out of me.

Reverend Prince yells, "Mala, open up. Your food's getting cold."

My face flames hotter. I swallow hard, not trusting myself to sound normal. I crack open the door, only to have a plate shoved through the crack. I grab it from the rev's hands with a muttered "Thanks," and close the door.

The greasy eggs slide across the plate as I set it on the counter, and my stomach gurgles. I take several deep breaths, eying the toilet. The kids like to leave floaters. Every so often, Axle will call me into the bathroom to show off a particularly large specimen. Once he even had one in fluorescent green. I think the culprit was a heaping bowl of Apple Jacks, but really, I've got no idea what he ate to turn his poop that color. Those boys just aren't right in the head.

My stomach settles after a few deep breaths. Happiness over not puking up my guts gives me the courage to tackle the important matter I've put off for over a week. With shaking hands, I pull the brown paper bag out of my jumbo-size bag of sanitary napkins—the one place none of my male houseguests would touch. The directions on the test say to pee on the stick first thing in the morning. It takes a couple of minutes for my bladder to relax, and all the while, those damn individually wrapped maxi pads seem to mock me. It's been almost two months since I bought them, and if I'm really unlucky, those pads will survive for another eight unbloodied months.

My toes curl on the cold floor. *Barefoot and pregnant. My life's a cliché.*

Pee splashes on my fingers.

No! Everything will be fine. Landry and I used protection. I put the condoms on him myself, except that *one* time. But I'm also on birth control. So what if my tender breasts, weight gain, and nausea are all symptoms of pregnancy. When put together, they could mean many things.

Another hard knock rattles the door, and I almost drop the test stick into the toilet. "What now?" I yell, studying the white center of the test stick. Is that a…no, it's too soon. *Oh hell.* Are those two faint lines? Are two lines good or bad?

Bang, bang, bang.

"I'm coming!" *Damn it!* I flush the toilet. "Hold on."

I stuff the test stick back into the bag of napkins, wash my hands, then grab a rubber band and wrap it around the buttons on my jeans to hold them together.

I'm breathing hard by the time I finish pulling on a baggy, purple sweatshirt, about ready to blow up. Whoever's outside better have a damn good reason for disturbing me. The boys know they should keep away when I'm in here. I fling open the door. "What?"

"We've got trouble," Carl says. The look on his face sends a chill down my spine.

It doesn't take but a second to figure out what's wrong with this picture. I press my hand against my rolling stomach. "Oh no. Not again…"

Daryl strides down the hall. "We've searched everywhere we can think of at our place. Landry's gone."

Great! My maybe-baby's daddy has wandered off in his sleep again. Pray to God he hasn't walked into the swamp. "Keep your voice down," I whisper, rising on tiptoes and craning my neck to see over Daryl's shoulder into the kitchen. Reverend Prince continues to spoon scrambled eggs onto the plates in front of Axle and Jonjovi.

Landry will kill me if his dad finds out he's sleepwalking. He's been very, very determined to keep his affliction secret, no matter how much I argue the need for honesty.

I grab the twins by their arms and drag them toward the front door. "Do you swear this is a legit walkabout? You're not trying to scam me into letting you stay home from school, right?"

The twins tag-team the promise, fingers crossing their hearts. Their identical blue eyes widen with barely checked panic. "No…" Carl begins.

"…way," Daryl finishes. "He was missing when we woke up this morning. We searched the whole property. Even the…the…lodge where we found him the last time."

My stomach twists at the memory of Landry asleep beside the bloodstain on the floor. Vomit burns the back of my throat. I swallow the sourness down. No time to puke.

I lean my head against the cool wall, then push off. "Okay, the rev will drive you to the bus stop. I'll search for Landry. He can't be far."

"But you'll need help," Carl says.

"You're going to school, Carl Acker." I stab the end of my finger at his chest. "No excuses. You're a minor and legally bound to attend classes. I know you think getting a job will better your situation, but you're gonna screw yourselves into getting the government involved. Social Services will snatch Axle and Jonjovi and put them in foster homes if you act up."

"No, I'm staying with you," Axle wails, running into the room. He throws his arms around my waist, almost knocking me over. I curse under my breath as Jonjovi slowly follows him into the room. *How did this happen?*

"You were yelling," Reverend Prince says, answering the question I didn't know I had asked aloud from the kitchen. He doesn't even stop washing dishes to come into the living room. When did this become my normal life? The kids look scared, and I feel like shit for making them feel this way. Which pisses me off even more. My emotions are topsy-turvy, spinning all over the place like a damn Tilt-A-Whirl. And I can't control them.

"I'm sorry. It's just that I can't lose you guys." Tears sting my eyes. "I swore to Dena that I'd protect you. Don't make me into a liar."

A knock on the front door sends a wave of relief coursing through my body. *Landry's back.*

Carl echoes my grin and throws open the door. "Where have you been? *Oh no…*"

I'm moving before I fully have time to process what I'm going to do. Instinct has me yanking Carl behind me while grabbing a baseball bat from the umbrella stand at the same time. I raise it over my head, ready to defend the kids from whatever danger stands on my doorstep.

The older woman slaps the bat aside with her clipboard. Her piercing scream sends the chickens scurrying across the yard. My heart falls into my stomach and lands in a lump of "Oh, shit."

I've screwed up. Big time. How am I going to fix this? Excuses run through my head. I'm frozen with them. The kids' social worker is halfway across the porch, heading toward the sheriff's deputy standing at the base of the stairs.

Deputy George Dubois shoves his gun back into the holster when he realizes the only danger is me making an ass out of myself. He grabs the woman by the arm. "Everything's okay, Mrs. Moulton." He fixes a hard glare at me. "Mala Jean?"

I stumble across the porch. The twins huddle at my back, whispering. Axle peeks his head around the door. Reverend Prince takes matters into his own hands by bypassing the kids and heading toward the social worker who cowers behind George.

"Genève Moulton, what an unexpected surprise." He grins his infamous congregation-worthy smile and holds out his hand. "What has it been? Ten years?"

The woman steps around George to take it. Her firm, no-nonsense pump and release of his hand reasserts her sense of authority. "Why, Reverend Prince, it is indeed a pleasure to see you again. I imagine it's closer to fifteen. My husband and I now live in Lafayette and attend services there. The Acker case was transferred to me yesterday, and I thought a visit would be appropriate."

"Ah, so you're here on official duties."

Her smile could crack ice. "I admit to being curious about Ms. LaCroix's application for guardianship. And your involvement with this family seems *unusual*." Her eyes practically glitter with curiosity. She waves toward George. "I never imagined I'd be greeted so violently on a routine home inspection. I'm certainly grateful that Deputy Dubois arrived right after I did."

George shuffles his feet. "I'm here on official business…"

My eyes widen, and I wave for him to *shut up*! She's going to assume someone called the cops on us for being disorderly. "Deputy Dubois isn't here *officially*, officially. He's my brother. Right, Georgie?"

"I'm not your brother."

"Adopted…"

My cowardly, nonblood-related, older brother raises his hands and steps back. I'm on my own. Start with an apology. "I'm sorry, Mrs. Moulton. This is all a huge misunderstanding. I thought…I didn't exp—"

Her glare stuffs the words back down my throat. Her wrinkles perform a gremlin act, multiplying across her forehead to form a scowl. "I assume you are Malaise Jean Marie LaCroix? The *girl* who filed to be the Acker children's guardian?"

I nod, trying to speak over the lump forming in my throat. I wipe my sweaty palm on my jeans before holding out my hand for her to shake. She stares at it with a moue of distaste, and I let it drop. Her eyes scan the kids clumped around me.

"And you older boys must be Carl and Daryl."

The twins exchange a raised-eyebrow grimace. Daryl speaks for them. "Yes, ma'am. I'm Daryl and he's Carl."

Mrs. Moulton taps her long nails against her lips. "Which means you're Jonjovi and Axle Rose." She glances back at Reverend Prince. "Is there a specific reason why the boys aren't going to school today?"

"The bus…" I glance at my watch and then clap my hands. "We still have ten minutes. Everyone grab your backpacks. Let's move."

The kids scramble back into the house like rats after chicken feed. I leave Mrs. Moulton in the capable hands of Reverend Prince. She probably hates me now. Anything I say will only make my situation worse. I hope he can explain why I almost brained her with a baseball bat. After all the attacks I've been through the last couple of months, I have a react-first, think-later kind of mentality. Which is not helpful now that all of my enemies are dead, in jail, or locked in a mental hospital.

George follows me into the kitchen. He stands beside the table while I hand out bagged lunches. "I really am here on official business, Mala," he yells over the chattering kids. "I have a case I want to talk to you about. A murder…"

I cover Axle's ears. "Not in front of the little ones, Georgie. 'Sides, I can barely hear myself think. Unless it's an emergency, it can wait until after you drive the kids to the bus stop."

"Me, drive?"

"I need to stay here and take care of Mrs. Moulton. Somehow convince her I'll be a fit guardian for the boys."

"Yeah, you totally screwed that up," Carl says with a snicker.

Daryl snorts. "Idiot."

"Brats, get to school." I swipe at them with a lunch bag.

A clearing throat spins me around. Reverend Prince and Mrs. Moulton are standing in the living room, and once again I want to crawl through the floor. George takes pity on the disaster that has become my daily life and helps to hustle the kids outside. Of course, they freak out over riding in his patrol car. Axle talks him into turning on the siren, and they ride off down the driveway accompanied by blaring wails.

I spend another minute contemplating whether to run for it. The only reason why the kids were placed in my home while they did the Kinship Placement assessment is because Reverend Prince is friends with someone in authority at the Department of Children and Family Services. He convinced them that the kids had been through enough trauma and that keeping them together in the same community would help them heal. Besides, at fifteen, the twins would just run away from a foster home.

As first impressions go, this is the worst. I already had my age, lack of a degree, and current unemployment as a deterrent to being found suitable. Not to mention my stint in a mental institution. *Gah*. When considered on paper, even I wouldn't find myself a suitable parental figure. I rub my belly, silently apologizing to the pea-size embryo that may have taken up residence in my uterus.

Mrs. Moulton and Reverend Prince exit the house. "So Axle and Jonjovi sleep in the second bedroom. Where are the twins staying?" she asks.

I answer her question. *Can't keep being a coward.* "They're staying at their own house with my boyfriend, Landry."

Reverend Prince cuts in. "As you've pointed out, Mala's home is too small for seven people. My son, Landry, is of age. He and the twins are doing some home renovations. Once those are complete and Landry and Mala walk down the aisle, we'll all move into the Big House."

Walk down the aisle? I avert my gaze before Mrs. Moulton can read my shock. Why am I so surprised? Reverend Prince hasn't exactly been subtle about his "no sex before marriage" rule. And living in the same house before we're hitched is definitely out. It's just that I only turned twenty-one a couple of weeks ago. I deferred this semester because I wanted to devote all of my time to the kids' adjustment to being in my care, which means I've still got a whole year before I'll earn my Associate Degree in Criminal Justice. It's like the universe deliberately keeps side-lining my educational goals. And marriage, well, it's just another trap to delay me. I'm too young to be saddled with the responsibility of being a wife.

And I'm sure as hell too young to be pregnant.

Tears fill my eyes again, and I dash them away. *Damn hormones.* Mrs. Moulton asks for a tour of the rest of the property. She takes notes on everything, searching for potential dangers to the kids. Rightly so. Only it still sticks in my craw when she points at the rusted nails poking out of the boards of the chicken coup. If she'd seen the Acker place before Landry started fixing it up, she'd think the kids had found paradise. Pure heaven on earth.

I scowl at the dangling chain on the chicken coop. One of the kids forgot to lock it. I pull open the door and freeze so suddenly that Mrs. Moulton crashes into my back. I spin around, shoving her back with one hand while slamming the door with the other. My hands tremble as I fumble for the chain, slipping the lock through the links one-handed while the door shakes from the body smashing against it, over and over.

Then stops. I press my ear to the door, listening. The quiet is even more unnerving than the initial violence.

"Ms. LaCroix?" Mrs. Moulton's voice in my ear totally freaks me out.

I let out a shrill screech, which Mrs. Moulton echoes. Her clipboard rises, and I wave her down. "We're okay." I lean against the door, pressing my hand to my throbbing heart. The clipboard drops. "I'm sorry, but I can't let you in there."

Her scowl returns. "Why not? What's in there?"

Why? Why? "A, uh, r-rabid raccoon got into the chicken coop. It's not safe. Or a sight you need to see. I'll call someone out to put it down." I swallow hard, working to push back the bile burning my throat. Nausea causes me to break out in a cold sweat. Maybe I look as sick as I feel because Mrs. Moulton steps back right before I vomit into the bucket of chickenfeed beside the door.

The woman doesn't show any compassion. She hightails it back to the house. I hunker before the door with my eyes squeezed shut, too scared to open them again and see what is already branded crimson in my mind.

A naked Landry lying on the ground, covered in bloody feathers, while hugging a half-eaten hen to his bare chest.

Chapter 2

Landry

Tastes Like Chicken

My sister crouches beside me in the thick grass. Her long black hair tangles around a face so emaciated, it looks like she's been hitting a crank pipe in the afterlife. Not that drugs should affect Lainey at all since she's dead for almost six months. This must be a dream. Which explains the whole me not feeling at all ashamed about my big sis seeing my dinky waving in the wind for the first time since we ran around the backyard naked as kids.

Terror fills me to the brim and leaks out to form pools of cold sweat on my bare skin. Each breath burns in my chest, coming shallower and shallower. The bushes to my left rustle…low to the ground. Leaves crinkle beneath a heavy, slithering form.

Words claw their way from my tightening throat. "No, not again."

Lainey spins on her toes, facing me. She presses her hand against my mouth and lifts a finger to her lips, shushing me. Yeah, stupid. Now *it* knows exactly where we're hiding. We've been lucky to stay under its radar for so long. Big sis used some mad mojo to put up a mystical retaining wall of sorts around us. It kept the demon contained in a corner of my mind, but like an idiot, I punched a hole in the barrier when I let the thing out to fight Red. At the time, I didn't think I had a choice. I couldn't fight him and Clarice on my own. And Dena…well, I wasn't really thinking straight after she got shot.

I squeeze my eye shut.

Lainey punches my shoulder. "Come on, baby bro. Don't fade on me again. I need your help."

A vein throbs in my forehead. "Mala thinks you're a product of my subconscious. Not real, but a manifestation of the part of me trying to fight the demon."

"I'm real enough to save your scrawny butt," Lainey says with a grimace. Her gaze darts to the bushes again. I think they represent the barrier in my head. It's pretty realistic. Hell, this whole dream is.

"You're not dreaming, Landry. The demon's taking a ride in your skin. It's in control, and you're too much of a chicken to come out of hiding to see what it's doing. You let it free. If it kills, it's your fault."

Lainey's right. I tried not sleeping, but it didn't matter. With exhaustion comes the lowering of my resistance. I couldn't escape, and now I'm cowering in this fake forest so I don't have to acknowledge the truth of all the horrible things it does when it takes over my body at night. Denial is the only way I can preserve my already strained sanity. I'm not ready to face the inevitable, and so far, I haven't hurt anyone.

I need to leave before that changes, but I just want a little more time. That's not too much to ask for, is it? Time to say my good-byes.

Lainey takes my hand and squeezes. *She feels so real.* "Leaving is the right choice. I can't draw it back inside your mind for much longer. My protection as your ancestral guardian extends only so far. I'm sorry, baby bro. You need help from someone more powerful than I am." She gives a sad grin. "But I have the juice to shove it in deep, one last time."

By shove it in, she means it's *here.*

I lunge backward, but Lainey's hand wraps around mine. Her grip is so tight that my bones grind together. She keeps me from running away. 'Cause it sure isn't pride making me hold my ground when the smooth skin of the giant snake rubs across my ankles. Its head, followed by its thick body, twines around my torso. My hand tightens around my sister's. Goose bumps rise on my arms, and despite telling myself I need to relax, I tense up when its dry, musty smell hits my nose.

God, I hate snakes. My breath hitches in my chest, but I grab hold of myself. I fight my gag reflex and open my mouth, letting my jaw stretch wider than humanly possible. The huge snake's head shoves past my lips to slide across my tongue. Its scales tickle the roof of my mouth, then the back of my throat.

* * *

I've got gas. Not the explosive kind, but the type that settles in my intestines and presses against my internal organs until my guts are about to burst. My skin itches. Something feathery brushes the tip of my nose. It tickles. I blow out a heavy breath, then inhale the sharp, coppery scent of blood and the acrid stench of chicken shit. Uncontrolled sobs filter in next, sending a full-bodied shiver through my body. I'm fully awake now and afraid to open my eye—to confirm what I already know.

I'm not in my bed at the Acker's house.

And Mala's crying.

Whatever the demon snake did while walking around in my skin is worse than anything it has done before if it broke Mala. I crack open my eyelid and wince at the shaft of sunlight shining through the opening door. A shadow hunches against the door frame. My body aches as if I'm suffering from the flu. Tight muscles protest when I sit up. A weight falls from my arms, and I stare in horror at the headless chicken on my lap. The yell comes from deep inside, bursting out. I fling the carcass across the shed and scramble on hands and knees toward the door.

Mala looks up when I reach her. She flinches from my bloody hand. The horror in her eyes stops me from moving closer.

"Mala," I whisper.

"You a-ate Tabitha." She wipes her eyes with the back of her hands, sniffing. "S-she was my b-best laying hen."

"Are you okay?"

"Do I look okay?" she wails.

"I'm sorry…"

"It's not your fault. I don't blame you. It's just…" Her dark-eyed gaze scans the inside of the chicken coop. "This is beyond…I'm so scared, Landry. You've never traveled so far while unconscious. Never k-killed before. That *thing* inside you is getting stronger, and we can't hold off any longer. I think it's time to call Magnolia."

I've been holding my breath, knowing, yet dreading what Mala would say. Air seeps from my lungs as a resigned sigh. "Call her," I say.

Mala bites her lip and nods. "I'll tell her about Dena too. Better to kill two birds with one stone. No pun intended." Her smile looks forced. She's doing her best to comfort me. I'd rather hear her cussing me out than this false cheer. It's fucking creepy.

"We've got other nonmagical problems," she says.

"What does that mean?"

"The kids' DCFS social worker thinks a rabid raccoon is in here. We don't have much time. I've got to go head her off before she gets your dad and Georgie all worked up and they come back with a gun. I can't explain this"—she waves her hand over me—"away. Especially since I almost hit her in the head with a baseball bat."

Social worker, bat, Georgie Porgie…Damn, what a shitty morning. I focus on the thing I can sort of control. "Why is Deputy Dawg here?"

Mala shrugs and pushes to her feet. She wavers a moment, eyes closing. I jump up, lightly touching her shoulder in case she passes out. Which appears to be a distinct possibility given how ashen her skin looks.

Her hand trembles when she pushes mine away. "I'm okay."

Hurt burns in my chest and I step back, crossing my arms across my sticky chest.

Mala peeks at me through one eye. "Don't get your undies all twisted. I'm not pushing you away because I don't love you, but because I don't want my clothes to get bloody. I'll get rid of everyone as fast as I can. Don't come out until it's safe. The last thing we need is for one of them to see you like this."

I glance down. *Naked and covered in blood.* Yeah, yeah. Got it. I look like I stepped out of a slasher flick. Still, Mala didn't answer the question about George, and I don't have time to ask again because, by the time I look up, she's already jogging toward the house with her head down and her shoulders slumped.

Another few minutes pass with me flicking off dried flecks of blood from my skin before a mass exodus occurs at the house. Dad escorts the woman who must be the kids' social worker to a tan sedan. They both climb inside, and the car backs down the driveway. Mala and George stand on the porch arguing, from the way they're gesturing, and…Oh shit! They're heading in my direction. The small wooden chicken coop has only the one exit. There's no way for me to get out without them seeing my naked ass running for the woods.

Mala's high-pitched voice echoes. "It's okay. I can handle this."

"A rabid animal is no joke."

"But it is a joke, really. Georgie…stop."

I peek around the corner. Mala holds on to George by the arm, keeping him from walking forward unless he wants to drag her. I duck behind the door and scrunch down. If he just sticks his head in, he might not see me.

Yeah, right. Who am I kidding? I'm so screwed.

I can already picture George's reaction when he sees me. *"You're dangerous, Landry. A rabid dog, and I'm putting you down."* Pow. Head shot.

Mala is talking fast, and probably looking sexy as hell, to convince him she lied about the rabid raccoon so the woman wouldn't inspect the chicken coop. I'd be impressed by her skills if I wasn't worried. "Mrs. Moulton already dinged me in her notebook about a rusty nail," she says. "Can you imagine what she'd say if she saw I haven't cleaned the coop for days? I know it's wrong to lie, but I was desperate. I screwed up earlier."

"What were you thinking to come at her with a baseball bat?"

"Obviously I wasn't thinking." *Uh-oh, George's gone and pissed her off. Dumbass.*

I stare through a crack in the siding. They stand face-to-face, glaring at each other. George in his tan uniform with his shiny star winking in the morning light. Mala with her arms crossed and foot tapping. If he knows her like I do, George will be able to tell she's lying by the way she refuses to meet his eyes

He throws his hands in the air. "Fine, whatever. We've wasted too much time anyway. I didn't come to babysit the kids or get involved in your personal drama."

"Why are you here then?"

"I need your help."

"Are you kidding?" She sounds as skeptical as I feel about George's sincerity. What's he up to now? I want to go out there and confront him. I even stand up, then remember, yeah, I'm fucking naked. And covered in blood.

"There's been a murder. A hiker found the body of a teenage boy in the woods. He's been torn to pieces. Like an animal ripped into him, but the bites were made by human teeth."

My stomach clenches.

"And…why come to *me*?" Her voice only breaks on the one word, but I know the same thoughts running through my head are going through hers. I stare down at my bloody fingernails and clench them into fists. My heart races. There's nothing but a foggy cloud in my head when I try to think back to what I did while possessed. I purposely kept myself from seeing what the creature did for this reason. I didn't want the memory of hurting someone to be stuck in my head. Except now I need to know. Is it possible? Did I…

I swallow. Wrong move. A metallic taste coats my tongue and I gag. George said teeth. Human teeth. It takes everything I have not to run the tip of my tongue over mine. *No. No. No. This can't be happening.*

"Once upon a time you would be asking all kinds of questions about the crime scene. You'd ask who the kid is, his age, how he was murdered. Whether I had any suspects lined up." George pauses, and I hold my breath. "Aren't you curious?"

"Yes," Mala says, choking on the word. "Yes, I'm curious. But why come to me? Sheriff Keyes already said I wouldn't be able work for the sheriff's office unless I pass a psych test, and we both know that's gonna be tough since I've spent time in a mental hospital."

"But you're not insane. You see ghosts."

"Like anyone at the sheriff's office—other than you—will believe me if I tell them 'I see dead people.' I haven't even told Bessie my secret."

"Maybe you should." He touches her arm, and my gut clenches. "Prove to her that you're telling the truth. Just like you did with me."

"'Cause that confession went over so well," she drawls. "Mr. Acker almost killed me."

"So you're giving up on your dream?"

"Not giving up," she says slowly. "I'm evaluating my possibilities. It's not just me anymore. There are the kids, Reverend Prince, and Landry. I've got a family to support. I can't be selfish and foolishly follow a dream that may not come true. 'Sides, dreams change."

"Exactly my point."

"Huh?"

Man, I really wish they'd take this conversation inside. As much as I don't want him talking her into anything crazy, I'm even more anxious to get out of this chicken coop and take a shower. My skin itches. And I can't stop thinking that it's that dead kid's blood. That I killed him. Ate him.

What if a finger is in my stomach? The DNA evidence slowly being digested. I swallow the chunks trying to crawl up my throat. Puking will make too much noise.

"You want me to do *what*?" Mala shrieks, and I almost fall on my ass. I roll onto my knees to peer through the crack. My girl has a curl wrapped around her finger, and she looks like she's trying to rip it from her scalp. She spins on her heel and stalks toward the house, yelling over her shoulder, "Everyone thinks I'm crazy, but Deputy Dubois, you've lost your ever-loving mind."

Oh, crap! What'd I miss?

Chapter 3

Mala

Ghost Detective

My feet move fast, but not nearly as quickly as my brain, which is racing to process what George just proposed. The idea of actually doing what he asked makes my stomach roll.

"Ridiculous!" I mutter, throwing a glare over my shoulder. It's crazy—a death wish of an idea. A ginormous, squishy ball of *stupid*. Yet part of me, the obviously insane-ain't-got-no-brain part, thinks this might be the perfect test of my skills.

"Mala, wait!" George yells, running after me.

I pick up speed, only to trip over a stick. George catches my arm before I fall flat on my face in a mud puddle and embarrass myself further.

I jerk my arm free and spin around. "Let me get this straight, be-cause I swear I didn't hear right." My finger stabs at the bulletproof vest under his shirt. "You want me to go with you to the crime scene and *ask* the murder victim who killed him?"

George's green eyes sparkle as a smile lights up his face. "Yeah, isn't it brilliant?"

"Brilliant's the last word I'd use." *Potentially suicidal, maybe.*

"Why?" He places his hands on his duty belt and rocks back on the heels of his black tactical boots. I clench my fists to avoid giving in to the temptation to shove his ass into the puddle he saved me from. Maybe he sees the glitter of intent in my eyes because he steps back before continuing. "I've been thinking of ways for you to use your abilities ever since I found out." He rubs his hands together like Dr. Frankenstein dreaming up how to raise his mad monster from the dead. "Can you imagine how many murder cases could be solved by asking the victims who killed them? You could be famous."

My mouth drops, then shuts with an audible snap. "Saints, Georgie. Mama died from her infamy. My gift isn't something I want broadcasted all over town, much less the world."

"Okay, scratch being famous."

"You're totally missing my point."

"No, I got it. Keep my ghost informant a secret." He pretends to lock his lips and throws the imaginary key over his shoulder.

He's wearing his stubborn expression. How do I talk him out of this plan when the more I think about it, the more appealing the idea becomes? One of us has to use good judgment. And since I'm the one at risk, it should be me.

"Look, it's great that you want to use me to help solve cases. But there are hidden variables to consider. For one, there's no guarantee this spirit's still lingering or if it'll even be able to communicate. Also, do you have any idea how crazy some ghosts get after they die? How powerful and strong? How scary they look?" Goose bumps rise on my arms. "Remember how Lainey and Acker tried to kill me? The ones who die by violence…the trauma drives them insane."

My breath hitches as I force the words past the fear tightening my throat. My voice sounds hollow in my ears. He has to understand the magnitude of risk involved in what he's asking. "Most of the time, the ghosts can't speak outright. Like Lainey, they burrow into my dreams and show me visions of horrible things. I experience their pain, feel their fear, read their last thoughts before dying. It's horrible. And the worst part is…I can't get rid of them. They haunt me until I do what they want."

"Then do what he'll want you to do. Help me find his murderer." George's hand lifts but I step out of reach. His voice softens. "I know you're afraid, but think about the victim. He would've been in the same grade as the twins. They probably knew him."

Low blow, Georgie. He knows how to manipulate me since we've known each other forever. It's not hard for him to cloud my judgment. But I can't let him. The decision is too important. If I do this, deliberately use my gifts, I could really help someone. On purpose. My choice, unlike the times I did it only to survive or got guilt-tripped into it.

I helped Ms. Anne find her daughter's ring. Because of me she moved on. Gloria Pearson disappeared after Red and Clarice got arrested. They never found her or Rathbone's bodies, but she's now at peace. I hope. If I take this step into the supernatural realm, I can never go back. I can never have a normal life.

I gnaw on the end of a ragged fingernail. The manicure I got in New Orleans didn't last through falling into the tomb and raising a zombie. My life hasn't been normal for months. It's time to accept this fact. "I'll go," I say before I change my mind.

Yes, this might be the worst decision—ever. But after all the horrible things that have happened, I'd like to use my abilities for good and not evil for once. 'Sides, Landry's still barricaded in the chicken coop. I need to get George out of here. Fast. And in truth, I'm a bit relieved about moving "call Magnolia" and "check pregnancy test" to the very bottom of my to-do list.

"What did you say?" George asks.

"I said it's time to do some ghost-busting."

"You're not funny," George says shaking his head, but he's smiling. He has a bounce in his step when he walks, while I drag my feet. I wish Landry was coming. I haven't had to deal with a ghost solo since he woke up with the power to see the dead.

"Should I change clothes? I'm kind of ratty." I bite my lip, staring down at my white rain boots. "I have a pair of dress slacks and a nice shirt in the closet. How do you plan on justifying bringing a civilian to the crime scene to your superiors anyway?"

"You don't want to wear nice clothes where we're going."

"Oh?" I follow him to the patrol car.

"The crime scene has already been processed. We'll be the only ones there." George opens the passenger door.

I slide in and buckle up, waiting for him to get in and start the car before asking, "When was the body discovered?"

"Yesterday." He gives me a tight smile as he pulls down the driveway. "You know, I'm surprised you agreed to come with me. I thought I'd have to go down on my knees and beg for your help."

"Ha, coyness doesn't suit you, Deputy Dubois. You said exactly what I needed to hear to convince me." I laugh, shaking my head. "I'm so predictable."

"Not lately. I can't seem to figure you out anymore."

I twist to study his face. "Is that a good or bad thing? 'Cause, let's face it, I used to be boring as hell. All I cared about was school and work. But lately"—I sigh—"half the time it feels like I'm running around like a bull in a china cabinet. My life feels out of my control, and I hate it—and to be honest, kind of love it."

"Never a dull moment?"

"Boy, ain't that the truth."

"And it's bull in a china shop." He grins and continues, "But you still want to be a detective?"

"I do, but I also have to be realistic about what I can accomplish given my situation." I wave away my words. "Enough. I'm starting to get depressed. Tell me about the crime scene. What exactly am I walking into? You said a teenage boy's body was found?"

"Yeah, but I kind of exaggerated the body part." George bites down on the tip of his thumb nail, then grimaces. He returns the hand to the steering wheel, making me a lot more comfortable. He blows out a gust of air. "Sorry for being evasive. You know I've got a problem with dead bodies, which is crazy given my line of work. At least Lainey was intact."

Oh… "And the kid wasn't?"

"Yeah, I didn't want to freak you out by divulging the whole situation upfront." His lips twist, and he swallows hard. "Pieces of the victim were found scattered across Old Lick Road—an undamaged right hand, severed at the wrist, and the index and pinky fingers ripped from the missing left hand. The fingerprints were matched to a local missing teen, Dylan Monti."

I swallow as hard as George did. "What about the rest?"

"We haven't found the rest of him yet."

"Earlier you mentioned there were signs he'd been eaten?"

"Teeth marks were found on the recovered parts. Mala, this is the fourth missing boy in the last month."

I stiffen as the implications settle in. "What the hell, George? Why haven't I heard anything about this before?"

"Sheriff Keyes decided to keep the news out of the media. Can you imagine the panic if it got out that someone's kidnapping and eating kids?"

"God, yes! I've got kids. Four boys I'm responsible for keeping safe." And maybe another on the way if the stupid condom broke. Shit! Landry and I could be having a baby…a child we'd protect with our lives. But the world's a dangerous place. I swear I just felt a hair turn gray from this news. How do parents survive knowing some unforeseen danger could be lurking down the block, yet still allow their kids to walk out the door without them? "What justification did Sheriff Keyes give for covering this up?"

"There wasn't any evidence that the missing boys were anything other than runaways. We have teens taking off to the bigger cities all the time. Nobody expected foul play in Paradise Pointe. And we still don't know if the other boys' disappearances are related."

"But *you* think they are, or you wouldn't have mentioned them."

He gives me a frustrated grimace. "If those boys are dead, then there's a serial killer on the loose. Help me prove it so I can call in the FBI."

The word *serial killer* scares the hell out of me. *Craptastic.* I don't want anything to do with some Hannibal Lecter or Jeffrey Dahmer wannabe. Bad enough I've got Magnolia wanting a kid from me and

Landry, which makes me highly suspicious of the whole pregnancy thing. Since I know we used protection…*Stop! Focus, Mala.*

These thoughts…so not helpful. I've got to contact the ghost of the traumatized kid soon. He would've been terrified. *God, please don't let me relive his death.*

I brush away the tears filling my eyes. I can do this. I'm stronger than I was when dealing with Lainey and Acker. *I'll be okay.*

The storm predicted this morning has rolled in from the southeast, darkening the sky to the same pissed-off gray that Landry's eye would get if he knew what I was about to do. Fingers crossed that the rain holds off until we search the crime scene. Now I know why I didn't need to change out of my grungy clothes.

Old Lick Road borders Bayou du Sang, which meanders through a boggy wooded area so dank and impenetrable that I wouldn't be surprised if Bigfoot has taken refuge inside. The undeveloped land has a darkness about it. A miasma seeps out of the earth, like the land is alive and filled with hate.

"Who was the hiker?" I ask. "Why was he even there? Everyone avoids Old Lick."

George shrugs. "The hiker's a she—a professor from New Orleans conducting research. Apparently, Old Lick is a botanical treasure trove for homeopathic medicinal research."

"Do you even understand what you just spouted?"

George laughs. "Not at first. I gave you the *Botany for Dummies* version. I was too embarrassed to ask her to idiotproof it even more. The gist is that she was out searching for plants that might have medicinal uses. She had a whole bag full of twigs and berries."

"She stayed that long? Didn't she feel *it*?" I rub my tingling arms.

George shrugs. "My guess is she ignored her unease. Not many people pay attention when their spidey sense tingles. I bet she will in the future. She got quite a shock finding those body parts."

We spend the rest of the drive chatting, but really we are lost in our own thoughts. It has a déjà vu feel. I always think that if I had a crystal ball to see my future, I never would've pulled Lainey from the bayou. Now I'm not so sure. I kind of like my life. Yeah, there are some horrible parts, like Mama and Dena, but I've got a family. I'm not alone.

Saints, I'm a selfish witch.

When we drive past the cemetery gates, I close my eyes so I don't inadvertently make eye contact with one of the spirits. I concentrate on forming a shield over my thoughts. I'm not that great at holding it for extended periods of time yet. But it helps in situations like this. The shield blocks whatever psychic wavelength the ghosts tap into to contact me.

George parks at the entrance to Old Lick. It's a single-lane road. Potholes and broken chunks of asphalt litter the roadway. I follow George out of the car, breathing in air thick and heavy with moisture, while he pops the trunk and pulls out a raincoat for himself and an extra poncho for me. "In case the storm hits."

"Thanks," I say, giving the steadily darkening sky the evil eye and wrapping the poncho's sleeves around my waist. "How far in do we have to hike?"

"About half a mile to the crime scene. Are you ready for this?"

"Yeah, but I'm glad we don't have far to go. I'm already getting the willies." I hold out my arms so he can see the raised hairs and then follow him as he sets off at a brisk pace. "So, have you heard the old stories about this place?"

"I never believed in ghost stories," he says with a sideways grin. "At least until you. Wasn't there a massacre out in the woods somewhere?"

"Ha! Try multiple. The first happened back in the 1700s. Local legend says the massacre occurred during the war between the Chitimacha Tribe and the French, but nobody bothered to write down the exact story. A skirmish supposedly happened here during the War of 1812. And in 1918, a black family from Mississippi settled here. The parents and their four children were found murdered in their beds. No witnesses. After that, everyone decided the land was good and cursed. It reverted to the town. A lot of innocent blood stains this ground."

"How do you know all this?"

My face heats, and I duck my head. "I've taken to researching all the areas in the parish where there may be ghosts, so I can avoid them. You owe me an expensive dinner at Jacques for agreeing to this."

"How about a dinner party?"

I quirk an eyebrow.

"Aunt March's birthday party is Wednesday night. You should've received the invitation weeks ago, but you never RSVP'd. She asked me to follow up."

"I never received anything in the mail."

He gives me a long look, then shrugs. "Maybe it never arrived."

Or maybe it did. Landry picks up the mail at the box by the crossroads, but he usually stacks it on the kitchen counter for me to go through later. "I've got a bunch of unopened mail, mostly bills." A few hate letters too from friends of the psychotic Delahoussaye siblings, blaming me for what happened to Redford and Clarisse. They can't seem to believe that those nut jobs attacked me first, not the other way around. "It's been so crazy lately…"

"Ah well, it's nothing fancy. Just a small, informal dinner for family and friends. She asked me to invite you and Landry and Reverend Prince." He glances at me from the corner of his eye. "I'm bringing Isabel. Dad and my mom are also coming."

Realizing I've fallen behind, I take a running skip to pull even with his longer stride. "Isabel?"

"Interesting how you focus on Isabel first."

My cheeks heat. "It's just that I thought you broke up."

"She agreed to give it another go once I told her you and Landry are together."

"My relationship status shouldn't have anything to do with yours."

He gives me a lingering sidelong look. "But it does, and Isabel knows it. So try to look lovey-dovey with Landry at the party. Only not while I'm around to watch."

I break out a smile oozing with false innocence. "I always do."

George snorts. "Except when you're fighting."

"Landry and I don't fight. We discuss. Life's too short for fighting." I sigh and shrug. "I guess I should feel honored to even be invited, given the attendees. George senior hasn't acknowledged my existence. Much less claimed me as his illegitimate offspring. Does he know? Or is this one of Aunt March's grand schemes to throw us together?"

"He knows it's one of his sister's schemes, but I think he's secretly happy about it. He's been walking on eggshells since Mom learned about you. She was shocked. For about a month, I thought for sure they'd split, but she's still fighting for their relationship. Granted, she's not happy about him cheating on her, but I think she's willing to accept you."

"Wow, I'm so lucky," I drawl. "Fine, Landry and I will *discuss* going to this big, happy family gathering. And I'll let you know whether you're on your own with Isabel." A plan to use Landry as an excuse not to go immediately forms in my head. I don't think I'm mentally prepared for face-to-face rejection. I'd much prefer if my sperm donor and his wife continued to pretend like I don't exist. That's so much easier than suffering their scorn in person.

A warm hand wraps around mine, and I look up at George. "Sorry, but you seemed a bit lost."

"Oh? What did you say?"

"We have to go off-road."

The deer trail he points to heads toward Bayou de Sang. The underbrush thickens around us to form a tunnel of vines and leaves. George has to stoop to keep from being poked in the head. The path widens after about three hundred feet, revealing trampled grass and police tape attached to stakes in the ground.

"That's where the professor found the hand. The fingers were scattered around. Andy brought out his K-9, but Rex couldn't sniff out the trail. It's like the body parts fell from the sky." He turns his frown onto me. "Are you picking anything up?"

"Do you mean on my ghost radio?" I shrug, spinning in a circle. "Like I said, I'm not really good at controlling my powers yet. It's not like I can find the right station at first. It's more like scanning for the right…um, psychic frequency." I take a deep breath and close my eyes.

"What are you doing?"

My eyes pop open. "Shh, I told you. Scanning. It's kind of like meditating. It means shut up and don't question me every two min-utes."

He grunts, but mimes locking his lips. Only this time he throws the imaginary key at my head, and I involuntarily flinch, getting a chuckle out of him. He walks over to sit with his back against a tree and props his arms across his upraised knees and then, with a negli-gent flap of his hand, gives me permission to continue.

My eyes shut again, and I focus on the shield around my thoughts. I picture it like a brick wall that I built piece by piece, and I deconstruct it the same way. Slowly. One brick at a time, all the while scanning the area. Goose bumps prickle. With each piece of the wall removed, my range increases, extending outward in a radiat-ing circle. Wind picks up the ends of my hair. The stench of rotting meat fills my nose. I turn my head in that direction, inhaling deeply. Raspy whispers fill my ears, barely audible, more timbre than words, resonating through my body. My mouth dries.

I breathe out a puff of icy air, whispering, "He's here."

"Where?" George asks, calmly. Too calm. As if his voice were forced from deep within his chest. It sounds like he's moved from beneath the tree. That he's close enough to reach out and touch. "Do you see him, Mala?"

My lips feel dry, cracked. I let my tongue moisten them before speaking. "I'm scared to open my eyes." My voice shakes. "I feel him."

The cold spot surrounds my body. I'm trembling, chilled. A crack of thunder blasts overhead, and I jump. My eyes pop open with my scream, and then I see what I only felt deep in the marrow of my aching bones.

No. "Oh God, Georgie."

George grabs my arm when I try to bolt. "Mala, what do you see?" He wraps his arms around me. "Is it the boy?"

No…can't. I drag in a breath of icy air. It burns in my lungs. I press back against George's chest. My eyes dart from side to side, trying to protect my mind from the horrors appearing one by one in front of me, but no matter which direction I look, there's no escape. The circle of dead boys creeps closer. With bloody stumps outstretched and mouths open in silent screams, they're like something out of a horror movie. Only it's real.

"We're trapped, Georgie. There's too many of them. We're surrounded."

Chapter 4

Landry

Secrets and Lies

After showering away the blood and feathers, I throw on clean boxers, jeans, and a sky-blue T-shirt and a gray hoodie. I'm already late for my appointment with Mala's uncle, and my skin tingles with his spirit's pissed-off energy. Only I don't move fast enough in Gaston's opinion. The house rumbles with his displeasure, and the floor buckles beneath my feet. I grab on to the edge of the sink to keep from sliding across the wet floor. Mala's box of sanitary napkins, which are sitting on the counter, tips over. Pads rain down across the floor.

"Hold on, Gaston. I coming," I yell, dropping to my knees. I shove the pads back into the box, but stop upon feeling a plastic stick. I freeze with it in my hands, brain stuck on stupid as I process exactly what it means. And why it's in this house.

My breath catches as I flip the test over and study the results.

Two red lines. Is that good or bad? Or rather is it positive or negative? 'Cause right now good and bad are all relative in our sit-uation. I'm not opposed to having a kid with Mala—the face of a chubby-cheeked little girl with curly black hair and Mala's smile flashes through my mind. My daughter would have me wrapped around her tiny finger the second she left her Mama's womb. I'd spoil her rotten. Except that's a fantasy. I banish her tiny image from my heart before she gets lodged inside, along with any lingering threads of hope. It's past time I accept reality. I won't be around to see my kid's birth.

"How long are you going to stare at that stick?" Gaston asks.

I turn around, holding the pregnancy test up for his inspection. "Do you know what this means?"

"Means you're about to be a daddy."

"Yeah…okay, that's what I thought too."

"I take it Mala hasn't told you the good news yet?" He follows me out of the bathroom, looking dower. He fingers the trigger on his ri-fle like he's wishing he could blow my head off for defiling his niece. I feel like I should let him.

"Oh God, Ms. Jasmine's gonna kill me."

"Kill you for what?" Ms. Jasmine's distracted voice comes from the bedroom. I peek inside to see her lying on the queen-size bed, watching her soap opera. She rolls onto her side and gives me dagger eyes. "Knockin' my daughter up, you mean?"

"Shit, you know about it too?" My face burns.

"I'm her mama. Think I wouldn't know the signs?"

"But—" *How is this happening?*

"Knew you couldn't keep your promise about keepin' your dick in your pants. Now you've got to take responsibility. When you gonna propose?"

"I don't—" —*even have a ring. I'm broke.*

"Better do it soon. Don't want those snooty pricks in town labelin' my grandchild a bastard like they did my daughter. You ain't got much time left. Best drive to city hall and take care of the formalities there. You can always have a church wedding after you're no longer possessed."

"Do you really think I can get this thing out of me?"

Ms. Jasmine and Gaston wear identical expressions of pity.

I groan. "Let's go, Gaston. We're already late."

Gaston doesn't have to walk with me, but he does. For an ancestor spirit who's not even family, he's all right. He knows the value of silence. Apparently, I have super sperm. My little swimmers made it past the layers of contraceptive protection we used and impregnated Mala. I'm going to be a dad.

Mala's having my baby.

Breathe. So far, I've avoided the impending panic attack flittering at the edges of my brain. Maybe because I know that between her inheritances from Ms. Jasmine and Magnolia—when she passes—Mala will raise our child in luxury. Once I'm dead, George can swoop in and play the uncle. Or if he's really lucky, Mala will give him a chance to take my place.

The baby's face flashes before my eyes again, and my heart twists. *She's mine.* Not George's. I want to be the one to see her first smile. Hear her first laugh. Threaten the first boy she brings home and walk her down the aisle. It should be me who Mala grows old with, not George.

My jaw clenches against the shaking of my body. "I can't die. I'm not ready, Gaston. There's got to be some way to fix this. Mala needs me."

"Nothing's promised in this life," he says, studying me from the corner of his eye. "Death comes to everyone. It's just the timing that's up to the heavens."

"I'd rather it be later rather than sooner." I take a deep breath, reveling in the scent of the earth beneath my feet. The sun warms my back and the top of my head. "I'm not ready to give up. Especially now."

"Then don't."

The way he says it makes it sound simple. And for some reason, it eases my anxiety. I don't know how, but I will fight until the end. I push aside a low-hanging branch and step onto the trail leading into the woods. I should pay more attention to where I'm going, but with Gaston around, I'm not afraid of anything sneaking up on me. His energy crackles around him. Animals sense his presence and scurry off through the underbrush.

I pause at the edge of what Mala calls the "Dark Place" and breathe deeply in preparation. No matter how often Gaston brings me here, I never get used to it. This time, when I step forward, I put up the shield to wall in my thoughts, blocking the spirits from screwing with my perceptions but porous enough for me to see them.

"He's arrived," Gaston cries, raising his hands. "The father of the newest LaCroix. Welcome him to the family."

Silver lights spin in dizzy zigzag patterns in the air. The spirits flicker, then pulse, forming from hazy to solid within seconds. Mala's ancestors surround me with the warmth of their congratulations, and it finally sinks in. No matter how painful the road ahead might be, Mala is bringing a new life into this world. A baby that has a part of me. I've found another reason to live.

All my worries and frustrations melt away, and my dopey smile says it all. "I'm gonna be a dad."

"Felisitasyon, mon ami!" The familiar accented voice turns me around. The large man brushes a branch from the path and enters the clearing.

"Thanks, Ferdinand. I think."

"This is a wanted child. Many will eagerly await its birth." He uses a handkerchief to wipe the sweat from his bald scalp, then folds the cloth neatly and puts it in his pocket. His dark eyes search the area. "Where is the expectant mother? Don't tell me she's playing hooky from lessons again. The only reason Magnolia lets me come to this rinky-dink town is to teach Mala how to control her abilities. You're just a tag-along."

"I had another episode last night. Which I think may be the reason why Mala was driven off in a cop car this morning. It's a long story. I'll tell you over coffee later." I shrug my arms out of the hoodie and drop it to the ground, then pull the cotton T-shirt over my head. My skin prickles in the cool air, and I wince at the pain of strained muscles when I shiver. Bruises mottle my flesh. Some have faded to yellow, while the newest ones are dark blue.

Ferdinand hands me a bottle of cinnamon-scented oil.

I pour a dollop on my palm and rub it across my chest and ask him, "Why did it take you so long to arrive today?"

"Landry was uncommonly stressed out about being late," Gaston tells Ferdinand with a laugh. "It seems his impending fatherhood has made him more responsible."

Ferdinand's dark, almond-shaped eyes slant upward with his wicked sliver of a smile.

The bushes to my right rustle, and Sophia steps into the clearing as if making a grand entrance to a party, and her sultry green eyes linger on my abs. "I slowed him down," she says, with a tinkling laugh. "Hello, Landry." The tip of her tongue sweeps across her pouty lower lip.

I scoop my T-shirt from the ground and wrap it around my chest. "What the hell, Ferdinand? Why did you bring her?"

Ferdinand rubs a hand across his hairless scalp. "We've been working together for over a month with no progress. I'm desperate. I thought you were too. Do you deny that you planned to call Magnolia this morning?"

I scowl at him. "Are you reading my mind?"

Sophia laughs. "Yes."

"You both have this ability?"

"It's an easy skill to learn." She glides across the bare earth. Her hips…damn, she knows how to draw the eyes. "I can teach you, if you like. Of course, you weren't a fan of my teaching methods in New Orleans. Has this feeling of…revulsion that you experience in my presence waned? Does the mother of your child recognize how much she needs my help to keep her budding family intact?" Her head swivels, and she draws in a deep breath. "The air is full of power here, isn't it, Ferdinand?"

"*Oui*, I've found it to be so."

"The spirits accept you, but they resist me."

"That's because they know you're untrustworthy," Gaston says from behind her.

Sophia whips around. The glamour spell she weaves over her features to restore her youth drops for a moment as her eyes narrow on Mala's uncle. Gaston cradles his rifle against his shoulder. His wide-legged stance is at ease, but I've seen how quickly he reacts to supernatural attacks. The man lobs a grenade like it's the ninth inning and he's pitching with bases loaded. If Sophia tries anything witchy, he'll protect me. I think.

Except the longer I watch their interaction, the more I'm not sure. Gaston isn't behaving like his usual stoic self. He's not exactly giggly, but he's given himself a makeover that would make *GQ* magazine proud to feature him as a model. Rather than his usual burned appearance, I see him as he must've appeared as a young recruit fresh out of basic training. Damn, the old ghost has game.

Sophia saunters over to Mala's uncle. "Will you allow me to help Landry?"

"Depends on what kind of help you plan on giving him." He turns in a slow circle, keeping his eyes locked on her as she walks around him. Looks like he has trust issues when it comes to this woman too. He keeps his voice low, calm. "I heard about what you did to the boy in N'awlins."

"Did you now."

He steps forward, and Sophia sucks in a breath. Minute trembles wrack her body. "He's my family, Sophia."

Her hand reaches out, stopping inches from his unblemished cheeks. "So am I," she whispers. "I've missed you."

A shine washes over his features, and when it disappears, Gaston's burned visage returns.

Sophia's fingers clench into a fist, and she swallows hard. "Must you?"

"This is what I am now," he says. I see his teeth moving through the ragged hole in his cheek. "But then, you've known where I was for the last forty-five years." Bitterness lowers his voice. "So no more games, *my love*. You made your choice long ago."

Between one breath and the next, Sophia's features shift. Maybe pain flickers in her eyes, and regret twists her lips. Or maybe my eyes are playing tricks on me, 'cause it's gone now.

She steps back. "Ever the pragmatist. This is why our relationship died with you, Gaston. But I'm a forgive-and-forget kind of gal. All you have to do is say the word. You're family. Magnolia would make you whole, if you only ask." Her arms open wide to encompass all of the spirits. "I could stitch you all the most perfect bodies."

"Don't listen to her, Gaston," I say.

"Ferdinand's right. You really are a party pooper," Sophia tells me with a pout. "Why involve yourself in this? It's his decision."

"Mala told me how Magnolia tricked her into bringing a child back from the dead. And how doing so killed the man who murdered her." I shake my head. "The price isn't worth it."

"Of course the cretin died." Sophia cuts her eyes toward Ferdinand, and he shrugs. Like *I'm* the idiot for having morals. "Magic is about balance, Landry. A life for a life. So what? Karma's a bitch, and he deserved to die. He murdered that little girl in cold blood. Mala felt the terror that child experienced at the moment of her death. The unfairness of the whole sordid hit-and-run. And during the moment of transition, she chose the side of justice. She chose to bring the child back."

"Mala didn't know that guy would die."

"True. But she knew the price when she tried to bring her cousin back to life. Yes. I'm aware of that debacle in spite of Mala's refusal to beg for help. It's sad. If she didn't have an attack of morality and hesitate, Dena wouldn't be lingering on the edge."

How does she know about Dena?

"Get out of my head!" I snap. "You have no right to judge."

Sophia chuckles, waving her manicured hand. "Sorry. It's just too pathetic. As the last LaCroix, Mala has inherited the power of her ancestors. How many people have gotten hurt because she's too afraid to use it?"

"Mala's weak," Ferdinand says, going to the bloodstained altar stone. He opens his backpack and pulls out candles one by one. "I never should've told her the price for returning a soul to its body. She seemed tough, like her aunt. I didn't think she'd get all squeamish about death."

"About *murder*," I protest, but it's like talking into the wind. "Tell it like it is. To bring Dena back to life, she has to murder Red. How the hell is she supposed to do that?"

"I'll do it," a voice says, and I turn to see Carl stepping out from behind a tree. "I'll kill Red if it'll bring my sister back."

Damn it, I thought George would've made sure the kids got on the bus, not just dropped them off at the bus stop and called it good.

Carl stares at me, and then his gaze moves to Sophia then to Ferdinand and the altar. How must this look to him—the candles, oils, the fucking chicken in a cage? Right, like we're crazy cultists about to do a spell to summon a demon. Which is the sad, pathetic truth.

The expression on the kid's face screams that he's been listening in on our conversation for far longer than I'd like. He shakes his head and gives a wry snort. "You're all crazy. It feels like I'm in *Twilight*."

"Zone or glittery vampire?" I wave him quiet when his mouth opens. "Forget it. I'd rather know why the hell you ditched school."

His jaw hardens. "Like that's important compared to what you just said about my sister. Which is weird. But what's weirder is how ya'll keep talking to somebody named Gaston, and I don't see nobody else in this field but you three."

"Gaston is a ghost," Sophia says, brushing her long, black hair over her shoulder and meeting Carl's eyes with her own green gaze. "Surely you believe in ghosts. You'd have to, living with Mala LaCroix, heiress to the Hoodoo Queen Magnolia's power."

Carl's mouth drops. "You're shittin' me," he says all in one breath, then looks at me.

I shake my head, rushing to his side. "Go back to the house. I'll get the truck and take you to school."

I lay my hand on his shoulder, but he shrugs it off. "Did she say Mala's gonna be a Hoodoo Queen when she grows up?"

Sophia smiles. "Yes."

"Stop, Sophia." I feel like tearing my hair out. "Carl—"

"Dumb Mala who can't even kill Red to bring my sister back to life?"

I suck in my breath at his words. "Carl—"

"You think I'm stupid, but I'm not. I heard you talking about saving my sister. I also know you're sick in the head, Landry. So as much as I'd like to believe that Mala can save Dena, I don't really believe all this."

"Fine. Don't believe it. We're all crazy." I pause, frowning, as I try to come up with an excuse—any excuse—to get the glitter out of his eyes. "Look, you can't say anything about what you've heard."

"Ha. Like anyone would believe me. Still, I'm not going back to the house. Or to school. That's my condition. I won't tell the *rev* about you all being insane, if you let me stay and watch your insanity play out." He sits down on a rock and folds his arms. "Go ahead. Ignore me."

This certainly wasn't part of my plan.

Not that I have one. It went out the window the second Sophia and Carl stepped out of the forest. Still, it's too good an opportunity to pass up. Mala's not around to stop whatever happens. Sophia has the know-how to contact the demon inside me. And I need to find out what it wants and how to stop it. Pronto.

"Okay, stay. Just be quiet."

"Sure. Oh, by the way. Congrats on knockin' Mala up. I've always wanted to be an uncle."

I lurch toward him, arms stretched out, lips in a snarl. Maybe Dena won't mind losing one brother. She's got three more, after all.

Gaston appears between us. I almost run right through him, which would've been gross and cold. Not to mention rude. "Mala needs help," he snaps.

My feet tangle, and I almost fall on my ass. "What? How?"

He closes his eyes, body flickering like a lightbulb about to lose its spark. "She's screaming." His voice comes from far away, an echo. "I can't go to her."

"What does that mean?" Panic makes me trip on my words. "Where is she? You're her spirit guardian. You're supposed to protect her."

Gaston faces me with a bleak expression. "A spell blocks me. It's wrong, dark magic. I can sense her pain, her fear, but the spell acts to imprison the souls trapped inside its circle. And right now, Mala's soul is stuck in there, and I can't get in."

Chapter 5

Mala

Something Wicked

The spirits come in mass, far too many to count.

Blood covers severed limbs, slashed throats smile, and cloudy eyes seem to see right into my soul. I rear back, trying to escape, but a solid presence blocks me from behind. Arms wrap around my chest, becoming the bars of my cell. I scream, bucking to break free.

The stump of an arm, with the jagged bone protruding from the wrist, brushes my face. The spirits' memories barrage my mind, flashing images of people I've never met, places I've never been, all coming at me faster than I can process. Then the reflections slow and solidify into a vision of a single moment.

My vision narrows, darkens.

Rain falls across my face. I shiver from the cold, hunkering deeper into a too-small rain jacket. My stomach clenches, grumbling from hunger. Exhaustion weighs heavy, bowing my shoulders until it takes all of my strength to remain standing.

Headlights shine in the distance, and I stretch to my full height and stick out my thumb. Desperation makes me whimper.

At first it seems like the car will blow by, spraying muddy water over me as it passes like the others tonight. When it slows, my heart leaps. My thumb drops, and I hold my breath as the mud-streaked white car pulls onto the shoulder of the road. I shade my eyes, blinded by the rain and the lights in my eyes. The windshield wipers flicker, barely keeping the glass clear of rain. I can't see the driver, but I don't care. Get me out of the cold and I'll do whatever I'm asked. I've done things in the past to survive that I'm not proud of. What's one more?

Shivering, I run to the door, and it pops open. With a grin and a shout of "Thanks," I throw my backpack onto the floorboard, slide inside, and slam the door. A blast of heat from the vents warms my frozen cheeks. The seat belt is twisted, and I try to untangle it—moving quickly so I won't annoy the person waiting for me to finish. The belt buckles with a low click, and I turn toward the driver.

A fist fills my vision. The force of the blow snaps my body sideways, and the right side of my head rebounds off the glass. Pain strikes—explosive and raw. I lift my arm, but a heavy body throws itself across my chest. Its weight pins my arms to the side. A wet cloth covers my nose, and a cloying sweetness follows my inhale. My eyelids grow heavy. Close. I drift.

I wake to pain and claw my way to the surface.

Stars twinkle through the leaves overhead. The stink of a rotting animal makes me gag. Vomit clogs my throat, and I try to swallow it back down. But I can't. I'm suffocating. The rag in my mouth soaks up some of it, but I also breathe some in. My chest and nose burns even more.

I'm dying. My point of view shifts out of the body.

A hunched shadow crouches in front of me. His arms move back and forth. The sound reminds me of sawing wood, only different. Wetter. He stops sawing, reaches for something, and drops it. My hand thumps onto the ground. He picks up the saw again.

I stagger backward. He's cutting off my hands. Why?

Why am I seeing this? Who am I?

I wrap my arms around myself. The hug reminds me that I'm not the shell of the boy lying on the ground. I'm here as a witness. I'm Mala. And the guy is nothing but a nightmare. I take a deep breath and tiptoe closer, careful with each step. I need to get close enough to describe him to George.

I can do this.

My next step lands on a branch. The crack of the break draws a startled gasp from me. My eyes dart upward. The shadow turns, handsaw rising. He swings it at my neck. Screaming, I throw myself backward. Yellow eyes meet mine for a second and then sharp pain fills my cheek. My head snaps back.

I blink rapidly, focusing on the clearing with the yellow crime-scene tape while the vision fades. A shadow crosses my face, and I look up to find George standing over me. A worried scowl brings his copper eyebrows together.

I raise my hand, covering the throbbing in my cheek. "You slapped me?"

"Damn right I did. You started hyperventilating, then stopped breathing. What did you expect me to do?"

What indeed?

I raise my hand to George, and he helps me to my feet and brushes the dirt off my jeans. I'm still too shocked by what happened to protest the invasion of my personal space. "Sorry…and thank you. I think you saved my life."

"What happened?" he snaps. "And don't leave anything out because you think I won't believe you."

"I'm sick of lying." My eyelid twitches. Shadows flicker in and out of the corners of my eyes. "They're all still here. The murdered kids."

George turns a full circle. "Kids plural. Not just the one we found?"

"Yeah, that's why I lost it. I wasn't prepared for an assault. I can usually handle one or two spirits, but five's a bit much. I saw how one of them died. He was hitchhiking, and someone driving a white sedan stopped to pick him up. The kid didn't see the driver's face. Almost as soon as he got into the car, the killer punched him. He woke up out in the woods. Either here or somewhere nearby." I pause to take a deep breath, still tasting the puke from when I was inside the boy's body.

"Did he see the killer before he died?" George asks.

"No, he choked to death on his own vomit. The killer cut off the boy's hands after he was dead. I tried to see his face, but…" *Yellow eyes. He's got eyes like Landry's when he's possessed by the demon.*

A surge of denial rushes through me, and I chase after it like a starving dog after a bone. I know Landry's heart like my own. He'd never do this. Or let the demon use him to kill. I release a heavy breath, my momentary surge of doubt fading in the face of my faith in Landry. Besides, I saw two eyes. Not one.

The boys don't appear in solid form, but I sense their presence.

Their need for justice shouts louder than words, and I want to cover my ears and hide. My heart still races from being trapped in the dream. I hate losing my sense of self—of being assimilated as if I'm nothing more than a mirror—a dark reflection of the other side, giving voice to the voiceless.

George rumples my curls, and the affection in the action startles me. "Are you okay?"

I glare at the muddy toe of my boot. "Yeah, I'm just sorry it's not much of a lead."

"Hey, don't get down on yourself. It's a hell of a lot more than what I had before."

But not enough to catch this guy. He'll kill again. Over and over, until he's stopped. The next time it could be Carl or Daryl, unless I duct tape them to chairs in front of the Xbox. And then there's Landry. I know it's not him, but he'll think the worst. It's his nature to protect, even if it's from himself. If he finds out, he's sure to believe he did this while under the control of the demon. No telling how he'd react.

"Maybe one of the other kids saw more details. I should try again." The words come out before I can stop them, and I'm kind of glad. I'm not so good with long-term planning. If I think too much I'll cage myself in my fear. It's time for action. "Now that I'm prepared, I'll strengthen my mental shield so I don't get overwhelmed by their emotions."

George shakes his head. "Nope. Landry will kill me if anything happens to you."

"I'm a grown woman, Deputy Dubois. I make my own decisions, and this is work. Think of me as being a contracted consultant and keep this transaction strictly on a business level." I touch his arm.

"Look, it's not like this is my first rodeo. I know the risks. If I don't help these kids, who will? The murderer disposed of their bodies in a way that even a K-9 with a sniffer like Rex's couldn't pick up. Come on, isn't this the whole reason why you dragged me out here, Georgie?"

He squints, scanning the clearing as if trying to see what is hidden to him yet so obvious to me. When his gaze returns, I see resignation. If he really understood how dangerous this is, I couldn't have convinced him to let me connect with the spirits again. He only understands the results. Not the consequences that might befall me while trying to get them. And I don't plan on enlightening him. If I stop breathing again, I have faith he'll bring me back. And as long as the kids don't attack me like zombie puppies starved for brains, mouth to mouth will *not* be necessary.

I fan my heated cheeks, totally embarrassed by the flashback of the kiss Landry and I shared way back before we admitted our feeling for each other. I wonder whether we would still be together if we had sex that day. Would he have stuck around after poking that virgin notch in his belt like the player he was rumored to be? His continued relationship with me led to a whole lot of pain for him. Well, more pleasure than pain lately.

God, I'm so glad George can't read minds. *Go away, dirty thoughts. No time for you.*

George's hands land on my shoulders. "You talk a good game, but can you really handle this?" His thumbs rub my collarbones, and I twitch. "You're a bit jumpy."

I pull free of his hands and turn to give him a sickly smile. "I ain't afraid of no ghosts," I sing. "Seriously, I'm good." Not great, but I'm not screaming and running away anymore.

"Okay. Walk me through your plan. If it sounds logical, then I'm onboard. But I'm the team leader of this investigation. I call the shots. If I think things are getting too dangerous, I'm telling you to stop."

"Sure," I agree, ducking my head to hide the panicky chewing of my lower lip. If this works, I won't be able to *hear* him. "Basically, my plan is to slip my skin. If my soul is free of my body when I contact the spirits, I don't get overwhelmed. It's like I'm on a level interdimensional playing field."

"Uh, you can do that? Astral projection?" He rubs his chin. "I read about it while researching your symptoms."

"You say it like I've got some rare disease."

He laughs. "In a way, you do. What do you need from me?"

"Watch over my body. If I stop breathing, then wake me up. Fast." I lean over to brush twigs and rocks from the ground and lie down. I fold my hands across my chest.

"You look like a B-movie vampire in its coffin," George says. "I vant to suck your blud, *muwahahaa*."

"Shut up. If you make me laugh, I won't be able to concentrate." I lay my palms flat on the ground. "Okay, here goes."

My eyes close to block the flickering light of the sun shining through the branches overhead. Warmth from the earth and a tingling energy soak into my palms. The energy in this place feels like nothing I've ever experienced. Like it's a focal point or a convergence of magical lines—ley lines, that's what they call them in books. Could this be that sort of place? Were the boys murdered here because of this energy or was this some sort of coincidence? Either option is bad. Option A: Some random serial killer chose this place because it has a creepy reputation and nobody comes out here.

He probably would've been able to hide what he's been doing longer if that professor hadn't found the body parts.

Onto option B—which is the same as option A—only insert random witch/hoodoo doctor/Satanist cult member with delusions. Unfortunately, after seeing those yellow eyes, I'm going with option B.

Okay, speculation at this point is getting me nowhere but amped up. Must chill.

I tense and relax my muscles, starting with flexing my toes, then moving up my calves and thighs. While at the same time, I count backward from one thousand. With each number I tick off, my body grows heavier. I sigh. My spirit trickles from between my parted lips. I hover above my body, watching the sluggish rise and fall of my chest. It still unnerves me to see myself so vulnerable. What's even freakier is the silver glow around my stomach.

I turn away from myself, still not ready to face that particular shiny revelation. I prefer to live in denial for as long as possible. Well, at least until dinner time. I can accept anything if it's followed by sweet potato pie and whipped cream, even if said dessert is made by the rev.

Lick Creek's reputation for giving off bad vibes is compounded in spiritual form. What I felt before as creepy crawlies skittering across my flesh is magnified tenfold. The dirt beneath my feet oozes blackness, like tar. Then I look at the boys and gasp. Hundreds of blue-winged butterflies flutter around their spirits and crawl lightly across their exposed wounds. Their shocking presence brings an ethereal beauty to an otherwise horrible scene.

"Where are you?" I ask the boys.

The kids roil around, excited balls of sparks, and then they fade into misty wraiths, mixing with the butterflies to form a silvery-cobalt cloud. I will myself to follow. Trees pass in a blur. *I'm moving too fast.* The scream breaks free of my locked throat, scratching it raw on exiting. I bury my face in my arms and then remember that I'm incorporeal. *Nothing can hurt me. I am in control.*

With that thought, my speed decreases. I drop to my feet, sucking in air, as my spirit instinctively reverts to my normal bodily functions. When I stand, vertigo sends my thoughts spinning, and I waver like Mama used to when trying to pass a field sobriety test. It takes a few seconds to get my balance, and then I freeze. I've landed at the edge of a pond. Green scum coats the water. Gas bubbles rise to the surface, popping to release a sulfurous stench. I turn in a slow circle to get my bearings. I'm on an island, surrounded by this nasty water, with no visible way to cross back to the other side without going for a plunge. Bet leeches would like that scenario. Thank goodness I don't have to rely on something as mundane as walking. Relief at being here in spirit form fills me once again.

The caw of a crow whips my head back. The white oak's branches stretch outward. Bloodred sap oozes from the rents in the curling bark. My gaze flies past the lump on the branch overhead, then dances back. My brain doesn't want to interpret what I'm seeing. My subconscious erects a shield to protect me from the horror, but when it crashes, I fall hard. My stomach twists, but I don't look away.

I'm here as a witness. I must be strong.

Putrid corpses are tied to branches with rotting ropes, decorating the oak like macabre Christmas tree ornaments, celebrating death instead of life. Each boy reflects a different stage of decomposition. And all of their bodies show signs of being picked apart by scavengers, like the murder of crows hopping from branch to branch, feasting on eyeballs and entrails and the butterflies, wings fanning the air as they suck the moisture from the decaying flesh like it's the sweetest nectar.

I bat away the butterfly fluttering around my face, disgusted. I knew some butterflies ate the dead, but I've never seen it. And I wish I hadn't now. A large scavenger must've dropped the hands and fingers at the original crime scene. It's the only way to explain how they were removed because the rest of the boys' amputated hands are nailed securely to the trunk of the oak.

I squeeze my eyes shut. "I don't want to be here," I whimper, speaking as much to myself as to the boys' eternally trapped on Horror Island. I've seen what I need to lead George here. Time to go back. I focus on returning to my body, straining to whoosh back to reality. The rubber-band-like cord connecting my soul to my body stretches, lifting me, then rebounds with a snap. I tumble backward, slamming into the ground.

The earth feels dirty, contaminated, and I feel tainted by touching it. Scrambling upright, I brush my hands on my jeans. *No!* I strain forward again, but the effort of returning to my body sends pain arcing through every nerve. *This isn't right.* I've slipped my skin more times than I can count, and I've never failed to go back. *This is not happening.*

I breathe through the pain and fight back the panic. If I stay calm, I can figure this out. The trauma of seeing the boys must be messing up my mojo. Once I pull myself together, I'll be in control again. *I'm not stuck here.*

The earth trembles beneath my feet. Dirt erupts, peppering my body with clods and stones. Vines, thick as ropes, climb out of the holes left by the erupting dirt. They curl around my ankles—alive and full of thorns that leave oozing, paper-thin cuts on my skin. My legs look like the tree. Oh Saints, how can a spirit bleed? And if I can bleed, does this mean I can also die? What kind of shitty place is this—tampering with the rules of the other side?

"Stop!" I jerk my leg, trying to break the vine. But it's like I'm a catfish jerking on a hook. The more I fight, the tighter the vines wind around my body, and the more the thorns imbed into my skin. "Help! Gaston, help me."

Oh God, what's going on? I scream, arms flailing as I lose my balance and fall forward. I stretch out my hands to catch myself, but only my fingertips brush the ground. I'm hanging vertically, dangling from the vines wrapped around my ankles. More vines whip around my torso. They manipulate my body, lifting me higher and higher. Bark and hard wood press against my back. Vines twine around my chest, tying me to the branch. To my left, a skull grins in welcome. Patches of leathery skin sticks to the bones. A butterfly crawls from the open mouth and scurries down the jaw.

I close my eyes as the light tickle of wings brush my cheek. "Please, please, Georgie, wake me up. Someone help me."

Chapter 6

Landry

Deal with the Devil

*M*ala's trapped within a circle of black magic? Where? How?

I search Gaston's scarred face for clues, but his blank expression shouts louder than if he showed his fear. My fists clench to keep from shaking the spirit to get his attention. I can't touch him. Can't do anything. I tremble with the overwhelming weight of my frustration as I yell, "Tell me where she is. I'll go to her if you can't. Gaston!"

The guardian spirit stares into space. He doesn't hear me. Hopefully he's trying to get to Mala in his own way. I hate to think of her being alone. Afraid. Trapped God knows where. She needs me to find her, and I'm wasting time. *Gotta move.*

I grab my jacket from the ground and turn to head back to the house to get my truck. George kept yammering about finding a dead body. What if he dragged her off to the crime scene, wherever that is, and the killer came back and snatched her? Now she's being held as a hostage by a psychotic cannibal. Damn that rent-a-cop. Mala doesn't know anything about being the law. She doesn't even own a gun. He's gonna get her and my baby killed.

Sophia blocks my path, and I flinch away from the hand she raises to stop me. "Running around like a chicken with its head cut off is no way to help her."

"I can't just stand here with my thumb up my ass." I swing around her, but her hand lands on my shoulder, sending a wash of revulsion through my body. I shudder, flashing back to her lying on top of me in the graveyard. My stomach clenches.

Sophia's head tilts to the side, and her eyes slit, as if she's listening to inaudible voices. And maybe that's the case. The ancestral spirits in the clearing seem agitated. Their energy glows brighter as the silver balls swirl through the air.

"Gaston," she calls. "Are you able to pinpoint where Mala's being held captive?"

"The ground is warded." He shakes his head like a dog coming out of the water. His eyes are cloudy when they focus on me, as if he is still searching the other realm for clues. His hand rises to stop my words, and my mouth closes. "It's not Mala's physical body that's in danger, but her spirit."

"What exactly does that mean?"

Gaston blinks quickly. "She slipped her skin and traveled to the other side."

Oh, shit! I press my hand to my chest, feeling the rapid thumps of my heart beneath my palm. I breathe out the pent-up breath I've been holding. "Yeah, she's addicted to the whole astral projection thing. She got a kick out of spying on me in the shower while I was in jail. She even saw Dena when Red was holding her prisoner. Why is this time different? And how can anything hurt her in spirit form?"

"I don't know," Gaston's says. "I'm blocked from going to her. It's like she stepped behind a brick wall, and I can't break through it. But she's screaming, Landry. Screaming…"

Not helping, Gaston.

"Show me," Sophia says, holding her hand out to Gaston, and I jump. I'd forgotten that she and Ferdinand, two of the most powerful practitioners of magic, stand before me. If anyone can figure out how to break a black-magic circle, it's Scary and Scarier.

Gaston stares at Sophia's hand like it's covered in dog shit. The corner of his lip curls. I glance at Sophia and catch a flicker of pain in her eyes, but it's gone so fast I want to punch myself for believing the wicked witch is capable of experiencing emotion. She wiggles her fingers, beckoning him forward as if he's a child.

Gaston's shoulders straighten, and the corners of his mouth dip in resignation. When their fingertips touch, sparks fly. His hand passes through hers. In a few more steps, he fades inside of her.

Sophia shivers as she takes the spirit into her own body. A slight ripple of light races across her skin. She remains silent for what feels like an eternity, but when she finally speaks, her voice sounds like a merger between herself and Gaston, rumbling from deep within her chest. "Okay, the circle's strong. It was erected by someone twisted but talented. It's meant to trap spirits inside."

"It can be broken?" Ferdinand asks in his quiet, yet authoritative voice.

"Perhaps if we use the spell of unbinding and combine our energy. Landry would have to be the one to make contact."

Ferdinand nods. "Ah, because of his blood tie to her?"

"Out of all of us here, he's the only one living who is linked to her by blood."

My head's spinning, like that girl from the old *Exorcist* movie, and my stomach churns with nausea. Any minute I'm going to start hurling green vomit. Just once, I wish I understood what the hell was going on. Especially since it involves me. "What does that mean?"

"The child Mala carries is a legacy from you both. Its blood links you together, allowing you to travel across the plane to find them." Sophia holds out her hand. I take it without pausing to consider the consequences. She's either telling the truth or lying. I'll know soon enough. And there isn't time to waste on debate. Not if what Gaston said is true.

"I'm also blood to Mala. I want to help too," Carl says, coming over.

I'm already shaking my head before he gets out the final word, but Sophia takes his hand and draws him forward. "Ah yes, I forgot about you. Good, this should make the link stronger." Her lips pucker. "I should warn you both. This will be very painful."

Huh? A flash of agony rips through me. Dimly, I hear Carl screaming in the background, but the sound is mostly drowned out by my own yell. My back arches, and I drop. My head slams onto the ground, and I roll onto my side, cradling my knees to my chest in a fetal position. I fight to remain conscious.

"Let yourself go!" Sophia yells.

Fuck no! The battle within my mind rages. The second I lowered my guard the snake woke. I sense it beneath the surface, crawling upward by tiny increments. With each slither, a chill crawls up my spine. If it breaks free, it'll take over my body. God only knows what kind of damage it will do to these people. Why didn't I think of this before agreeing to Sophia's plan?

My head throbs, pulsing with the creature's awareness. It probes my memories with reckless abandon, like it's scrolling through television channels and scanning the contents of the show before moving on. *"Stop fighting."* The words float before my eye, dripping with bloodred ink. What the hell? *"Mala needs your help."*

My hands squeeze the sides of my head, trying to keep my skull from splitting open from the pressure. Pain throbs up my neck. The roof of my mouth and nose tingle with each pulse. *"You don't have a choice. Let go."*

It's right. Mala…the baby. They need me. Desperation claws at my insides, shredding my resistance, but I can't just let go. The demon snake is stronger than before. I sense the difference. I don't think I'll come back if I hide again. But I need it to cooperate and maybe it needs me. For the first time, I confront the creature head-on rather than running and hiding.

"Help me!"

Blackness washes across my vision, but in the darkness, a sliver of light shines. Metaphysical eyes open in my head and stare back at me in cold assessment. Windows into my soul slam shut. I can feel Sophia and Gaston pounding on the walls of my brain, trying to reenter my mind, but the snake wants this conversation to remain between the two of us. And I agree. Whatever it wants, I've got to decide whether I'm willing to give it. Whether it's worth it to save Mala.

A feather-like sensation brushes across my mind. The roof of my mouth tickles. Ah, I think it's laughing at me. Way to make this an even more uncomfortable experience.

"Name your terms," I think.

"Let me free."

I wince at the response. *"Can't do that."*

"Not even to save the one you love?" Its chuckle vibrates inside my skull. *"Why ask if you're going to deny me?"*

"I thought you'd come up with a plan that we can both agree on." Anger makes my thoughts jagged. *"Don't be so greedy."*

It laughs again.

I'm wasting time. It can drag this negotiation out for days. This doesn't matter to it. Mala's the one who's going to get hurt. Already hurting.

"Fine, I'll let you free." I regret the necessity of the promise and narrow the terms of my service as much as I can. *"But only when I'm awake. You don't sneak out and run crazy while I'm asleep. We share this body. If I say no, then we come to a compromise. And no killing."*

"Why are you trying to block all my fun?"

"No killing. Unless I agree."

"Agreed."

"And no more eating raw meat. If I get salmonella poisoning, this body's dead. Then what are you gonna do?"

"Regret runs on two legs."

"Whatever."

I let go of the barrier compartmentalizing him in a detached section of my brain. Its awareness spreads, seeping into the spaces I kept safe from its intrusion. Now we fuse together. No longer separate, but one entity. My soul erupts from my mouth on an exhale. I'm moving forward so fast that everything around me blurs. I only slow down when I get to Mala's body. George has her cradled in his arms. A closer look shows me the faint rise of her chest. He stares into the distance with glazed eyes, more bored than worried. Whatever is happening to her hasn't affected her body... *yet.*

A hand lands on my shoulder, and I turn to see Gaston. "Don't move another inch!"

I freeze. "What's going on?"

"The black-magic circle begins here. One more step and you would've crossed the same boundary as Mala. You would've been trapped."

"How did you get here? I thought you couldn't find her?"

"You brought us here," Sophia says. She glows in this realm, as beautiful and terrifying as ever. Darkness smudges her aura. The spirits of Mala's ancestors begin to appear, one after the other, until the clearing is full. George shivers, feeling the cold spots surrounding him. He squeezes Mala tighter against his chest, and I want to rip her from his arms. How did he get her into this mess?

"Where are we?"

"A place of sacrifice," Gaston says. "Immense power has soaked into the land and built up over the centuries due to the deaths that occurred here. With each death, the tie to the land of the dead grows stronger. The person who drafted this spell increased its potency by adding in the sacrifice of innocents. The young and particularly vulnerable bring strong magic."

"How do we get Mala out of here?"

Sophia answers this time. "I can't break the circle. But we can tie a metaphysical rope around you. You go in and grab Mala. Then we'll pull you both out, hopefully before the rope breaks and traps you inside."

"The hopefully part doesn't inspire confidence."

"I'm winging this particular spell. I've never seen anything like this in my life. And as you know, I'm older than I look." Her eyes close as she begins to chant. Her words dance on the breeze. Power winds around my body.

"It's ready. Go forth," Sophia says.

Gaston holds up his fist, and I give him a fist bump. For some reason, the act lessens my anxiety. I step forward. The air parts around my body. I focus on Mala's scent, her laugh, the feel of her body when it's connected to mine. I think about the life growing inside her. I whoosh forward again. This time I'm prepared for the whirlwind sensation, and I grit my teeth.

I stagger on the landing, arms outstretched to catch my fall. A dark miasma crawls in through my nose when I inhale, and my gut twists from the foulness. It's hard to breathe. Which strikes me as strange, since I'm not in my physical body. I cough, trying to clear my lungs, and scan the area for Mala. I'm on an island in the middle of a pond of green goop. Nasty.

A choked sob comes from above. The branches stretch in all directions from the trunk of the biggest, ugliest tree I've ever seen. I swallow hard, mouth dry, and blink a few times. The image doesn't go away. Nothing in my wildest nightmares prepared me for seeing decaying corpses, covered in tiny, blue-winged butterflies, tied to the blood-seeping tree above me. This is nuts.

"Ah, at last. The reason for my existence." A sense of satisfaction follows those words, and I remember that the demon observes from my eyes. It doesn't elaborate on this statement, and I don't ask. Bad enough I feel its pleasure. Does it enjoy this type of death? Did these sacrifices draw it here? I don't want to know or care about the answers because, right now, they don't matter. Finding Mala and getting us off the island in one piece does.

I turn in a circle. "Mala?" I yell, listening for a response. Her spirit drew me here. She has to be around somewhere. The island isn't that large. Only holding the tree. Another sob comes from the branch to the left of the trunk. Vines encircle the body, but I see a sprig of brown curls. Once I know what I'm looking at, I see the curve of Mala's cheek, her bold nose, and her bloodstained lips. Her eyes are sealed. Butterflies blanket her exposed flesh in a silent horde. Folds of bark and lichen grow over her skin. Sores weep blood. It's like she's an insect in the maw of a Venus flytrap, slowly being consumed.

"Mala," I scream. "I'm here. Mala!"

She doesn't stir. I can't even detect the rise and fall of her chest. Is she breathing? Does she need to breathe in spirit form? Again with the useless questions. I've got to get her down. The problem is that the trunk stretches a full twenty or so feet before the lowest branch. There is no way for me to climb up to her.

"Spirits don't need to climb. Float."

Demon's right. Again. God, I hate being dependent on a smug parasite.

"How?" I ask. "Think happy thoughts like in Peter Pan? I don't have any pixie dust to sprinkle over my head."

"Will yourself to her."

I knew that. I'm just panicking. It's the same principle as how I found her. I close my eye and focus on light thoughts. A game Clarice and I played as kids floats through my memory. "Light as a feather, stiff as a board."

A sense of weightlessness lifts me from the ground. I stretch my arms overhead as I rise to her. A crack of thunder booms and lightning flashes in the sky. Wind lashes out and smacks my body. I yell, spinning in a circle and flapping my arms like I've got feathers.

Which I don't. I'm nothing but an untethered spirit at the island's mercy. And it senses my presence like a living creature would.

Vines whip out, snapping their tips at my face. Thorns cut into my flesh. I use my upraised arm to shield my eye. I've only got one that works. Can't lose it or we're screwed. Even with all this opposition, I don't stop struggling to reach Mala. The vines wrap around my legs and arms, but whenever they touch my skin, the ends sizzle and blacken.

"Are you're doing that?" I ask the thing inside. It chuckles, but doesn't answer.

When I reach Mala, I grab the vines and start yanking them off her. Smoke rises as they burn beneath my touch. Her eyes open, and she screams, bucking upward. Tiny blue-winged bodies burst into flames like candle wicks and float to the earth as dust.

The rest of the vines disintegrate, and Mala drops into my arms.

I cradle her against my chest, breathing hard. Cries fall from her lips, and she fights to get free. The blankness in her eyes show she's not fully aware of where she is or who I am. It reminds me of the panic attack that took her at Acker's farm. She attacked without knowing I held her. I hate the helpless feeling of not being able to rescue her from her own mind. Hopefully when she returns to her body, she'll be back to normal. Or at least as normal as she can get.

"Sophia, Gaston, I've got her," I yell, sending the thought from my mind to theirs. I hope. There's lots of hoping and not enough knowing going on.

A slight tug jerks my head back. My arms tighten around Mala. Then I'm snapped away from the island. I inhale, rearing backward. My head slams into a rock. Bright lights fill my vision, and I sit up, rubbing my head.

"Are you okay?" Carl cries, crawling over to sit beside me. "Did you get my dimwit cousin? Did you? Say something before I punch ya."

"Shut up, Carl." I rub my eye, trying to get the goopy film off my eyeball, then blink up at Sophia and Ferdinand. "Did I? Is she back in her body?"

"She's back. Gaston stayed behind. He'll let us know what's going on."

"Good," I say, then let blackness wash over me.

Chapter 7

Mala

Two-Tongued Snake

I can't breathe. My lungs tickle, like legs are crawling inside my chest. The sensation builds, tightening and squeezing, until it erupts. I roll onto my hands and knees, coughing. A hand pounds on my back. A blob of phlegm breaks free, leaving a coppery tang on my tongue as I spit it out. The clot of blood and mucus lands in the mud between my hands. It shimmers, wriggling like gelatin from the death throes of the iridescent thread-like larvae.

Worms. I pull back with a choked cry. *Inside me.*

The scream rips from my chest, searing agony through my damaged lungs.

A shadow looms overhead, and I strike at it. Hands pin me.

I'm trapped. Infested.

The arms pull me against a wide chest. "Calm down. It's me."

The yell penetrates my panic, and I glance up. *Landry? No.*

George stares down at me with shimmering, jewel-like eyes of gold-flecked emerald. *So pretty.* I force my gaze away before I get lost in them and search the ground for the bloody stain. Nothing. It's gone. Like it never existed. *A hallucination.*

George's dark copper hair is soaked from the raindrops leaking from the sky like tears. Water drips into my eyes, and I squeeze them shut, trying to remember why I'm on the muddy ground. Memories slide through my mind in sluggish pieces. *Fingers…a hand, but no body.* George and I drove to Old Lick together to talk to a murdered boy's spirit. He protected my body while I went to find…*What did I see?*

Darkness. Blood and suffering. Pain.

I bite the inside of my cheek so I don't scream. A full-bodied shiver rips through me as the memory returns of being trapped in a tangle of vines. George hugs me against his warm chest. *I'm safe.* My fingernails dig into George's shoulders. *Then why can't I stop shaking?*

George winces and pries my fingers free. "Holy hell, Mala! Your hands feel like ice." He cups my hands in his, raises them to his lips, and blows warm air across them. "Are you okay? What happened?"

My mind feels fuzzy. Drained. "I found the kids." Lightning crackles overhead, and a thunderous boom sends us cringing together. Smoke rises, and flames light up the sky in the distance. I point in the direction the screams are coming from. "Over there…the boys' bodies." My voice chokes on a sob. "After he murdered them, he cut them into pieces and tied them to the tree."

His eyes widen when he follows the direction where my finger points. The uppermost branches of a tree is engulfed in flames. *The tree.*

I'm not sure how I know, but it feels right.

Gaston flickers into existence and crouches beside me. "Mala…"

I rock forward. My hands pass through his body and drop onto my lap. "Uncle Gaston, it was horrible." Tears trickle down my cheeks, and I try to breathe through my clogged nose. "I was so scared. Vines grabbed me and tied me up. I couldn't get away. Did you save me?"

"Who are you talking to?" George asks, pulling me back against his chest. "Is it the kids again?"

"No, my uncle came. He saved me."

Gaston rocks back on his heels. His hands flutter like he wishes he could touch me too, and his eyes have a wildness to them that I've never seen before. "No, it was a team effort. Ferdinand and Sophia came up with the spell, but Landry went in to grab you."

"Landry was there?" Yes, I remember now. I thought he was a hallucination. A part of the nightmare I couldn't wake up from. The tree trapped my spirit. It sucked at my energy, draining me inch by inch. Any longer and I would've been a goner. With my spirit sucked dry, my body would've died soon after. Poor Georgie would've been stuck holding a lifeless body. And Landry wouldn't have known why this happened.

"Tell me everything," I beg. "Is Landry okay?"

"Not now. The spell has been broken. The boys' spirits have been set free. We'll deal with the rest later." Gaston fades before I can try to weasel out more information.

My gaze travels back to the tree, and I swallow hard. Time to get it together. Business first. "George, the tree is burning. We'll lose all the evidence if we don't act fast. Call it in to Dixie."

He pauses a moment, then nods. He's handling this better than I expected—better than me—but then he'd be a hypocrite if he didn't believe me after he came up with this crazy plan. He radios the sheriff's office and explains the situation. The dispatcher says she'll notify the local Forest Protection branch to dispatch a wildland fire crew. The crime-scene techs have a thirty-minute ETA.

George and I follow the smoke through the woods to the edge of the pond. It looks just as scummy in real life as it did on the other side. The oak burns. The bark crackles. Shrieks like nails on a chalkboard send the willies down my spine, and I cringe, clenching my jaw. A mix of decomposition, swamp rot, burning flesh, and acrid smoke makes my stomach roll. George, with his sensitive stomach, gags, and I pat him on the back as he hacks up a gob of phlegm and hawks it into the bushes.

"Are those black lumps the bodies?" He wipes his upper lip with the back of a trembling hand. "Who would do something like this? It's sick."

"I don't know, but I'm going to find out." I meet his gaze with determination. Whoever killed and displayed the kids like this is twisted. And powerful. Not the normal, everyday variety psychopath, but one who knows how to manipulate the natural world. Dark magic taints the air. I don't know what this guy needed so much power for, but it can't be good.

We head back to the main road to wait. Sheriff Keyes and Detective Bessie Caine arrive in the sheriff's fancy gray Buick. Andy with his K-9 partner, Rex, and Deputy Hale park right behind them. George leaves my side to run over to the sheriff and Bessie and quickly briefs them on the situation. They give me nods of greeting, but smiles don't crack their lips. They're not happy. Not that they should be in this situation, but it's more. They're wearing their pissed-off expressions.

I hover in the background and try to go unnoticed as we wait for Dr. Michelle Montague, the new parish coroner, and her assistants, along with the crime-scene techs to unload their van. Bessie likes her. Says she actually cares more for the job than holding the position to take bribes. Watching them unload their gear reminds me of the day I found Lainey's body. That business led to a lot of crap falling on me. I hope this time won't be the same.

The full force of the storm hits. Cold rain pounds us hard enough to sting. By the time we reach the edge of the pond, the fire has burned out. The flames never reached the bodies tied to the lower branches. While George advises dispatch to cancel the forestry crew, the techs start inflating a rubber raft. The rest of us stand on the bank and stare.

Bessie shivers, wiping her face. "What a miserable place. How in the world did the two of you stumble across this? And why didn't Rex sniff it out earlier?"

"Hey, LT," Andy protests, laying a hand on his dog's head. "We covered this whole area. I never saw this place."

"That's what I'm saying," Bessie says. "It reeks of death. How could you miss a tree strung with decaying corpses?"

My mouth opens to explain about the area being warded with a spell to keep intruders from finding it, but I shut up. Gah, almost babbling like a lunatic about supernatural forces. Mother Mary, that's a whole can of worms I'll never be comfortable opening. At least not while I still dream of having a normal life.

Andy shrugs, but unease narrows his eyes. "Rex and I will take a turn around the area. See if we missed anything else." He and his K-9 walk off, leaving me alone with Bessie and Chief Keyes.

Bessie shifts her glare in my direction. "And what are you doing here, Mala Jean? Did you wrap George around your little finger and convince him to bring you to the crime scene?"

I gasp. "Bessie, I'd never—"

"*Cher*, don't forget I helped raise your little ass. I know exactly what you're capable of."

My cheeks heat. "Well, I didn't. I was at home minding my own business when my brother showed up. I didn't know anything about that professor finding body parts. So how could I even think of finagling an invite to a crime scene that, for all intents, had already been processed by the time we came out here?"

Sheriff Keyes zones in on me. "Then why are you here, Mala?"

"George asked me to go for a hike. Do some sibling bonding. Why? Is there a crime in going for a walk and experiencing nature at its finest?"

Thunder cracks and lightning flashes across the sky. I flinch, ready to be struck dead. Saying that George and I went hiking, well, it's partly true. Same with the sibling bonding. I can't lie to Sheriff Keyes. It would be like lying to my own father. Well, not my bio-dad. The sheriff has been more of a father to me than Dubois Sr.

I avoid his eyes by glaring at the rock beside my boot. It slides an inch, and I gasp and then swallow hard. *Holy telekinesis! Stop before someone notices.*

Sheriff Keyes traces his thumb and index finger down his handlebar mustache. "Why do I sense I won't get the whole story from you?" At my shrug, he shakes his salt-and-pepper head. "Deputy Dubois, get over here and explain why you brought a civilian to the crime scene."

George darts a frantic look in my direction. Obviously he doesn't want to lie to Sheriff Keyes either. I surreptitiously swipe my hand across my throat in a knifing motion and widen my eyes as I silently threaten him with beheading. If he doesn't keep his big fat mouth shut about my business, I will go King Joffrey on his ass.

"Son," Sheriff Keyes says, folding his hands over his rotund belly and looking more like Santa Claus than the head of the local law enforcement agency, "tell me the truth."

My older, but not so wiser, brother's shoulders slump and his mouth opens. "I brought Mala to find the bodies. She can talk to ghosts," he blurts out, thus sealing my doom.

All eyes turn in my direction. *Kill me now.*

"Is this some kind of joke, Deputy Dubois?" Bessie's voice snaps him upright. His cheeks flush bright red, and he rubs his hand over his wet head. He looks at me with a pleading expression, but I'll be damned if I help him out. Hell, I'm already damned. Bad enough they thought I was crazy after being locked in the mental ward. Now he's confirming the crazy and adding a whole new level to the madness.

What was I thinking? I never should've told him my secret. Never should've agreed to coming out here with him. Should've known he wouldn't keep his mouth shut. I forgot what a double-dipping, two-timing snake my brother can be when he wants something. I'm seriously gonna rip out his guts and eat them like chitlins.

"Mala, please?" he begs.

Please? Ha. Let's see how he feels being locked up in the psycho ward. Maybe then he won't make arbitrary decisions about other people's lives. He took my choice away. If I never shared my secret, so what? What business is it of his if this giant lie has been eating me up inside. Or that I'm sick of hiding a part of who I am from those I love.

I stare at the faces of people who have known me my entire life. People I respect. What's the point in denying the truth now? It's out. Might as well face it head-on or I'll be trapped in a forever loop of lying to cover up my true nature. "Fine! He's telling the truth. Sheriff, you've got your very own Ghost Whisperer. Use me at will. I don't care anymore."

"What are you saying?" The shock in Bessie's eyes almost breaks me.

I swallow around the lump in my throat. "I'm admitting to being able to communicate with the spirits of the dead. It's sort of an inherited family gift. Sorry I didn't tell you sooner." I wipe my eyes with the back of hand. "I didn't want anyone to know. Hell, it took me almost dying to figure out what was happening to me. You all saw how that turned out. Lainey possessed me in the hospital, and I got locked up."

I wrap my arms around myself, shivering from the cold. I search their faces, but see nothing but skepticism reflected back. "Oh, come on. Don't just stare at me like I've lost my mind. Please."

George comes over to wrap his arm around my shoulder. "I didn't believe her when she first told me about Lainey Prince haunting her. But since then I've seen proof." He points toward the island. "Now so have you. What more do you need to believe us?"

Sheriff Keyes clears his throat. "How exactly did you find the bodies, Mala?"

I shift from one foot to another. "Well, the thing I've learned about spirits is that they have a strong sense of justice. Those boys wanted to be found. And they want their murderer captured." My nostrils flare. Anger simmers below the surface and builds with each word. "This guy's a psycho. Full of arrogance and smug in the belief that he's smarter than everyone else. He thinks he won't get caught, and up until now, he was right. Hell, Georgie said nobody even realized the kids were missing."

I stab them accusingly with my gaze, then shift my glare across the pond to the smoking tree and the blackened bodies of the children in its branches. The rage inside dampens my embarrassment. I won't be selfish anymore. Whether they hate or fear me now doesn't matter, as long as they believe I'm telling the truth. Finding the murderer and stopping him from killing another kid is all I care about. "A serial killer has been building his very own trophy island in Paradise Pointe. He came to our town in a white car. Picked up our kids from the side of the road. Once he got them inside, he knocked them unconscious and brought them to the island. That's where he dismembered them and set them up for display."

"And you know all of this how?" Sheriff Keyes asks.

"Those kids told me." My cell phone vibrates, and I sigh in relief. Saved by the buzz.

I slide the phone from my pocket. I read several alerts for missed messages from Landry. Gaston said he'd tell him that I'm okay so I'll check in with him later. What gets my heart racing are the three missed calls from the attendance clerk at the high school.

I look back at Bessie and Chief Keyes. "This news is probably a shock. I need to make an important phone call. Why don't you listen while George tells you about his experience, then discuss this among yourselves? I'll answer your questions when I'm done."

"Mala, this is pretty important," Bessie says, rubbing her arms. "If what you're saying is true then…Hell, I don't even know what to think."

"I know." My lips twist from the sour taste in my mouth as I say, "I'd ask you to just trust me, but that's ridiculous. What I'm saying is pretty hard to believe, even with proof of the supernatural. I won't hate you if you can't wrap your mind around the fact that the information I got came from ghosts. As long as you don't ignore it. Right now, it's your only lead."

I walk toward the trees, leaving Sheriff Keyes and Bessie in George's hands. "Mala told me she could see spirits after Dena was kidnapped by Redford Delahoussaye..." he says, his voice fading the farther away I get.

Part of me wants to start running toward the main road and never come back. But the other part is hopeful to the point where it physically hurts. George is the only one who gets how much I want to become a detective. He understands how my desire to right a wrong and bring justice to the victims makes me forget common sense and jump into situations feet first without thinking about the consequences, because he's the same way. I'd forgotten how much I love the feeling of being at a crime scene. I'm glad George recognized this and brought me here. Even if he had to spill my deepest, darkest secret to justify my presence.

I take a few minutes to get my emotions under control. As keyed up as I feel, it would be a shame to take it out on the attendance clerk even if she deserves it. Gladys Huxton has a disagreeable stick-shoved-up-her-ass personality, and she treated me like dung stuck to her shoe all through high school. After becoming the twins' guardian, I learned nothing's changed since I graduated.

The attendance clerk picks up on the fourth ring. "Paradise Pointe High, Mrs. Huxton speaking."

"Hi, this is Mala LaCroix. I had a message?"

"Yes, thank you for finally returning my call. Are you aware that Carl didn't come to school today?"

I pinch the bridge of my nose, breathing hard. "No, ma'am, that's

not possible. He got on the bus this morning. He should be there."
Footsteps crackle through the ground cover. I turn to see George
walking in my direction and wave him over.

"They're ready for you," he says when he reaches my side.

I shake my head, covering the receiver and whispering, "They'll
have to wait. The school says Carl never made it to class. You saw
him get on the bus, right?"

He scrubs his fingers through his hair and shrugs. "Uh, no, I
dropped them off at the bus stop and came back."

I let out a low hiss.

"What about Daryl, Mrs. Huxton? Did he make it to any of his
classes? Has he seen his brother?"

"He's showing to be present. The problem is Carl—"

I cut her off, my voice rising with growing panic. "But what did
Daryl say? Did Carl get on the bus this morning?" *Where do I even
start to look for him? The house? Town?*

"I don't know."

"What do you mean, you don't know? If Daryl's there, then ask
him. I need a place to start searching. What if something happened
to him?" *What if the killer snatched him?* My voice cracks as I say,
"Carl's my responsibility."

Her gusty sigh forces me to pull the phone away from my ear.
"Exactly, Ms. LaCroix. Carl is your responsibility, not mine. Unless
he's on school grounds. And he's not, which is the reason for my call.
He has more absences this semester than days present. The principal
and guidance counselor want to meet with you and Carl. When is a
good time?"

"I don't know." It's almost noon now. How long will it take to
track the kid down? "I'll have to call back later."

The line goes quiet.

"I'm not trying to make light of this situation. I know it's important, but I need to find Carl before I can bring him in to meet with the principal."

"Call back by the end of the school day."

The line disconnects. My heart feels like it's about to be ripped from my chest.

"Little shit tricked me," George says. "He probably doubled back after I dropped him off and is at home playing video games with Landry."

"Right, yeah." I settle for the easiest conclusion. The other is too scary to worry about.

"Landry feels so bad about Dena that he overcompensates by spoiling the kids rotten. Stupid Xbox is frying their brain cells." I punch in Landry's phone number. "I keep telling him that the boys need consistency and routine." The line connects on the third ring.

"Mala, thank God. It's Sophia," she says, her voice warbling. "Why did it take so long to call?"

Panic spurts. "Why are you answering Landry's phone?"

"We have a bit of a problem. The situation is contained for the moment, but you need to get here as soon as possible."

"Is he hurt?"

"Only minor injuries. That's why I said a *bit* of a problem. I'll fill you in when you arrive." Her last words are muffled like she puts her hand over the phone to drown out the distant shouts.

"What the hell's going on, Sophia?"

I hear a muted yell. "He's breaking free. Pin him down."

"Mala, just get to the Acker farm. Quick. Before it's too late."

Chapter 8

Landry

Butterfly Shit

I wake with a shout. Ice cold water drips down my face, and I wipe my eyes. Ferdinand, Carl, and Sophia, who's holding a canteen, stand over me. Worry etches deep frowns on their foreheads. "What the hell?"

"We thought you died." Carl rubs his hands together like he's cold. "But you only passed out. What happened?"

My head throbs, and I touch the lumps on the back of my skull. "Hit my head on a rock again."

"Nobody cares about your hard head. I mean with Mala." He grabs my arm and helps me stand. "You said you got her before you passed out, but you didn't tell us how. What did you see?"

A chill runs down my back at the memory. "Something I hope to never see again." I squint at the empty circle. The ancestral spirits are gone. Hopefully they're still with Mala, protecting her. "I can't even...Death. Corpses strung up in a bleeding tree. Carnivorous butterflies. What the hell is going on, Sophia?"

She casts a sideways grimace toward Carl, who looks between us with bugged-out eyes. "We'll talk about this later."

Good idea. "What about Gaston? Is he still with Mala? Have you heard from her yet?"

"He says she's recovering," Ferdinand says, holding out a blue glass bottle. Herbs float in the coffee-colored liquid. "It's time for you to do the same. Drink this."

I hold my breath before drinking and shudder at the sharp, minty taste. "What was that?"

Carl shakes his head. "Maybe you should've asked before drinking it."

Yeah, not bad advice for the future even though it came from a punk like him.

Ferdinand puts the bottle into his backpack. "Thank you for your trust. It'll help purify you."

"Because I'm tainted."

"Blessed," whispers the voice in my head. Then it laughs.

Crap, I'd forgotten about my deal with the devil. "It feels like I've got a layer of scum on my skin, as if I took a bath in that nasty pond."

"That's the touch of dark magic. It infects," Ferdinand says. "The medicinal cleanse will purify you, and we'll need to do the same with Mala. Otherwise the taint will begin to rot her from the inside out. Wait too long, and it's impossible to remove. Dying in such a manner is painful."

"Will she turn into a zombie?" Carl asks.

Something about the thrum in his voice makes me pause. He seems a bit too eager for this to be a concern. What is he thinking?

"There's no such thing as zombies," I lie. The kid's eyes narrow in sus-picion, and then he shrugs.

I need advice, but Sophia's right. Talking about this while Carl's around means nothing but trouble. Mala will be pissed when she finds out how much he's learned about this crazy, magical world we live in. Plus he's scared. He's hiding it well, but I don't miss the slight tremor in his hands.

"My truck's over at the Ackers' place," I say to Sophia and Ferdi-nand. "If you don't mind riding with us while I take Carl to school, we can talk in private on the way back."

"Hey, I told you I'm not going to school." The punk-ass kid steps backward, arms crossed. "That was our deal for me keeping my mouth shut about what's going on. You're going to renege? Turn into a lying sack just like my mama and daddy?"

I freeze at his words, stomach churning. But that's what he wants. He and his brothers are masters at manipulating my emotions. I still remember how devastated the Acker kids were when their mom ran off four years ago. And if that wasn't bad enough, their dad lost his ever-lovin' mind and became a conspiracy theorist who booby-trapped their property, kept everyone away except his own group of friends, and effectively isolated the kids from having a social life out-side of school. Then he tried to kill Mala. His parents weren't the best role models. And apparently, neither am I.

"Sorry, Carl," I say. "You caught me off guard. I never should've agreed to the deal. Not holding you accountable for your bad choices was wrong. So, unless you want to explain why you're skip-ping to the rev, you'll go to school without whining."

"How do you expect me to concentrate on geometry after every-thing that's happened?" he grumps, stomping away. Still, he doesn't complain while he helps us pack up the magical supplies, even cracking an unfunny joke by holding two of the candles against his chest. He plays with the wick nipples, cooing.

"If you want to learn how to handle real breasts, I can demonstrate," Sophia says, cupping herself with both hands and adjusting the fit of her bra with a wicked smile.

"Sophia!" I say. "Don't encourage him."

She titters and blows a kiss in Carl's direction, and the boy ducks his head and blushes. Even Ferdinand breaks his traditional silence to chuckle.

Children. I'm surrounded by children.

"*I bore witness to the creation of mankind…*" the voice in my head hisses indignantly. "*Despite the fact that the human form has evolved significantly within that time, female and male sexual reproductive organs vary little from your primate origins. I am immune to the evocative nature of a female's breasts. Unless they belong to Mala LaCroix. She, as humans say, has a fine rack.*"

"*Shut up!*"

The creature chuckles in response to the surge of anger flowing through my body, pleased it got a rise out of me. I guess I've become its new favorite toy. I share my glare with the others. "Behave. All of you."

Carl's face flames. "Sorry, Ms. Sophia," he apologizes with an Adam's-apple-bobbing gulp and shoves the candles into Ferdinand's open backpack. He picks up the chicken cage, making me extremely grateful that I don't have to carry it. My mouth waters every time I look at the bird.

I use the walk through the woods to settle down, avoiding actual thought as much as possible. My head throbs, stuffed with my thoughts and the creature's. It seems to find everything amusing.

From the way Sophia minces through the woods like she doesn't have a care in the world—only letting out a curse when her high heel gets stuck in the mud—to the last of the orange and gold leaves falling from the almost-naked branches overhead like butterflies flitting from flower to flower.

After seeing those butterflies on the corpses, I'll never appreciate their innocence quite the same ever again.

"Jaded. You have no sense of beauty."

"They were eating those kids," I say. "It was gross."

"What?" Carl asks, throwing a look over his shoulder.

My shoulders twitch. "Nothing. Just talking to myself."

"Eats to live. Eats to poop. Everything eats. Including butterflies."

It's got a point.

The path takes us past the pond. Sophia pauses on the bank and stares across the water for a long moment. "Oh, I'd forgotten how beautiful this area is." She points toward the same tree that Mala and I made out under the first time she brought me to the pond. "I lost my virginity to Gaston right over there." She sighs. "We were sixteen and so in love."

"TMI, Sophia." I tilt my head toward Carl. The kid's getting too much in the way of a sex education today. I'm such a bad guardian. 'Course, I could be overreacting. Lots of boys his age aren't virgins, but I don't think he'd blush this much if he had any experience.

Sophia winks. "No matter how experienced the man, one night with me is like popping your cherry all over again. You got a small taste, so you know I speak the truth."

"Get out of my head, Sophia."

"What's she talking about?" Carl asks, shifting the cage from one hand to the other. It takes a minute for the words to fully process, and his eyes grow wide. "Oh my God, she's got telepathy. She's reading your mind."

Shit, that was close.

"Did you cheat on Mala with her?"

God, help me.

"I shall do my best," the demon answers. It shoves my consciousness aside and speaks using my mouth. "It was only a brief dalliance. Drugs were involved."

"Stop! You're breaking the agreement."

"You asked for my help." The rustle of scales fills my ears.

"I said, 'God!'"

"Exactly. To what other god would you commune with if not me?"

The throbbing pain behind my eye messes with my thoughts. How do I explain the difference between big-G God and little-G god without insulting the creature? Or is it messing with me? I rub my temple, unable to speak. It takes a minute to notice that Carl studies me with narrowed eyes. Whatever he sees quirks his lips. He crosses his arms and shakes his head.

"Nah, you're messing with me. Mala would kill you. Kill you both if you ever cheated on her." Carl mimes pointing a gun at my head and pulls the thumb trigger. *Pow,* he mouths. "My cousin doesn't play. You shouldn't even joke about something like that."

"I remember," Sophia says in an odd tone. No longer teasing. I catch her staring, and my hand drops. If she's really able to read my mind, has she sensed the change in my relationship with the creature?

"Worry not, host. I don't care to share this tasty brain. The female likes to play, but I'm the master of games."

This basically means that I'm screwed. Do not pass go.

We've reached the fence dividing the Acker and LaCroix property. "How about if you lead the way, Carl," I say.

"Sure." The kid smiles shyly at Sophia. "Be careful to stay on the path, Ms. Sophia. My dad booby-trapped the heck out of this place. We destroyed all the ones we could find, but you never know."

"He's been crushed," Ferdinand whispers in a low rumble. He slaps my shoulder, and I wince. "It's sex magic. The boy didn't stand a chance."

"Couldn't she have dampened it a bit? He's barely fifteen. He'll have unrealistic expectations for any normal girl he encounters in the future."

"Aren't most first loves like that? The attraction is only physical. A heart binding isn't involved. It will fade."

I nod in relief. What he said makes total sense. Mala's my first love. But the physical attraction only played a small part. It wasn't until she tried to comfort me in the morgue garden after Lainey died that I started falling for her. My emotions grew stronger each time we spoke, until I finally reached the point where I couldn't imagine life without her.

The Ackers' two-story, plantation-style farmhouse comes into view. I've put a lot of work into renovating the place. I sold the junked cars and machinery for scrap metal. I used the money to replace the rotten boards on the wide porch and hung up new hurricane shutters. The twins repainted the house a buttery yellow because it was Dena's favorite color. They also take care of her garden, which sits in a corner of the property.

An empty white Toyota Camry is parked in the driveway, and the front door stands wide open.

"Someone's stealing our stuff!" Carl yells, lurching forward.

Ferdinand grabs his arm. "Let us." He lifts up the back of his shirt and pulls out a 9mm semiautomatic. "I'll go in first," he says.

Hell yeah, he goes in first. Like I want him at my back with a gun. I haven't been acquainted with Ferdinand long enough to know whether or not he's a good shot. And everyone in town knows Acker's dead and that the kids are living with Mala. Whoever's bold enough to break into the house during daylight might be crazy enough to come armed.

Carl and Sophia duck behind the white car, which blocks them from being seen from the house, while I follow Ferdinand, taking the steps up to the porch in twos. He motions for me to stand on the opposite side of the door frame, and once I'm in position, he yells, "Come out with your hands up!"

Muted voices filter from within, one pitched high like a woman's, the other deeper and pissed. A shadow darkens the doorway, and Ferdinand moves faster than I can react. Hell, by the time I remember to blink, he's grabbed the guy by the arm, yanked him from the doorway, and pinned him to the outside wall. He presses the gun barrel to the base of the guy's skull.

A middle-aged woman with fire-engine-red hair stands in the doorway with her hand pressed to her mouth. Screams roll forth, ending in a choked wail. I thread my arms through hers, locking her wrists up behind her back. The last thing I need is for her to lose what's left of her mind and try to defend her man. Her voices rises an octave when she realizes she can't break free.

"Shut up and don't move or I'll blow his head off," Ferdinand snaps at her, and she shrinks into the fabric of her peasant blouse and ankle-length skirt, looking like a wilted flower child—a holdover from the sixties era or a poster child for a cult. My pick goes to the cult angle, since the smarmy guy she hooked up with gives off an oozing, drink-the-Kool-Aid-Jim-Jones vibe.

Ferdinand must sense the aura of danger floating around the guy too. He still holds the gun, but at least it's no longer pointed at the guy's brainstem. No need to accidently splatter the newly painted walls with gore simply out of twitchiness. "Hey, kid, get up here and cover us," he yells, tipping his head toward the woman.

I glance at Carl, who stares at the woman with wide eyes. Sophia has her hand on his shoulder, and he visibly trembles, like he's about to fly apart. A sob bursts from deep in his throat, and he shakes off her grip.

"Mama," he cries, running forward. He clears the steps in one jump and then staggers to a halt about five feet from the woman. "Is that you?"

My arms drop when it dawns on me who I'm touching. The woman steps aside, giving me a clear view of her face, and dashes tears from her eyes. Too late, I notice the resemblance between her and her children. I always thought Dena favored her father, but seeing Pepper Acker again after four years brings a stab of pain. This is what Dena will look like someday, if she survives.

"Daryl…no, it's Carl, isn't it?" Pepper staggers forward with her hand stretched toward her son.

Carl flinches. His foot slips off the edge of the porch. I lunge forward, like I'll be able to catch him before he topples backward. Lucky for us both, he white-knuckles the railing, holding on for dear life, and I'm glad I replaced the rotten wood or it never would've held his weight.

"What are you doing in my house?" His gaze moves to the cardboard boxes on the porch, and he frowns. "Are you stealing from us?"

Pepper gasps. "No, of course not. I've come home."

His eyes trace the curve of her face. His chest heaves from his rapid breaths. Pain flashes across his features. Then he lets out a deep breath and his expression hardens. "This isn't your house. Hasn't been for over four years. Why are you here now, when we don't need you anymore?"

She flinches, eyes flickering to the man that Ferdinand now holds in place by the arm.

"Don't look at him. I asked *you* the question," Carl yells, pushing off the railing. His back straightens and his chest puffs out. Once again, I'm reminded that he's not really a kid anymore. Even though he's stupid as a rock, he's becoming a man. And he's determined to protect his family, even if it's from his own mother. "Are you brainwashed or something? What do you want?"

"Stop it, baby. Please, don't be mad." She takes another faltering step toward him. This time he holds his ground. "I only heard about your daddy dying a few weeks ago. I came as soon as I could."

"Why?"

Her face crumples. "How could I not? My baby girl's in the hospital. You boys are all alone. You need me. Us. That's my boyfriend, Judd. We came to take care of things."

"Is he the man you ran off with?" Carl's eyes dart toward Judd, but come back to his mother. "Nah, I doubt that guy stuck around for long. How many guys have you shacked up with since you decided to abandon your own kids?"

"Hey! Don't talk to your mama like that," Judd yells, jerking his arm. "Treat her with respect."

"Respect is earned, so shut the fuck up. Nobody asked for your opinion." Carl's hands double into fists. He faces his mother again.

"You chose that piece of shit over me. Over Daryl, J.J., and Axle. Over Dad and Dee. You left us. So scurry back to wherever you've spent the last four years before I call the cops and have you arrested for trespassing. Nobody wants you here. Either of you."

"Ain't your property," Judd says. "We'll go when we finish what we came for. Wrap up the reunion, Pepper. The realtor will be here in two hours. We need to finish inventorying the property."

Pepper sighs. "Sorry, Carl. I tried to do this the easy way, but you've gone and made it hard. Best accept the fact that I'm not going anywhere until I set my affairs in order, no pun intended. Your daddy's and my divorce never finalized. Legally the house and property are mine to sell, and I'd be a fool to hold on to this backwoods piece of swamp. You and your brothers are mine too. I'm taking back everything that I gave up to get away from him. So go pack your bags. You and your brothers will be moving to New Orleans with me."

A drawn-out silence follows as we process her words.

"You're a selfish bitch!" Carl yells.

Judd shoves past Pepper, knocking her against the wall. He's a big guy, but now that he's closer, I see he's not as big as Carl. Pepper must not have told him how Carl grew up. The kid's been fighting his whole life, starting with beatings from his dad and then on to schoolyard bullying. The boy's no saint. And he punches hard enough to break bone. Judd swings at him, but Carl ducks. He pops Judd square on his bulbous nose. The audible crack and flying blood causes Pepper to scream. Carl grabs the guy around the waist, lifts him up, and body slams him to the porch. Once Judd's beneath him, Carl's fists fly in a flurry of punches aimed at Judd's head.

Ferdinand stands off to the side, watching with a slight smile. Can't say I'm not enjoying the show either. The jackass deserved to get his ass beat. And seeing the boy handle his business like a man fills me with fatherly pride. Still, I can't let it go too far. I let him get in a couple more punches then yell, "Carl, stop! You're gonna kill him!"

When he doesn't even pause, I wrap my arms around his waist and haul him off Judd. He swings his elbows back, catching me in the gut. Air woofs out of my chest, but I don't let go. It's like hugging a bobcat, spitting and clawing in my arms.

"Damn it, Ferdinand. Help me."

Judd sits up, holding a hand to his broken nose. "I'm gonna kill you, you little bastard."

Carl kicks out at him. "Come on!"

"Stop antagonizing the kid or I'll let him finish what you started," I yell at the man who remains huddled in a ball with his fingers pinching the bridge of his nose to stop the bleeding. Ferdinand grabs Carl's legs and helps me carry him down the stairs.

"Drop him," I say, and Ferdinand nods.

Carl hits the ground butt first, and I wish I'd let go before Ferdinand. Dropping him on his head might've knocked some sense into him, but he's too pissed to feel pain. He tries to scramble up. So I shove him back down with a boot to the center of his ass. He bucks and twists beneath me, strong with his anger. Normally I wouldn't need help with him, but not today. I squat to press a knee to the center of his back. "He's breaking free. Pin him down."

Ferdinand sits across his legs.

"Better get Judd to the hospital while you have the chance, Pepper," I yell. "I don't plan on holding your son indefinitely. Maybe you should arrange to have this conversation later. *And leave Judd at the motel the next time.*"

Chapter 9

Mala

Destination Crazytown

George overhears my end of the conversation. He follows silently when I sprint for the main road and his patrol car, not that I give him the opportunity to protest. He only pauses after unlocking the door to pick up the radio and advise Chief Keyes and Bessie of an emergency situation in progress, then slides into the car beside me and asks, "Where are we going?"

"Something is going down at the Ackers'." My voice trembles as I say, "I heard yelling in the background. Sophia said 'only minor injuries,' but I don't know what the hell that means. The woman can bring the dead back to life. A broken bone is like a paper cut to her."

George turns on the engine and pulls slowly out onto the dirt road. The drizzle from earlier changes into a heavy downpour, and water runs down the windshield with each swipe of the wipers. "Who is this Sophia person?"

"She's an apprentice to my Aunt Magnolia."

"Oh? Is she the woman who drugged Landry in New Orleans?"

I gulp. "I told you about that?"

"You were in the hospital and highly medicated from the shock of what happened with Red and Dena. You told me a lot of things you probably wish you never spilled."

"Did I tell you about my Dena dilemma? No." I shake my head, muttering, "I never told you about that." Even delusional I wouldn't be idiotic enough to tell George that I could bring Dena back from the dead if I murdered someone. As a peace officer, he'd be against the idea for obvious reasons. I should be against it for the same principles, but it's basically less about my ideals than what type of guilt I can live with.

George flips on the siren as soon as we exit Old Lick and drive onto the main road through town. I try to get through to Landry's phone but there's no answer. I give up, staring out the window as the scenery flies past. A white car captures my attention for a brief second. The woman driving looks so much like Dena that my heart tries to leap out of my chest and chase after her.

I blow out a heavy breath. "This is killing me. I hate not knowing what's going on."

George reaches over to rumple my curls. Kind of annoying in my present agitated state, but the expression of emotion inspiring the gesture also brings comfort. "I'm sure everything is fine," he says. "If it weren't, Dixie would've gotten a call to send out an ambulance."

"True." The image of Landry in the chicken coop pops into my head. I pinch my eyes shut, knowing I shouldn't say anything, but the words spill out. "Landry's been sleepwalking."

"Seriously?" He frowns. "No wonder you're freaking out. Is it a side effect of the whole possession thing?"

"Yeah. When he's asleep, his defenses lower, allowing the demon to take over. It comes out to play, then returns to wherever it hides inside him. Landry wakes up with no memory of what happened." I turn sideways so I can study his expression. "You know I don't scare easily, right? I don't want to lose Landry, Georgie. You almost shot him the last time. But you also hesitated when the demon attacked. You both could've been killed."

He meets my eyes in the rearview mirror. "Why are you telling me this?"

"If you're in danger, take him down. Don't wait. I'm not saying to shoot him in the head, but use your Taser. Knock him out with your baton, if you have to. Don't let him get close enough to injure you. Otherwise, you won't have any choice but to use your gun. Like I said, I don't want to lose either of you."

George remains silent. After a while, I face forward again. My mind races through possible scenarios about what I might find once we reach the Ackers'. And I'm glad I warned George in case the demon has broken free again. Forewarned is forearmed.

We pull down the Ackers' driveway. Sophia and Ferdinand stand by Landry's truck. I jump out of the car as soon as it stops moving. "Where is he? Is he in the house? You said he's hurt." I veer around them, running for the steps.

Landry strides out the front door, followed by Carl. He lifts his hand, and I almost keel over in relief. He meets me at the base of the stairs with arms stretched, and I throw myself into the hug, squeezing tight. A puff of air releases from his lungs with a little "*Oof*" and a wince.

"Oh Mother Mary, you're hurt?" I pull back, lifting the bottom of his T-shirt. My fingertips trace the slight redness on his tight abs. "How did this happen?" I step toward Ferdinand. My voice rises an octave, and I wince at the shrillness of my tone, but I'm too angry to turn it down. "Did you hit him?"

Landry wraps his arm around my shoulder and tucks me against his side. I try to shrug him off but he won't let me go. "Retract your claws. It wasn't Ferdinand."

"It was me," Carl says. He slides the toe of his tennis shoe across the red dirt. "It was an accident. Sorry."

I point my finger at him. "Sorry doesn't cut it, buddy. You're in so much trouble. If George wasn't here to witness your death, I'd wring your scrawny neck. What were you thinking? Ditching school, fighting with Landry—do you want to get taken away from me so badly?"

"Mala, I—"

"When Mrs. Huxton said you didn't arrive at school, I almost lost my mind with worry! I thought someone kidnapped you. That you'd been—" I inhale and hold in the word that's tap dancing on the roof of my mouth, but it flashes through my mind anyway—*murdered*.

George meets my gaze and nods. He'd been thinking along the same lines. Good to know I'm not just being freakishly overprotective. The boys need to be warned about the threat. They're far too independent to be running around town without being aware of the danger.

While I try to find the words to express my fear in a way that won't give him nightmares, Carl cuts in. "Will you stop yelling long enough for me to explain, please?"

Tears pop in his red-rimmed eyes. Snot runs from a Rudolph the Reindeer red nose to mix with the tears. He wipes his face with the bottom of his brand-new T-shirt, avoiding the mud stains and…I squint, leaning closer. "Is that blood?"

He drops his shirt. "Yeah, but it's not mine," he says quickly, and upon seeing my panicked glance up at Landry, says even faster, "I'm not crazy. Landry would kill me if I ever punched him."

Landry rubs his stomach. "Right, but elbowing me is just fine? A little lower and I wouldn't be able to conceive children."

Carl grins. "Good thing Mala's already pregnant."

All the air in my lungs releases in a strangled rush. "W-w-what?" Heat floods my cheeks as five pairs of eyes turn in my direction. Surprise flickers in George's gaze, but everyone else smiles as if the announcement's no big deal. Like they've already heard…*What the hell?* "That's bull. Who says I'm pregnant?"

"I found the pregnancy test this morning." Landry pulls the test stick from his pocket and holds it out to me. "See, two lines equals: 'Surprise! You're my baby momma.'"

My eyes cross as I try to focus on the squiggly, blurry lines. The urge to run gets my feet moving, but the fuzziness in my head causes them to cross and tangle together. I stumble, and Landry's grip on my shoulder tightens. He twists me around until I'm facing him.

I can't even look him in the eye. "Let me go!"

"Why? I'm not mad. Just hurt that you didn't tell me."

"How could I when I didn't even know myself? The twins came to tell me that you were missing before the result came in. Then everything went to hell. Maybe it's a false positive. That can happen if you wait too long to read the test. The box says so," I say, voice rising with false hope. 'Cause yeah, dream on, baby!

Landry's jaw hardens. "We'll talk about this later."

Now I've gone and hurt his feelings. I want to crawl into bed, pull the covers over my head, and bawl my eyes out, but I can't. I've got to suck it up and try not to explode into a gooey mess in front of my friends…and the witch Sophia. I bury my face in Landry's chest, wishing I could disappear.

Footsteps shuffle forward and a throat clears. I peek over my shoulder. George stands a few paces behind me, looking as green about the gills as I feel. "If there's no danger here, then I'd better head back to the crime scene."

"Sure." *Please go before I die of humiliation.* "Bessie will have a bunch of questions. I hope you don't get disciplined because of me."

He ruffles my curls, ignoring Landry's grunt. "Hang in there, little sis."

Warmth fills my chest at his words. I always wanted an older brother. Guess hearing confirmation that Landry and I are expecting has kicked his fraternal instincts into high gear. Before he can leave, I say, "If they let me, I would love to work this case. I know I can help. You'll vouch for me, right?"

Landry's muscles flex beneath my hands. "Hold on—"

George ignores Landry as if he didn't speak. "The situation's more complicated than I initially thought." His eyes drop to my belly, and I cover what I now know for sure is a baby bump with my hand. "You'll probably have Bessie on your doorstep tonight. Run it by her then."

Landry tries to step forward, but this time I hold him back from going after my brother. "Look, I held off on kicking your ass because Mala came back safely, but there's no way in hell I'm letting you drag her deeper into this case, George. She almost died."

"What are you talking about?" A frown furrows George's brow.

"Nothing. He's just being overprotective." I swallow hard, squeezing Landry's bicep in warning. "I'll fill him in on what happened after you're gone."

Landry's mouth opens then shuts when he catches my pleading expression. He blows out a heavy breath. "She's right. Just ignore me. Obviously Mala can take care of herself." He pulls his arm free to rub a finger along the underside of his eye patch, like it itches. A telltale sign of his discomfort that shouts even louder than the tension in his rock-hard body. He runs the same hand through his hair, dragging his fingers through the ebony locks until they hang like a curtain over his face.

My stomach twists at the movement. It took forever to convince him to wear his hair back, so I could stare at his face whenever I want like a lovesick fool. He uses his hair to hide his feelings. Like I can't tell how upset he is right now. But despite his discomfort, I still don't want George to know about the danger I put myself in. Knowing I'm pregnant is bad enough. He doesn't need another reason to bar me from this case. I'm being selfish. I know it, but I don't want my dream to get snatched away again. Especially since I'm closer to reaching it than I've been in months.

"Deputy Dubois, can you drop me and Sophia off at my car? It's parked at the crossroads," Ferdinand says, drawing George's attention from the silent argument Landry and I are having. When he notices his words have captured our interest as well, he explains. "I need to get back to New Orleans and update Magnolia on what has happened."

"No problem. Let's go."

"Oh no," Sophia says, waving them off. "I think it's best if I stay."

"I'll be there in a minute," Ferdinand says, waiting until George walks over to get into his car, then turns to Sophia. "What now?"

She rolls her eyes. "What do you think? The magic used to break that spell was powerful, and it's left a path directly to Mala's door. I don't think she's at all safe on her own."

Ferdinand frowns. "Do you think he'll come for her?"

"Wouldn't you in his situation? He would've looked for her out of curiosity alone, but not only did she break his circle but she stole his totems. He'd been amassing energy from those sacrifices for a long time. He won't be pleased to learn they've been stolen."

"Stolen?" I swallow hard. "I didn't take anything."

"Never said you did," Sophia says, glancing over at Landry. He flushes but remains silent, only tipping his chin up in a good-bye to Ferdinand. I study Landry with narrowed eyes, wishing I'd learned her handy skill of reading minds. What's going on in that head stuffed with demon fluff? And why do I suddenly feel so frightened?

Not up to an argument, I decide to take a page from Carl's distractionary playbook and shift the focus off myself. "So what exactly happened here?"

Sophia twines her fingers through the ends of her long dark hair and studies the tips with a slight frown. "Do you want the long, exciting version, which includes your timely rescue from dark magic, or the shorter, equally thrilling bit, where the boys' mother returned?"

It takes a minute for her words to sink in. "Sophia!"

She blinks and drops her hair. "What?"

"Carl, why don't you go into the house? I need to speak with the adults alone."

"You're a little late, Mala. I'm not deaf. I know all about how you talk to ghosts," he snaps. "I even met your uncle Gaston and helped drag your sorry ass out of the dark-magic circle. So don't treat me like a stupid kid."

"And how exactly did you get dragged into this mess?"

My boyfriend shrugs. "Sorry."

"Don't blame Landry. I overheard him talking about bringing Dee back from the dead. You're going to save her right? Red shot her and tried to kill us." He steps closer, and I realize he's almost as tall as Landry. He looms over my head, a dark cloud filling his blue eyes. "He doesn't deserve to live after what he's done. And you know it!"

My breath comes out in rapid bursts. "Stop, Carl. Don't…"

"Leave her alone," Landry says. "It's Mala's decision. She'll have to live with the consequences, not you."

He turns to Sophia. "Then you teach me."

"It's not so easy." She smiles, looking him over. "You'd have to die first. Are you willing to do what it takes to earn the power?"

"No, he's not!" I grab Sophia's arm. Her skin burns my fingers, and I pull my hand away with a hiss. "It's my job. I'll do whatever needs to be done. Leave him out of it."

"As you wish."

Saints, what a mess. Carl throws a glare in my direction. Obviously he won't be happy unless I save Dena. Landry grabs his arm and drags him up the porch stairs. He's jabbering the whole time. Hopefully he'll talk the kid off the ledge.

"Is this why you called me away from the crime scene?" I ask Sophia. "You made it sound like someone was about to die. Was it to talk some sense into Carl?"

"Well, at the time it seemed like a close call from my point of view. As I mentioned earlier, the boys' mother returned. Said she planned on selling this place and taking the kids with her to New Orleans. Needless to say, your boy was not pleased at the news. Or with her new man trying to assert his authority. The blood is all the other guy's."

A rush of panic flows through me, and I fight off the urge to run to the school, pack up the kids, and hide them in the bayou where Pepper Acker can't find them. I promised I'd protect them, but maybe I'm being selfish.

Dena loved her mom, a lot. Hell, I loved her too. She acted like a surrogate mom to me when I visited as a kid. She didn't view me with the same disdain as her husband. When she took off, it devastated her family, but especially Dena. She ended up taking on her mother's role in the home. At least her dad didn't beat her like he did his wife and the twins. "Oh, I think I saw her. Was she driving a white car?"

"Yes."

A white car. Like the one the murderer drove to pick up the kids. Nah, it can't be that easy. The guy didn't seem stupid. Why would he drive the car all over town? It has to be a coincidence. "Where did she say she was going?"

"Probably to the hospital. Carl broke her boyfriend's nose."

I need to find out what's really going on from the horse's mouth. I can't give the boys up without learning her intentions. They've suffered enough loss without having their mom come into their life only to abandon them again.

Chapter 10

Landry

Parasitic Pest

We pile into my truck. I hold the steering wheel in a death grip as I drive down the road leading off the Acker property. It's twisty with muddy potholes big enough to eat my tires. Over the last few months, I've adjusted to having only one working eye. I rarely get nauseous anymore from vertigo, due to compensating for my lack of depth perception. And I added extra-wide mirrors to the truck to cover my blind spots. As long as I don't lose focus or get distracted by shiny things, I do okay behind the wheel.

Mala sits in the passenger seat, leaving Carl stuck in the back next to Sophia, not that he complains. I catch him in the rearview mirror peeking down her blouse. To point it out would be a dick move—bringing embarrassment to all parties. Well, probably not to Sophia. I doubt she'd care. Plus, she egged him on earlier.

I clear my throat, hoping to catch his attention. But his eyes don't lift. Oh well, I did my best. If he gets caught, the consequences are on his head. A soft snore comes from my girl. She sits with her chin resting on her chest, her eyes closed. Her cheeks are flushed bright pink, and her luscious lips are slightly parted. She looks pretty, but clearly exhausted, although she'd never admit it. She acts like she's got to be the Energizer bunny at all times.

"Fetuses suck the life out of their hosts far faster than I do."

I blink at the pitted road, shaking my head. Maybe if I shake it harder the parasite will fall out of my ear like a blob of earwax. *"Are you talking to me?"* I think to the muttering voice.

"Yes. You seem discomfited by my presence. I merely point out that a prenatal human is far more invasive, or parasitic, per your insult to me. They suck their nutrients from the host. I, however, have found an alternate food source. Chicken. Plus, I provide an invaluable service. If not for me, you would have perished at least a handful of times, and that number only includes those instances when I bothered to wake." Smugness radiates through my body.

"Why do you have to be such a tool?"

"Watch the road, host!"

My attention shifts back outside my head.

How did I miss all the screaming? Mala has both hands on the steering wheel, and her foot slams on the brake pedal just before we careen off the road into the drainage ditch. When the truck stops, she turns and repeatedly slaps my shoulder, screaming, "Wake up! Wake up!"

I grab her hands. "I'm awake." A sob rolls from her, and I pull her quivering body into my arms. "It's okay. We're okay."

Carl punches my already throbbing shoulder. "Asshole. You almost killed us."

"I know. I'm sorry." I squeeze Mala a little tighter, expressing my guilt through bodily contact that doesn't absolve me of anything. I should've been paying attention to the road instead of engaging with the demon.

This is your fault, I think-yell to the thing in my head.

"No, I saved your life again. Your debt grows."

I shiver at the threat in its tone. Death might be preferable to what it wants in compensation, but the terms of any future deal are open to negotiation. I'll worry about my payment plan later. Right now, Mala and the baby are my first priority.

My fingers thread through Mala's curls, brushing off the strands clinging to her wet cheeks. I press a kiss to her forehead. "You're not hurt?"

"No thanks to you." Mala shoves out of my arms. "I was screaming, but you didn't respond. What happened?"

"I got distracted." I rub the lump on the back of my head. "Maybe I have a bit of brain damage," I joke. "I hit my head twice today."

"Or maybe you should admit that you're no longer alone in your thoughts," Sophia says, busting me out.

I wait for the explosion, but Mala doesn't seem to catch on to what she's implying. I'm okay with that. Springing the news about my deal with the devil this way will only bring pain. I need to ease her into the right frame of mind to accept the implications of how this will affect our relationship—preferably once she's satiated after a night of rambunctious sex followed by wine and chocolate truffles.

I lick my lips at the image of Mala eating the chocolate off my body. The increasingly kinky fantasy does nothing to help refocus my thoughts enough to navigate this road. Umm, shiny things. So very shiny.

"How about if you drive, Mala," I murmur. "Between my vision and the headache, I shouldn't be behind the wheel anyway." Which is kind of the truth, but I expect the third degree. So I'm surprised when Mala jumps out of the truck and switches places with no further questions asked. We both seem to be stuffed full of secrets and concerns today.

"Where are we going first?" Mala asks. "To drop Carl off at school or to the hospital?"

"Pepper and jerkwad might be gone if we wait too long. And I didn't ask what hotel they're staying in."

Carl wraps his arms around the headrest and Mala's neck. She stiffens until she realizes he's not trying to choke her unconscious, but hugging her. "Do you know what you're going to tell my mom, Mala? You won't give us up to her, right?"

One of her hands releases the steering wheel to pat his head. "I don't know yet. Guess we need to know her intentions. She didn't make the best first impression by letting her boyfriend assault you. If I'd known before George left, I would've asked him along."

A spurt of jealousy hardens my jaw, but I force the words out in a light tone. "You got me." I tilt my head to study her expression with my good eye. It's times like these when I miss having peripheral vision on my left side. Sidelong glances are a distant memory. My throat closes while I wait for her response.

The corner of her lip lifts in a crooked smile. "Yeah, but you don't have a badge to flash if this guy gets out of control again."

The breath releases in a low sigh. I hoped she'd acknowledge my ability to protect her, but Mala's like a mockingbird when it comes to the shiny gold star winking on Deputy Dawg's chest. And here I am thinking shiny things distract *me*.

"Your obsession with dog rivals mine with chicken. I also prefer breast meat. Do you plan to cook him before you eat him?"

"I think he'll taste better flame broiled."

The creature laughs at my joke. Well, hopefully it knows I'm not serious. My smile fades when I catch Mala's sidelong grimace, and I shrug. "Carl kind of brought the wrath down on himself. Pepper seemed reasonable at first. Said she wants to put her family back together." I twist around to face Carl, but he avoids my gaze by staring out the window. "I know you're mad, but you've got to admit your dad treated her pretty shitty. I'm surprised she didn't bail on him sooner."

"Then she should've taken us with her." He slumps back in his seat and crosses his arms. The stubborn expression he wears doesn't hide his hurt.

We pull into the hospital parking lot. None of us move from our seats. We each dread what's coming for different reasons. Tension radiates from Mala in waves strong enough to raise the hairs on my arms when she clutches my hand. She's never been comfortable in hospitals, and now it's worse.

Ghosts flock to her like she's got a homing beacon attached to her forehead. I don't get hit with the mojo quite as bad. I see the residual spirits. We've been practicing blocking them when we train with Ferdinand. Hopefully our shielding will withstand the oncoming barrage or we'll be ready to punch someone in the face before we find Pepper.

"Let's get this over with." I release her hand and open the door. She waits until I come around to help her out rather than making the long jump to the ground herself. Her arms wrap around my neck, and I hold her close, inhaling. Her scent wraps around my body. She presses her nose into the side of my neck. Her warm breath blows across my skin, and my gut tightens when she presses a kiss to the underside of my jaw.

"Hold on to me, Landry," she whispers. "Don't let them get me."

"I've got you. Always."

Her lips press against mine. The taste of her mouth with each pulse of her tongue is like honey and melted butter. My tense muscles relax as the kiss deepens. My worries fade, leaving a golden brown haze in their place.

Finally, she pulls back with a slow inhale and whispers, "No matter how bad things feel, one kiss from you puts everything back into perspective."

"Too bad about our audience. If we were alone, I'd really rock your perspective." I give her a quick dip with a neck nuzzle that leaves her giggling, then set her on her feet. Sophia sticks her head out the open door. "I'm beat. I'm going to take a nap while you take care of business."

"Carl? You staying in the truck too?" I ask.

"Nope!" He slams the door and races for the entrance as if afraid we'll call him back.

Mala threads her fingers through mine, walking on my blind side. She's my other half. With her next to me, I don't worry about crashing into unseen obstacles. My presence becomes important to her once we enter the emergency room lobby. Her sweaty hand clenches mine. I glance over to see her glazed eyes shut as she inhales. When the breath releases, her eyes open.

"I'm okay," she says with a grin. "The shield's holding, and Caspar is not invited to this party."

"Good, I didn't want to kick not-so-friendly-ghost ass."

Her laugh cuts off in a snort. "Whoops."

"You're adorable."

She pinches my cheek. "So are you, sweetie."

"Ugh," Carl yelps. "Stop with the lovey-dovey talk before you totally turn me off relationships. I don't see my mom, but her asshole boyfriend is sitting over there with an icepack pressed to his nose." He steps forward, but I jerk him back. "Stay here and protect Mala. I'll go talk to him."

"Babysit her from what? Evil ghost nurses?"

Mala whirls on him. "I'm about sick of your smartass attitude. Don't disrespect Landry or I'll tell the rev."

I leave them to their bickering. Of all the Acker boys, Carl's the most like Dena and Mala. They like to argue just for the fun of getting one over on the other. It seems like an exhausting waste of energy to me.

I thread through the rows of empty chairs. Judd straightens in his seat when he sees me coming. His gaze darts to the security guard standing by the check-in counter. I raise my hands. "Look, I'm not here to finish anything. I brought the kids' temporary guardian to talk to Pepper about her plans. Where is she?"

"You don't talk to her without me." He half rises from the chair like he thinks he can stand up to me, but unlike Carl, I'm not a teenager.

I scowl and rest my hand on his shoulder. All the construction work I've been doing has bulked up my arms, and he winces when I give him a little squeeze. I also do my best to loom over his head to add emphasis to the unspoken threat. Judd drops back into his seat with an audible gulp. "Like I said, where's Pepper?"

His eyes widen, and his Adam's apple bobs as he licks his lips. "She went to visit her daughter."

I slap his back hard enough to rock him forward. "Thanks for your assistance."

Mala and Carl have subsided into sullen silence by the time I reach them. "She's upstairs visiting Dena."

Carl gasps. "I can't handle seeing Dee all hooked up to those machines. I'll be in the truck with Ms. Sophia."

Mala watches him run off with almost the exact same expression. Guilt spins the wheels behind her eyes. "I'm not sure if I can confront Pepper like this either. Not in front of Dena."

"I'll be with you the whole time. The last thing we need is Pepper showing up at the house unannounced to pick up the kids. Carl freaked out bad enough. Can you imagine how Axle will react? She left when he was five. He barely remembers her."

Mala drags her feet the whole way to the long-term-care unit. Pepper stands in front of the room with Dena's doctor signing some sort of document. Mala gasps when she sees her. She breaks free from my grip and runs over to them. "What are you doing?"

She tries to snatch the clipboard from Pepper's hand, but the woman shoves it at the doctor and steps protectively in front of the older man. "Have you lost your mind, Mala LaCroix? I don't care how old you are. I'll swat your backside like I did when you and Dena ate a whole pan of banana bread."

Mala stiffens. "Don't you dare, Mrs. Acker. You've no right to play the parent card now." She addresses the doctor over the woman's shoulder, ignoring her sputters. "Dr. Estrada, is that the form authorizing Dena to be taken off life support? I told you I wouldn't sign it. Ever."

"Ms. LaCroix, according to the legal documentation from Dena's mother, you're no longer in charge of what happens to this patient."

"When did you go to court? And why wasn't I notified?"

"Why should you be?" Pepper asks.

A wild expression fills Mala's eyes. "But you can't kill her." She grabs onto the doctor's coat when he tries to scoot passed. "Please, don't let her do this."

The doctor jerks out of her grasp. I grab Mala's shoulders and pull her against my chest to keep her from following as he flees down the hall with his tail between his legs. Huge sobs choke her up, and her bewildered, inconsolable tears break my heart.

Pepper watches her with moist eyes. Her hand flutters toward Mala and then drops. She turns her pleading gaze to me. "Landry…please."

"I can't…" I shake my head. "She's right. Give Dee a chance, Pepper. It's too soon to give up hope. Miracles happen all of the time." Especially since this might be the incentive Mala needs to finally make her choice. But the woman before me doesn't know this.

Her shoulders straighten, and a hard glint wipes the sadness from her gaze. "I'm Waydene's mother. This is the most difficult decision I've ever made. I need you and Mala's help explaining this to the kids."

"Explain murder?" Mala cries. "How?"

"She's brain dead, Mala. Dena's gone. It's only her body that's being kept alive. My daughter would never want to linger like this. In your heart, you know it's true."

I don't think Mala can even hear her over her sobs. Her body shakes, and I hold her close to keep her from collapsing. Her swollen eyes search Pepper's face. "Is it because of the hospital bills? I have money. I'll pay for her care until she wakes up. Please don't do this, Pepper. I'm begging you."

Pepper takes a step closer and lays a trembling hand on Mala's arm. "It's not about money. I have to do what's right for my sweet baby girl—no matter how much pain it causes me. Dena's organs will be donated. She'd be happy to know that others have a chance at a healthy life because of her. I won't change my mind. You have three days. It'll give us all time to say our good-byes."

"What about the boys?" I ask. "They'll never forgive you if you do this."

Pepper's eyes tighten. "I owe you a debt I can never repay for taking care of my family, but I'm back now. I'm coming for my boys next. I spoke to their social worker. Mrs. Moulton says she'll contact you tomorrow to arrange for a smooth transition into my custody."

"No," Mala cries, voice strangled. "This is all wrong. Don't do this, please."

Pepper pats Mala's arm and walks off without looking back.

"She's killing Dee. She's really gonna die. I can't let this happen." She shoves open the hospital room door and staggers over to the bed holding her cousin. Dena looks like a wax dummy. Nothing of her usual vibrancy remains in the shell before us.

"Pepper's right. Dena's brain dead. She's not waking up on her own, no matter how much we want her to. You know what you've got to do."

"But what if she comes back wrong? Like Etienne."

"She might. There are no guarantees. You've got to decide whether or not taking the risk is worth losing her. I'll back you all the way, no matter what."

Chapter 11

Mala

Sir Hotness

Save her or let her go? The words flash-bomb the shield around my thoughts, peppering the wall with seeds of doubt and anguish until I'm too upset to concentrate. The protective barrier breaks, and I stagger toward the hospital bed. Landry grabs for me, and I hope he'll catch my fall, but he misses. I topple across Dena's legs. The second my hand touches her, my vision goes black like a trash can lid slamming shut and locks me inside.

I freeze, afraid to move. My heart races, using up the oxygen in my straining lungs. I inhale a shallow breath of frigid air. The aching cold settles in my chest and chills my flesh. My bones ache. I search the darkness for a hint of light, but see nothing. Feel nothing, but emptiness. It's maddening. A total absence of sensory stimulation.

I'll go crazy if I stay trapped here. Problem is, I don't know where I am or how to free myself. Should I call for Gaston?

Humiliation twists my stomach at the thought of begging for help again. Bad enough I screwed up so horribly this morning that I needed a five-person rescue team to drag my ass out of danger. And whatever's happening is nowhere near as bad as being trapped in a dark-magic spell designed to eat my soul. *I hope.*

Okay, stop! No wimping out. This is an opportunity to practice controlling my abilities. I can't learn if I cry for help at the first sign of trouble. I got here by myself, and I'll figure a way out on my own. Just be calm. Analyze the situation in a logical manner. One step at a time.

Okay, first observation: This place feels different from the times I traveled to the other side in the past. Before, it had the feel of an alternate reality. One based on the same physical principles as the real world, only slightly off in texture, sight, and sound.

I squeeze my hands together until I feel pain. I touch my cold cheeks and shiver. I exhale a heavy breath to warm my cupped hands. *This is me.* Wherever I am, I have a sense of self.

My feet shuffle in place. My toes curl on cold stone. No shoes. *Am I naked?* A quick pat down confirms the holy grail of all nightmares. *Crap!*

I squat to hide behind my upraised knees and cross my arms over my chest. *Okay, don't freak. It's dark. Nobody can see me, and so what if they can? Do I care what they think about my nakedness? No, because if they're stuck in this limbo world, then they're just as screwed as I am. And they're probably naked too.*

Moving on to the next step: Determine if I'm the only one trapped in this hellhole.

"Hello?" My voice echoes, cracking on the *O*, as if I'm yelling in an underground cavern full of winding passages. The sound reverberates in my ears. I lift my hands to muffle the sound, and then realize, if I do that, I can't hear a response. I hold my breath, ears straining, and almost choke up a lung when a broken sob, followed by a tiny, familiar voice, breaks the unending silence.

"Help."

"Dena?" *It's her, I know it is.* "Where are you?"

"H-help…" Sob, then echo, growing louder and louder. "Help!"

Pain. The word stabs into my brain, poking holes in my thoughts. I drop to my knees and cover my ears. It hurts. "Stop shrieking, Dee. Please, you're hurting me."

The screams cut off. The final echo ends with a slight hiccup, as if she's holding it in with effort. Am I in her mind? Or is this purgatory, a place for souls who can't break free of the bonds of flesh? Hell, it doesn't matter. I'm not leaving her trapped here. Once I find her, I'm bringing her out. I can't hesitate this time.

Guess this means I've made my decision.

"It's Mala." My voice bounces off unseen walls. I grit my teeth against the pain. A whimper comes from my left. Facing in that direction, I stretch out my hands and shuffle forward. "I'm here to help you."

"Shh, he'll hear you." Footsteps hit the ground, moving away from me.

"Dena, please."

"Told you… Now it's too late to save yourself," she whispers, close enough that I feel her warm breath in my ear.

I spin, arms waving. The tip of a finger brushes across her icy skin, and I lunge toward her, but she's already gone. "Stop running from me."

"He's coming."

"Who?" I hold my breath, straining to hear.

Only Dena's voice pierces the darkness as she laughs, and the madness in her tone raises the hairs on the back of my neck. "Thinks he's so sneaky." She singsongs the words, as if using this conversation with me to taunt this unknown person. "He can't catch you if you don't stay still, can you, Redford? You try and try, but you can't catch me."

A wave of hatred flares like a fire lighting up a moonless night.

Redford Delahoussaye's voice comes from right behind me. "I'll kill you."

I drop to my knees with a shriek and I crawl away as fast as I can. I think I move at an angle, but the dark disorients me. The echoing nature of this place makes it difficult to determine where sound comes from. It plays with my senses, deceiving with every turn.

Oh God, Red's trapped in here.

With Dena. Me. That murdering psychopath's continuing to terrorize my cousin. Bad enough he kidnapped and beat her within an inch of her life, then shot her. Now they're trapped together in this limbo…and it's all my fault. Their fates are linked. When I tied Dena's soul to her body, it also left Red in a vegetative state. My fear doomed my cousin to an eternity of bondage to the person who tormented her.

Revulsion floods through me. I can't breathe it's so thick. I return to my body and sit up, gasping for air. Spots dance in front of my eyes. I blink, and the spot condenses into a giant, blurry blob. A second blink and the blob forms into a scowling face. Landry flips his chin-length black hair out of his face, and my chest tightens with the surge of love flowing through me. His bristled jaw flexes, and I throw my arms around his neck. "I'm so happy to see you."

Our bodies cling together so tightly that it's almost as if we're one. I let his scent fill my nose and soak into my skin. He doesn't speak for several minutes, just rubs my tense shoulders until my breathing slows and the tears dry up and then he leans back. "Are you with me now?" He cups my cheeks between his palms. His stormy gray eye stares deep into mine as if trying to read my thoughts. I jerk my head aside, and his hands drop. Some thoughts are best left private.

A spasm rips through my lower back from being propped against the side of the hospital bed. With a grimace, I set my hands on the cold floor and try to push upright, but my body doesn't cooperate. Maybe I'm still in shock. "Help me, please."

Landry stretches my legs into a more comfortable position before speaking again. "What happened? One minute we're talking. The next you're falling. Then your eyes roll up in your skull. Freaked me the fuck out."

I rub my sticky tongue along the roof of my mouth. "I need some water."

His nostrils flare, but he slaps his hands down on his thighs and pushes to his feet. He reaches out, and I let him lift me to my feet. Dizziness almost topples me back over, but he wraps his arm around my shoulders. Maybe he does read my mind because he senses I can't be in this room another second. He helps me walk to the water fountain by the elevator, and I drink until my stomach hurts.

I clutch the fountain with one hand and press the other against the wall, letting my head rest in the crease of my elbow. I've never fallen asleep while standing up, but...My eyes drift shut. Not even the stomach-dropping sensation of falling pries open my eyelids because I'm caught and lifted before my mind processes the reason for my vertigo. I lay my head on Landry's shoulder and shut off my brain. Or try to.

It doesn't really work.

My thoughts race, fighting my control. I focus on rebuilding the shield, but each brick I shove in place crumbles. I can't conjure the finesse needed to lay them in orderly rows. The spirits haunting the hospital sense my presence. They swarm like a plague of locusts, set on leeching away my remaining energy. Cold fingers tug at my hair to get my attention. Voices whisper in my ears, pleading for help. Gruesome images of death and carnage pass behind my eyes, and I dissolve into a quivering mess.

"Mala Jean," the voice breaks through the shouting mass. I crack open an eye. Bessie blocks Landry's exit from the elevator. "What's going on? What's wrong with her?"

"Nothing that getting out of this place won't cure," Landry says impatiently. "Follow me if you want to talk." He sidesteps to get off the elevator before the doors slide shut, but when he tries to go around her, she blocks him again.

She rests the back of her hand against my forehead, and I shiver from the coldness of her touch. "She's burning up."

I lift a trembling hand and wave my fingertips in her direction. "I'm okay, Bessie."

Her dark eyebrows draw in to an intricate knot on her mahogany forehead. "Girl, I've felt enough fevered heads in my lifetime to know you've come down with a cold. Probably from stomping about in the rain with George this morning."

"Be better if it were a cold," Landry mutters, hugging me tighter. "Stupid—"

"Did you call me stupid?" Bessie lurches forward.

Landry steps back to keep her from chest-bumping us. "No! I called—"

"Do you think calling Mala stupid is supposed to make me feel better?" Bessie's got the scary don't-bullshit-me glint in her eyes and tone. Saints, she's royally pissed, and this has nothing to do with whether or not I've got a cold. Oh no, this anger comes from deep within, a brimming pot seconds away from boiling.

"Enough!" I snap the word like a sopping wet rolled-up towel, hoping the sting sets them back a notch. It works better than I imagined.

Bessie's eyes widen. "Malaise Jean Marie—"

"Don't throw all three names at me, Elizabeth Faye Caine," I cut in before she works herself into full-froth. "I'm not a child, and I don't deserve to be scolded like one."

Bessie sucks in a startled breath, and a spurt of satisfaction flows through me. I've always shown her the utmost respect, and I'm quaking in my rain boots at talking back to her. Still, I've neither the energy nor the patience to deal with her diplomatically. "Put me down, Landry. Bessie and I need to talk in private."

Landry sets me on my feet, and I pretend like I don't see the slight quirk to the corner of his lips. He's laughing at me. I know he is. Bet he thinks I can't handle Bessie. That she's going to recover from her shock, eat me alive, then spit out the indigestible chunks. Maybe he's right. But it's time to try. I can't let her treat me like a child forever. Not if I want her to see me as an adult capable of consulting on the murder investigation.

"I'll meet you at the truck," he says, walking off. Right before he gets to the door, he throws a last I-double-dare-you grimace over his shoulder. Ha, I'll show him.

I blot the dots of perspiration off my forehead with the back of my hand. Bessie's right about the fever, just not the source. *Stupid spirits.* They manifest by drawing on energy from their surroundings, including the living, but they're especially attracted to people who are aware of their presence. Like me. Too much exposure to spirits wears the body down bit by bit. This is why the shield's so important. I learned that much when Lainey haunted me. I didn't realize she was the cause of my runny nose and aching muscles, not the flu.

"I need to sit down," I mumble and stagger over to a bench beneath the WASHED HANDS SAVE LIVES sign. My stomach rolls at the picture of an open sore labeled methicillin-resistant Staphylococcus aureus. I take a few deep breaths to fight down the nausea.

Bessie gives me the dirty eyeball. "Tell me again why you're not sick when it's obvious you're suffering?"

The habitual lie sticks to the end of my tongue, and I swallow it. Now that Bessie knows the truth about my abilities, I don't have to hide what's really wrong. "Hospitals tend to affect me like this. All the voices in my head sap my strength." My lips purse...*Hmm, that sounds like I'm having a psychotic break.* "These halls are full of the dead. Too many ghosts in one place can be draining. Once I get out of here, I'll be fine."

"About that..."

"Don't you dare say you don't believe me!"

"What do you expect? I've known you since you were a little girl. Are you saying you've kept this secret all this time? That you didn't trust me with the truth?"

Now the real reason for her anger comes out. "I'm sorry, Bessie."

"Sorry?" Her eyes close for a minute, then pop open. "So if

George hadn't spilled the truth, you never would've said anything. How do you think that makes me feel?"

"How do you think I feel?" I snap, then realize how my loss of control must appear to her. *Mother Mary, help me stay calm. Be rational.* I force my words out in an even tone. "Do you think it's been easy? Letting everyone think I'm insane because sharing this secret would only make it worse? At least PTSD from seeing Mama murdered seemed like a probable explanation for my supposed breakdown. But saying I see ghosts, well, that's an ongoing psychosis, isn't it? You believed Dr. Rhys' diagnosis easily enough. Even tried to force me to go to therapy and stay on those horse pills."

"I was trying to help. Jasmine—"

"Yeah, Mama. Let's talk about how well seeing spirits worked for her."

"Mala, you're not your mother."

"But I could be, Bessie. This is how it started for her. In a few years, I could be a drunk too. That's what seeing ghosts does. It messes with the mind. Turns a sane person insane. Makes a mother abandon her child." *Where are all these words coming from?* "That's what's in my future. Why I was scared to tell you."

"Oh, *cher*," she whispers, opening her arms.

I step into her embrace. *"Mo chagren..."* My tightening throat chokes off my apology. My eyes burn with unshed tears, and I struggle to hold them back. When I think I've got my emotions under control, I step aside but remain close enough to study her expression. "I need you to believe me. It's the only way you can help me stay sane. Mama tried to hide from her gift by denying it. She didn't get help to learn how to control it. That's why she drank." I swallow around the bitter taste in my mouth. "I'm lucky. I've got Landry, but he's in the same situation."

"As in he sees ghosts too?" Her eyes do a quick roll before she catches herself. "Sorry, it's just…"

"When he died in jail, he came back able to see spirits."

"Okay, that's asking a bit much for me to take in."

I can't help but laugh. She's got a point. Bringing a demon possession into the mix will only make the situation worse. "Fine, let's leave full disclosure for a later time. So how did you find me to have this conversation, anyway?"

"I didn't actually come for this reason. I came to interview the victim of an assault by"—she pulls out a notepad and reads verbatim—"'a big-ass black guy' who held his victim at gunpoint while Carl Acker beat him up." She gives me a sideways glance. "Bet you can guess where this all went down?"

"That son of a bitch!"

"The victim was here getting treatment for a broken nose. Says he wants to press charges."

"Did the so-called victim also tell you that he's the boyfriend of Pepper Acker, Carl's mother, or that he attacked Carl first? If anyone's gonna press charges, it should be Carl. The victim's a grown man, putting hands on a kid."

"Hey, I understand. Sounds to me like the kid defended himself, but he signed a citizen's arrest form. It's out of my hands unless he drops the charges."

"But that's not fair. Was Pepper there when he made his report?"

Bessie shakes her head.

"Are you seriously gonna arrest Carl?"

"He's already in custody. Deputy Winters picked him up when

she saw him in the parking lot. That's why I'm here getting the statement. We're a bit shorthanded while we finish processing the crime scene you and George found. Once we get Carl's statement, you can pick him up from the station."

I head for the exit doors at a fast pace, and Bessie matches my stride. My heart races as I imagine Carl's expression as he's locked in handcuffs and hauled off in the patrol car. Poor kid. Sure, he can be a brat, but he's never gotten arrested before. He must be terrified.

Sunlight stabs at my eyes, and I blink at the patch of blue in the cloud-filled sky. Judging by the position of the sun, it's almost time for the boys to get out of school. Guess Carl and I won't be making that appointment with his principal after all. No telling how long it'll take before he's released.

Landry has the truck pulled up by the curb. When he sees me, he honks. I hold up a single finger in answer, and he gives a jerky nod. "You'll need Landry's and Sophia's statements." I talk fast, not caring to waste time. "Pepper's too. Hopefully she'll be honest and back up her son. The 'big-ass black guy' must be Ferdinand. If he hasn't left town, I'll ask him to come in."

"George was transporting your friend Ferdinand when Dixie dispatched the call. He brought him down to the substation, and Ferdinand provided a corroborating statement to what you just told me." Her lips twitch. "I must say, Ferdinand Laffite is quite impressive."

I'm not sure I like the awed, lust-struck husky tone to her voice. Far as I know, Bessie hasn't been interested in a man since her husband died. He was killed on duty during a traffic stop. "Yeah, Ferdi's been a big help to my family."

She stops walking to stare over my head with slightly glazed brown eyes. "Did you know he served twenty years in the Marines before starting his own private security firm? His employees are hired to protect some pretty famous stars when they visit New Orleans."

I glance over at Landry. He tilts his head in a come-on gesture, and I shake mine in return. "I didn't know that."

She blinks. "Really?"

"I always see him with my aunt Magnolia. I didn't know he was the president of his own company."

If the president's guarding Magnolia, I guess that makes her pretty important. But more important than those rich billionaires? This information puts a whole new spin on his motivations for helping me. Is he licking her boots out of loyalty or is the Hoodoo Queen of N'awlins holding some sort of magical blackmail over his head to gain his compliance?

Bessie nods. "Well, he gave me a business card and showed me his permit to carry concealed. The background check came out clean. He single?"

"Good Lord, Bessie. As tough as you are, I don't know if you can handle Sir Hotness."

"Humph, better ask whether he thinks he's up to the challenge of handling me."

Chapter 12

Landry

Playing Possum

Mala gives Bessie a bone-crushing hug, then drags herself over to the truck like each step hurts. My chest constricts at seeing her obvious strain. When she reaches the truck, I lean over and pop the latch. She stands in the doorway, staring at me with dark eyes glittering with pain, and I force a grin. "Score one for my girl. Bessie didn't eat you alive."

A smile flickers then blooms. "Did you really doubt me?"

"I'm no fool. I've seen you back down to spare someone's feelings, but I've never seen you lose in a fight. You're too damn stubborn. And cute…" *Come on, think of something to shake her out of her funk.* "Too amazingly sexy to ever be able to stay mad at for long."

She snorts at the cheesiness of my compliment. "I don't think Bessie sees my hotness as a factor in whether or not she'll forgive my lies."

My eyebrows shoot up. *Lies?*

Rather than climbing into the truck, she folds her arms on the seat and rests her chin on top of them, totally creating a gap down the front of her T-shirt. Her breasts strain upward from being pressed together—twin mounds, within easy reach. My mouth waters, imagining the taste of her smooth skin, and I run my tongue across my lips.

Her long eyelashes sweep down and then flicker upward. "George blabbed to Bessie and the sheriff about my ability to see ghosts when they asked how we found the crime scene. She's still in the denial phase, but I'll win her over."

"Oh shit, seriously? He told?" *Damn him.* "Is he trying to get you killed or locked up in some government facility or—"

"Calm down. That won't happen. I was pissed at first, but it's for the best. I couldn't hide how I found the crime scene if I wanted them to take my vision seriously. It's the only way to catch the killer."

"Why the hell not? Did he tell them about me too?" I tap my head, and she shakes hers so hard that flyaway curls tumble over her eyes. I fall back in the seat with a sigh, all my lusty thoughts dried up at the insta-panic I felt when I thought Bessie had learned about the demon.

"No worries, I handled the situation like a pro." She brushes her hair back and straightens with a shrug. "I faced it head-on. I won't run and hide from this anymore. It's a part of me…us. It's time to use our abilities to help others. Don't you think?"

I rub my hand over my chest, afraid I need to pull my inhaler out of the glove box. I draw in a breath, then another, willing my heart to slow. Everything's okay. Mala will be safe. They won't try to burn her alive. Bessie and Chief Keyes, they're good people. They'll see the benefit of having Mala on their side. Just like George did. Course this line of bullshit doesn't make me feel much better given how much trouble he's gotten her into today.

The lopsided curl of Mala's luscious lips captures my attention. That's my girl, cocky and sexy as sin. I grin, stuffed with my own bit of pride now that the sadness has drained from her eyes, and I lose myself in the sparkle, like a jeweler mesmerized by an onyx gemstone surrounded by diamonds. I've got to remember this thought when buying her engagement ring. Course, I need cash. Which means I need to find a job, since I don't need to worry about fixing up the Acker place anymore.

"Hey," Mala says, snapping her fingers and waving her hand.

"Sorry, love." I reach out to grab her trembling hand, silently promising to hold on to her for as long as she needs me. With a quick tug, I pull her up onto the seat. She collapses against my shoulder and nestles into the curve of my body. Her fingers clench mine hard enough to cut off circulation.

After a heavy sigh, she whispers, "I'm beat."

I wish I could let her rest. "Well, deep breaths, 'cause it's not over." I nudge her head with a lift of my shoulder. "Carl got arrested. The deputy said we can pick him up from the station."

"I know, Bessie told me." She points out the window. Her voice deepens as it takes on an English accent, "Make it so, Number One. Warp speed ahead."

I laugh and untangle her fingers to get the truck into gear and then pull around the ambulance parked by the curb. Mala rests her hand on my thigh, and my muscles clench. Only a couple more inches to the left and she'll feel how very aware of her agile fingers I am.

A quick glance in her direction shows she's far from operating on the same wavelength. She glares out the window with a pinpoint gaze sharp enough to burn a hole through the windshield. Her chest heaves faster and faster with each breath. Finally she snaps. "What's wrong with that woman?" Her fingernails dig into my thigh. "First she decides to pull the plug on Dena, and then she lets her son get arrested. What kind of parent does that?"

I pry her fingers free before she accidentally skewers my balls into shish kebabs. "The kind who abandons her children for years with no word." I flip on the turn signal, checking for oncoming traffic before pulling onto Main Street. "Do we really want to know what goes through that woman's head? Even if we could read her mind, we'll never be able to understand her. She's lived a different kind of life than us."

"You'd think she would've learned after getting away from Acker, but then she goes and hooks up with that loser Judd. How hard is it to choose a decent guy?"

I shrug. "Luck plays a huge part. There's only one of me in the world, and you're the only woman I want."

"Luck's got nothing to do with it. Even when you were angry and grieving for your sister, I sensed the goodness in you. I couldn't help falling in love with you, Landry Prince." Her hand returns to my thigh. She gives it a playful squeeze.

I shift in my seat, trying to ease the pain from the swell in my jeans "I'm your kryptonite," I say, in a voice hoarse with repressed sexual frustration. Man, if only Carl didn't need us right now. My hands grip the steering wheel so I don't accidentally-on-purpose turn down the street leading to the Super Delight.

Mala's hand slides higher up my thigh. "Mm, I feel like I'm dying every time you do that twisty-swirly thing with your tongue." She shivers. "How about pulling down that alley so we can take this discussion into the…back." Her voice cracks on the word. She throws a quick look over her shoulder, and all the air explodes out of her. "Saints! How in the world did I forget about Sophia? Where is she?"

I point to the sticky note I'd crumpled up and tossed onto the floor. "I found that stuck to the steering wheel. Guess she got tired of waiting and walked back to the hotel."

"That woman's driving me crazy. I understand her even less than I do Pepper. Why is she so determined to help us all of a sudden? She knows how much we despise her, but she's sticking to us like a piece of gum on the bottom of a shoe." She glances down at the floorboard as if she really had gum on her boot. When she leans over, I guess it's the case, but she lifts a blue glass bottle and tilts it up to the light shining through the window. "What's this?"

"Ah, the note. Sophia said for you to drink this. It's for cleansing your body of the residual taint from being trapped in that spell circle." My nose twitches. "It tastes like minty licorice…pretty gross. Better hold your breath when you drink it."

Mala throws a skeptical grimace in my direction. "Are you really advocating that I drink something that Sophia left? You do recall she's the one who drugged our champagne."

"Sure, but—"

"Plus, who knows what's in this. What if it's not okay for the baby?"

That shuts off the internal argument I've been preparing to convince her to trust Sophia. She has a point. I don't know why I believed the woman. I guess seeing the pain in her eyes when she saw

Gaston today made her seem less sinister, more human. Plus how helpful she was in freeing Mala from the trap lowered my guard. I can't deny that I feel some sort of bond with her, but I don't know why or where it came from. And I'd be a fool to trust her with Mala and the baby's safety when she's lied to us in the past.

"How about if you wait until we find out exactly what's in it," I say slowly.

"My thought exactly."

Still… "Ferdinand also said it's important."

Mala lays the bottle on the seat. "I trust them about as far as I can throw them." Her fingernails drum a rhythm on the glass. "So what do you think about the whole pregnancy thing?"

Loaded question. "Uh, how do *you* feel about it?"

She shrugs. "I'm kind of still in shock. I mean, you'd think I would've had time to adjust to the idea." She glances at me. "It's been a few weeks since I missed my period."

"How far along do you think you are?"

"Maybe about six weeks. I think…my birthday."

My lips flicker at the memory of how we celebrated her twenty-first birthday. Dad watched the kids while we went to a performance by her favorite zydeco band, along with a shared platter of crawfish, beer, and a quickie at the Super Delight Motel. Mr. Khan even gave us a half-price discount for our hour in the "honeymoon suit." The Super D isn't the most romantic of settings, but we got more than our money's worth out of the vibrating heart-shaped bed with leopard-print bedding. I doubt anything compares to Magnolia's suite where we had our first time. But compared to the toolshed, in the heat of the moment, it was hot.

Unfortunately we didn't have much time with Dad babysitting

the kids. He's stricter about our curfew than when I was in high school. Now his worst fears have come true.

"We're pregnant." I draw out the breath that follows the word. "It's happening sooner than I thought."

"Sooner… How about I hadn't planned on getting married until after I finished college. I wanted to at least have Axle in high school before even thinking of getting pregnant."

I cut a glance in her direction. "I don't have that long, Mala."

She hisses. "Landry…"

"This might be my only chance." I grip the steering wheel. "I know it's not part of your long-term plan. Being with me and all, but…

"Of course, you're part of my long-term plan. Who do you think I'm planning to do all this with? You're *not* leaving me alone. Especially if we're having a kid, so wipe that doom-and-gloom thought right out of your head. We'll find a way to save you."

I nod, not trusting myself to speak. "Anyway, I know it's a shock. But I'm happy."

"I'm not sad," she says slowly. "How can I be when I'm having a child with you? It's just that the timing sucks. For us, at least. I still wonder about Magnolia dipping her magic fingers into this mess. I mean, we were careful, Landry. This doesn't feel like an accident. It feels planned."

That or we're the butt of a cosmic joke. The universe's ultimate punching bags.

I turn into the parking lot in front of the Bertrand Parish Sheriff's Office and park in front of the flagpole. The shadows of the flags blowing in the wind cross Mala's face. I cup her cheek and lean in. Her lips part as they meet mine. Her fingers clench in my hair, holding my face to hers as her tongue explores my mouth with a scary, yet sexy desperation. Her scent invades my nose with my quick inhale. She smells different than usual, sweeter. I've noticed the subtle change for the last few weeks. Is it pregnancy hormones? All I know is I feel super protective of her. I want to hold on to her and never let her leave my arms.

She pulls back with a hitched breath, then presses one last lingering kiss on my lips. Tears sparkle in her eyes, but don't fall. "Ready to go kick Judd's ass?"

A lump forms in my throat, and I swallow hard, then say, "I'll let you handle him. I'm so pissed, I might lose my shit with him this time."

"*Tsk*, you saw how well I did with Pepper at the hospital. Weeping and wailing. Pathetic."

"You were in shock. Should we call an attorney? I kept the public defender who represented me on speed dial in case something went wrong again."

"Smart, given the horrible luck we have." Mala opens her door.

I grab her arm. "Hold on, let me get you."

"Wow, special treatment. I think I'm really going to enjoy being pregnant."

"Yeah, I'm gonna spoil you both rotten for as long as I can." I jump out and slam the door on her automatic protest. It doesn't matter what she says about finding a way to survive. I need to prepare for the worst while hoping for the best. I've already decided to fight. No matter what, I won't give in.

"*Do you hear that?*" I think to the creature sleeping in my head. It doesn't stir. Maybe it doesn't feel like wasting its time on an answer.

I walk slowly around the truck, forming a plan to drive her so crazy with thoughts of ripping off my clothes that there's no room for sadness. I pause in front of the open door. Mala must've spent her time doing the same because the look she gives me from beneath her lashes sends a spike of heat straight to my groin. Just thinking about her wrapped around me, so hot, tight... *Ah hell*, it takes everything within me not to lay her back on the seat. Sweat pops on my forehead, and I wipe it off with a trembling hand.

"Are you okay?" Mala asks, voice husky. Her fingernails sear a trail of fire around the back of my neck, and I shudder. I can't *not* touch her. My arms wrap around her firm ass cheeks, and I drag her out of the truck. Her legs wrap around my waist, thighs clenching, to seal the space between our bodies. She rubs up against the strained seam of my zipper with a tiny moan. Her face tips upward, and she purses her lips slightly.

Wicked girl! One more wiggle, just one, and I'm spent. Does she sense how close she is to breaking me, or even care? Do I care? Then I dimly remember we're in the parking lot of the sheriff's office so we can get Carl.

I gather the shredded threads of my control and tie them together in a frayed knot. I go for safety over satisfaction. Instead of claiming those pouty lips, I brush the tip of my nose across the end of hers. Eskimo kisses always make her squirm, and this is no exception. She licks her lips, straining forward. I dip my head again, but pull back before claiming her mouth. She lets out a low moan as I slide her down my body, angling my knee slightly so she rubs down it. Her hands grip my shoulder, nails digging into my skin, and her knees buckle.

"Behave," I whisper, pointing to the security camera attached to the flagpole. "Wave to whoever's watching us."

Mala gasps and jerks back. "You tease."

"Thought you needed a taste of your own medicine, but I'm the one paying the price." I wince, shifting my stance until I'm hidden from view by the open door. "Give me a few minutes to recover. I'll follow you inside."

Mala's gaze dips to the bulge in my pants. Her laughter bursts out, and she waggles her finger at me. "Ha, serves you right."

Yeah, it does. Should've known better. I'm a glutton for punishment. And I throb, aching for her. Unlike me, Mala doesn't seem to be physically handicapped by our interlude in any way, other than her puffed-up ego. She slams the door and almost skips toward the front entrance, probably mentally patting herself on the back the whole way. Just before she goes inside, she spins around and blows a kiss in my direction. Do I catch it? Hell no.

I lean back against the side of the truck, stretching out my legs and adjusting myself slightly to make more room inside the crotch. My eyes close, and I focus on anything but my mouth sucking on Mala's tits, which is hard since I'm once again thinking of my tongue teasing her nipples until they're hard little nubs.

I've got Mala on the brain, both of them. You'd think I'd be used to blue balls. Sure it's torture, but by tonight Mala will be so hot and ready. I won't even have to make the first move. She'll drag me off to some secluded corner, rip off my clothes, or not, and fuck my brains out. Then when we've calmed down, I'll make sweet love to her until she screams.

My grin curdles at the skid of tires on pavement. I straighten just as a white car shoots into the parking space beside my truck. The front passenger tire barely misses my toes. Even with steel-toe boots that would've hurt. Asshole parked too close. I won't be able to open the door without scratching the other car. Which turns out to be the lesser of my worries.

Judd exits the car with a loud curse. Rage flushes his face beet red. He waves a piece of paper over his head. "This is your doing, isn't it?" Before I can ask what he's talking about, not that I really care, he races in my direction. It doesn't take him long to reach me, but I've got enough time to decide on how to counter his aggression.

I don't try to avoid his punch.

Swing, baby, I think, staggering backward when his fist connects with my jaw. *This is all getting caught on video.*

Chapter 13

Mala

Faking It

Thank goodness the lobby's empty. My body still throbs with the heat generated by Landry's kiss. Sweaty curls cling to my forehead, and I swipe them back with a trembling hand and huff, releasing the buildup of sexual frustration tightening my chest.

With a dab of my finger, I ring the buzzer. The records clerk takes her sweet time turning away from her computer. I must've caught her in the middle of a thought. Go figure. For Sana Lane, those are far and few between. My finger hovers over the buzzer, ready to give a long blast to show my irritation, when she finally rolls her chair back and rises. I'm glad I held back when her face lights up in recognition.

"Oh hi, Malaise." Her microbraids end in curls that bounce on her shoulders as she hustles up to the window. "Hang on a minute."

She steps out of sight. I know from the time when I used to work with her that she's headed into the hallway. I go over to the door and form a cup around my eyes, trying to see through the one-way glass. The door moves beneath my hands, and I take a huge step backward when it swings open. Lane stands there with a grin. "Come on back. Winters wants to talk to you."

Yay for me. I step inside and let the door swing shut. She leads me into the dispatch center. I look for Dixie, but another woman sits in front of the radio, talking into the headset. I don't know her. She must be new. She eyes me for a brief second and then nods, but she doesn't stop typing the call she's receiving into the computer.

"Who is she?" I ask Sana, who fiddles with her skirt.

"I don't remember her name," she whispers, then shrugs. "I didn't even bother to remember yours until you'd been on the job six months. I think she might last. She used to work for Lafayette PD, so she's experienced."

I nod. "You said Winters wants to speak with me? Are you gonna take me to her?"

"She's done with the interview. She'll bring Carl to you." Footsteps sound down the hallway, and Sana leans out the doorway. "Here they come."

I move into the hall to see Carl walking toward me. His face appears lifeless. Straw-colored hair hangs over his downcast blue eyes. He rubs his wrists, as if trying to wipe away the memory of the handcuffs that have just been removed.

Deputy Winters has the cuffs in her hands and she places them into the handcuff holder on her duty belt. She follows a few steps behind in silence. Not much expression crosses her sharp features, but her hawk-like nose twitches when she sees me. She's Bessie's niece by marriage and is a few years older than Maggie and me.

We never really bonded as children. I think she sees me as a rival for Bessie's affections, but I don't feel the same way about her. I respect the fact that she wants to move up in the ranks at BPSO without abusing her aunt's position of authority or creating any rumors of favoritism.

I give her a civil nod, then focus on Carl. "Hey, brat, you okay?"

His head pops up. When he sees me, Carl shuffle-runs down the hall. I expect him to stop, but instead, he falls into my arms, almost taking us both to the ground. Saints, he's too big for me to hold, but I don't say it. Next thing I know, he straightens up and lifts me into the air. It freaks me out a bit, but I just pat him on the back, wishing I could do more to comfort him.

"Are you really his guardian?" Winters asks.

Carl suddenly realizes there's an audience to his less than manly reaction to our reunion. He drops me to my feet. I grip his shoulder to catch my balance, but he slips back and crosses his arms. I grunt. "Yeah."

She shakes her head and holds out a yellow carbon-copy paper.

My head pounds at the smirk on her face. I snatch the paper from her hand; a quick glance down shows it's a citation. "Are you kidding me? You're charging him with battery? What about the so-called victim?"

"Judd Helmert? Lieutenant Caine cited him for child abuse." Her large brown eyes glow. "My guess is he'll be contacting you soon to see if you'll drop the charges on him."

Ah, he'll want to make a deal. "Yeah, not happening."

"Handle it any way you want. I doubt DA Cready will file on Carl anyway. Helmert's the aggressor, and I'll put the witness statements in the report to back it up." Her composure cracks as she drawls, "What a jerk. Is he really Pepper Acker's boyfriend? She has the worst taste in men."

I scowl, throwing a warning glance toward Carl, and Winters grimaces, mouthing *Sorry*.

I'm so ready to be done with this day. "You ready to go home, Carl? I'll ask the rev to make you a jailbird-special meal. What do you want? A bacon cheese burger, pizza, steak and lobster? All of the above?"

"It's not funny, Mala," Carl says with a sniff. "My mom had me arrested."

Damn, this really has messed the kid up. As much as I want to find Pepper and punch her in the face, I can't let Carl see my anger. No matter what, she's his mom and should be shown respect, even when she doesn't deserve it. If Carl had remembered that in the first place, we wouldn't be here.

I swallow my anger so it won't show in my voice. "Nah, Pepper didn't have anything to do with this. I bet Judd called all on his own. She'll be furious when she finds out."

"I don't think she will." He stares at me with blue eyes so full of pain I want to hug him again.

"Holy shit!" Sana yells.

I jump at her voice. My hand flies to cover my thumping heart. The woman stands in front of the flat screen showing a live video feed of the parking lot, then turns with a horrified, yet slightly giddy expression. "Some guy's getting his butt kicked in the parking lot."

Oh no. "Landry—" I reach for the door knob.

Deputy Winters grabs my arm and jerks me back. "Stay here until I clear the scene," she says to me and then barks to the dispatcher, "Get me backup."

She's out the door before I can tell her to go fuck herself. Landry's in danger. The only reason I haven't followed yet is because of Carl's death grip on my elbow. I jerk and twist my arm, finally resorting to prying his fingers free one digit at a time.

While I'm struggling to get free, the dispatcher calmly relays Winters's request for backup over the radio. The bathroom door in the hallway slams open, and I whip around, then scoot back against the wall as a deputy the size of a tank, which is why it's his nickname, comes out adjusting his duty belt. He runs past us, and I'm right on his heels.

It's only when Carl follows that I spin around and slap a hand on his chest. "Wait here."

He shakes his head. "No way."

I don't have time to argue with this hardheaded brat. "Then keep back until Deputy Winters says it's safe."

"You too. If you get hurt, Landry will kill me."

Landry… My chest squeezes out all the air in my lungs at the thought of his being hurt. The deputies move fast, but not fast enough to stop someone from getting away. The white car skims past, barely missing Tank. He yells for the guy to stop, but the car speeds out of the parking lot. He watches it go while putting out a description over the radio. Hopefully a patrol car is in the area, but in a parish this big and with so few deputies, they're spread thin.

Winters reaches the screaming woman who stands over a body stretched out on the ground. A body wearing my boyfriend's boots.

I race across the parking lot with a burst of energy spurred by panicked-fueled adrenaline. Even though I'm at top speed, Carl outpaces me with his long legs. He skids to a halt in front of his crying mother. When she sees him, she throws herself into his arms while wailing like someone's dead. Which scares the crap out of me.

Panting for air, I press my fist against the stitch in my side and apologize to the baby for all of the running. Fingers crossed she didn't get seasick. Both deputies are crouched down beside Landry. Tank's wide, like a solid brick wall that I can't see over. I slide between them. "Is he okay?" I stoop down. "Landry?"

He looks up with a faint smile and raises his hands. "I didn't start it."

Relief drops me to my knees, and I press my forehead against his chest. My heart hammers in my ears, making my voice sound gruff. "Did you finish it?" I demand. "'Cause if not, I will."

"Judd's got enough problems." He caresses my hair with a shaky hand. "Hey, seriously, I'm okay."

"Well, I'm n-not"—my voice cracks—"so give me a minute."

His hand shifts from my head to my cheek. His breath catches and holds, then releases in a rush. I tense, expecting him to say something about the tears, but he doesn't. *Protecting my dignity in front of Winters and Tank.* I sniff. *How sweet.*

Deputy Winters shifts beside us, her impatience obvious in the sharpness in her tone as she asks, "Can you give us a description of the perp?"

"It's *her* boyfriend. Ask her." Landry tilts his head toward Pepper, who still has her arms draped over her son's shoulders and her face pressed into his chest. Carl seems shell-shocked. He pats her on the back like she might suddenly turn rabid and bite his hand.

"That guy? I guess he decided not to try to negotiate a settlement."

Landry huffs. "Oh, Judd tried to negotiate, but with his fists. The guy's seriously thwacked in the head. He came at me, yelling a bunch of nonsense, then punched me. He's lucky I've already been incarcerated. I didn't want to go back to jail because of that loser. Even if it meant taking a beating," he finishes in a grumble.

"Smart," Winters says with a nod. "Even with a justification for self-defense it can backfire into a mutual combat situation. The whole incident was caught on video in any case." Winters turns to Tank. "I'll get Pepper's statement."

My tears dry up as soon as I realize Landry is playing possum. He let Judd hit him on purpose. I don't know if I'm impressed by his restraint or if I want to shake him for scaring me half to death. I settle for sitting up and crossing my arms. Landry darts a quick look in my direction. *Oh yeah, buddy. I'm not happy about your getting hurt.*

Tank, who still has toilet paper stuck to his boot, holds his hand out to Landry and lifts him to his feet. I make note to slather Landry's hands in sanitizer because I doubt the deputy had time to wash before running out of the bathroom.

"Do you plan on pressing charges?" Tank asks.

"Hell, yeah. I don't know if the guy's on drugs or mentally deranged, but he's dangerous." Landry turns his attention back to me. "I don't want him around the kids."

"No, of course not." *My boyfriend's brilliant.* "Tank, uh, I mean Deputy Toussaint. What now?"

He shakes his bald, glistening head. "Dispatch broadcasted a description of the vehicle and suspect. It's only a matter of time before we arrest him."

"Mama, no," Carl yells, drawing our attention.

Tank gives a pained sigh, muttering, "What now?"

I've got to agree.

"I'm not going with you," Carl tells Pepper. When he sees us watching, he starts backing up on our direction. His mother follows, fingers outstretched. "Everything that's happened today is your fault. Why did you bring that guy here?"

"I didn't know Judd pressed charges against you." Pepper's hand drops as she turns to us. "I was with Dena when Judd called in the report. I didn't even find out until he drove us over here, ranting about 'not going to jail.'"

Not good enough, at least in my opinion. Judging from Carl's expression, her excuses hold about as much weight as a bag full of cotton balls. "But you were with him when he assaulted Landry," I accuse, not willing to let her off the hook. I'm still too angry with the whole sordid situation.

"I tried to calm him down, but he was so pissed."

Deputy Winters nods. "Ah, so Judd Helmert assaulted Landry Prince in retaliation for his acting as a witness in the assault on your son." She gives a tiny smile and glances at me. Bingo. All of those days spent manually entering old records into the computer burned the criminal codes into my brain. Judd just screwed himself big time by adding intimidating a witness to his crime.

"All of your excuses don't mean a thing," Carl says. "I'm out of here."

Pepper draws in a deep breath. "Fine, no more excuses. If you need proof that I came back for you, that I love you, then I'll show you."

It sounds good. Carl may not believe her, but I hear the sincerity in her voice. So why do her words send a shiver down my spine?

Chapter 14

Landry

No Privacy

I glance over at Mala. We sit on either end of the sofa. I want to lean over and touch her, but I'm scared to move. Not only because am I afraid of waking Jonjovi and Axle, who are snuggled up between us, but because she's been stewing in her anger since we arrived home. She glares at the television, not even cracking a smile when Hulk smashes Loki into the floor, her favorite scene in *The Avengers*.

I wonder how much longer she'll be able to keep it contained. She stayed in control while we dealt with filing the report on that asshole Judd. I can tell she's still pissed that I got hurt by not defending myself, but she respects my decision. And it all worked out in the end. It's going to be hard for Pepper to get the kids unless she gives up Judd. The woman talked a good game. I always thought Dena got her temper from her dad, but Pepper proved how she got her nickname. Her temper blazed hotter than a cayenne when Deputy Winters told her Carl risked going to juvie. If Judd had been present, she would've burned him to ash with her insults.

Even Mala seemed impressed. Carl though…maybe it was a case of too little, too late. The woman should've predicted how her son would react. Carl refused to acknowledge her existence—just walked out of the substation without a word to sit in my truck until we finished the paperwork. Between him and Mala, it was a quiet car ride home.

The younger boys didn't handle hearing about their mom's return any better than Carl did. Axle and Jonjovi clung to us, afraid to let us out of sight because they thought they'd get snatched. Carl's anger didn't help calm the situation so Dad took the twins back to their place and promised to stay with them.

It was midnight before Axle and Jonjovi finally drift off.

"I don't trust her," Mala mutters, lightly running her fingers through Jonjovi's hair. She catches my eye and clarifies in a whisper, "I can't stop thinking about Pepper's reaction. I don't think she would've said what she did if he had been there."

There she goes, reading my mind again. "I was wondering about that myself. If we look at it from her viewpoint, she's been victimized her whole life. Acker's gone, and Judd's going to jail. If she doesn't get Carl on her side, none of the other kids will forgive her. She needs them."

"Now. But what happens when she doesn't anymore?" She tips her head back against the sofa and sighs. "Will she abandon them again?"

"I don't know. Now that Acker's dead, it's all hers—the house, what little money they have, everything, including the kids. Judd can't kick her out on the street if she disobeys. Maybe she'll finally figure out that she's in control."

Her eyes meet mine. "If she's willing to fight for them, it won't be such a bad thing if she gets her kids back. They'll be better off with her. She obviously loves them. And after suffering so much loss, they need stability. We can't give that to them, no matter how much we want to. Our lives are too chaotic right now."

My eye drops to her stomach. "I know."

Mala lifts Jonjovi's head off her lap and lays it gently on a pillow, then gestures for me to follow. "Let's go."

I ease Axle onto the sofa and drape a blanket over the boys. Mala takes my outstretched hand and leads me to her bedroom. The minute the door closes, she shoves me against it. Lust makes her eyes smoky and sends an answering surge through my body. Her hands slide beneath my shirt. God how I love the warmth of her touch. I wrap my arm around her while I fumble to lock the door behind us.

I catch her pouty lower lip between my own. Her tongue darts out to dance with mine, but I ignore the temptation, continuing my exploration of the contours of her mouth with teasing kisses. Her breasts rub against my chest with each rapid breath. She presses closer with a tiny growl of impatience. Fuck that, I'm taking her slow tonight.

I break the kiss to whisper, "If the kids wake up and find us in here alone, they'll blab to Dad, and I'm dead."

"Then keep your voice down." Her eyes never move from my mouth. She rises on tiptoes, threads her fingers through my hair, and tugs impatiently. All I have to do to reclaim those luscious lips is lower my head a couple of inches. But I lean back.

"How about if you shut me up in a nicer way?"

Mala's eyebrow rises and then her lip quirks. Oh yeah. That's my girl—never backs away from a challenge. Judging by the gleam in her eyes, she's out to win. I'm cool with...*Hot damn*, she's going balls to the wall. Or rather tits, not balls. In a swift move, she lifts her T-shirt over her head and tosses it into the corner of the room. Her breasts strain over the top of the bra. The front clasp pops open with a flick of her finger, and the straps slide slowly down her shoulders. The bra falls onto the bed. My tongue flicks out to wet my lips, but I force myself to remain still so I can enjoy the show.

She throws a wicked smile in my direction. The tease. She knows just how to get me hard. Her hands rise to cup her breasts. "They're so sensitive. The slightest touch hurts."

"Pregnancy hormones?"

She frowns. "Yeah, guess so. Be gentle. Okay?"

"Are your nipples also sore?" I lean forward to cover the areola with my lips and brush the tip of my tongue over the nipple. Mala groans, back arching. "Did it hurt?"

"Not enough for you to stop."

"Then it did hurt. Sorry, I promise to be gentle." I pull back, leaving my hands in my pockets so I don't give into the temptation of touching her.

She lets out a little growl. "Help me out of these jeans."

She unwraps a rubber band from the buttons holding them closed and tries to shove the denim past her hips. Impatient, I lift her onto the edge of the bed. Her hips tilt as I slide my fingers into the waistband of her jeans and tug. They slide down her thighs, taking her panties with them. My heart hammers, and my hands tingle with the need to caress her smooth skin. She kicks her feet until the jeans drop to the floor and then she wiggles backward until she's in the middle of the bed.

"Your turn," she says, breathless.

"Help me. I've had a rough day. I'm a bit sore from getting an elbow to the ribs. Plus my head. Two rocks and a punch to the jaw, remember?"

"Poor Landry, maybe you're not up to exerting yourself. That's a shame. We haven't been able to use a bed since my birthday." Her lip pokes out in a pout, but her eyes sparkle. She grabs my belt and tugs me forward. Her nimble fingers undo the buckle and unzip my fly. "Sure you're up for this?" she asks.

My hand skims up her thigh, and she shivers. "What do you think?"

"I think you're wasting time." She lifts my T-shirt up over my head with the same speed she removed hers and tosses it in the same corner. The belt and jeans go next. I climb onto the bed on my knees and kneel over her. Her fingers fist in my hair. "Kiss me," she says. I love when she's all greedy and demanding. So fucking hot.

Her tongue slides past my lips. The taste of her mouth reminds me of mead, the sweet honey wine I drank once at a party. Her kiss intoxicates. The more I drink her in, the fuzzier my thoughts. I palm the back of her thighs, kneading her tight muscles. With a quick lift, she straddles my lap. Her warmth presses against my hardening length. Her hand goes between us, and she guides me into her in a quick inhale. Her muscles clench around my shaft, drawing me deeper inside. And a sudden thought hits.

"Wait. What about the baby?" I pull out of her and roll her back on the bed. The tiny bump on her belly suddenly looks ginormous.

Mala blinks up at me with a blank your-words-don't-compute glaze to her bitter chocolate eyes. "Huh?"

"What if I break open the sac she's in?" My gaze focuses on Mala's belly, and I picture air bubbles filling the water in the amniotic sac as my baby girl screams in horror. "My God, what if I poked out her little eye?" My hand flies up to cover the eye patch, and I shudder. I've scarred my daughter for life, and she hasn't even been born.

A flash of amusement cuts through my panic and is followed by a rolling laugh. My head drops between my knees to thump on the soft mattress. How did I forget I wasn't alone in my head? *It* had a front-row seat...It would've been along for the ride while I made love to Mala. Now it's laughing because I'm scared of hurting our baby, who would also be another member of my audience.

"Stop laughing." The mattress muffles my voice, but I put the full force of my anger into the words, hoping to make an impact. "This isn't funny."

"You are terrified your offspring will be traumatized by your giant dick? That is your worry? And you think my ego is large."

"Asshole."

Mala touches her stomach. Her voice trembles. "Uh, who are you talking to?"

"Better lie or you'll never get in her again."

My head snaps up. "Shut up!"

Mala crawls backward until she's stopped by the wooden headboard. "You're scaring me, Landry."

I focus my glare in her direction. "I wasn't talking to you."

"No shit, Sherlock," she yells, throwing the pillow. It smacks me square in the face, and I toss it off the bed with a growl. "Think I didn't figure that out fairly quickly? Why do you think I'm terrified?"

I crawl toward her. "Mala—"

She lifts the other pillow and holds it above her head as if ready to beat me if I try anything hinky. "Stay back!"

I freeze, staring into her eyes, afraid to look away and break the connection. We're in a Western-style standoff. One false move and she'll think she's under attack and commence with the beating. A minute ticks by. Mala's tense muscles tremble, and her breathing doesn't noticeably slow. If anything, with each second that passes, she gets more amped up. Sweat runs down my forehead and burns my eye, but I don't dare blink. My chest hurts from the shallow breaths when all I want is to drink in huge gulps of air.

When I can't take it anymore, I lick my dry lips. "Are you ready to listen?"

The pillow quivers above her head, and I flinch.

She lowers her shaking arms until the pillow covers her bare chest. "Depends. Is it you speaking or the demon?"

"I dislike the term 'demon.' It has many negative connotations in this era."

"Please, you're not helping the situation," I say back to it, then smooth out my frown. Because judging by the panicky look on Mala's face, she can tell I'm holding a conversation with it in my head by the changing of my expressions. I'm such an idiot. I should've told her about the deal earlier. We should've talked about everything first, but I wanted a few moments to connect before wading into the shit again.

Her breathing hitches as she speaks. "W-why isn't it trying to kill me?"

"Huh? Why do you think it would try to kill…" Oh yeah, 'cause it tried to kill her the last time it broke free. She had to kick me in the face to knock it out. *"Why did you do that?"* I ask it.

"How would you react to being woken from a sound sleep by an unknown threat? I did not know or care to take the time to discern who my enemy was. Neutralizing the threat was paramount for the preservation of my host's life."

"What did it say, Landry?"

"He says you're not his enemy."

"I am a lover, not a fighter."

A magnified image of Mala's breasts pop in my head, and I almost punch myself in the face. As if that would do any good. "Never!"

"What?" The pillow now hides all but her eyes, muffling her high-pitched voice. "Tell me what it said."

"It's got a dirty sense of humor." I grab our clothes from the floor and toss Mala's onto the bed. Then turn my back to let her dress in private. "When you got trapped in that spell, I made a deal with it to help me free you. Basically, I promised to let it experience life through my eyes."

"And what did it promise you? You did ask for something, right?"

I swallow hard. "It swore not to kill anyone or take me out for a test drive without permission."

"And no raw chicken." The disgust runs through my head. *"Although, dog seems to be acceptable, if flame broiled. I assume cooked chicken is not off limits. I have heard of this Popeye's Fried Chicken place."*

"Popeye's is fine." I catch Mala's frown. "He has a thing for chicken."

"I'm cool with taking him to Popeye's if he leaves my hens alone. Same with not feeling the need to kill me. And thank him for rescuing me from that spell."

"You're handling this part way better than I thought you would."

"Well, I'm alive. All other things are relative, right?" She doesn't make eye contact, but a slight grimace, which might be a pained smile, flickers across her lips. "But it's probably like how I'm sort of immune to the gore on *The Walking Dead*. If I overreact to every jacked-up thing we experience, I'll go insane." She waves her arm to encompass the tiny room. "This, us, is my reality, and I'm rolling with it. Can't you see, I'm rolling…Going with the flow. There's no need to panic. I find out I'm pregnant. Get trapped in a magic spell and almost eaten by a tree. Then find out Dena's stuck in limbo while being stalked by Red and it's my fault. If that isn't enough to toss me over a cliff, I don't know what is. But I'm fine."

"Are you sure? Because you don't sound fine. It sounds like you're about to scream bloody murder or grab a chainsaw and go *Friday the 13th* on somebody."

She lets out a heavy sigh. "*Texas Chainsaw Massacre*…and you're right. I'm not okay."

I sit on the edge of the bed. She hesitates for a long enough moment to make me think she doesn't want me to touch her anymore, then sighs again. She crawls onto my lap. Shivers wrack her body, and I wrap my arms around her. She lays her head on my shoulder.

"I'm scared for us, Landry. How can we bring a baby into the world when our lives are so chaotic?"

"We don't have a choice," I say. "Unless that pregnancy test was a false positive, you've got a baby on board. We've got nine months—"

"Thirty-four weeks…We've got eight and a half months to get our shit together."

"That's less than I thought."

"Blame your super sperm. I'm still trying to figure out how it got past the condoms." She rubs the tip of her nose against my shoulder. "You don't think Magnolia used a spell on us, do you?"

"Yeah, I kind of do. Ferdinand and Sophia didn't seem very surprised by the news. The new LaCroix heir. Your family is pretty excited. I still worry Ms. Jasmine might go all ballistic on my ass and learn how to throw knives. Still, I know you'll be a good mother. No matter what happens to me, you and the baby will be taken care of."

"You *will* be here to help me. Now that you've made a deal with that parasite." At my silence, she sits up and slaps my shoulder. "Please tell me you asked the demon for immunity from liquefying your brain. Please."

"I was more concerned about rescuing you at the time."

"Oh…" Mala grimaces and waves a hand. "Well, get on with it then. Better late than never."

I close my eyes. *"Hey, you still there?"*

Silence in the other end of my brain.

"I think it decided to give us some privacy. When Sophia and Ferdinand come in the morning, I'll see what we can find out from it now that we're communicating."

"I'm also ready to bring Dena out of limbo. I won't leave her to be terrorized by Red. He had a chance to reform, but instead he's continuing his evil ways. I didn't want to be the one to decide his fate, but…" Her shoulders straighten. "He brought this on himself."

"I'm cool with getting Dena back."

"What about Magnolia? I'll need her help."

"Ferdinand said her royal highness will arrive tomorrow night."

The corners of Mala's eyes tighten for a second and then the tension seems to drain out of her. She grins and traces her hand down my chest. "Since we've got the kinks in our plan worked out, how about a little foreplay?"

"No penetration involved until we talk to the doctor to find out if sex will hurt our daughter."

"Who says it's a girl?"

I gently rub Mala's belly, and she giggles. "Doesn't your family have a bad track record at conceiving boys?"

"There ain't been a male LaCroix since Gaston," Ms. Jasmine says from the corner chair. Mala and I break apart and dart to separate corners of the room. My heart races so hard I think I'm having a heart attack.

"Mama, stop! I'm seriously going to add warding to this room if you keep barging in on us like this," Mala cries. "What if we were having sex?"

Ms. Jasmine shrugs. "Then I'll have to figure out how to use a Ouija board and tell Reverend Prince you've broken the no-sex-before-marriage clause in your contract. Not that he won't figure it out soon since you're poppin' out your pants."

Chapter 15

Mala

Betrayal

I lay in the brown grass on my stomach with my chin propped on my folded arms. The blue wings of a butterfly flutter open and closed. The corpse it crawls on has dried out in the sun, its dried skin stretched across the skull. Scavengers have pulled apart the rib cage. Cracked bones litter the field like bleached white sticks. I roll onto my back. Red rims the clouds above, making the sky seem like it's on fire.

Screams come from a distance, and I moan. My body feels heavy. I should go to the boy, but I don't want to witness his death. The evil one saw me the last time. He sensed my presence and tried to kill me even though I was there only in memory. Now he knows the scent of my blood and sweat. The rich taste of my magic. He fed on me before. He'll be waiting to do so again.

I know this. Somehow.

The boy cries out in an undulating wail. Sympathetic pain radiates through my wrists as a blade hacks remorselessly through muscle and bone. Why doesn't he kill him first? Is it that he enjoys inflicting pain? Gets his mad mojo on by seeing the child suffer? *Sick bastard.*

I close my burning eyes, unable to leave him to die alone. They open to see the boy, splayed in the dirt. I double over with a cry, afraid to go closer. His cries trail off into low whimpers, fading. Then stop. Blood pools on the earth, turning it to mud and draining into a grooved circle cut into the dirt. It bubbles, letting off a layer of reddish mist. It's the edge of the spell. Cross the circle and I'm trapped again.

I edge backward. This place seems familiar. Like I've seen this place before, only I can't think of when or where it might be located. It's not White Oak Island, but somewhere else.

How many kids has he killed? How many circles of power has he made? How will I stop him before he figures out how to find my physical body? He senses me spying on him, like I sense his eyes burning through the veil. A whisper of sound from behind whips me around. My arm rises to block the swing of the knife. Its sharpened edge slices across my forearm, and I stumble, screaming, "Landry!"

The overwhelming odor of putrid flesh rushes in when I inhale, and I cough. The cloaked figure moves faster than I can react, launching forward. The knife cuts the air, and I dive out of its path. My shoulder and back slam into the ground. I roll onto my side in the flattened dry grass and curl my legs up to protect my stomach. I moved just in time. His foot connects with my thigh, and he lets out a mad howl that sends chills coursing through my body. I gasp for breath, my lungs straining. He moves until I lie sandwiched between his outstretched legs. The blade stabs down.

I grab the guy's wrist, but he's stronger than I am. He uses his body weight to press down. The tip of the knife inches toward my chest. My arms tremble from the pressure. I can't hold him off much longer. Panic builds. A heated rush of adrenaline courses through my body and triggers the abnormality in my brain that controls my ability to use magic. Thank God I'm a genetic freak because I grasp onto this lifeline with the desperation of the damned. Power surges from deep within, boiling in my belly, radiating heat from the inside. And like a bomb detonating in my core, it rips me apart.

With a scream, I thrust this power upward. It stabs him in the chest and flings him into the air. Only he lands on his feet. Before I can catch my breath, he's racing toward me again, like he's got nine lives to spare and has no fear of my stealing one of them. I can't kill him. It took me too long to figure this out, but I know now. It's my dream, but he's the one in control.

"Landry, wake me up!" I scream. *Wake up*.

He's a step away. I can't avoid the strike.

Then he's gone. A familiar back blocks my view of him. Mama didn't raise no fool, and I scramble to the side to avoid being smack dab in the middle of the battle. A rush of elation courses through my body when my awesome boyfriend catches him by the scruff of his cloak, and like he's fueled by 'roid rage, lifts him into the air.

I shake my fist in the air and cheer, "Yes, go, Landry!"

The guy's feet dangle inches above the ground. I swallow the lump rising in my throat as my euphoria is dampened by the memory of the last time I witnessed Landry exhibiting this much strength. Landry's stronger than the average bear 'cause he works out regularly, but he's no superhero. Or should I say, super villain. He'd pinned Redford Delahoussaye to the wall as easily as hanging a picture frame only because the demon had control over him. It saved us from certain death, like he's saving me now.

As if he can read my mind, a yellow eye turns in my direction, and I shiver. So, not Landry. But the demon. He came into my nightmare and holds a mass murderer in his hands. I'm not sure which one of the two scares me more.

The cloaked guy slashes at Landry's handsome face, but Landry knocks the knife from his hand. It falls at my feet, and I grab it off the ground, hissing from the coldness of the bone hilt. My palm hurts, then goes numb. I direct the pointed end outward and hold it up before me.

"What kind of demon plays with its food? Kill him before he escapes," I yell, silently acknowledging the irony in my request. But the saying "desperate times call for desperate measures" seems perfect for this sort of situation.

I shift the knife higher when the yellow eye moves in my direction again, and he says, "No, it's not my dream."

Unexpected response. "But he's the bad guy. He's killing kids."

"Yes…but per my agreement with my sleeping host, I only eat chicken. Nor has he given permission to kill this vile permutation of evil."

"Color me confused, but isn't a demon calling this guy evil a bit like the pot calling the kettle black?" My hand wavers, and the knife lowers. "What the hell are you?"

The cloaked guy twists and kicks the demon between the legs. Whether real or a facsimile of my boyfriend, the distraction works. His grip loosens, and the bad guy's running at me faster than I can skitter away. With a cry, I slash wildly at him. He flinches from the touch of the blade.

Arms snake around my waist from behind. I scream as I fall backward.

I try to sit up.

A heavy weight pins my upper body to the bed. I yell again, right in Landry's ear. With a choked snort, he rears back, teetering on the edge of the mattress. I grab his arm before he rolls off the side.

"What the—" He blinks, confusion swirling in his gray eye. Then he focuses on my outstretched arm. He grabs my wrist. Blood runs from a slice in my forearm. "God, what happened?" He pulls his T-shirt over his head and wraps it around the cut.

My teeth chatter against the cold pain in the wound, reminding me of the knife I still clutch like it's fused to my palm. "How…It's his knife. He tried to kill me with it."

"Where did this come from?" He reaches for the blade but draws his hand back with a hiss. He shakes his fingers. "It stings."

"I know." My breaths come in ragged gasps. "I dreamed about the murderer. The one killing the kids we found at the crime scene yesterday. He murdered another boy and cut me with this knife and…" I pause, not sure if I should tell him about the…whatever-entity living inside him saving me. I'll figure out this newest mystery later. Focus first on the most immediate threat, like the fact that I can be hurt in my dreams and bring items out of them.

Oh no, worse thought: What if I can *affect* things in my dreams? What if instead of wasting time watching butterflies, I'd followed the screams. Could I have saved the boy?

I trace the hard edge of Landry's bristled jaw with my gaze. He'd be so disappointed if he knew how selfishly I behaved. I squeeze my eyes shut. My head dips forward to rest against his muscular chest, and I count the rapid thuds of his heart. He grips the T-shirt and wraps his other arm around my shoulder, waiting to speak because he senses I'm not finished.

"He's coming to kill me." The idea of being hunted again sets off a mass of shivers. I'm shaking so hard the bed trembles.

"Let him come. It'll be the last thing he does." His implacable tone comforts me. Landry thinks that I don't trust him to protect me. In truth, I know it's exactly the opposite. He's so strong, so brave, he'll charge right into a dangerous situation to keep me safe. He died once because of me. I'll be damned before I let that happen again. Better to call George. At least he's got a gun, training, and the backup of the sheriff's office to bring to a fight with a psycho serial killer. All Landry has is me.

Of course, I don't play stupid by saying this out loud.

Landry wraps the sheet around the knife hilt and pries it free from my fingers and then wraps my hand around the T-shirt as a bandage. "I'll get the first-aid kit."

"It's under the bathroom sink."

He unlocks the door and freezes in the open doorway. I rise to my knees to try to see around him. A cluster of human forms block his exit. I fall back onto the bed and pull the covers over myself right before Axle squeezes underneath Landry's arm. He rushes into the room with Jonjovi right behind him. Both boys throw questions in my direction so fast that I can't focus on individual words. But worse than the boys catching me in the bedroom with my boyfriend is the fact that their sourpuss social worker, Mrs. Moulton, also stands in the doorway. Her wrinkled face shouts her disapproval, and her eyes blister my skin.

Totally busted. This is worse than being caught by the rev.

Then I remember what I told Mama. Damn it. I'm a grown-ass adult. And this is my house. I've done nothing wrong. Landry and I slept fully clothed after Mama interrupted our make-out session. There's no reason for this stupid rush of shame making my cheeks burn.

Landry throws a quick grimace over his shoulder. Only the pink tips of his ears, holding his hair out his face, show his embarrassment. Otherwise he seems perfectly calm and collected as he says, "Mrs. Moulton, could you please go back into the living room?" He doesn't touch her. She'd probably flip out if he did. Instead, he steps forward, using his bulk to drive her down the hallway with each slow step.

More voices filter in from the living room. It's like a party going on out there, except without the guests of honor. And I sure don't feel up to celebrating. I want to hide like a frightened child from the coming drama, but I can't leave Landry to face this alone. Axle taps my shoulder and shakes me out of my dazed stupor. The boys sit almost smack in the middle of my blanket-cushioned lap, trying to get my attention.

Axle's lower lip quivers. "You're bleeding."

I glance at the makeshift bandage. "I had a nightmare and fell off the bed. I cut my arm on something, but I'm fine. I just need a real bandage." My voice lowers to a whisper. "What is Mrs. Moulton doing in here? Did you let her into the house? You know you're not supposed to open the door to strangers."

Jonjovi crosses his arms and looks stern. "We heard you screaming. And when we knocked, you didn't answer."

Axle imitates a bobblehead doll. "Jonjovi said Red broke out of the hospital to get revenge. That he's killing you, and we had to stop him. That's why we let Mrs. Moulton in."

"Don't blame this on me," Jonjovi snaps. "It sounded like you were being killed. You should've opened the door. We didn't know Landry was in here. The rev's gonna kill him when he finds out you two slept in the same bed."

Axle nods. "Yup, kill you dead."

On a roll venting his annoyance, Jonjovi points a finger right between my crossing eyes. "Now Mrs. Moulton knows all our business too, and it's your fault. She said she's here to take us to our real mom."

"I don't want to go," Axle wails, throwing his arms around my neck. I fall backward, wrapping my uninjured arm around his waist as he buries his face into the side of my neck and sobs.

Jonjovi crawls off the bed. "You're gonna stop her, right?" His red face and eyes focus on me, and I read the hope written in them. He expects me to save them, but I don't think I can. Still, that doesn't mean I won't try.

"Go back into the living room with Landry while I clean up this cut. I'll be there in a minute."

"No!" Axle's grip on me tightens. I don't want to pry him off.

Jonjovi grabs his brother's arm and yanks him backward. "Let her go."

"I don't wanna." He twists from his brother, lunging toward me again.

I hold up my bleeding arm. "Please, Axle. I need a bandage."

His eyes widen, and he sniffs. Jonjovi drags him from the room and shuts the door behind them.

I heave a huge sigh. What a crappy way to start the day—terrorized in my dream only to wake up to an even bigger nightmare. What the hell?

I climb from the bed, woozy and nauseous from a combination of shock, blood loss, and stinking morning sickness, and race for the bathroom. After completing what has become my morning routine of making friends with the toilet, I pull the fully stocked first-aid kit from the cabinet. A quick dab of antiseptic and a bandage later, I head for the living room. Mrs. Moulton paces around the room like a caged tiger. And worse, George stands in the doorway with his arms folded. His frazzled hair sticks up in copper spikes from running his fingers through it. I seem to bring this nervous habit out in him.

"Great! You're here too," I say, then stifle my groan. Duh, statement of the obvious. Blood loss has obviously affected my reasoning skills. "Let me rephrase…"

"Don't bother." He holds out a stack of paperwork. "I'm here to do a stand-by while Mrs. Moulton picks up the kids. They're court-ordered to return to their custodial parent."

Landry slams his hand against the wall, and I jump. "Not like this, George." He takes a step forward. "Look, man, we get that Pepper has the legal right to her kids, but come on. She abandoned them for four years and then shows up with a new boyfriend and the first thing he does is takes a swing at Carl. You know this isn't right."

Mrs. Moulton's head swivels from Landry to George, and the folds between her eyebrows deepen with each word. "No, it's not an ideal situation, but Mrs. Acker has assured me that she'll call the police if Judd Helmert tries to contact her or the children."

Landry turns his glare in her direction. "And you believe her? What do you know about that guy? And have you even asked the boys if they want to go with their mom? Don't they get a choice?"

"Typically children don't get to decide who they live with, although in the twins' case I've made an exception." Mrs. Moulton shrugs. "Legally my hands are tied when it comes to Jonjovi and Axle. I promise I'll closely monitor the situation to ensure that Mrs. Acker follows through with keeping Mr. Helmert out of the home."

I collapse against the back of the sofa. Maybe my ability to imagine the worst possible scenario for every situation that might arise involving the boys' safety is a curse. "You did a background check on him, right? Anyone with a temper like his must have something to hide." *Oh, bad thought…* "What if he's a sex offender?"

Or a murderer. His car's identical to the one in my vision.

"The criminal-history check came up clean," George says.

Mrs. Moulton clutches her briefcase to her chest. "I know how to do my job, Ms. LaCroix, and while I'm not happy about Mrs. Acker's choices, my more immediate concern is what I witnessed this morning. I heard the screams coming from your room. The boys were terrified you were being murdered, and you've obviously been injured in some sort of domestic incident."

Landry rises to his full height. He stares from the woman to George. "What the hell? Are you accusing me of beating up my pregnant girlfriend? I'd never hurt Mala. George, tell her."

My brother stares at him intently. "How am I supposed to know what happened behind closed doors? I bet if you think on it hard enough, you'll admit you're of two minds about this whole situation."

Landry surges forward with a low growl. I slip between them and slap a hand on each of their puffed-up chests. "Low blow, Georgie. That's totally uncalled-for."

His gaze doesn't drop from Landry's. "Tell me you don't think it would be safer for the kids if they were as far from him as possible."

All the breath rushes from my body, and I stagger back to lean against Landry's chest. His muscular arms form a cocoon of strength to hold me up, and his warm fingers wrap around my clenched fists. Red spots flash before my eyes, and I struggle to regain control.

How could George even utter that out loud for Mrs. Moulton or the kids who huddle in the corner with their arms around each other to hear? A hollow feeling settles within my chest, growing wider and wider. I can't even comprehend what's going on. My lips feel numb as I beg, "Don't do this, Georgie."

George steps so close that I'm squished between them. The elevated levels of testosterone makes my head swim. "Be honest"—he stabs me with his eyes and then refocuses on Landry—"both of you. With everything going on, do you really think the kids are safe in your care?"

I want to spit out the word "Yes!" but my throat constricts.

Landry's hands tighten on my arms, and a throbbing ache radiates from my wound. "Mala..." He breathes my name softly.

I blink the burn from my eyes. "I promised..." I whisper. But there's a guy out there murdering kids. He knows who I am, and he has the ability to hurt me. I couldn't protect myself and I barely escaped death, because obviously, if he could slash open my arm with that damn knife, he could've gotten my throat. The only reason I'm alive is due to the demon possessing my boyfriend. A damned creature that refuses to kill without Landry's permission. Way to keep an inconvenient promise. I told Dena I would keep her brothers safe. I already let one kid die tonight through inaction. What if he uses the boys to get to me? I want to say this out loud, but too many ears are listening. "I can't be selfish. Not again."

"This is wrong." Landry's arms drop from around me. "You know I'd never let anything happen to you or the boys."

"Don't you get it, Landry?" George says. "You're the danger."

I don't think he is, but I can't say the same about the demon. I don't know why it helped me. Or what it is. Landry's a fighter. A protector. He won't let the boys go without a fight, unless he thinks it's in their best interests. The hurt in his eye almost breaks me. "George is right. And if safe means their mother, then I've got to let them go."

"No, stupid head," Axle cries. "I'm not goin' and you can't make me." He lunges toward the door. George blocks him and lifts him into his arms. The kid's on fire. Kicking and screaming. "Put me down."

Jonjovi bites his lip, staring from face to face. His eyes harden when he sees the decision has been made. "Shut up, Axle."

His brother stops in midscream.

"You're the biggest liar of them all, Mala. You said you wouldn't give us up without a fight. But now you say you'll let us go. Well fine, we don't want to stay here if you don't want us."

"It's not that I don't want—"

"Let's go pack, Axle." He grabs his brother's hand and drags him to the bedroom.

I want to shout that I don't want him to go, but I know it will only make the situation worse. Better to have the boys leave without a fight. It'll be less traumatizing this way, I hope. I don't know. None of this feels right. I feel like pieces are being carved out of my heart and set on fire. Yet I know it's the best choice.

Landry shoves past George. "This is wrong, Mala. You're going to regret this decision. You should've trusted me." He exits the house and runs down the stairs without a backward look. It takes all of my strength not to chase after him, but I do watch to see that he heads in the direction of the Ackers' property. Maybe the rev can calm him down enough that I can explain later why I made this decision.

The kids pack up their belongings in silence and then file outside. I'm shocked to see Daryl in the front seat of Mrs. Moulton's car. He gives me a wave and shrug. They must've stopped off at the Acker place first. I try to give Axle and Jonjovi a hug and kiss good-bye, but they turn away and climb into the backseat. The tears I've been trying to hold back release, as I watch them pull down the lane.

A hand falls on my shoulder, and I shrug away from George's touch. I'm still not sure if I can hold a civil conversation. All I want to do is punch him in the face. "What about Carl?"

George rakes his fingers through his short hair. "He refused to go. I didn't feel like forcing the issue. Daryl says he wants to talk to his mom before making a decision. Plus, once he found out we'd be taking his little brothers, Carl said one of them needed to go to protect them from Judd, and it couldn't be him since there's already bad blood between them."

"Where are they staying?" I ask.

"Robicheaux's Bed and Breakfast."

"Don't worry. I won't drop in and mess up their reunion. I wanted to facilitate this differently. It would've been better to introduce them to Pepper so they got to know her before being ripped away from me. I'm not sure how long it'll take before I can forgive you for this."

George's eyes go flat as he buries what he feels behind an emotionless façade, but his words flay me. "You say you want to be a cop, but then act surprised when I do my job. Being a cop sometimes sucks. Besides, you know getting those kids out of here is the right thing to do. How do you expect to raise four boys, a baby, and go to college? You're twenty-one."

"So is Dena. She would've done it."

"Only because she didn't have a choice. Her mom's back. Those kids are her responsibility. Not yours. She birthed them. It's about time she took responsibility for them."

Chapter 16

Landry

Hard Choices

I barrel down the staircase and sprint for the woods as if the hounds of Hades are chomping at my ass, so pissed that I'm seconds from exploding. I can't believe how that jackass played on Mala's fears. He manipulated her as if her brain's a soft, doughy pretzel, weaving his words until he convinced her to hand the kids over to Pepper without a fight.

Spots flash before my eye, making my vision wonky. I slow down once I hit the dirt path, not willing to crash into a tree simply because I'm too fired up to see where I'm heading. Which raises the question…where do I think I'm going? Not to dad. Sure, he'll say all the right things, like Pepper's their mom and she's got the right to parent them. That it's her property, and she can decide whether or not to keep it. Blah, blah, fucking holier-than-thou bullshit. But I've had my fill of moms. Mine destroyed my bright and shiny image of motherhood—set her halo on fire. Now it feels like Mala's doing the same.

It scares the hell out of me that she thinks she'd do a poorer job of raising those boys than the woman who abandoned them. And what about our kid? Is she gonna give our baby up when it gets too tough? Like after I'm gone.

This is what really shakes me. Her lack of trust in me or our relationship. The fact that she thinks I can't protect my family. And then George goes and deliberately feeds into her fears by bringing up the uncommonly quiet parasite in my head.

"Why aren't you chiming in?" I ask the thing lurking behind my eyeball. "Not like you to hold back the sarcastic quip. I know you've been listening in this whole time. I can sense when you're awake."

"My presence has caused enough chaos in your life."

"Never stopped you before," I mumble, shoving aside a vine. The path forks up ahead and rather than heading left to reach the Acker property, I head to the right. I shove my hand into my pocket to search for my phone, but come up empty. Even if I wanted to call Mala to see how she's doing, I can't.

"If you weren't concerned, why bother searching for your cellular phone?"

"Shut it."

"You would not be angry unless some part of you did not acknowledge the truth in Mala LaCroix's actions. Her reasoning was sound. The children are in danger so long as the evil one hunts her."

A chill runs through my body. "What does that mean? She said he sensed her in the dream. That he would be coming for her. That wasn't just paranoia talking?"

"He drew her mind to him. He wanted her to witness his sacrifice.

He tapped into her magic to form a bond with her when she was trapped in his circle. Now he can manipulate her at will. We must break the bond between them before it's too late."

"How do you know all of this? And why do you care?"

"The strength of her fear sucked me into her nightmare. I saw what she faced. He is not a simple man, but the essence of evil. The very creature who drew me to this plane of existence. The one I have fought against for eons. He who takes many faces and has many names. Who seeks to consume and destroy."

"Kind of dramatic, aren't you?"

"I tried to keep it simple so your puny brain could understand."

"Yeah, big words hurt brain." I shudder. The overcast sky coupled with the water-saturated air presses heavily around my body. No matter how crazy his words come across as, I sense how serious the situation has become. "So dumb it down even further for me, 'cause I seriously don't understand what the hell's going on."

"Demon. This is what you call me. Why, I do not know. The definition of such an entity more closely resembles that which Mala faced this morning. I am its adversary. Drawn from the dawn of time to combat that which infects and feeds on the horrors perpetrated by mankind."

"So, what…" I laugh at the ridiculousness of my thought. "Are you some kind of angel?"

"I'm no angel." I feel its mental shrug. *"But if it eases your mind to think of me this way, so be it."*

"God, you're hurting my brain."

"That is another name by which I've been called throughout time immemorial. God, with a little g, of course." The angel/god thing in my head laughs. Not funny.

"I need to speak with someone who understands this more than

I do." But who? Sophia or Ferdinand. Even Magnolia calls this creature a demon. If they don't know the truth of its origins, who would?
"Why did Magnolia say you were a demon?"

"Why did you believe her?"

That's a fantastic question. Mala's been screaming about Magnolia being evil since we met. Her great-grandmother even cut ties with
her twin sister because she practiced the dark arts. There's a reason
why Magnolia's the Hoodoo Queen of New Orleans. A woman who
raised zombies and tried to convince Mala to do the same. We believed what she said because we didn't know any better.

"Ah, so you work through to the truth of the matter."

"Huh?"

*"The fact that you place your trust in those who are the least trust-
worthy."*

My feet continue to move down the path. I know where I'm
heading now. The place where Mala's ancestors gather.

"Gaston, I need you," I yell, bursting into the empty clearing.
"Gaston!"

One minute I'm alone, and then I'm not.

As soon as I lay eyes on him, I get heated again. He's supposed
to be her protector, but he didn't show up when she needed him.
"Were you in the house when all that went down this morning?"

Gaston squints. "Is there a reason you're acting like a jackass on
loco weed?"

"The murderer entered Mala's dream, cut her with a knife, and almost killed her. She brought the knife he used out of the dream and
into the real world."

"And this all happened in a dream? She didn't slip her skin?"

"Yeah, that's what my rider says. Oh, and he also says he's not a de-

mon but also not an angel, unless I want to think of him that way…"
I squeeze my eye shut. "Ah, I'm so confused."

The cheek flap stretches, showing Gaston's gums when he starts to laugh, which is disturbing since I've rarely seen Mala's uncle so much as crack a smile. "An angel. Like the winged variety? Harps and cherubs."

"You say that like it's impossible. But why couldn't it be true if demons exist? Something to fight against the forces of darkness, like Magnolia?"

"My aunt hasn't done anything suspicious lately."

"Shows how much you know." I point my finger in his direction and then snatch it out of reach when he gives it the evil eye. "You've dropped the ball. Let her minions get a stranglehold over us. What happened to the guy who threw a hissy fit when Magnolia first came into the house? Did Sophia work her sex magic on your ass? Got you pussy whipped so you can't see the truth."

Gaston's hand clenches around the barrel of his ever-present rifle. Once again I'm thinking I should've kept my mouth shut. 'Cause if Mala can be hurt in a dream, could I get shot by a ghost if Gaston gets pissy enough?

Calm down. "Look, I don't mean to disrespect you, Gaston. I'm frustrated. And worried. We've got no idea who this guy is or why he's killing those kids and making those power circles. Somehow, Mala's tied to him. She thinks he's coming after her. If it's a supernatural attack, then you're the one who's in charge of defending her. Problem is, he's also got a foot in the real world. He's really kidnapping and hacking up those boys."

I tap my head. "The one up here is concerned we don't have enough information, and the only ones who have a clue about what's going on are Magnolia and crew. But who's to say they're being truthful with us? They've got their own agenda. And they're not sharing."

Gaston stares at me like I've lost my mind. And hell, maybe I'm not wrapped tight. The skin around his mouth puckers. At least he appears to be thinking about what I'm saying. "What do you need me to do?" he asks.

"We need their help, but we also can't blindly go along with what they tell us."

Gaston turns his head. "They're coming."

I turn to see two shadowed forms on the path leading from the crossroads. Ferdinand favors one leg when he enters the clearing. Sophia's face lights up, and a smile forms on her pouty lips, but her amorous expression isn't for me. Her eyes drink in Gaston like he's a tall glass of water. And I know she's seeing him as he appeared before his death. He knows it too. And he's not as unaffected as he would like to portray.

For a brief second, his image shimmers to reflect his unburned appearance. Like he can't control it. Maybe he doesn't want to. For all his big talk, Sophia still gets to him. Guess it's true what they say about never really getting over your first love.

"Landry, you look lovely," Sophia calls. Today she's dressed more appropriately. Instead of a skirt and high heels, she's in tan khakis and flat leather boots. A wide-brimmed, Curious George–type jungle hat rests on top of her silky, black hair. All she needs is an elephant gun and she'll be ready to go on a wild-game safari. She saunters over and, before I can pull away, plants a kiss on my cheek.

Revulsion flows at the touch of her moist lips, and I pull back, rubbing her red lipstick off with the back of my hand. "Don't touch me!" The words spring from deep in my gut.

Her lips form a pout. "I thought we got over our feud when you begged for my help yesterday."

"Today is a new day."

"Indeed it is." She brushes dried blood off the altar stone with her bare hand and sits down, crossing her legs. "Where is your baby mama? I seem to recall telling her to meet us here today. We need to purify her."

Ferdinand throws his backpack to the ground, then turns. "Fuck this! I have better things to do with my time than stay in this town, twiddling my thumbs while waiting on the two of you. I told you the side effect of not ridding the body of the pollutants. Yesterday should have taught you how much you have left to learn about controlling your gifts."

I share a quick look with Gaston. "Damn, Ferdinand, tell me how you really feel."

"Don't mind him. He slept poorly last night," Sophia says, waving her hand in his direction. "One downside to getting old is waking up with random aches and pains and not knowing how you injured yourself in your sleep."

I forgot that Sophia is a lot older than she appears. If she and Gaston were hanging out before his death, she's got to be at least sixty, yet she looks half that age. "I know it's not polite to ask a lady her age, but…"

"You've seen my true appearance. And while I've aged well, without the glamour, I don't appear quite this beautiful. Nor does my body feel as youthful as I'd like. The sort of spells for immortality come with a high cost."

Ferdinand snorts. "Not that you're not vain enough to contemplate casting one."

Sophia's face flames. "Contrary to popular belief, I have no desire to damn my soul simply to live forever."

"Whoa, come on. Let's not fight," I say. "There's something I need to talk to you both about."

Sophia rolls her green eyes. "Why? Will you trust what I say or continue to look upon me with suspicion?"

"Stop acting like an *enfant*," Ferdinand says.

This whole situation is ridiculous.

"They endeavor to keep you distracted from the real issue, host. Listen to the hidden."

"Can you please stop speaking in riddles?"

"That is not my nature."

The weight of eyes on me brings me to the present. "Something happened to Mala this morning," I say, and proceed to lay out everything I've learned. Well, I leave out the parts about her bringing the knife out of her dream, my suspicions about them, and the demon not being a demon in the biblical sense. So basically, they get the mega-edited version.

Ferdinand and Sophia share a long meaningful look.

"It's as predicted," Ferdinand says.

Sophia nods like a lovely puppet on a string. "We may be too late. We should have performed the cleansing ritual yesterday. All the drama." She sighs. "I thought it would be fine to wait. Now that he's connected to her, it will be tougher to pry him free. Where is she?"

"At home."

"Then let's go get her before it's too late," Ferdinand says.

Chapter 17

Mala

Professional Courtesy

As much as I long to drop-kick my brother's ass off my property, I can't. It's a sad fact that no matter how angry he makes me, I always end up forgiving him. 'Cause I'm stupid loyal to my friends and family, and while it pains me to admit it right now, Georgie's both. Though he sure as shit doesn't deserve the benefit of the doubt half the time. It's usually only when I look back on his actions that I can see he isn't a self-serving jackass and has my best interests at heart. It's just how he goes about making his point that I hate.

Same with this situation. He knows about the demon. He knows about the murderer. He knows, and I know, that the kids are in danger. No matter how much I would like to deny it, I'd be an idiot to risk their lives to thumb my nose at George. I just wish Landry could put aside his anger long enough to trust me and acknowledge the pitiful reality of our situation. It would make my life simpler, 'cause

I get tired of always being the bad guy in our relationship.

I lead the way up the stairs and ease myself into one of the rocking chairs, careful not to bump my injured arm. George sits across from me as I say, "I'm not happy with this situation or you right now. Just promise you'll find Judd."

He drums his fingers on the table. "Don't worry. We're searching for him. Pepper said he hasn't contacted her since he fled the scene yesterday, but she'll notify me if he does. She'll remain at Robicheaux's tonight, then move back home while she packs up their stuff and sells the place."

"She's also planning on pulling the plug on Dena." My eyes meet George's. "Did she mention that?"

He focuses on the table. "Yeah. It's time, don't you think?"

I contemplate telling him my plan to raise her. But it's only something else he can use against me whenever he wants. Forget that. "Dena's strong, and as long as she's still breathing, there's hope she'll make it back to us. Pepper pulling the plug is taking away that chance."

"So you'd rather she suffer."

Tears fill my eyes. Even without knowing Dee's trapped in limbo with Redford, he hits the nail on the head. I need to change the subject quick, but I can't speak around the emotion clogging my throat.

George nods toward my arm. "So what really happened? And don't say you tripped and fell. Did Landry hurt you?"

My mouth tightens at the suspicion. "He would, never hurt me. Neither would the creature in his head, but I don't suppose you'll believe that without proof." I lean forward. "Last night, I had a nightmare that wasn't. I dreamed about the murderer. He picked up another boy."

He breathes in with a hiss. "What did you see?"

"Nothing helpful in figuring out who is he is. But the kid's dead, and I think…" *I could have saved him.* But I can't admit that out loud. "He has another trophy spot. It's a field full of bones. Those damn blue butterflies and a sky on fire. I'm not sure which of the details are real. But that guy knew I was there. And he cut my arm."

"How the hell did he hurt you in a dream?"

My head bobs. "Don't know, but I've got the knife he used."

"What?"

I give him a tight smile. "He dropped it when he fought with the demon possessing Landry."

"Girl," he says, blowing out the word with a snorted breath, "you're not making a lick of sense."

"Tell me about it. I'm totally freaked." I push out of the chair. "Come on. I'll show you."

George follows on my heels, literally, and I jab my elbow toward his stomach. He skips back a step with a muttered "Brat."

The knife's still wrapped in the sheet on the bed, right where Landry left it. Part of me had worried it would have vanished like the misty details of my dream, but I'm not so lucky. Its cold presence is a reminder of how deadly my situation is. A residual fire races up my palm, and I'm careful not to touch the bone hilt. "This is it. Do you think we can get prints?"

"Did you touch it?"

"Hell, yeah. He tried to kill me, and I was unarmed. Picked it up as soon as he dropped it. Landry touched it too. Can you dust for prints anyway? We can give you ours for elimination."

"Yeah, it's possible to get prints off skeletal material. Probably should use a silicone rubber compound to lift the print. We also might be able to get some DNA, if there's any left in the marrow. Determine if it's human or animal. Let's take it to the station."

My nose scrunches. "I think it's a ceremonial knife."

"Would your aunt know anything?"

I grimace at the thought of Auntie Magnolia, but he's got a point. "Let's run this by the professionals first."

"There's someone else I want you to meet while we're in town."

I raise an eyebrow.

"Remember I told you a professor found the boy's remains. Well, Deputy Winters said she called and requested a meeting with you this afternoon. Says she has some information and it's pretty important, but it has to be in private. You up for it?"

"Sounds weird. I don't know why she'd want to talk to me, but I'm game if you are."

I try to call Landry to tell him where I'm going, but his phone's in the living room on the charger. He stormed off without it. And I've got no idea when he'll be back. I write him a note and stick it to the TV.

"Where to first?" I ask.

"The station. Bessie wants to talk to you, and we can ask the tech what he thinks about the knife." He dons latex gloves and pulls a plastic Ziploc bag from one of his cargo pants' pockets, then removes the knife from the sheet and drops it into the bag.

* * *

When we reach the crossroad, I feel a spike of guilt when I see Ferdinand's car parked by the side of the road. I'd forgotten we were supposed to meet this morning. But before I have a chance to ask George if he'd mind stopping, we're turning onto the road to town. The Bertrand Parish sheriff's office and fire department are located in the same brick building off Main Street. We pull in through the gated back parking lot, and I draw in a deep breath. Giddiness fills me. My gaze travels over the parked patrol cars and the fenced-in shed that houses confiscated property that won't fit inside the evidence room. Unlike yesterday, when I went in through the front like every other private citizen of Bertrand Parish, entering though the restricted access feels like coming home.

The firefighters have an engine parked out back and are busy scrubbing it with long-handled brushes. Pete Lemaster, who was a total tool in high school but pulled his head out of his butt to become a productive member of society, turns the water hose in my direction.

"Hey!" I yell, skirting the puddle.

He laughs, lifting the hose again. "Mala Jean, missed ya, girl. Let me show my appreciation for those fine legs of yours. Dance for me, baby."

"You're the only thing I don't miss about working here. And I guarantee, if I ever come back to work here, you'd better duck and cover." I mime shoving a pole up where the sun don't shine.

He blows a kiss in my direction.

George raises his hand, palm up. That's it. He doesn't say a word, but Pete lowers the hose with a chagrined expression. When George looks away, he rolls his eyes, and I shrug. My brother's lost his sense of humor today. Not that I blame him, given what we're here to find out. I'm upset too, but I also can't stifle my excitement about being here. I finally get the chance to be of use. No more helpless, silent witness. I'm gonna hunt this creep down before he turns the tables and finds me.

George enters his password into the keypad, and I follow him into the building. I breathe in, loving the smell of burned coffee wafting through the air. It's been too long since I graced these halls, but nothing has changed. When we file past the interview room, I peek through the window to see Andy inside with a handcuffed man. Rex lies in front of the door. His tail thumps on the ground when I pass, but he doesn't move.

"Do you want to say hi to Dixie?" George asks.

"Oh? She wasn't on duty when I stopped by yesterday." I glance toward the dispatch center down the hall. Dixie sits in front of a large computer screen with her headset on and microphone down. Her fingers fly across the keyboard. I shake my head. "I'll talk to her later. Is Bessie in her office? What do you think she'll say? I really think I can help with this case."

"Best way to find out is to ask."

I square my shoulders and head toward her office. Her voice filters down the hallway, and I also recognize the sheriff's voice coming from the room. And my name. *Oh crap, they're talking about me.*

I freeze outside the door, not sure if I should go in or turn around and run for the swamp. Instead I peek inside. Sheriff Keyes lounges in a chair in front of Bessie's desk with his hands folded over his round belly, while Bessie paces in front of her bookshelf. They don't look happy. Maybe it's best if I come back later. I step backward and bump into a solid chest.

George reaches around and knocks on the partially open door. "Mala's here to talk with you."

I throw a dirty expression over my shoulder. He shrugs and hip bumps me through the doorway. I stumble forward and mumble "Hi" around the lump in my throat. "Sorry I had to leave so quickly yesterday. I know you both have questions. I'll do my best to answer them, but the thing is, I may not know the answer. This is all pretty new to me too."

I wipe my sweaty palms on my jeans. Silence fills the room. I clear my throat. "I was telling George earlier that I think the guy killed another kid yesterday. In my vision the boy looked to be about sixteen, with brown hair and a fair complexion. Maybe about five-nine, but I'm not sure since he was lying down. I don't know where the suspect killed him. The crime scene seemed familiar, but I can't place where it could be."

Bessie shares a sharp look with Sheriff Keyes before she steps over to her desk and picks up a manila folder and pulls out a picture. "Is this the boy you saw?"

Biting my lip, I take the picture with a trembling hand. My breath catches when I see the boy smiling from the school photograph. "Yeah, it's him. What was his name?"

"His name *is* Marcus Wright. His parents reported him missing last night. The boy's from one parish over. Sixteen. Someone saw a white sedan pick him up off the side of Route 23 and called it in."

"Any identifiers on the vehicle?" I ask, reverting to language I learned while working in dispatch with Dixie. Back then, instead of calling the deputies by their name, I used their radio call signs. Instead of calling a fight a fight, I called it by the criminal code designation. Such an easy habit to fall back into. Comforting. And I need it right now, because I'm all kinds of shook up. For some reason, seeing the boy in the dream, even getting cut by the killer, didn't make him feel as real as seeing his picture.

"We've got a partial Louisiana plate number. We're running variations of it now to see what we can come up with in this area."

"The murderer was driving a white car in my vision yesterday." I stare down at the boy's face one last time as I gently place the photograph on the desk. "Pepper's boyfriend Judd also drives a car identical to the one I saw."

"And you're only just mentioning this?" George says.

I bite my lip, ashamed. "Thought you might think I was being prejudiced since he's an ass. Plus, the probability of him being the killer is so low. But he's someone we should definitely question, if only to rule him out. Don't you think?"

"Mala, how do you know all of this?" Bessie drops into her seat and steeples her hands on the desk. "It's so hard to believe."

"Then trust me. When have I ever lied to you, Bessie? Do you think I'd make this up? That I'm sadistic enough to go around murdering boys so I can pretend to solve their case, because that's the only other explanation for how I knew where to find those bodies. Or that this boy's missing."

Sheriff Keyes still hasn't spoken a word. This scares me more than Bessie's question. He studies me with expressionless eyes, so unlike his usual twinkle. He used to like me. Now I'm not so sure. And that hurts worse than anything.

Tears well up, but I blink them away. "I guess I've wasted your time. Let's go, George. I doubt they want me walking unescorted through the halls."

"This is nuts!" George bursts out.

"Deputy Dubois," Bessie says, "get ahold of yourself."

"No, this is bullshit. Are you seriously letting her leave like this?

Even if you think she's a suspect, then you should at least interrogate her to find out what she knows."

"George—" I back away from him. Is he saying to stick me in that tiny room where that homeless guy sat, stinking up the chair, and question me for hours on end? "I've already told you what I know. You don't have to treat me like a criminal."

"We're not saying you're a suspect," Bessie says. "We think you're confused. I called Dr. Rhys, and he said you could be delusional if you're off your medication."

"Oh, I see. You're planning on locking me back up in the psych ward. Well, I'm not going without a fight. So you might as well arrest me now for assault on a peace officer."

"Mala Jean! I'm concerned."

"No, you're in denial and trying to find excuses. You know I'm telling the truth, but you're scared to admit it. What do you need? More proof?"

"Yes." Bessie glances at Sheriff Keyes, who nods. Why is he letting her do all the talking?

"Fine, if that's what it takes. But I warn you"—I step forward, holding the gaze of her onyx eyes—"if you make me do this, you're the one who will suffer. And I'm sorry."

"Why are you apologizing?" Her voice hitches on the question, and her eyes widen. Part of me wants to spare her the coming heartache, but it's too late for regrets. For either of us.

I let the protective shield in my mind drop. Not a lot. Just enough to encompass this office. Whatever magic that draws spirits to me like iron to a magnet engages.

An icy draft flows through the room. Bessie shivers, fingers fumbling with the cuffs of her rolled-up sleeves. "Why is it so cold?" she whispers, and vapor forms in the air in front of her. "Did the air conditioner kick on?"

Sheriff Keyes rises from his seat and waves a hand in front of the air vent. "No. Are you responsible for this, Deputy Dubois?"

My brother raises his hands. The tips of his fingers have turned blue. "Mala…"

I grit my teeth so they don't chatter. I want to appear to be in control of my powers. Sure, I still suck at controlling spirits, but to show my fear would undo whatever trust I gain from this situation.

A blurred figure appears behind Bessie's shoulder. I focus on drawing it from the other side. When he solidifies, I walk over to her bookshelf and pull the picture of the young, uniformed man from the shelf and hold it out to her. "Your husband has something to say."

Bessie stiffens. "What did you say?"

"Daniel's here." I cock my head, listening. His voice sounds distant, as if the wind blows it away. "He has a message for you."

Her hands slap the desk. "This isn't funny." She pushes up from her seat. The chair rolls back to slam against the wall. Bessie's deceased husband steps closer, and a full-body shudder wracks her body. "Stop this, please," she begs.

And I want to. I really do, but I can't. It's too late.

The spirit's voice drops directly into my brain, and I speak for him. "Daniel says he's been watching out for you and Maggie. He's so proud of his daughter. And happy she found Tommy. You raised her right. But it's time for you to find a man and move on."

Bessie hisses. "I can't believe you'd use my interest in Ferdinand against me."

My shoulders hunch in pain at the hurtful accusation. But I understand why she's lashing out. "Daniel says he's tired, but you won't let him move on. You've got to stop holding on to him—talking to him." I lay the picture face down on her desk. "You got to let him go."

"Mala…"

"You kept his badge. And the last note he wrote to you before he went out on patrol the day he died. They're in the top right desk drawer."

"How did you k-know?"

"Same way I know you've got a dress in that dry cleaning bag behind the door for the date you were thinking about canceling. He says to stop feeling guilty about being alive. Go and have fun."

Tears stream down Bessie's cheeks. I've never seen her cry. It rocks the very foundation of my world. She stares into space, which happens to be where her husband stands, gazing into her eyes, as if she senses his presence. "Have I been selfish holding you here?"

His outstretched hand caresses her cheek.

She shudders, whispering, "Daniel…"

He gives one last sad smile, then fades. "He's gone."

"No, call him back!" Bessie yells. "There's more I need to say to him."

"He's heard everything you've ever said to him, but he's gone now. For good this time. This is what I do. I help the dead pass over to the other side." My head's killing me. Every time I drop the barrier I get a wicked headache. This time it's worse. The overhead lights create a pulsing throb behind my eyeballs, and I squint. "Do you believe me now?" *Please don't make me call up your dead mama or something. Please.*

She folds her arms on the desk and presses her face into the crease of her elbow.

Sheriff Keyes watches Bessie with an intensity that sets my heart thumping. How did I never notice before? The man's in love with Bessie. Does she know? Damn…

When she doesn't answer, Sheriff Keyes waves his hand in a shooing motion. "Do what you've got to do. We won't stop you. But remember this: You're a consultant. Nothing more. No peace officer powers. No gun. Deputy Dubois, you're responsible for keeping her from getting herself killed."

"I won't put her in harm's way," my big bro promises, taking my elbow and steering me from the room. Sheriff Keyes' voice follows us into the hallway, nothing more than a dull rumble.

"Come on, Mala. Let's get the knife to the techs."

"Why didn't you mention it to Bessie?"

He shrugs. "We've got no way to prove this knife was used to kill the kids. The chain of evidence won't hold up in court. And I don't particularly want to answer questions about how it came to be in your possession. They were suspicious enough without producing the murder weapon."

My phone vibrates, sending a thrill through my ass. I slip it out of my pocket. "It's Landry."

"He's probably calling to bitch you out about letting the kids go. You'll have to call him after we finish with Ernesto. Reception's nonexistent once we enter the dungeon."

The evidence room is like an underground bunker, with concrete block walls and rows upon rows of shelving and boxes. Ernesto Diaz, the evidence technician, sits at his desk with his feet propped up on a chair. His computer monitor displays a game of Spider Solitaire.

When he sees us, he sits up with a groan and clicks the minimize button. "What's up, Dubois? Catch a new case for me to process?"

"Need to see about lifting some prints." George pulls the baggie with the knife from his pocket and hands it over. "What do you think?"

Ernesto holds the bag up to the light. "Whoa, man, where'd you find this?"

"Don't ask. Let's just say I'm calling in that favor you owe me."

Chapter 18

Landry

Cranky Pants

The house is empty when Sophia, Ferdinand, and I arrive. Mala left a note saying she's taking off with George but doesn't say why or where she's going.

I shove my phone into my jean pocket. "She won't answer."

Ferdinand drops onto the sofa and picks up the remote. "Magnolia won't be arriving until late afternoon anyway, and fuck if I feel like dealing with it now. I slept wrong, and I want to rest up for the ritual."

Sophia glances at me, and I shrug. I can't blame him for being pissy. Still, I've got to ask. "But don't we need to do this ASAP?"

"If Mala doesn't care, why should I? 'Sides, we can't do shit without the queen," Ferdinand says with no inflection. The big guy's already got CNN on the screen, and he lounges with his legs crossed and arms folded in front of him.

Sophia motions toward the door. "Ferdinand can stay and wait for Queen Magnolia if you'll give me a ride to my motel. I need to get some supplies."

"Yeah, whatever." Better than sticking around here with Mr. Cranky Pants. Plus, I have a few places in town I can check for my runaway girlfriend. "Let's go."

Once we're in the truck, I ask, "Where exactly are you staying?"

"Robicheaux's B and B. Until that obnoxious woman brought her brats over this morning and interrupted my complimentary breakfast, it was a nice, quiet stay."

I shoot her a quick look.

"Your boys threw a fit the moment they got dropped off. They didn't take the reunion well, and they're giving their mom hell. As deserved." Sophia laughs, buckling her seat belt. "I've been meaning to apologize for what happened in the graveyard."

Did I just hear her right? I'm half blind, not half deaf. Maybe a bit crazy 'cause the sincerity in her tone has me questioning everything, like the whole nature of the universe—Big Bang versus seven days and nights—the totality of it all. If the woman who puts the capital *B* in *Bitch* could apologize, then perhaps my demon rider really is an angel. And I'm not going to hell in a hand basket. "Sophia…are you seriously sorry about molesting me?"

She gives a haughty sniff and waves her manicured hand. "Not like you're a virgin."

Ah yes, order in the universe restored. "Doesn't matter…" I shake my head. "You know, if you're so twisted you can't recognize that what you did was wrong, nothing I say matters."

"I apologized, didn't I?" She stares out the window. "I knew it was immoral, but I didn't have a choice. When Magnolia gives the order, I obey."

"What happened to free will?"

She chuckles. "I chose beauty over freedom. The only time I regret it is when I see Gaston. Except he still desires my body. I doubt he would be as interested if he saw the sagging skin of a sixty-year-old hag."

"Harsh. I guess the saying 'beauty's only skin deep' doesn't apply to you. So, what happened? It's pretty obvious the two of you still have feelings for each other."

"I was apprenticed to Magnolia at birth, as payment for some service she provided to my mother. I never saw my birth family again. Not that I care. Magnolia provided all I ever needed and more." She pauses with a sigh, and I wonder what she's thinking. Is she really okay with being sold? Or not knowing her family origins...*who* and *where* she comes from?

Her shiny emerald eyes turn in my direction. "Would you be happy knowing your only value to your mother was as something she could barter? Why would I want to meet someone like that?"

"Sorry..." I let the apology trail off.

The bushes up ahead part, and I press the brakes. A buck steps cautiously onto the road and glances in my direction, then makes a run for it, followed by the rest of the herd of deer. I watch them in silence, hyper aware of the woman sitting next to me. I'm not sure what more I can say to help ease the pain she obviously still feels but doesn't want to acknowledge. Her willingness to open up this much shocks me.

Sophia stares at the creatures bounding across the road with a slight smile. "Gaston and I met as children, before his mother and her sister parted ways. We grew up together out here, roaming these woods. It was a beautiful, magical childhood spent with my first and only love." Her sigh hums with longing and regret. "He promised to marry me when he returned from Vietnam, and I vowed to wait for him. And I did. When Magnolia and Cora had their falling out, I had no choice but to follow my mistress to New Orleans. Even there, I remained faithful to Gaston. He's the one who broke his promise to come back to me."

"He died, Sophia."

"We both know death is not an excuse." The corner of her lip curls with the raw, bitterness in her voice. "He *chose* to remain on the LaCroix property despite knowing I was forbidden to return."

My gut clenches in sympathy. Not only for her losing the man she loved, but also at the thought that this could be my fate. How did Gaston find the strength to leave her? Did he think he was doing her a favor by setting her free to live her life? What I do know is that I couldn't do it. *No way.* If given a choice after I die, I'll tie myself to Mala and the baby. No matter how difficult it might be for her to see me when I'm dead or how much it hurts me to be unable to touch them. Even if I've got to watch her move on with another man, I won't abandon them.

* * *

The Robicheaux's Bed and Breakfast is a converted two-story Victorian painted the same color blue as my dead sister's eyes, with white trim around the windows. It's a pretty place. My mom and the owner, May, were childhood friends. We used to visit after church on Sundays. Lainey and I would play hide-and-go-seek in the garden while May and Mom sat on the porch swing and gossiped.

Those memories of happier days fill me with pain, and I shove them into the back of my mind. I hope, someday, I'll be able to re-visit them without the heavy sadness choking off my breath. I help Sophia out of the truck in silence. She still hasn't come out of her-self. It's a day for dark reflection.

"Dark reflection," Sophia says, sighing out the last word. "My, Landry, you're quite the poet."

I grunt, waving for her to take the lead. Sure, we seem to have struck a truce, but I still don't trust her at my back. Or walking on my blind side.

As soon as I reach the bottom of the front staircase, a kid screams bloody murder and blurs across the porch. A tiny body launches it-self from the front step. My arms open, and I don't even have time to pray I don't miss, what with my depth perception being all screwed up, before Axle slams into my arms. "Landry, did you come to take us home?"

I hug him tight, breathing deeply to calm my pounding heart. I force myself to set him on his feet and run my fingers through his baby-fine hair with a trembling hand. "Why aren't you in school?"

"Pepper said she wanted to spend the day getting to know us bet-ter. If she cared so much, she wouldn't have 'bandoned us, right? It's bullsh"—his eyes widen—"poop."

"Where did you hear that, 'cause I know you didn't come up with it yourself?"

His gaze drops, and he shrugs.

I squat down until I'm at eye level. "Where's Jonjovi?"

"He ran off, but don't tell."

"Axle…"

"Said 'This is bull…*poop*' and he's going home, but he wouldn't let me come 'cause I'd tell Pepper-mama. But I can keep a secret."

Shit! This just gets better and better. I knew this would happen. "Where's your mom?"

"Probably doing the nasty with ol' Judd the Stud. They kicked me out of the room."

Instant rage flares at hearing Judd's with Pepper, but I force myself to remain calm so I don't scare the kiddo into thinking he's the source. "Axle, where do you get this stuff?"

He rolls his eyes, reminding me of Carl. "Dad gave me the sex talk when I was seven. I'm not a kid."

My head's about to explode. TMI overload. "And Daryl?"

"Said he's going to Playtown Park. He wouldn't let me come either. Dena would've made them take me."

Damn it, Daryl might be the smarter twin, but when it comes to family, he doesn't have the sense God gave a toad. Selfish little bastard left his baby brothers to fend for themselves after swearing to Carl that he'd watch over them. Soon as I find him, his ass is gonna get up close and personal with the toe of my boot.

"Let's go find your mom." I grab Axle by the back of the shirt when he tries to make a break for it and steer him into the B and B. "Where's your room?"

He points down the long hallway past the dining room. "Number three, but I'm not going in there. Judd said he'd smack me into next week if I disturbed them."

I'd like to see him try that with me. "I'll take care of him."

Axle punches his fist into the air. "Yeah! Take his a-a...butt out. One-two punch."

A throb of pain pulses behind my dead eye.

I don't want him to witness what happens, especially if his mama's really doing the nasty. "Go get some pie while I talk to your mom,"

I say, waiting until he takes the ten-dollar bill I hold out and heads into the dining room.

Sophia took off the minute the kid played Superman and launched himself into my arms.

I pound on Pepper's door, then press my ear against the wood. Filtered whispers and rustles come from the other side. The door flies open before my twentieth knock connects, and I pull my fist back so I don't accidentally punch her in the face.

She stares at me with wide eyes through an untamed mop of red curls and pulls the gaping top of her robe closed. "What do you want? Ms. Moulton told—"

"Told me what? That you said you'd take care of the boys. Keep your boyfriend away from them? Next you're gonna tell me you were playing with yourself just now."

She gasps. "That's disgusting."

"How do you think I feel saying it?" I shove open the door, forcing her backward so I can see into the room. The bed's empty, but a breeze ruffles the curtains hanging in front of the open window and blows the ripe stink of cologne through the room. "Where is he?"

"I don't know."

"When are you going to learn, Pepper? Like Carl said, 'Respect is earned.' Your sons won't forgive your crap just because they love you. You've got to earn their trust, and this isn't the way to do it."

"Wow, Landry. Didn't think you'd grow up all holier than thou, but I guess I should've expected it given your daddy. Course, he's a big ol' hypocrite too, talking about turning the other cheek. Guess he meant that literally, since he never did anything about my husband beating me even when he saw the bruises. Maybe that's why your mama turned out nuttier than Ida Jean's fruitcake."

It takes all my strength not to lash out at her words. Dad wouldn't condone domestic abuse. *I won't let her manipulate me into feeling sorry for her. Judd's her choice.* "Ida Jean's dead, Pepper. She died two months ago. No more nuts in the fruitcake. Or cake period, but then, you'd know that if you'd stuck around."

Her cheeks turn as red as her hair. "Fine, rub my face in my bad decisions. Think I don't know how badly I've screwed up my family. All I have to do is go to the hospital and look at my dying daughter." Tears well up in her eyes, and my heart constricts. Not sure if it's sympathy or heartburn, 'cause I'm pretty sure those tears are fake. Damn! I'm getting cynical in my old age.

"Just do right by the kids you've got left. Don't leave them to wander around alone. There's a killer on the loose." I pinch my lips together. Maybe I shouldn't have said anything about the case George is working, but…fuck him. "I'll give you twenty minutes to get dressed, and then we're going out to gather your troops and bring them back together. After you apologize for being a shitty parent, take them to Munchies for pizza. No pepperoni, just cheese."

I turn before I regret trying to help her out. It's this or rounding up the boys and hiding them in the sticks where she won't be able to find them. Chances are she'll get bored with being a parent. My guess is the only reason she came home was to get the property Acker left when he died. Judd probably put her up to it. Plus, four kids means a fat welfare check in the mail every month.

Man, the negativity's bringing me down.

I go to the front desk and schmooze May Robicheaux, pulling on a strained smile and not wincing at her cheek pinching, until she caves and gives me Sophia's room number. With a final kiss on her plump hand, which gets me a girlish giggle from the middle-aged woman, I head upstairs to find out if Sophia needs a ride back to the house. There are only six rooms on the second floor. From down the hall, I can see that Sophia's door is cracked open.

A sliver of unease slides down my spine. I've learned to not ignore it when my spidey sense gets to tingling. My heart pounds as I creep down the hall and slowly push the door open wide enough to peek inside. Piles of clothes litter the floor. Drawers hang out of the dresser at precarious angles.

"What the hell?" I throw open the door so hard it bounces off the wall. Someone trashed the place.

I don't see Sophia. *Did she walk in on the guy? Where is she?* "Sophia?"

A muffled groan comes from the far side of the bed. I run over and drop to my knees beside her prone body. She has a nasty cut on her temple. Her eyes flicker open, and she stares up at me with glazed eyes. "W-what happened?"

Relief that her brain isn't scrambled makes my words harsh. "You tell me?"

I put my arm around her shoulder and help her to her feet. Her legs shake with the effort of rising, and once she sits on the bed, she slumps over, half falling off the edge. *This won't do.* I slide my arm under her legs and lift her, crawling across the mattress to deposit her in the center of the bed. Her trembling hands land on my shoulders, and her fingernails dig into my skin.

"He was here," she whispers, eyes wild. "He knew. Somehow."

"Who, Sophia?"

"The man…from Mala's dream. He came for me."

A gasp comes from behind me. "What's going on?"

My head whips around at the familiar voice. Mala and George

stand in the doorway. Shock twists her face, and I know she's re-membering the time in the graveyard. "Mala, it's not what you think—"

"Is it what *I* think?" George interrupts, pushing past Mala to en-ter the room. He pauses beside the bed, bottle-green eyes flashing as he takes in the scene of my assumed crime. 'Cause I know that asshole's not giving me the benefit of the doubt. "What happened here?"

"George, shut up and listen. Someone broke in and attacked Sophia right before I arrived. Move your doughnut-eating ass and go catch him."

"What does he look like?"

"Didn't see him." I glance down at Sophia. "Did you?"

She shakes her head.

For once, George doesn't argue. He pulls out his radio while running for the door. The corner of Mala's eyes tighten, and I yell, "Don't you dare."

Her shoulders slump. "Fine. You're right. No attempted heroics." She comes over to the bed and sits on the edge. I slide my hand up her spine, feeling her shiver. Her voice breaks only a little when she asks, "Is she okay?"

Sophia's eyes slowly lift. "I'll be fine if you lower your voices. You're making my headache worse."

"Are you sure you didn't see who did this?" Mala asks.

My hand drops. "Leave her alone. She already said she didn't."

"Even the smallest of clues might help." Her nostrils flare. "Why are you being so protective of her?"

"Children, behave. And I can speak for myself, Landry." Sophia takes Mala's hands. "But it's better if I show you."

Mala stiffens. Her eyes slide up behind her eyelids, leaving only the white, and I shiver over the creep factor. Her eyes roll faster and faster in time with her heaving breaths and then her back arches. She lets out a gasping moan. Her head falls forward as she collapses face-first onto the mattress.

I stare at her for a long second, waiting for her to sit up. "What did you do to her?"

Sophia doesn't answer.

I lay Mala on her back so she doesn't suffocate. *"Did you see all of this?"* I ask my visitor…Damn, I need to think up a name for him.

"I saw. Sophia inserted her memory of the attack directly into Mala LaCroix's mind. They will be insensible for a few minutes."

"Were you able to see the vision?"

"Your girlfriend didn't let me enter her. Even when she mistook me for you. Be grateful I've never taken her offerings in the past."

The dual meaning of his words leaves me sputtering, "I… you…Damn it, if you ever touch—"

Mala's hand covers my mouth. "Stop yelling."

I wrap her fingers in mine. "Are you okay? What did you see?"

"I'm fine." She shrugs up on the pillows until her back rests against the headboard. "Sophia showed me the attack. He was already in the room when she came in. She didn't see his face, but the stench of his aftershave is burned into my nostrils. It's pungent." She sniffs.

Sophia rolls onto her side and lays her cheek in her cupped hands. "Aha, you even picked up the sensory details. Good girl."

"Don't congratulate me too quickly. This place still reeks of Old Spice. I've hated that cologne since I was a kid. One of Mama's regulars bathed in that mess, and she always came home stinking of it."

"Pepper Acker's room smells of the same cologne as I smell in here." I crawl off the bed, mindful of how this will look to an outsider and the door's wide open. "Axle told me Judd was with his mother, but he was gone by the time I confronted Pepper. Do you think he hid in here and then panicked when Sophia came in?"

"Pepper would've told him that he's wanted for assaulting you. That's enough to make him desperate."

Sophia grabs my arm. "I was *not* attacked by accident. He tried to hide it, but not even Old Spice can mask the stench of dark magic on his skin."

But why would Judd stink of… "Then—"

Mala grabs my arm. "Judd drives a car just like the murderer in my vision." She starts to crawl off the bed, but I push her back. "Oh God, Georgie should be back by now. What if Judd got the jump on him?" Her voice rises. "Landry—"

Damn it. "Stay here. I'll find him."

I'm out the door before she can think to come with me. The last thing I need is her charging into the middle of a fight. I run for the closest exit, knowing I didn't pass anyone on the way up the stairs. He would've gone out the back entrance to keep from being seen.

I stand on the upstairs landing, scanning the large yard and street until I find George. He's running through the yard, but doesn't appear to be chasing anyone. When he sees me, he waves.

I clump down the stairs, yelling, "George, we've got a problem."

He slows to a walk, breathing hard. "I searched the grounds, but I didn't see anyone suspicious. I've got deputies en route for backup. Once they're on-scene, we'll do a more extensive search. I think Judd Helmert's here too. I ran the license plate on a car in the parking lot matching the description of the one he was driving."

"Yeah, he—"

The dispatcher's voice comes over his radio mike. "BPSO eighteen, license plate is registered to Ace Rental Car."

"Ten-four," he says. "Is medical en route?"

"Affirm, ETA in five."

George takes off again toward the parking lot, leaving me no choice but to follow on his heels. His blatant lack of respect pisses me off. Here I am trying to warn him his suspect could still be hanging around, and he ignores me like I'm still the kid he used to babysit. This is so typical of him. He's doing the same thing in my relationship with Mala, inserting himself in the middle like he's got that right.

It ends now.

He's in the driveway by a white sedan. I grab his shoulder and shove him against the car. His back hits the door with an audible *thunk*, but he pushes off and raises his hands. "Back off, Landry."

"Not this time. Listen—"

"Look, whatever you're pissed about, get over it. I've got a suspect on the run so forgive me if I don't take your temper tantrum as seriously as you'd like."

His holier-than-thou tone sets my teeth on edge. "Damn it, will you listen to me? This is Judd's rental car," I say quickly, before he can interrupt again. "Sophia thinks Judd assaulted her. He must have been hiding in her room and attacked her when she walked in."

"Why didn't you say anything earlier?"

The urge to punch him almost overwhelms my self-control. "She also thinks he's the one who's been murdering the kids."

"What?" George frowns. "Wait…Do you smell that?"

My nose scrunches up. I step closer to the trunk, then step back from the overpowering stench of Old Spice mingling with the sweet, sickly odor of decay. The smell triggers a memory I've tried my best to suppress. But I'm back in that moment, seeing my sister Lainey lying on the autopsy table. Her chest cut open. Her heart on a scale. The smell…it's the same. My stomach rebels over what I suspect is in the trunk.

I point to a red-brown stain on the metal trunk handle. "Is that blood?"

George looks like he's also about to throw-up. He nods and pulls latex gloves from a pouch on his duty belt. "A dried thumbprint."

"Don't tell me you're opening that?" I step back, breathing through my mouth.

"He could still be alive." Doubt colors his tone. He reaches for the latch, and his hand trembles slightly. "It's unlocked." He looks at me, then swallows. He pulls the trunk open and staggers back, hand rising to cover his mouth. The smell brings tears to my eye.

I stare at the lumpy, black plastic garbage bag. "Don't open it."

He leans forward, and I close my eye. I hear the rustle of plastic and then the closing and slamming of the trunk. Rough breathing follows, then gagging.

My eye pops open.

George stands doubled over with his hands on his knees a few feet from the car. He sucks in air through his nose, then hawks up a wad of spit. "We're too late." He pulls out his radio and goes over the mike to calls in the murder to Dixie.

A voice that sounds like Deputy Winters comes over his radio. "BPSO twelve and fourteen, on scene at Robicheaux."

A patrol car pulls into the parking lot. We step out of the way as it parks behind the car. Winters gets out of the patrol car, followed by

Deputy Toussaint from the passenger seat. Another patrol car pulls into the parking lot. I see the K-9 Unit lettering.

I grab George's arm when he starts to walk over to them. "If this is Judd's car, then he's probably on foot." *Oh shit, Mala.* "What if he doubled back to finish what he started?"

Chapter 19

Mala

Butterflies & Champagne

Landry leaves me alone with Sophia as he goes to assist George. While a bit of my unease subsides, I'm still shaking. A tiny piece of me wants to go help, but I can't risk hurting the baby. I have more than just myself to think about now. I have to believe that, between the two of them, they can handle any threat.

I bite my lip and pull my gaze from the doorway. Sophia looks so pitiful that I don't mind the skin-to-scales contact when I help the viper sit up in bed. I even feel a twinge of guilt for mentally comparing her to an animal that swallows its prey whole.

"How are you feeling?" I ask, filling my voice with so much syrupy concern that it almost gags me.

"I'm fine. A bit dizzy." She lightly touches the tips of her fingers to her cheeks. "Did my glamour slip?"

I snort-groan, pressing my fist to my stomach. "Saints, you're vain."

"Don't I know it." She points to her Louis Vuitton suitcase. "Bring that over here for me, please."

"Do it yourself" hovers on the tip of my tongue, but I control my impulsive retort since she's injured. Plus she even used the magic word.

I nod, knowing it's best to keep my mouth shut so I don't say something I shouldn't. The instinctive rage I felt upon seeing her on the bed with Landry lingers. For the split second before my brain processed the scene, I lost it. My fingers hooked into claws, more than ready to rip out her flowing, fake locks again. But then I took a breath, which cleared the fog of my fury.

I knew I was overreacting because I trust Landry to keep his guard up. He won't drink the poisoned Kool-Aid or anything else she gives him, ever again. And there's no way he'd ever go to her willingly.

The suitcase is too heavy to lift but it rolls. "What in the world do you have in here?"

"Open it for me, Malaise."

I rock it over until it lies flat on the ground. "It's locked."

"It'll open for you," she says.

When I glance over, I see she has her eyes closed. My fingers hover over the latches. The air between them feels dense. The latches vibrate and then pop. "Whoa, what just happened?"

"It's coded to your biometric tag…your magical signature. I worried for my safety, and I wanted to make sure you could get into this if you needed too."

"How?"

"Believe me, it wasn't easy. And we don't have enough time for me to explain." The serious tone of her voice has me biting my lip.

Usually she's all about the quips, but not now. It makes me pay more attention…to everything. I lift the lid, expecting to see frilly lingerie, but she must've packed those in another suitcase.

"Books, oils, candles." I pick up a small glass bottle and hold it up to the light. It contains a black and violet-blue butterfly. White spots and orange circles are on the tips of its wings. They look like eyes—for camouflage, I guess. "I've trolled the swamps my entire life, but I'd never seen this type of butterfly until yesterday."

"That isn't the same species of butterfly you saw, although it's part of the same genus. I found that specimen while visiting Northamptonshire: *Apatura iris,* the Purple Emperor. It's a Eurasian butterfly not found in the Louisiana swamps." She presses her lips together and raises an eyebrow, like I'm supposed to know what the hell she's talking about.

"Okay," I say, drawing out the last syllable. "So what type did I see? And more important, why should I care?"

"Because the butterflies you saw, while similar, aren't indigenous to this realm. They're a species found only in the land of the dead. And while that butterfly you hold in your hand once consumed rotting flesh, the *Apatura livid* is a *vorator animi*—a soul eater."

My lip curls. "Seriously?"

"Of all the things you've witnessed, you find this strange?"

Not really. "So why is *Apa*"—I stumble over the Latin pronunciation, then spit out—"this butterfly so important that you encoded my biometric magical signature to your suitcase?" *Man, I would chew off my left arm to learn how to work that level of spell casting, but I won't beg her again.*

"Because it is the key to keep you from falling prey to the demon eating your soul."

Saints! I huff a curl off the tip of my nose. *How many demons are there, and why did they all seem to be concentrating their culinary efforts on me and my boyfriend?* "Did I swallow a butterfly while on the other side? You know…I've had this strange tickle in my throat." She doesn't crack a smile at my joke or roll her eyes to insult me.

I shiver, wrapping my arms around myself. A memory pops up of the larvae I coughed up after being pulled from the circle of power trap. "Damn, if you're reading my mind, then you saw what I just remembered."

Sophia nods.

"You'd better not be messing with me."

"Do I appear to be joking?"

I swallow the tickle. "So, by 'demon,' do you mean the creature inside Landry?"

Please say yes. Landry's learning how to handle that wannabe brain-sucker.

"My, aren't you feisty today," Sophia says drolly, and I cringe. She laughs at whatever expression crosses my face, which makes my belly burn. I hate acting the fool for her benefit, yet I always seem to go to the idiot side when dealing with her. She waves a lazy hand as if to erase my momentary lapse into incompetence, and I swallow the sour taste of gratitude. "I don't know what inhabits your boyfriend. I'm talking about the *loa* who tied his soul to yours while you were held captive. The one Queen Magnolia told me to contact while I was out here."

I freeze. "What are you talking about?"

"Deputy Dubois brought you here to speak to the person who discovered the crime scene. Who do you suppose it could be? Since he brought you to my room." She arches her eyebrows and blinks her insanely long eyelashes. *Glamour does a body good.* "Please don't tell me you're really this dense, Mala."

"Hey! I get what you're trying to tell me. No reason to be snotty about it. Let me process this." *'Cause I'm falling headfirst down the rabbit hole again.* "Explain what Magnolia's role is in my mass-murder case. Don't leave out anything."

"All I know is she told me to go to Lick Creek. I found the body parts strewn across the ground, almost as if they were left deliberately for me. So I reported it."

"Did you know I would be part of the investigation?"

"I don't have the gift of prophecy."

I lick my dry lips. "Does Magnolia?"

"She is queen. The limits to her powers are so vast they cannot be seen. As are her ultimate goals. All I know is you went there, you got trapped, and we saved you. In the process, you were exposed to the evil one. He is now connected to you and draws on your power. It must be broken..."

I bounce back onto the edge of the bed. Right now, the dreams I have are my only lead. Break the connection and I won't be tied to him anymore. Won't be able to see where he is or what he's doing. Does she know this? Is her I'll-help-you act genuine or a deliberate attempt to keep me from getting more information on this guy? And if it's really Judd, then does it matter anymore if I'm tied to him? It's just that no matter how much evidence points to Judd being the culprit, I can't picture him as a serial killer. A hotheaded asshole yes, but...

Maybe Sophia's reading my thoughts again because her gaze drops to the bedspread. "Magnolia will arrive this afternoon. Don't trust her…" She trails off, her gaze lifting over my shoulder to focus on the door. "Ah, you're back," she says.

Landry and George burst into the room. Tension radiates off both of them, visible in the stiffness in their shoulders and around their eyes. "Did you find Judd?" I ask.

"No, but we located his car in the parking lot." George sits next to us on the edge of the bed. His hair stands on end, a sure sign of his agitation. He takes my hand.

My eyes flick toward Landry to gauge his response but he doesn't react, stressing me out even more. "Okay, so what's the problem?"

"I found the body of the missing boy, Marcus Wright, in the trunk," George says.

The air rushes out of me in a gasping hiss.

George gives my hand a squeeze. "We have deputies on the premises conducting a search, but I'm here to protect Sophia until I can get her safely onto the ambulance. Once the hotel is cleared, we'll process the room for evidence."

Landry asks, "How much longer before the ambulance arrives?"

"The paramedics won't come in until they're sure the scene is secure." George gets up and walks toward the door as he radios dispatch with the question.

Dixie's response is clipped. "Medical's at the staging area. BPSO twelve reported the scene has been secured. Medical's cleared to enter."

"Good," Sophia says. "I can use a vacation. Being in the hospital is almost as relaxing as going to the day spa. Only the food isn't quite as tasty."

She laughs, but white lines are etched beside her lips. She's obviously in pain. The fact that she's willingly going to the hospital shows how much. "Mala, take my bag and keep it safe until you can go through it in private. Tell Ferdinand and Magnolia that I'll be waiting for them at the hospital." She gives my hand a squeeze. "It's a magical day. Family will be reunited."

She means Dena.

She nods. Ugh, she read my mind again.

I try to lift the suitcase, forgetting how heavy it is, and grunt. George reaches for the handle, but Landry gets to it first. He hefts the bag over his shoulder without breaking a sweat. I trace the contours of his biceps and pecs. The fitted T-shirt leaves nothing to the imagination. I can clearly see each defined muscle. And I thank God that I washed all of his cotton shirts in hot water.

My tongue darts out to moisten my lips, and I twitch when he pokes my side with the tip of a finger. "Let's go," he says gruffly.

I nod, stomach churning with guilt. Even imagining Landry naked doesn't remove the picture of Marcus Wright from my mind. How can I even consider renting one of these rooms for an hour when the boy's body lies cold in the trunk of a car?

"Wait," George calls. "What about our investigation? I'm sure Bessie will let you watch while they process the vehicle. Maybe Marcus stuck around and you can do a little ghost talking."

A sliver of excitement stirs. I've been at the scene of two crimes, and I didn't get to participate in either. And I want to see firsthand exactly what goes on in processing a scene for evidence. Books and drama-land can only teach so much. I want to experience the real thing, even if contacting the boy's spirit might give me nightmares.

"We don't have time," Landry says, popping the fantasy bubble in my head.

George acts like we're alone in the room. His voice lowers, cajoling and oh so tempting. The devilish imp riding on my shoulder urges me to listen. "Are you sure, Mala? I bet Ernesto has an update on the—"

I wave my hand, breaking in quickly. "Tell me later."

He swallows back his surprise, but he gets the hint and shuts up. I don't want him talking about the knife in front of Sophia.

"Pepper lost track of the boys," Landry says. "I promised to help her round them up, but we're running short on time. We've got about five hours before Mala's great-aunt gets to town."

Magnolia's coming. Is it sad that I'd rather chase a serial killer than meet with my aunt? I nod, shivering. "I'm sorry."

George tilts his head toward his shoulder mike, listening, then tells Sophia, "The ambulance is here." He turns back to me. "Wait for me to hand Sophia off to the paramedics, and I'll go with you to talk to Pepper. I have some questions for her about Judd."

Landry puts his arm around my shoulder and gives a slight nudge. I can't stop thinking about what Sophia said. She always seemed like a good little minion, acting on Magnolia's orders without hesitation. Yet today, it feels like she switched sides. Her warning rings loudly: *Don't trust Magnolia.*

Well, duh. I've been saying that for months. I also don't trust Sophia.

"What are you thinking?" Landry asks once we're in the hallway.

"That I don't trust anyone."

His arm drops. When I realize how that might be construed, I throw his arm back over my shoulder and snake mine around his back. "Obviously you aren't included."

"No," he says, drawing the word out. "I think you said it right the first time. Maybe you don't realize it, but you really don't trust anyone. Even me."

"That's not true." I squeeze his hip as we go down the front staircase, lending my support since his balance is off from carrying Sophia's suitcase. I do it naturally. He doesn't even notice. I usually don't either, but today feels different. Everything seems crystal clear. "If I've done something to give you a reason to think this, I'm sorry. You know I love you, right? Love comes from trust. I wouldn't be with you otherwise."

"Then why did you stab me in the back this morning?" He twists away. The move rips his T-shirt from my fist when I try to hold on to him. The bag drops onto the step. "You let the kids go without bothering to discuss the situation. Now look at what's happened."

"That's not fair! I didn't think Pepper would play crazy and take Judd back after what he did to Carl. And I certainly didn't predict that he's a damn serial killer."

"Doesn't matter. Don't you get it? We're supposed to be a team. The decision wasn't yours to make alone. I understand as well as you do that the kids are in danger with us. If you'd given me a chance, I would've had your back like always. But you didn't have mine."

My mouth hangs open wider with each venomous word. He's been holding in this anger too long. It's been festering inside him—a gangrenous growth filling him with poison. And it's my fault for not communicating with him. I need to fix it.

I close the distance between us until only a few inches separate our bodies. My hands slide up the thin cotton T-shirt, which doesn't pad his chest at all. I can feel each muscle tense beneath my sensitive fingertips. His heart thumps beneath my palm. I meet his steady gaze without flinching. "I didn't mean to hurt you. I'm sorry."

He studies my face with a dark gray eye. The black patch stands out against his pale skin. A constant reminder of what could happen if I don't trust him to protect me with his life. He ran into my burning house to rescue me. And I charged into one with a guy holding him at gunpoint. Neither of us are the brightest stars in the sky when the other's in danger, but we're loyal.

I rise up on tiptoes. He holds back for a second, then sighs. Our lips brush, sending that spark through my body that only his kisses create. My arms steal around his back, and I clasp my hands together so he can't pull away even if he tries.

Clumps on the stairs signal that someone's coming down behind us, but I simply press Landry back against the banister.

George clears his throat. "Can't you do that somewhere more private? People are staring."

Landry's tongue in my mouth prevents me from answering. But from the corner of my eye, I see his hand waving George around us. We stand on the bottom step for a while. When we finally break apart, I rest my head against his shoulder while I try to catch my breath. By the time I look up, George is holding open the front doors for the paramedics carrying a stretcher.

"I know this sounds weird coming from me, but I hope Sophia's okay." I mean it too. Surprise, surprise.

Landry's arm wraps around my neck. He hugs me close, dropping a kiss on the top of my head. "I'm surprised you've held a grudge as long as you have."

I squeeze him tight. "If Sophia had only hurt me, I probably would've forgiven her by now. But she hurt you. She's lucky I don't know how to fix a curse or she'd look like a plucked chicken by now."

Landry laughs. Together we step aside so George and the paramedics can get past us. We watch until they vanish upstairs, then turn in the direction of Pepper's room. Deputy "Tank" Toussaint blocks the entranceway to the restaurant. Another deputy guards the hallway leading to the back door. The perimeter is indeed secure, and judging by the smiles on their faces, we provided quite the performance for our audience.

A blush heats my cheeks, and I avert my face. "Sophia told me something interesting while you were outside."

"I got worried when George told me he brought you here because she wanted to speak to you in private."

"He told you about her being the professor who found the body parts?" He nods. "Well, she also warned me that Magnolia might be in cahoots with the murderer—Judd. But if that's the case, why did he attack her? Plus, being so forthcoming is totally out of character for Sophia. Either her reunion with Gaston has affected her loyalties or she's working some other twisted angle with my aunt."

Landry hisses. "First of all, *cahoots*? Second, what the—"

"Sorry, but that's what seems to be going on."

He glances around the room and sighs. "Let's deal with Pepper first, then break it down for me. I need to know what we're getting into before Magnolia arrives."

"Yeah, I guess a conversation about soul-eating butterflies and murderous *loas*, unlike deep-throat kissing, should wait until we're in private."

I raise a hand and wave at Axle, who stuffs half a cheeseburger into his mouth, ducks down to scoot between Tank's legs, and runs out of the restaurant.

"Don't run with food in your mouth," Landry barks, and I hide my grin.

Damn, he'll be such a good father.

Chapter 20

Landry

Line of Fire

Axle slides across the floor until he comes to a halt right in front of us. His jaw works up and down, and his face scrunches as he swallows, then coughs. Mala pats him on the back until the rough hacks ease. "Don't worry," she says, eyes twinkling when she looks at me. "Someone who *claims* to be first-aid and CPR certified once told me, if you're coughing, you're breathing."

"Probably someone with a sick sense of humor," George says, coming from behind. He slaps my back hard enough to make me flinch from the sting. *Ass hat*. "Sophia's on her way to the hospital. Let's go interrogate Pepper."

"Axle," Mala says, pointing toward the massive deputy standing across the hall. "We need to talk about adult stuff with your mama. Deputy Tank over there will keep an eye on you while you go grab some dessert."

Toussaint gives a short nod, but his eyes don't stop scanning the area despite the all-clear given earlier. Until Judd's in custody, everyone will remain on alert.

The little con-artist holds out his hand and wiggles his fingers.

Grumbling, I reach into my pocket to pull out my ever-thinning wallet. "Why do I feel like I'm getting scammed?"

"Because you are," Mala says, scowling. "The kids have you wrapped around their little fingers. You're spoiling them rotten."

"I know they're rotten, so don't blame me."

She snorts, not even deigning to get into a debate when she knows the truth…that yeah, I plan on spoiling them for as long as I can. Maybe I won't win Parent of the Year, but I'll beat Mala at the job as best surrogate parent ever. *They'll miss me when I'm gone.*

A few doors down, George stands in front of Pepper's room. He has his head cocked to the side, probably listening to our conversation and getting ready throw out another insult. To head him off, I say, "I told her to be ready—"

George stiffens. His hand snaps up. "Something's wrong."

I drop the suitcase and freeze. *It's too quiet.*

George unsnaps his gun holster. He speaks quietly over the radio, alerting the other deputies to his suspicions. Tank and the deputy by the rear exit start in his direction while I head in the opposite, dragging Axle and Mala by the arms back down the hall. My vision narrows and the hallway stretches, growing longer like some crazy optical illusion.

"Pepper, it's the sheriff's office. Are you in there?" George yells.

No answer.

"Pepper, I'm coming in." A bang echoes down the corridor from his foot connecting with the wooden door. More yells drowning out individual voices until it's a dissonant symphony of curses and the sonic boom of Tank's rumbling bass voice.

Axle trips. His thin arm slides from my sweat-slick hand. He lands on his knees and stares at me with wide, fear-filled eyes. His lips move, but I can't hear him over the yelling. My body reacts before my mind catches up to the danger. So does Mala. She scoops Axle up, and I wrap my arms around them both, sandwiching Axle between our bodies. I shove them into a shallow doorway. Mala winces when her back slams into a doorknob, but she presses Axle's face into her chest, while I protect his back.

I fumble behind her for the doorknob. It's locked.

We crouch down in the small space between the closed door and the hallway. I drape my body over them to shield them from the image of the man holding a gun to Pepper's head as much as to protect them from any stray bullets, leaving myself totally exposed. Only Deputy Toussaint forms a living wall between the gun and us.

Mala's breathing hitches. I can barely hear the words she speaks through the mop of hair on Axle's head. "It's okay. We're okay," she repeats, doing her best to soothe the sobbing boy in our arms.

I wish I could believe her.

"Drop your weapon," George yells, and I flinch. His voice comes from my blind spot. To see him, I'd have to turn sideways, which would leave Mala and Axle exposed. But I *can* see Judd. He's got his left arm wrapped around Pepper's neck. The woman's face is purple from lack of oxygen. Her eyelids flutter, and she gasps, sucking in what little air she can as he forces her into the hallway. He's careful to keep his back against the wall, using her body as a shield.

"Drop your guns or she's dead," Judd yells. His hand shakes, but more from adrenaline than fear, judging by his body language. A wild look fills his muddy eyes when he sees me. His mouth stretches, a perversion of the Joker's mad grin, but scarier because he's real.

"I see you, girl…" He giggles. A sliver of ice goes down my spine at the mania in the sound. Grown-ass men shouldn't fucking giggle. But even worse is the reason behind his sudden burst of glee. His intent has shifted to Mala for some reason.

My back tenses, and I press closer against my family, trying to cover any exposed body parts with mine. He'll have to shoot through me to get them. He'll only get one chance because as soon as he moves the gun away from Pepper's head the three deputies in the hallway will take him down.

But so far he isn't making any stupid decisions.

He takes a slow step in our direction, dragging Pepper. "Stay where you are, girl. I'm coming. You have something I need."

Mala whimpers, her breaths coming faster and faster. "Landry?"

I don't know. My arms tighten around her. Doubt gnaws at my gut. What if he shoots? Would one or two, hell even a whole magazine of bullets, bring him down? He acts like he's on bath salts or LSD, some weird brain-eating drug that turns the user into someone who doesn't operate on normal, logical rules.

Judd must not be cutting off Pepper's air anymore. The woman inhales a huge gulp and lets it out in a piercing shriek. Axle echoes it, screaming into Mala's chest. The deputies continue to yell orders, but they don't risk Pepper by taking the shot. All of my focus remains on each slow step he takes in our direction. While trying to get away, the hall seemed a million miles long. Now it shrinks. The only thing keeping me steady is that, to get to us, Judd has to get past Tank, who positions himself as a guard in front of us.

To show his growing rage with the resistance he faces, Judd's finger flexes on the trigger. "I mean it. Back off and let me get what I came for. No need to mess up this lovely woman's face in front of her kid."

"He's going to kill her," Mala says, her words coming loud and clear as if she speaks directly into my mind. My body is more aware of her now than I have ever been. Electricity arcs from her through my arms. I don't know if Axle feels the building power, but it sets my gums to tingling.

It grows. Painful, biting…an exhilarating wave that builds, cresting over. Mala grits her teeth, and my jaw aches from doing the same. Between us, Axle whimpers. I almost tell her to stop because we're hurting him, but Judd steps forward again. His eyes remain pinned on us with laser-like focus, as if he's drilling through my body to reach Mala.

"Where is it?"

An image fills my mind. Bright and clear. *The knife.*

"He can't have it," Mala says. "I'm taking my shot."

Her fingers pry free of my shirt. A rush of energy flows through my body into hers, and I force my trembling knees to steady. "Do it. Now!"

Mala's yell starts deep in her chest as a low rumble and crescendos into a roar. Judd must sense what's coming because he releases Pepper, who crumples at his feet, and swings the gun toward us. He pulls the trigger as Mala flings all the power straight at him. The gunshot rumbles through the walls, but he fired too late.

The beam of energy strikes Judd's upper body, and he collapses inward as if hit by a car. His arms and legs fly up as he hurtles backward to slam against the wall.

He hasn't even hit the ground before the deputies reach him. The gun slides across the floor away from his hand. Tank presses a knee against Judd's upper back and twists his arms behind him to lock the cuffs on his wrists.

"All clear," George yells, then goes over the radio: "BPSO, one in custody. Send in medical."

Feeling in my body returns in a rush. My knees and back ache from being hunched over, but an even bigger worry hits, and I push to my feet.

The back of my T-shirt feels wet. "Shit, I think I've been shot."

"Oh no." Mala shoves Axle into my arms. They're still partially numb, with a slight tingling in the tips of my fingers, but I manage to hold onto him. Not that I could drop him with his thin arms squeezing my neck in a death grip.

Mala's behind me. Her hands run frantically up my back. "Blood. There's blood."

"I must be in shock." I shake my head to clear out the foggy feel to my brain. "It doesn't hurt."

A dry rustle sounds in my brain. *Do you think I would let you get hurt, host?*

"He shot me."

"He tried to shoot the last LaCroix. You were in the way." It's then that I realize with a soul-sucking horror that Axle's wet too. Did the bullet go through me and hit him?

Mala's fingers lift the edge of my T-shirt. "I-I don't see a wound." She turns me around to check my front. "No blood." She pulls Axle from my arms and sets him on the ground. He won't stop crying and he shakes uncontrollably, but he stands on his own two feet while she checks him over from head to toe. My lungs burn from the smell of gunpowder in the air, but beneath it is the sharp odor of urine.

We turn toward the commotion in the hall. George sits on the ground with Pepper leaning against him. Deputy Winters runs past us, followed by Andy. The unknown deputy and Tank have Judd detained, but he still lies in a crumpled heap on the ground from where Mala flung him, like a judo master, with the power of her *mind*.

I laugh, but it has a slightly hysterical pitch to it.

Mala blinks at me. "Are you okay? Really?" Her lips crumple in a frown, and fat tears gather in her eyes. "Is everyone else all right? Georgie?" She turns toward the group. "Where did the blood come from?"

Deputy Winters stops in front of Tank and says calmly, "I'll take over. Get to medical."

The big guy's eyebrows rise like furry caterpillars until they almost migrate onto his bald head. He follows her gaze down his body to stop on the blood running down his bare arm. The blood splatter across the carpet shows the path of the bullet, which went right through the underside of his bicep and lodged in the doorjamb only inches from where my head had been. If he hadn't been in the way…

I rub my forehead, swallowing hard.

A huge sigh comes from behind me. Mala presses her cheek against my back, and her arms wrap around my waist. I pat her clasped hands. "I know."

I feel her nod.

George passes Pepper off to one of the responding medical technicians. He stops to talk briefly with Tank, then heads in our direction. "Are you three okay?"

"We're fine," I say.

Axle hides behind my back and peeks around me. "You caught the bad guy."

George gives him a smile and pats him on the back. "Of course. I couldn't let him get away and hurt anyone else. I'm really proud of you. You were so brave."

"No, I wasn't." His voice rises in an inconsolable wail. "I was so scared…I pissed myself."

I wrap my arm around his shoulder, but George does even better. He squats down. "Hey, I almost peed myself too when Judd came out of the room."

"But you didn't."

"'Cause I'm used to bad guys coming at me."

Axle hiccups. "So you weren't scared?"

George shakes his head. "Of course I was scared. Everyone in this hallway was scared. It's normal to be afraid if someone tries to hurt you. But what makes a person brave is not letting fear stop them from protecting the people they care about."

Axle's head lifts higher, and he nods. "You were scared."

"Yes."

"So was I," I say.

Mala snorts. "I wasn't."

"Ha! Liar," Axle says, poking her in the stomach until she laughs, squirming. "Were too. You were shaking so hard that your boobs jiggled like Jell-O. Jonjovi's gonna be so jealous when I tell him that I touched them."

Mala gasps. "Axle, shh." Her face turns bright red as she sends a quick glance around the room and crosses her arms to hide the breasts that the eyes of every guy within hearing distance turn toward. A protective flash goes through me, but I force it back. She'd be even more embarrassed if I said anything to the deputies. Plus, the teasing sparkle is back in Axle's eyes. He still might have nightmares tonight, but I hope seeing Judd get arrested and knowing he's safe will help him heal from this faster.

George stands with a final pat on Axle's head. "Pepper sustained minor injuries. They're taking her to the hospital. She asked that you take the boys for the night."

Mala breathes out a long breath, as if she'd been holding it. "Yes, of course."

"Don't celebrate too soon. I have to notify social worker Moulton about what happened."

"Can you hold off?" I ask. "We don't know how much involvement Pepper had in the murders. Plus Jonjovi and Daryl are still missing. If they come back and Pepper's not here…"

George turns his gaze toward Axle, who has drifted down the hall. The kid doesn't get close enough to the action to be in the way, so I don't call him back. He watches in silence as paramedics lift Judd onto a stretcher, with Deputy Winters as an escort, and carry him toward the back exit. "She'll want to detain the boys."

"Right," I say. "I doubt that would be in their best interest. Especially if their mom's a victim, not a suspect."

"I'll hold off on contacting her until tomorrow. Lord knows I've got enough to deal with tonight."

"Thanks, big bro. We'll take them to the rev. They'll be safe with him." Mala gives his bicep a squeeze, and their eyes lock. *Super intense.* "Why does this feel wrong, Georgie?"

His shoulders tense, and he steps closer to her. His voice lowers. "So you noticed it too?"

I feel like an outsider. Even if I understood half of what they were going on about, I still wouldn't feel the same exhilarated rush that flushes their cheeks, like they're working through the clues in their minds and feeding off each other's impressions.

All of their gazing into each other's eyes frays my last nerve. I wave my hand in front of their faces. "What are you two talking about?"

Mala blinks. She grabs my hand and locks her fingers through mine, but doesn't look away from George. "Doesn't his capture...feel off? It's too convenient for some reason..."

"...like we're being set up," George finishes.

"Don't you think so?"

"Yeah, but we found the latest victim in the trunk of *his* rental. Plus, he held Pepper hostage and tried to shoot a peace officer."

"Mala," I interject. At least I can give a slight assist. "He wanted the knife. And he tried to shoot Mala, not me or Tank."

"Yes, yes, I know." Mala waves away George's argument. Not mine. I don't think either of them heard what I said.

I sigh and lean back against the wall. Why bother? I'll let them do their *Criminal Minds* act without me.

Mala begins to pace. "But look at the facts of the case. Judd and Pepper didn't get to town until a couple of days ago. That body dump had eight kids in various stages of decomposition."

George pauses. "I saw...and you said in your dream there was another site."

"Yeah, it's been going on for months. It doesn't seem logical that Judd did this alone. Maybe he has a local accomplice."

"Whether or not this crime is related to the others, I don't know. What I do know is we have a dead kid in his trunk. I've got to go. Bessie and Sheriff Keyes are on scene, and we need to give them our report. Are you coming?"

"We'll be outside in a minute. But we need to make it fast. We still need to find the boys."

George nods then heads toward the exit.

Mala watches him go, biting her lower lip.

"I know what you're thinking." I push off the wall.

She jumps, but upon seeing me, the tension riding up her shoulders releases. "That if Magnolia's involved, maybe she set up a scapegoat for some reason." She grabs my belt loops and tugs. I wrap my arms around her as she lays her head on my chest. "I just don't understand her grand plan, Landry."

"I'm sure it's convoluted and nefarious."

"Yeah, that's why I'm worried. I don't want the boys and your dad getting sucked in." Mala sighs, then pulls away. "I'll call Carl, see if he's heard from his brothers."

She goes to get Axle while I try to grab Sophia's suitcase from where I dropped it, only to find out it's classified as evidence (fucking blood splatter) and can't be removed according to the evidence technician. So is my T-shirt, which is also bagged after I take it off. Before going outside, I go to the front desk and ask the frazzled Mrs. Robicheaux to call me if the boys come back while we're gone. Her slightly glazed eyes focus on the activity behind me, but she nods. "Sure thing, sweetie." She leans forward. "Do you think they'd mind if I got a couple of pictures? The B and B's never seen this kind of action. Think it might be good publicity?"

"Depends on what type of clientele you want to attract, Mrs. Robicheaux."

She sucks air across her teeth. "Oh, guess you've got a point there."

Mala and Axle meet me on the porch. She gives my naked chest an appraising once-over, and I grin. I lead them to my truck first and grab a spare T-shirt from my duffle bag in the back seat. "Any news?"

Mala leans against the side of the truck, watching the bustle in the parking lot. George stands with Bessie, while Sheriff Keys talks to the new medical examiner. I can tell by Mala's sour expression that she wants to be in the mix. "Carl said Jonjovi rode the bus up to their place and is in his bedroom hiding from your dad. But no Daryl."

"I told you, he's meeting his girlfriend at Playtown," Axle says.

"What his girlfriend's name?"

"That top secret info comes with a price," Axle says, climbing into the back of the truck and holding out his hand. Mala caves to the bribe and gives him her cell phone so he can play games while he waits for us to come back from giving our witness statements. "Astrid Lebeau. She's a senior."

Well, no wonder Daryl never told us about her. Dad will flip when he finds out.

Mala doesn't look or sound happy as she growls, "If she's over eighteen…" She cracks her knuckles.

"Better get used to it," I warn her. "Daryl comes off older than he really is because he's smart. And nerdy, even though he tries not to let his brothers' notice. It's probably nice for him to be able to talk to someone on his intellectual level."

"Long as it's only intellectual, and not physical."

After giving our witness statements to Deputy Winters, we drive to Playtown, listening to Axle's knock-knock jokes and forcing ourselves to laugh at the appropriate times. The kid eats it up. It's rare for him to be the center of attention. The way his face lights up, I make a note to spend more one-on-one time with him. If Pepper lets us after today.

"They're probably at the skating rink," Axle says. "That way they can hold hands and slow skate together."

I glance into the rearview mirror and catch him making kissy face. He sees me looking and sticks out his tongue. "Bleck. Girls smell like dog butt. I don't know why you and Daryl think they're so great."

"Hey, I'm a girl," Mala says.

"Nope, you're a woman. Big difference."

Mala's cheeks pink, and her arms cross again. Her voice doesn't betray her embarrassment, 'cause Axle doesn't need the positive reinforcement, when she asks, "Does Carl like girls?"

"Nah, he'd rather go hunting. Like me."

I help Mala and Axle out of the truck. We walk hand in hand into the skating rink. A family. Damn Pepper for ruining everything. We were happy. Now everything has gone to hell. Rather than wandering around in search of Daryl, Mala marches up to the DJ's booth, hands him what looks like a five-dollar bill, then grabs the microphone. "Daryl S. Acker, you've got ten minutes. Kiss your geriatric girlfriend good-bye and meet us outside." She holds out the microphone to the DJ, then snatches it back. "And don't even try to escape out the back 'cause if I have to hunt you down, I will tell everyone your middle name…which rhymes with *flash*."

She hands the microphone back and then storms over to us. I'm holding my stomach from laughing so hard. Pepper's slicker than I thought. Deliberately naming her sons after eighties rockers simply to have leverage to hold over their heads if they misbehaved. *Wicked*.

But she's a toddler compared to the grandmamma of them all, our very own Wicked Witch of New Orleans. Time to get my bucket of water ready; Magnolia's waiting.

Chapter 21

Mala

Nefarious Hijinks

Daryl's face is flushed when he finally makes his way to the truck and climbs into the backseat. "You guys are so embarrassing. This is why I don't introduce you to my friends. What are you doing here, anyway? Mrs. Moulton said we're supposed to stay with Pepper. Does she know you're here? I don't want to get in trouble for being with you," he says, immediately going on the attack to deflect us from questioning him about his girlfriend. It's not the smartest move. We were distracted from what happened at the hotel, but it all comes rushing back.

Axle's face crumples. He doesn't cry, but his lip trembles. "You're stupid, Daryl."

Landry gives Daryl a smoky one-eyed glare through the overhead mirror. "Something happened. It's a long story, and I only want to tell it once. So we'll fill you in at the same time as Dad and your brothers."

Axle stares quietly out the window for the rest of the drive to the Acker place, which more than anything imparts the seriousness of the situation upon Daryl. Reverend Prince and Carl are outside, painting the fence around Dena's vegetable garden. When they see us, they come over to the truck.

"Everything okay?" he asks his son, hand squeezing his shoulder.

Landry nods and tips his chin toward the paint. "Helping Pepper get this place ready to go on the market?"

Reverend Prince wipes his paint-stained hands on a dishrag. "I spoke with the bank about getting a loan. If Pepper's determined to sell, then I might as well buy it for you kids. I doubt Pepper will get a better offer."

We gather the kids on the porch and fill them in on what happened at the B&B. We don't go into detail. Just that Judd had been arrested and Pepper was okay, but was taken to the hospital. Reverend Prince puts aside his curiosity for now. He promises to have a talk with Axle about what he witnessed and to lecture Daryl about his responsibilities to his brothers. It's hard to leave the boys after getting them back, even in Landry's dad's capable hands.

What's even more terrifying is pulling up at my house and seeing Magnolia's Cadillac parked in the driveway.

Landry parks off to the side. Neither of us reaches for the door handles. Only our heavy breathing breaks the silence in the cab until Landry leans back in his seat. The vertebrae in his back pop with his stretch, and he sighs.

I brush a tight curl off my face and lick my dry lips.

"Do I look as scared as I feel?"

Landry threads his fingers through mine. His palm feels clammy, but his warmth comforts me. "We survived a standoff with another lunatic with a gun. This should be no problem."

"Magnolia's crazy *and* uses magic. That makes it worse. Plus, we need her more than she needs us."

"Maybe," he says and grimaces. "Maybe not. Whatever plan she's working toward is a long game. She's been setting up her pieces for months…seasoning us for whatever her goal is. I just can't figure out what part we play in all of this. But whatever it is, I feel like we've moved into the endgame."

"I do too," I whisper. My gaze drifts toward the house and collides with Magnolia's. The old bat sits in the rocker on the front porch beside Ferdinand. Etienne hovers at her back, like a spindly stone gargoyle. Even at a distance, the weight of Magnolia's stare feels like a punch in the gut. She waves.

I swallow hard. "The queen beckons."

Landry glances at the porch. "Let's get a move on before she directs Etienne to make off with our heads."

"That creeper would do it too. No questions asked."

"I doubt he remembers how to string together a sentence. I swear, I can't figure out if he's the best or worst example of a zombie that I've ever seen."

"Hopefully worst. I don't even want to think of Dena coming back like him. Being trapped in a decaying body"—I shudder— "it's the stuff of my worst nightmares." Not including my latest foray into the mind of a demented killer. *Saints, I don't want to do this. But I have to. For Dee.*

Landry presses a kiss to the back of my hand. "Don't move. I'll come get you."

The seriousness of his tone cracks the frozen shards icing my heart. Warmth floods my body as I'm once again reminded of how lucky I am to have him. He knows me well enough that he feels it necessary to remind me not to jump out of the truck on my own. In this case, I don't think my stiff fingers can work the door latch let alone trust my shaky legs to hold my weight. Not that falling on my face in front of Magnolia would be a bigger humiliation than my last "incident"—rolling into an open grave and landing on a rotting corpse.

Landry holds me steady the minute my feet touch the ground. I inhale his scent, and his strength fills me. My shoulders straighten. We cross the driveway and climb the porch stairs as a united front. Prepared to face whatever she dishes out together.

* * *

Magnolia lifts Grandmère Cora's china teacup to her lips, but her eyes never break the connection between us. The air prickles with energy, flowing from her to me and settling in the pit of my stomach, drawn to the life I hold inside. She aims a gummy smile in my direction and raises her hands palm forward, like she's offering benediction.

"Hey there, *cher*," Magnolia says and cackles. "How you been?"

"I'm sure you know better than I." I lean forward and lay a peck on her dry cheek. A spark bites me at the touch, and I jump back. "You've heard Landry and I are expecting?"

"Been expecting for over a month, so it's no surprise to me. Ferdinand filled me in on your situation. Where's my Sophia?"

I glance at Ferdinand, but return my focus to Magnolia's eyes, watching for a hint of guilt, as I say, "Someone attacked her at the hotel. She's at the hospital."

Nothing. The old bat doesn't even blink.

Ferdinand clears his throat. He taps a finger against his cell, which lies on the table. "Sophia texted that she's been checked out by the doctor, and she's okay. She said she'd meet us at your cousin's room."

"Why?" Magnolia asks. She sets her empty teacup on the saucer and wipes her lips.

Surprised, I frown at Ferdinand. I thought he would've explained the situation to Magnolia. Or better yet, had not needed to explain. I thought she knew everything? Ferdinand and Sophia have no problem dipping into my thoughts. "Uh, I know you came to do some purification ritual, but today we're gonna get my cousin instead. If that's all right with you, ma'am."

"She's stuck in limbo," Ferdinand explains. "Mala didn't have the fortitude to bring her all the way back."

Magnolia raises an eyebrow, and my cheeks heat.

"Damn it, Ferdinand. I thought we were friends," I say. "Why do you have to go and make me sound all wussy? Sue me if I'm not on-board with killing someone as easily as you."

"So what's changed?" he asks.

"Red's trapped in limbo with Dena. He's torturing her, and it's my fault. I won't leave her in there with him."

Magnolia rocks back with a sly grin. "Miss High and Mighty tampered with the balance between life and death and now sees the consequences aren't necessarily a matter of black and white."

"No matter how I cut it, it's still murder if my actions are the cause of his death," I say.

"Ah, then you're willing to assume the consequence for such a dark act?"

I knew it wouldn't come without a price. "I've thought about my decision at length. I'm willing to pay whoever guards the gates to the afterlife if it means bringing my cousin back." Plus a tiny spark of hope still burns that maybe I can get around Red dying. "Isn't the situation different this time? She's not completely dead like the decaying girl in the grave and"—I lean forward to whisper from behind my hand—"Etienne."

Magnolia laughs and pats the silent man on the back. A puff of spicy and dust explodes from his suit, making my nose tingle. "He won't get his feelings hurt by hearing he's dead, *cher*. He knows better than anyone living the state he's in."

I guess. "What I mean is, since Dena isn't dead, Red won't need to die to balance out the sacrifice. Right?"

Magnolia shrugs. "I don't decide these things."

"But who does?"

"Someone with greater power than I, *cher*."

Saints! Oh…she does mean saints or God, angels, Loa of Death, a higher power. Scary thought. I'm tampering with the rules of life and death, and I don't know what they are. Evidently, Magnolia, for all of her big talk, doesn't either. That's a recipe for trouble.

Landry clears his throat. "So what exactly is the price? To Mala, I mean."

I'm not surprised he doesn't give a flying monkey about Red, but me…yeah, I can already see his wheels spinning as he tries to figure out the said and unsaid. And he's staring Magnolia down, not backing off from her.

Magnolia raises both silver eyebrows. "Is this you asking or your demon?"

"He tends to go quiet when you're around. Maybe he doesn't like your company."

The insult stiffens her crooked spine. She slams the end of her cane down on the wood floor, letting out a resounding thump. "Seems like it's a negative influence on your manners. You were always such an obedient partner for my great niece. It's why I let you live the night Jasmine died, despite Mala's desire to sacrifice you on the altar of her revenge." A dark shadow hovers above her skin, and her voice turns gravelly. "Don't make me regret my decision."

Landry's eye widens, so do mine. "So you really were in the road that night. You caused the accident."

"I saw you and your father's souls were pure. Not so for the other men involved in murdering my niece. Those who are no longer in this world, and the one who hovers on the brink." Her grin sends a chill down my spine, because where once there were only gums blackened by chewing tobacco, a row of sharp teeth flash between her narrow lips. The shadow beneath her skin rises to the surface once again, superimposing itself over my aunt. *Her true form.* I don't know where this thought comes from, but I know it to be correct. "A storm's rolling in, and we need the light of the moon for the purification ritual, so we'll deal with your cousin first. Tomorrow night is soon enough. Ferdinand, bring my bag."

The big guy gives us a warning frown and brings Magnolia's satchel over. He sets it at her feet, and I rub my hands on my jeans, remembering the oily feel it left on my palms when I last touched it. *Nastiness.*

Landry and I leave first for the hospital. Neither of us wants to be stuck in the Caddy with Magnolia. I have too many suspicions about her to be in such close proximity, especially when she's read my mind in the past. But I do want to talk to her about what happened at the B&B with Judd. Even though I think he might be working with her, I need to get her opinion on what I saw when I shot that spear of power into his chest.

Landry and I talked about it after we dropped off the boys. He said he watched the whole attack, but he didn't see it—the darkness that rose out of Judd's body when the energy hit him, like the power severed his shadow and it flew off on its own, à la Peter Pan. I saw something similar happen to Magnolia on the porch. Like something lived just under her skin.

We don't wait for Magnolia and crew to arrive, but go inside. I see Bessie and George standing by the emergency room door in deep conversation. Judd must still be getting examined. I wonder if his blood work will be positive for illegal drugs.

I veer from Landry's side, saying over my shoulder, "I'll get an update on Judd and Pepper while you wait for Magnolia."

"Okay, get to it." He gives me a tight smile, and I nod. Time for Operation Interrogate the Flunky, aka finding out what Judd has told George about his crime. Convincing George to buck authority and spill police secrets is a whole lot easier when I can bat my eyelashes and give him flattering looks without Landry around to get all *grr* with jealousy. I didn't expect our ill-formed plan to go into play this soon, but I can't pass up the opportunity. Who knows how long it will take to bring Dena back from the living dead or what sort of shape I'll be in after it's over.

"Hey," I call, running over to them. I don't wait for them to return the greeting but launch into my speech. "Judd's here, right? Did he spill anything?"

"Mala—" Bessie begins, but I cut her off.

"Look, I'm not some civilian off the street. Sheriff Keyes said I could work this case with George, and I've done more than my share. Don't cut me out now, when we're so close to finding out the truth."

Bessie raises a hand. "Maybe if you'd let me speak without interruption, you'd know that I had no intention of cutting you out of anything. The fact of the matter is that I need your opinion."

"What?"

"Judd's acting all kinds of peculiar," Bessie says, shaking her head. "Like being slammed against the wall scrambled his pea brain, however the hell that happened. Every witness to his capture mentions it, but nobody knows how or why." She gives me the beady eyeball, but doesn't voice her suspicion when she continues. "Anyway, he says the last thing he remembers is going to the Ackers with Pepper. After that it's a blank."

My lips twist. "Super convenient, or inconvenient, since amnesia won't help with an alibi."

George clears his throat. "Thing is, I don't think he's faking. He reminds me of you after…" He trails off, shifting from one foot to the other.

Bessie stares at him like he's lost his ever lovin' mind, then turns to me. "He means after your attack. Only I don't know why he just didn't go on and say it."

"Hey, that was a hard time for me," he protests.

"Harder for me, since I'm the one who had a ghost-fried memory." I poke George in the chest.

"See, LT, I told you," George says. "That's how he acts. Like he was possessed by a ghost. He has the same blank"—he waves his hands in front of his face in some wacky version of jazz hands— "'I don't know who you are or what I did last summer' glaze to his eyes. He actually started crying when I told him he held a gun to Pepper's head and had a kid's body in his trunk."

Bessie crosses her muscular arms. "I think it's less likely that he was possessed and more likely he's a remorseless serial killer who is setting up an insanity defense."

George turns to Bessie. "You didn't see his face in the hallway, Lieutenant."

"Yeah, I agree with my brother," I say. "You can't fake that kind of crazy. Or vice versa. He really wanted to kill me over that knife."

"Knife?" Bessie asks.

I cover my mouth. "Oops, damn. Sorry. Georgie and I planned to tell you about it if it turned out it had something to do with the murders."

"You found the murder weapon"—Bessie's voice rises with each word, and I cringe—"and didn't say anything?"

"It wasn't found under conventional circumstances. It can't be used as evidence in court. I mean, how are you to explain that I took the knife away from the killer in a dream and brought it out to the real world. See," I crow, pointing at her openmouthed expression. "That's what I'm talking about."

"So this knife—

"That's another problem," George says.

"Will you please stop interrupting me?" Bessie cries, hands rising to rub her forehead. I think we're about to break the unbreakable Lieutenant Caine. Not good. We need her sanity intact to keep us from going off the rails. I swear, half the time I cringe over the non-sense coming out of my mouth. The problem is that the craziest things are real: ghosts, zombies, demons, magic, love. *Nuts*. I remember thinking before Mama died that future-Mala's life would be boring. Boy was I wrong.

George has the grace to look contrite. "Sorry, Bessie. I'm trying to fall on my sword here. I just received a text from Ernesto. When he got back to the station, the knife was missing. Someone stole it while we were busy at the crime scene."

"What?" Bessie and I yell in unison.

George ducks his head. A nurse at the check-in counter scowls and puts her finger to her lips, shushing us. I can't speak anyway. I'm too shocked. "This person had access to the sheriff's office and a key to the evidence cabinet," he tells us. "The accomplice strikes again."

"Oh, damn." I groan, holding my stomach. I feel sick.

Bessie's fingers twitch. Either she's going for her gun or is about to grab George by the ear and march him to the naughty chair for holding back the information for so long. Time for this little witch to make a graceful retreat by using my buzzing phone as my magic wand. I pull it out to see Landry's text: *move ur ass*. A quick glance at the door shows Magnolia, Ferdinand, and Etienne walking toward Landry, who waves for me from beside the elevator.

"I have to go." I pull on a disappointed frown. "My aunt's here. We're going to check Sophia out and take her home. I'll connect with you tomorrow."

George touches my arm before I perform the next step in my act—vanishing. "Don't forget Aunt March's birthday party tomorrow night. You're going, right?"

Oh crap, I forgot to come up with an excuse to get out of it. "Surely you're not still partying, with everything going on?"

Georgie's green eyes narrow. "Our suspect is in custody. He's not going anywhere."

"Besides, I have a date," Bessie murmurs. "I'll see you there."

Crud, screwed again. "Yeah, we'll be there."

George smiles, but Bessie nods without meeting my eyes. "Good, we'll talk more over cake." She retreats down the hall with her work phone glued to her ear. If I were her, I would be investigating how someone could steal from the evidence room without getting caught on video surveillance. The problem is that it doesn't take much magic to burn out a camera.

I find it interesting this happened now that Magnolia's in town. Did she bring someone in? Or does the accomplice live in Paradise Pointe? I start to think about the people I know, 'cause lately the line between bad guy and friend has worn thin. I hate to suspect the people who are closest to me, but…I do.

Chapter 22

Landry

Adrift

I lead the group through the hospital. Sophia said she would meet us at Dena's room. With each step, my anxiety about what will happen grows. I turn to the one creature that might give me some assurances.

"Hey? You there?" My internal bellow reverberates off the back of my skull. An echo in the emptiness. The snake has been unusually quiet today, like it's gathering its energy. Even without it speaking, I sense its building restlessness. I just wish it would give me a hint about what to expect. Or confirmation of my suspicions that all the craziness around us stems from Magnolia, and we're just pieces on the board for her to move around and discard at will.

I don't know what I expected to gain from stupidly challenging Magnolia earlier. My rebellion didn't get me far. She slapped me down as easily as squashing a mosquito, and about as remorselessly too. The only thing I did confirm was my suspicion that she has been working for a long time toward furthering her hidden agenda. She left me alive for a reason. And while I'd like to believe she's on our side, I'd be three kinds of fool to do so.

Sophia seems like the sort to jump off a burning ship and throw mothers and children overboard into the frigid water to make room for herself in the lifeboat without a sliver of remorse. Yet she told us not to trust Magnolia. If the queen learns about this, she won't take such a betrayal lightly. I can see a skinned, deep frying in Sophia's future if she's not careful.

Still I won't complain. I've got my guard up now. So does Mala.

Sophia waits for us in front of Dena's room. A small, white bandage stands out against her skin. She brushes a lock of hair over her shoulder. "I've taken care of the nurses. They won't disturb us for a few hours."

"How?" I ask. "Did you fix a spell?"

"Of course she did," Mala begins, only to trail off when Sophia rolls her eyes.

"Children, please. Why use a spell when a wad of cash works equally well?" She holds open the door for Magnolia. The old woman smiles and sweeps into the room. Mala follows, but when I try to enter, the door slams shut on me.

I pound my fist into it. "Hey, let me in."

Ferdinand grips my shoulder. "That isn't the place for one such as yourself."

"Why the hell not?"

The big guy takes up guard position on the left side of the door and crosses his arms. "Having been pulled back once from the land of the dead, do you want it to notice you again? It's had a taste of your soul. It will try to suck you back."

I shiver, remembering the burning of the darkness that tried to pull me down its maw. If Mala hadn't held on for as long as she did, or if Lainey hadn't drawn me back, I wouldn't be here. And I wouldn't have El Creepy in my head. *"Is this true?"*

The rustle of scales fills my mind. *"Why do you think I hide, host? I'm not keen on going back into the dark any more than you."*

"Oh? So if I go in there, you might get sucked out of my head?" My hand reaches for the door, 'cause hell, this is the first clue I've gotten about how to rid myself of this pest.

My open fingers freeze an inch from the doorknob. No matter how hard I strain, I can't get my arm to move any closer. "Cut it out," I say. "You're breaking your promise."

"So are you."

"Who are you speaking to?" Ferdinand stares down at my trembling hand and then meets my eyes. "The rider? Does he control you now?"

I grit my teeth. "He says if I go into that room he'll get swept back into hell."

"You exaggerate, host."

"So you won't go to hell? Or back to the cave I found you in?"

"I'm here for a purpose. You would be a fool to give up your advantage when you need me the most. And you know it." My hand drops to my side, no longer out of my control. *"Trust is a two-way street."*

I lean against the wall with a sigh.

Ferdinand slaps a hand on my shoulder, and I flinch. "Are you in control?" he asks.

"Yeah, man. We have common ground. Neither of us is ready to die today. I can put up with his smug attitude a little longer." Energy flows in a wave across my arms, setting the hairs on end, and I straighten. I press my fingertips against the door and then bring my hand back with a gasp. "Do you feel it?"

"Magic," Ferdinand says, drawing in a deep breath. "Let the taste flow over your lips. Drink it in."

"You sound like a drunk savoring a glass of the finest whisky."

His eyes gleam. "No matter how much you drink, you always crave more."

Can't say I agree with him. Magic grows thicker. My gums ache and a bitter twinge hits my tongue. Squiggly lines flow in front of my eye, and I close it. Ferdinand's warm hand settles on my shoulder again, and I stagger beneath the weight, unable to remain standing against the pressure building in the air.

"What's happening?"

"Stay grounded. Focus on the here and now. Don't let it drag you in."

It's not affecting my body. At first I thought so, but it's more internal. Not physical but spiritual. My body fights to hold itself together, struggling against the overwhelming force tugging on my soul. I clench my teeth and grab onto Ferdinand's arm. He's solid and real.

"Hold on, Landry. Just a little longer."

A piercing scream comes from within the room. *Mala...* Her voice stabs my eardrums, and I lurch upright. The sound echoes in my head, pulsing with the rapid beats of my heart. I grab the doorknob, twisting it, and when it doesn't open, I throw my shoulder against it. Once, twice, the third time it breaks. I fall into the room. Ferdinand grabs for me, trying to hold me back, but I shove him aside. My mind is completely on the mother of my child and the need to kill anything that's causing her to scream like that.

A multitude of candles circle the hospital bed. Shadows dance in the flickering light, their flames painting the walls. Monstrous shapes...I can't even describe the nebulous forms. Dark magic thickens the air. The stench, like a mix of curdled milk and rotten eggs, burns my eye. I tear my watery gaze from the walls to search the room for Mala. A shudder wracks my body when I see her. She's kneeling on the bed, naked, with Dena between her legs. Her tangled hair wraps around her waist, writhing around her back with the energy flowing through the room like living snakes.

Magnolia stands beside the bed. Only it's not her. She appears the same she did the night she ran our truck off the road. A top hat sits on her silver hair. Smoke rises from the cigarette in her mouth. Her eyes imitate the candles in the room, glowing with an otherworldly yellow light. In one hand, she holds her cane and waves it over Mala's body. With the other, she sprinkles a fine black powder over Mala's upturned face. It drifts over her forehead, sticking to the sweat coating her skin. A deep-throated howl rips from Mala's throat. Her arms fly outward, and her eyes roll back as her hips rock, shaking Dena with each convulsion.

"Stop!" I stagger forward. Ferdinand grabs for me again, but I wheel around. My punch lands beneath his high cheekbone. He falls backward, and his head slams into the doorframe. He catches himself before his legs slide out from under him.

A body darkens the doorway. I meet Pepper's shocked gaze but rip free. I dimly hear her screaming and Ferdinand's answer behind me as I sprint across the room.

Sophia steps from a corner to block my path. She doesn't stop chanting, despite the fear widening her eyes. She's silently screaming at me. I can't hear her, but I sense it. I must stop this. Whatever's happening, it's wrong. A corruption. Evil.

"Help me, Sophia. Please."

She closes her eyes. Her voice rises. Each sound from her lips sets off a cascade of colors—a visual fireworks display erupts in my head. My equilibrium's shot, and my stomach rolls at the sensation of freefalling. With my depth perception skewed, I stagger toward the bed, unable to judge the distance.

Desperate, I reach for the creature watching silently from behind my eye, but it slithers out of my grasp, hiding. It hisses, *"This is not the time. It's too soon. Fight, host."*

The energy filling the room pulses, pushing me backward with every step. I shove through it, like I'm breaching a force field. My nerve endings burn until soon my whole body feels raw, like it's on fire.

Magnolia rubs a paste onto Mala's belly in a clockwise circle. Something other than raising Dena's going on. *What is she doing to the baby?*

"No!" I grab for her arm. My fingers sting before they make contact with her skin. It's like the energy shield originates from her. The darkness licks my fingers, hungry. The false overlay twists, and I stare into a double set of eyes—Magnolia, and always underneath her skin, the man in a top hat and long coat.

Fucker sees me staring and throws back his head and laughs. "You're too late," he whispers in a voice deeper than a sound boiling up from the darkest pit of hell. "It's done."

"What's done?" I ask hoarsely. "What did you do?"

Mala collapses on the blanket. She stares up at the ceiling—nothing moves in the dark depths of her eyes. She doesn't breathe. Then her lashes flicker and her chest rises. I cup her face with shaking hands. Her skin is ice cold. I lean forward to press my ear against her lips. A hand moves in from my blind side. I don't see it, but the heat from Magnolia's palm burns into my forehead. Everything goes dark, like I lost vision in my good eye. But it feels different.

I'm no longer in the hospital room.

"Where..." The word echoes, bouncing off invisible walls. I shiver from the damp chill in the air and wrap my arms around my naked chest.

A slither of scales comes from my bare feet, and I dance back. A long, sinuous body of a snake twines around my ankles, and I shudder. "Where are we? How did I get here?"

The snake's muscles constrict, tightening its grip on me as it winds higher up my torso. I tense in preparation, jaw already loosening, but instead of shoving itself down my throat, the head rests on my shoulder. Its tongue flickers against my earlobe as it hisses, *"The trap is set. Now we need the bait. Find Mala LaCroix, the last descendant of my line."*

"What? Oh, hell no!" I cringe when the shout bounces back. I cover my ears, but even when I whisper, it sounds loud. "Don't even think about using her for whatever you've got planned."

"As you wish. Leave her trapped in the void. It matters little to me."

"Liar." Don't let it trick you. My first priority is finding Mala. I'll deal with the weirdness of that proclamation later. "Is she here in this place?"

The head wraps around my neck like a shawl. *"You recognize it, don't you? The place you fell into after you passed over to the other side. Some call it purgatory. I think of it as jail."*

"You were in jail?" Sympathy fills me. Nothing good comes from being imprisoned. Hell, I died while on lockdown. No wonder it didn't want to come back.

"I am the jailer."

Oh…Still, this place should be condemned as being inhumane, not that the creature perched on my shoulder's human.

I shove aside my confusion when it chuckles, asking, *"What does the responsible jailer do when his prisoner escapes?"*

A yell echoes through the cave and distracts me from the question before I can shove my foot deeper in my mouth. It doesn't sound like a cry of pain. Oh, damn. Someone pissed off my girl. Her voice grows louder and louder. Soon it's so loud that I have to crouch down and cover my ears until it stops. Then I'm up and running in the direction I think it came from. The snake tightens around my chest, making it difficult to breathe.

I use a burst of air to yell, "Mala, where are you?"

"Landry?" Her shaky voice comes from the right.

Luckily I have my hands outstretched or I would've slammed face-first into the wall. I pat the weeping stone. "There's no entrance."

"Farther down," the demon/angel directs, hissing the words.

I slide my hand across the wall until I find the entrance to the tunnel and go through. Pain flares on the back of my head, and I fall forward. The snake drops from my neck, and I hear it slithering away. I touch the lump at the base of my skull. A whisper of sound jerks my hand down. I try to block the strike, but I can't see it. I can only hear the snap in the air. Feel the pain of a foot jamming into my stomach. When I double over, a knee smashes into my face. I collapse and curl into a ball, trying to breathe, but all the air shot from my lungs when the foot smashed into my solar plexus. My nose begins to swell.

A hand fists in my hair, yanking my head back. Rank breath blows into my face. "Welcome to my party, prick," Redford Delahoussaye says, then presses a wet, lip-smacking kiss on my forehead.

Shit! This must mean we're in Dena's head or the limbo she's trapped in. His foot repeatedly stomping on my gut keeps me from pondering too long. I wrap my arms around his leg and twist. I hear his knee pop. He screams as he falls. I roll on top of him and then straddle his chest. I'm glad it's too dark to see his ugly face, 'cause, yeah, plug-ugly. I grip his hair with my left hand and aim my punches for where I estimate his face to be. I count my punches at first. By twenty, my arm aches and his whimpers have stopped. The snake's back, perched in its spot on my shoulder. I didn't even feel it return.

"Mala, Red's down. Come out. You're safe."

"I can't let go of Dena. She's trying to get away."

"Where? I can't see."

Mala whimpers. "It's too bright."

"What is she talking about?" I ask.

"Magnolia cracked open the door to the other side, and Mala stands at the entranceway. If she gets too close she may be pulled in. Get her."

I don't know what he expects me to do when I can't even see this light Mala speaks of or figure out where in blue blazes she is. This place is like an underground maze, full of twists and turns. What a fucking mess.

"Tell me what to do?"

"We need a trade. A life for a life."

Red! I trade him for Dena. Simple as that. But that means getting him into the mouth of the vortex. I rub my hand across my chest, remembering the burning pain of the tentacles that latched on and tried to drag me into the vortex when I died. "Mala, hold on."

I feel on the ground until I touch Red's arm and grab it. He's heavy. But the slickness of the floor makes it easy to drag him. I follow Mala's whimpers. Down around the corner, I sense her before I see her. Her spirit calls out to a primal part of me. My heart hammers, and a black fear rises within when I see the shining silver and blue vortex lighting up the room. I squint against the brightness.

Tentacles stretch from the maw of the "door" and are wrapped around Dena's waist, the same way it grabbed me when I died. And like she held me, Mala grips her cousin with both hands. They're both on the ground and sliding inch by inch toward the opening.

I lift Red beneath his arms and drag him forward. Mala sees me and cries, "What are you doing? Get away from there."

A tentacle whips in my direction, and I duck. If they latch onto me, I'll be dragged in. Red stirs in my arms, and I lift him higher. He comes to, flailing his arms and screeching like a mad person. Which maybe he is, and was, even before getting trapped in limbo. I drop him. He staggers upright, swinging his fist. I dodge the punch and maneuver myself until he stands between me and the vortex. He throws another wild punch, too out of it to aim. I come up under his guard with an uppercut to his gut. He hunches in on himself, and I take a few steps back and then level a kick to the middle of his chest. He staggers away.

A tentacle whips out and circles his chest, and he shrieks. I scramble beneath another snapping tentacle and do a commando-style run that turns into a slide across the slippery stone over to Mala. She's struggling to hold on to Dena's hands. I wish I had a knife, something to cut her loose. But I don't.

"What do you need to do to free her?" I ask, grabbing Mala around the waist. I heave backward, pulling her and Dena back a couple of inches. "What's wrong with Dee?"

"She passed out." The panic in my love's voice hits me down low. "I don't know what to do. I can't think. Why isn't Magnolia helping me?"

"She has her own agenda. I'm not sure this was a good idea."

"You tell me this now?" she says and sobs.

Yeah, bad timing. I focus on holding them steady. We're not making progress breaking free, but we're also not moving forward. Red lets out a scream that raises goose bumps along my arms and sends a shiver down my spine and curls my toes with remembered pain. Those damn tentacles burn. Like fire ants crawling across your body, biting as they go.

Lainey suddenly appears. *My sis.* She's even more skeletal than the last time I saw her. She'd been fighting to put up a barrier between the demon and my mind for months. Keeping me sane for as long as possible. Her hand pulls at her tangled black hair, and she turns in a circle like a dog chasing its tail. "Why are you here, Landry? Why?"

A hiss comes from my shoulder. I'd forgotten him. *"Get her away from me."*

"No." She grabs the demon by the tail and yanks. His body tightens around my throat, cutting off my air. My hands slip from around Mala, and the pull on my body threatens to break my neck. Mala screams, sliding away from me. I lunge for her ankles, grabbing on.

Stars swirl in front of my eye as I suck in tiny gasps of air. "Lainey, no!"

I think—really think—I've lost my fucking mind. Part of me wants to stop her and tell her it's not a bad guy. That it's been helping me. But that's the crazy part. Why would I want this thing inside me? Especially when I have a chance to send it back where it came from.

"You still need me."

"So says you," I gasp out.

"Don't believe it. It's the father of lies, Landry," Lainey says, whimpering in frustration. She can't pry it free without my consent. And I can't say yes. What if it's telling the truth? The coils release enough for me to speak. "Back off, Lainey. Please."

She stumbles back, realizing I've made my decision. The serpent nudges my mouth. I pause a moment, then unlatch my jaw. Mala's too wrapped up in Dena to pay attention to what I'm doing, which is just as well since she'd probably freak out as much as my sister does.

No matter how much I want to be free, I can't be. If there is a murdering prisoner out there and the only way to stop it is through its jailer, then I need to keep him around. Of course, even if it's good, it doesn't mean it won't suck me dry in the end. 'Cause now that I'm here, I feel it using me up. I'll be the sacrifice if I have to. Maybe that will redeem all of my bad choices. Let me move on and not be trapped in this sort of purgatory like Red.

Lainey whimpers again. Her fingers claw at her face and then her hair. Her voice comes out low and full of sorrow. "I'm tired…"

Mala's shaking in my arms. She's holding on to Dena by her fingertips. Dena looks unconscious. Red is almost entirely covered by black ooze, but he's not being drawn into the vortex. Something still ties him here.

Mala closes her eyes. "It's really up to me." She leans forward until her forehead touches her cousin's hands. The blue light in the room condenses, separating into two smoldering balls. One zips over to float above Dena's body. The other drifts closer to the vortex. "Combine."

Dena's wrapped from head to toe in the silvery blue aura. It's so beautiful, yet darkness also spots it. I don't know what this means.

"Landry, get her out of here," Lainey says, then turns.

I figure out what she's about to do too late. There's no time to yell for her to stop or tell her good-bye. She runs for Red and launches herself at him. Her arms wrap around his neck, and her weight sends him flying backward. The vortex pulses, expanding to accommodate them, then collapses in on itself. And they're gone.

Chapter 23

Mala

Conflicted

My eyes crack open, and I squint against the overhead light. White spots flash across my blurry vision. My head's fuzzy, and my mouth tastes like a toad died and dried out on my tongue. It takes a few seconds to process the fact that, for some reason, I'm lying on an examination table with my feet in stirrups. A cold draft blows across my stomach, and I shiver. *Great.* I'm wearing a paper shirt, and it opens to the front.

What I can't figure out due to my current scatterbrained state is how I hurt myself. Again. But I do know that I'm pretty damn tired of landing in the hospital every few months. It's like the universe's idea of a twisted joke to keep sticking me in the only place that terrifies me to the very marrow.

With a sigh, I wipe away the gunk gluing my eyelashes together.

My movement triggers an answering shuffle, and I focus in the direction it came from.

Landry sits hunched over on a stool at my side. His hair stands on end, forming a black halo around his too-pale face, and his storm-filled eye studies me. "Dr. Mello, she's awake," he calls to someone, but doesn't break eye contact.

The intensity of his stare sends an echoing shiver through my body that has nothing to do with the cold air blowing through the vent overhead. He takes my hand.

"Are you okay?" he asks, voice husky, like he overtaxed it. "You scared the hell out of me."

Okay? No, I'm tired and confused. "What happened?"

He squints his eye, like he's trying to send me a message, but my head's too swimmy to read his mind. Not that I think I can replicate what happened during the standoff with Judd. I'm not even sure if the psychic connection between us was real or a figment of my panicked imagination. And I'm too afraid to mention it to Landry to find out.

When he realizes I don't know the answer to his question, he blurts out, "You fainted."

My head throbs, but I don't recall falling down. Plus… "I've never fainted in my life…well, except the times that Lainey…" I trail off at the deepening groves etching around the corners of Landry's eye and mouth. His sadness is raw and totally unfiltered. What happened while I was unconscious?

A woman in a white lab coat rolls a large machine that looks like a giant computer into the room, and I heave upright. "What in the world is that thing?"

Landry presses me back onto the table. "Dr. Mello said she'll do an ultrasound to make sure the baby is okay."

Oh no, the *baby*… My fingers slip from Landry's hand, but he grabs them when I try to touch my stomach. It feels funny. Before it felt full. Hard. I hadn't noticed how tight my uterus had become until right now. I feel empty, in more ways than this.

The doctor slips on a pair of wire glasses and smiles down at me. My muscles relax. She wouldn't smile if something was wrong.

"Hello, doctor," I say, wishing I could smile back, but I'm too nervous. "Nice to meet you."

"The pleasure is mine, Ms. LaCroix. Give me a minute to set this machine up, and we'll begin."

My toes curl against the cold metal stirrups. "Okay."

Breathe. Everything's okay. My hand tightens around Landry's, and he lifts it to press a quick kiss over the fluttering pulse in my wrist. I shift on the padded table, but keep sliding toward the bottom. And the arches of my feet ache. The crinkling paper sounds too loud in the otherwise quiet room. Each breath comes faster.

Why isn't Landry saying anything? The silence stretches, and I grit my teeth against the jittery anger filling me. Why is this taking so long? I don't want to be here anymore. I glance around the room and see my folded T-shirt and jeans on a chair. My socks are stuffed in my tennis shoes beneath it. *Why didn't they leave them on? My feet are cold.* I should go. This is a waste of time and money. The baby's okay. So am I.

Dr. Mello sets the machine on the opposite side of the exam table. The monitor faces her, not us. She turns to us with another smile and holds up a probe wearing a condom, which is what Landry should've doubled up on so I wouldn't be in this mess.

"I'll be doing a transvaginal ultrasound. This is a transducer, but I call it my magic wand," she says. "Once it's inserted inside you, sound waves will recreate images of your uterus on the screen. Your fiancé says you're over six weeks along?" She raises an eyebrow. I nod, not bothering to correct her on the whole fiancé business. "Then the gestational sac and the fetal pole should be visible."

"The what?" Landry asks for both of us.

"Yolk sac," she says. "We may even have a heartbeat. Now, this will be a bit uncomfortable, but it will be over before you know it."

I focus on happy thoughts while she inserts her magic wand. The pressure is more than a *bit* uncomfortable. And not at all as pleasurable as having Landry's wand inside me. She begins to move it around, checking stuff out, and I squirm, biting my lip to stifle an undignified moan.

Dr. Mello gives me a stern look. "I need you to hold still."

The muscles in my stomach tighten, and I hold my breath.

"It'll be over soon, Mala," Landry says, like he knows what the hell he's talking about. The doc should shove her magic stick up his where-the-sun-don't-shine. He needs to get a taste of what I'm going through. Man, this is making me all kinds of grumpy. I don't even want to imagine going into labor. I'm feeling twitchy just thinking about it. This sucks. And hurts.

"What's taking so long?" Landry asks, not looking away from my face. If my expression mirrors his in any way, I must look like I'm sucking on a pickle. "Shouldn't you see the egg yolk by now?"

"Yes," she says, drawing the word out between her teeth. She swivels the screen in our direction. "I should, but I don't."

Landry throws a wide-eye look at me. I don't know what she's talking about either. All I see on the screen are white lumps. I can't tell what internal organs they're supposed to represent.

She twists the wand sideways, stretching me, and I almost leap off the table from the pain. If Landry hadn't been holding my hand, I would've punched her. Why isn't she saying anything? And what happened to her earlier smile? It was false advertising in my opinion. Leading us to believe everything would be fine when clearly it's not.

I draw in shallow breaths and concentrate on forcing the muscles down low to unclench. The clock on the wall over the door counts down the seconds for me. I breathe in with every five ticks and release the air on the sixth.

At the two-minute mark, Dr. Mello finally sighs. She slides the wand out of me and removes the condom, throwing it into a red biohazard bin. "How did you find out that you're pregnant, Ms. LaCroix?"

I can't speak. My vaginal muscles are still quivering.

Recognizing my discomfort, Landry answers for us. "She took a pregnancy test."

"Did you get the result confirmed by your obstetrician?"

Landry shakes his head. "No, it's only been a few days since we found out."

Dr. Mello removes my feet from the stirrups and adjusts the head of the table until I'm no longer lying flat on my back. She sits down on a rolling stool and starts fiddling with the hem of her coat. "I don't know how to say this without being blunt." Her head tilts, and she pushes her glasses up the bridge of her shiny nose. "I'm not finding any evidence of a pregnancy."

Landry straightens in his chair. His hand squeezes mine too hard. "What does that mean?" He rubs the tip of the scar that ends beneath his eye patch. "I know what the words mean, but what do you mean?"

The doctor's glasses glint from the overhead light. The glare hides any emotion she may feel. She lays a hand on my shoulder. "I'm sorry, Ms. LaCroix. You're not pregnant."

The lump in my throat lands in the pit of my stomach. Landry and I share a quick glance, and I shake my head. *This doesn't make any sense.* "But I peed on the stick. It came back with two lines. That means baby-on-board, right? How could there be no evidence of the baby on the ultrasound?" I tug on Landry's hand. "Is the test still in your pocket? Show her."

The doctor waves her hands. "I believe you. But those over-the-counter home pregnancy tests occasionally give a false positive. It's rare, but it does happen for a variety of reasons."

I run my hands across my sore breasts. "But what about my symptoms—no period, nausea, soreness—"

Landry blurts out, "She's gained like ten pounds."

A rush of heat rises in my chest. "Is it okay if I kick him, Dr. Mello?"

Landry crosses his legs and twists sideways in the chair. "Sorry, but it's true. You look good with the extra weight. I'm just saying—"

"That I'm fat." I struggle to regain control. To understand what I'm being told. "The weight gain itself doesn't bother me. It's the fact that you say I'm not pregnant. That doesn't make sense. Not that I'm upset about not being pregnant." I point my thumb in Landry's direction. "He was excited, but I was scared to death. Still, I had two whole days to get used to the idea of having a baby. Now to hear that I'm not…" *Saints, I'm rambling.*

Am I happy or sad? Both? I don't know what I'm supposed to think or feel right now.

Landry stares at me, stricken, like his whole world is falling apart around him.

I sigh. "How could this happen?"

Dr. Mello studies my face, like she's trying to gauge my emotional reactivity before laying anything more on a potentially unstable patient. "It's not common to get a false pregnancy result. Most are the result of faulty tests. There's also the possibility that this is a chemical pregnancy, in which case you miscarried the embryo prior to implantation. The hCG hormone would still be in your system. Have you had any spotting or cramps?"

"Not that I remember."

I'm really not pregnant. My fingers tingle.

"More than likely the test is at fault."

A cool rush of air fills my expanding lungs. The tight ball of anxiety in the pit of my stomach releases. "I did buy it at the Dollar General."

Dr. Mello pats my shoulder as she stands. "Next time, stop by my office, and I'll confirm it for you. Also, if you are actively trying to get pregnant, then I suggest you begin taking vitamins with folic acid."

I wrap the paper blanket around my waist and sit up. "No, we're not, doc. This was an accident. I'm on birth control, and he's wearing a condom every time, from now until we *both* decide we're ready to have kids. Right, Landry?"

He stares at me and then turns to the doctor with a silvery sheen to his eye. "So, she's really not pregnant?" Pointing at the ultrasound machine he says, "Are you sure that's not broken?" He really can't seem to wrap his head around the idea that we're not becoming unwed parents. At Dr. Mello's head shake, he slumps on his stool. His hands fist in his thick hair. "Damn."

I lean forward, careful to keep my ankles crossed, and I wrap my arms around his shoulders. His nose presses into the corner of my shoulder. I rub my hands up and down his back. "It's okay."

He shudders, then pries my fingers apart and stands up. "Yeah, it's fine."

Apparently for him, it's not. "Try to think of this as a good thing. We're not ready to be parents."

The doctor unplugs the machine and pushes it toward the door. "I'll leave you alone so Ms. LaCroix can get dressed."

"Thank you, Doctor." Once she leaves, I slide off the examining table and press tissues between my legs to dry myself, then throw them into the biohazard bin. Landry stands on the other side of the room with his arms crossed. He doesn't even look at my breasts when I shrug off the paper shirt and start to get dressed, a clear indication he's not handling this well. "Now that we're alone, tell me what happened."

"You tell me." He blows out a harsh breath. "Do you remember what happened after you went into Dena's room?"

His question keys open a locked vault in my mind. Memory rushes in. "Oh my God, Dena."

"Do you remember now?"

"Sophia had prepared for the ceremony before we arrived. She had a bundle of smoking herbs, and she ran it under my nose. It made my heady fuzzy." I rub my temples. "Then I went to Dena, and like the last time, I got sucked into her head when I touched her."

"Do you remember taking off your clothes?"

"What? No…Do you mean I was naked?" My voice wobbles. *Merciful heavens.* "Did anyone else see me besides Sophia and Magnolia? Ferdinand—"

He shakes his head. "What about once you were inside her head?"

I squeeze my eyes shut. "It was dark. I hid from Red while I searched for Dee." My heart thumps, and I grin. "I remember we pulled her out."

"Only because my sister took her place by sacrificing herself and Red for us."

Oh my God, Lainey shoved Red through the door to the other side. "She's gone?"

"Yeah, for good this time."

"But Magnolia never said—"

"A life for a life, Mala. Your aunt didn't help you out of the goodness of her heart. She had another plan in play when I burst into the room, and I think it had something to do with why you're no longer pregnant. I saw her put something on your stomach." His body shakes with pent-up emotion. His head turns, and his eye scorches my skin when his gaze touches my stomach. "I think she killed our baby."

Light-headed, I fall back against the table. "Wait a minute...what?"

My hands fall on my stomach, and I dig my fingers into my skin. The hollow emptiness I now feel makes sense, and the relief I felt moments ago vanishes with my confusion. A slow, burning fury builds because if our child was stolen...taken from us...then how do we get her back?

I won't believe she's dead. Better to not have existed at all.

"Mala—"

"Let's go." I pull on my jeans with jerky movements. This time, they button easily. I don't bother with my socks, just stuff them in a pocket and slip my feet into the tennis shoes.

Landry swallows. "Is that it? That's all you're going to say after hearing what Magnolia's done?"

I calmly set my hand on the door handle. "What am I supposed to say? Do you want me to cuss her ass out? She's not here, and I'm too exhausted to think about this right now. Let's go check on Dee."

"Who cares about Dena? Our baby's dead."

"I care. So do you." I throw open the door and breath in fresh air filled with the scent of bleach and antiseptic. My head clears. I can think again. Plan. "We lost the baby because we wanted to save Dena. We have no idea if the spell worked. Or if it was just a trick on Magnolia's part. And the only way to figure out what's going on is to gather the evidence and confront the source. That means finding Magnolia."

"Or Sophia."

"Why do you think she's suddenly on our side?"

He stares over my head, then shrugs. "I think her past has come back to haunt her. Maybe this time she wants to make a different choice."

I shuffle from the room like a bowlegged old lady. Even my evil aunt moves faster than I do. My insides ache. Landry catches up pretty quickly and hooks his arm around my waist. His steady presence infuses me with strength and allows me to put one foot in front of the other when all I want to do is curl up into a ball and cry.

Or go on a rampage of destruction that'll make the Hulk look like a sissy. I sniff, rubbing my hand across my dry eyes. It's far better to feed my helplessness into the fire pit of my anger. I can't do anything with despair. But anger…it consumes. Burns.

I stoke it higher.

My back straightens. I pull free of Landry and quicken my pace.

A spot of frigid air is my only warning. I try to flee behind the shield, but it lies in crumbled ruins within my head. Demolished, as if a sledgehammer has decimated the bricks I built over the course of the last few months, leaving me completely vulnerable to a spiritual attack. The skeletal hand shoves through the wall. Sharp fingertips score scratches down my arm as the ghost latches onto me. Contempt rolls through my body. I jerk free with a twist of my arm. My own fingers hook into claws, and I shred the wailing wraith into micro-thin filaments and whoosh it away with a wave.

Landry stares, mouth agape. "What did you do?"

Destroyed it. "It shouldn't have touched me." Guilt sours my stomach. "What happened after you came out of the trance?"

"I don't know. Last I remember, Pepper had come into the room. Ferdinand kept her back. She lost it when she saw what was happening. Not that I blame her. I've never seen anything so terrifying in my life..." He trails off as the elevator door opens on an expecting couple. We step aside and allow them to pass between us. The annoyed grimace on the woman's face makes my lips twitch, and I watch them until they reach the nurses' station.

"Are you coming?" Landry asks.

"Yeah." I step into the elevator and lean into Landry's side, needing to touch him. "Finish telling me what happened."

"When I came to, you were still unconscious. I didn't wait around to watch the drama."

My fingers trace my shrinking belly again. I can't seem to stop touching myself. Maybe there's a dirty joke in there somewhere, but I can't find the humor in it. The rounded contours are deflating, like a pinpricked balloon. In a few more hours, it'll be even flatter than before my alleged pregnancy.

"I'm scared," I whisper.

"Me too."

I usually approve of his honesty, but in this situation I would've preferred an "everything will be fine," even if we both know it's a lie.

The door to the long-term-care unit is open. The nurse's station and hallway are empty but for the crowd of hospital personnel, far more than just the ones who work in this unit, gathered in front of Dena's room. They stare inside in utter silence. Tears streak many of their faces. A heavy weight fills the air like right before a hurricane hits.

Landry and I rush forward, elbowing our way through the staff. Pepper and Dr. Estrada stand in front of Dena's bed, blocking our view. The doctor has his arm around Pepper as she sobs into her hands. My own eyes burn at the sight.

I freeze in the doorway, too afraid to go inside.

"What happened?" Landry asks, tugging my hand, and I stagger into the room. He touches the arm of a woman in scrubs. "Did she pass away?"

The nurse wipes her eyes. "No, the opposite."

"She woke up?" I grasp her arm. "Is that what you're saying? Dena woke up."

The woman gives a little squeal and wraps her arms around me. Her cry breaks whatever hold kept everyone still. Soon everyone's cheering. I've never heard anything like it. Or expected it, given their occupation. Maybe it's because most patients who have been declared brain dead don't wake up let alone sit up in bed with an impish grin on their face.

I rush forward and throw my arms around my cousin. "You're back."

"Did I go somewhere?" Dena asks, arms lifting to wrap around my waist. She hugs me back weakly. She still feels so frail that I'm afraid I'll break her. When my stomach brushes her, she pulls back. "Good grief, are you pregnant?"

"No," I say lightly, but my voice hitches. "I've been stress eating."

Her freckled nose scrunches. I never thought I'd see her do that again.

Dr. Estrada shoos away the crowd. "Okay, enough. All staff needs to get back to their assigned duties. Only immediate family can remain in the room. Everyone else can visit after she finishes with the battery of tests I'm about to run."

Landry grabs my hand. "Come on."

We wind through the lingering crowd. At the end of the hallway, there's a gurney being rolled from the room where Redford had been. A white sheet covers the body. I can't take my eyes off it. Especially since I know he's beneath it. I agonized about my decision. Tossed and turned nights on end, too scared to sleep, too afraid to make the wrong choice to do anything. I tried to mentally prepare myself for the soul-crushing guilt I'd feel at taking his life.

But all it takes is glancing over my shoulder to see Dena, animatedly talking with her mother, to remind me that the asshole brought this on himself. A life for a life. *Ding dong, Red's dead.* And I don't care.

"He brought it on himself," Landry says, reading my mind again. "He tried to kill us again. If Lainey—"

"They're not together. That door they went through sent them to different places. I could tell."

"Yeah? How?"

"I'm a witch. I know these things." I shrug. "If you don't believe me, then ask what's his name."

"He's been quiet since we came out. I might've lost him in the void."

"Do you hope you lost him?"

He rubs a finger across his scar. "I'm not so sure. I think we need him. We're not strong enough to go against Magnolia on our own, and he's the only lead we have on fighting the evil she's in cahoots with."

I give a slight grin at the way he says the word "cahoots." Then shiver.

"Let's go talk to Sophia."

The problem is we can't find her in the hospital. And upon going to the Robicheaux's, we discover she and Ferdinand have checked out of their hotel rooms. The rat bastards are on the run.

Chapter 24

Landry

Reevaluate & Regroup

Mala gives me sidelong glances during our walk from the B&B to the truck. Tension squares her shoulders, and her fists stay clenched. She holds herself like she thinks she'll have to stop me from going off and busting shit up. Her hypervigilence continues during the drive home. It would serve her right if I swerved toward the ditch.

Truth is, I'm too numb inside to dredge up the energy. Between watching Lainey sacrifice herself and finding out we played right into Magnolia's trap, I can barely function through the grief. What's worse is the fact that Mala's emotions swing on a pendulum. One moment she's on the verge of going to war, and the next, she acts like she doesn't give a shit.

Or if she does care, she doesn't show it. Even if she was never pregnant, I feel like I've got a giant hole in my heart. In two days, the baby had become real for me. I'd imagined her tiny face. Her black curls. I wondered if she'd have Mala's skin tone or a blending of hers and mine. I imagined her with Lainey's eyes—a beautiful sapphire blue. But I didn't really care what she looked like. Only that she was healthy. And that somehow I'd figure out how to stay alive long enough to meet her.

Now she's gone.

If what Mala said was true, Lainey and Red went to different places. I hope that wherever she is, she'll care for her niece until I get there.

I roll down the window, needing fresh air to clear my head of the morbid thoughts. I hate being depressed. It's a fucking waste of time and energy. What I should be doing is figuring out what happened in that room other than freeing Dena. I can't blame paranoia for skewing my perceptions. Innocent people don't pack up and vanish without a word.

Exhaust fumes mingle with the cinnamon scent of dying leaves and the rotting egg stink of stagnant water from the bayou. The trees have lost most of their fall leaves, leaving them naked to the chilly wind. So far, it hasn't gotten cold enough to bring out the sweaters. Soon.

I glance over at my girl. Wind blows through the crack in her own window, blowing her curls around her face. She stares back with glittering eyes and gives me a tight grin.

My gaze shifts back to the rutted road. "Are you doing okay?"

"I've been better." She leans forward to turn on the radio, scanning stations until she hits on Adele's "Set Fire to the Rain," and sings softly under her breath. Her hand steals out to settle on my leg. It's enough.

The tension in my shoulders relaxes. A light rain dusts the windows. I turn on the headlights because it's getting too dark to see the turnoff to Mala's place without them. She sighs. Her head slides over to rest on my shoulder, and I'm finally able to put aside my pain.

I was so excited about the idea of being a father that I never tried to see the situation from Mala's point of view. She must've been scared to death. The responsibility of caring for a life, holding it safe inside her body, all the while knowing that every decision, even simple things like drinking caffeine or eating nonorganic foods, could impact the baby's health must've been overwhelming.

Everything has been moving so fast the last few days. She never had the chance to process the news. Hell, I didn't either. Otherwise I would've felt the same fear and sense of responsibility she did. I'd been living a fantasy. But the reality is that Mala and I have gone from one near-death experience to another. I was delusional to think either of us was ready to have a kid.

I park the truck in the darkened driveway. Mala throws open the door and jumps out before I pull the keys from the ignition. The door slams, and she doesn't look back. I watch until she's inside and then I follow. She's sitting cross-legged on the sofa with her new laptop propped on the coffee table and her cell phone pressed to her ear.

"I need a favor," she says to whoever is on the line. I settle on the other end of the sofa and pretend like I'm not spying on her conversation. "Can you get access to the suitcase we left at the crime scene?" She tilts her head, holding the cell with her shoulder. "I know the suitcase itself is evidence, but not the contents." Her jaw ticks. "Tomorrow? But I need it tonight…Fine. Okay."

She tosses the phone onto the sofa with a grunt.

"Was that Deputy Dawg?" Her nod doesn't even trigger the normal flash of jealousy at her turning to my arch rival for a favor.

A tiny furrow forms between her eyes in the wake of my silence. "Aren't you curious what that was about?"

I shrug. "If you want me to know, then tell me."

Her lips thin into a stern line. "Sophia wanted me to have her suitcase for a reason. She said she keyed it specifically to my biometric magical signature, so it unlocks only for me."

Of course. Why ask the obvious? I still won't understand. "Did she say why?"

"She was afraid something bad would happen to her. She was trying to warn us about Magnolia without coming right out and snitching. Hell, maybe Magnolia put a spell on her so she couldn't talk about it, or she still felt conflicted due to her loyalty to my aunt. Whatever the case, she wanted to help, but I didn't take her seriously…"

"You were right not to trust her. She left." I'm too tired to figure out her hidden motives. I kick my right leg up on the cushions and slide it behind Mala's back, leaving the other on the ground. I lay my head on the sofa's arm and close my eye, annoyed by the tick under my eyelid. It started in the truck

She clears her throat. "Sophia talked about a Purple Emperor butterfly. How it's drawn to the dead." The keys clack as she types, hypnotic. She shakes my leg. "Hey, wake up."

I yawn. "I'm just resting my eye."

"You were snoring."

I grab the sofa's back and pull myself upright. My muscles feel tight, and I roll my shoulders until I get a loud crack. Mala winces. She hates the sound. Says it makes her think of breaking bones.

Mala buries her face in the crook of her arm. "Okay, check this out. Does it look familiar?" She hands the laptop to me. On the screen is an image of a butterfly on a toad carcass. *Apatura iris.*

I run my finger across the wings on the screen. "Is this the same type of butterfly I saw swarming over the bodies"—*and crawling inside your mouth*—"in the spirit trap?"

"Nope. Sophia said what we saw on the other side is its cousin—a soul eater." She places the laptop back on the coffee table. Her fingers fly faster and faster, pounding on the keys.

"Enough," I say, sliding it from beneath her hands. "You're gonna break it. And you refused to buy the warranty."

She throws herself against the backrest, kicking out with her foot. The table slides across the hardwood floor. "That's 'cause warranties are a waste of money. A total scam. God, I'm so stupid," she cries. "Why did I trust Magnolia? We knew she was working on a plan. I just didn't think…"

I slide across the cushion. "The whole pregnancy was hinky in the first place. We knew that."

"Then why didn't we stop her?"

I shake my head. She's saying the same things I've been thinking since we left the hospital. Only hearing them out loud makes me reevaluate how much control we had over this situation. "What could we do? We didn't know what she planned. Still don't."

"But the butterflies. The murders of those boys. It's all connected, Landry. I know it." She swivels to face me. "I feel so empty inside. Like a piece of my soul was stolen, eaten. Our baby's soul." Her red-rimmed eyes look as hard as obsidian.

I reach over and grab her by the hips and drag her onto my lap. "As someone whose soul is being eaten by a demon, I kinda know how you feel. Question is why?"

"Did what's his name come back? He keeps saying he wants to help. Maybe he knows what's going on."

"Are you here?" I squeeze my eye shut and probe the dark corner of my mind where the creature likes to hide. Only silence returns, and I shake my head. "Maybe Gaston knows something."

"Gaston, we need your help," Mala calls, head tilting as she listens for a response. She calls a few more times, then switches to "Mama. Help." We both scan the room and then look through the window. The rocking chairs remain still. "Mama, if you don't come right now, I'm having sexual intercourse with Landry on your new sofa."

"Well, if that doesn't get her to come running, I don't know what will," I say. But it doesn't work. The house gives off an unusually quiet aura. My arms tighten around Mala. "Guess we're alone."

Mala's chest hitches like she just held in a watery hiccup. "Good, because I wasn't joking about having sex. I need you."

Before my body has a chance to react to the idea that I'm finally going to get laid, her heavy weight melts in my arms as if her bones congeal, and I'm the only thing holding her together. Hot tears run down my neck as she burrows her face in the crook of my neck.

The rawness of her grief adds to mine. I can't hold it back anymore. I've suffered too much loss. Lainey and her baby. Mom. And the baby I'd somehow pinned all my hopes and dreams onto.

Now nothing's left, but this woman in my arms. She grounds me. Without her, I don't know where I would be now. Lainey's death and Mom's betrayal almost broke me. Mala's the one who put the pieces of my shattered heart together again.

She tips her head back. Her wet cheeks gleam. Her fingers release their hold on my shirt and slide up my neck to curl into my hair. She draws my face down and trails tiny kisses up my cheek to my eye, then shifts around to straddle my lap, planting both knees on the sofa.

My hands run over her shoulders, and I work the hair tie from her braid. Once loose, it only takes a few flicks to unravel her hair. I know better than to try and run my fingers through her curls. Instead I pull the mass over her shoulder. The chocolate-peppermint scent of her new conditioner fills my nose, triggering a craving deep inside.

I trace my fingers down the smooth column of her neck, marking the territory I want to taste. Her sigh warms my cheek and then her head tilts. "I love you so much," she whispers against my mouth.

My lips part, but I don't have a chance to speak as her kiss-eats my words. Her tongue searches for more, exploring the roof of my mouth with a hungry desperation that I echo. The sounds in the room fade, until all I'm aware of are the little moans she lets out as the kiss deepens.

Her hips tilt as she shifts her weight off her knees and settles back on my lap. I lean forward, unwilling to break the kiss until she lifts her T-shirt and forces me to. I crumple the soft fabric in my fist and yank it over her head. Her greedy lips capture mine again.

I rock forward, glad I've had enough practice to undo the clasp on her bra by touch. Her breasts spill free, and I groan when they rub against my T-shirt. I want to be skin to skin.

Mala tugs on my shirt. "Take it off."

She works on slipping her pants off while I remove my shirt. It takes some juggling so we don't topple off the sofa. At one point, I'm flat on my back with her lying on top of me while I kick off my pants. I can't resist taking her earlobe into my mouth. I roll her golden ball earring over my tongue and get a giggle. My lips twitch, but I stifle my chuckle at her reaction. Instead I nip her earlobe until she flails. My hand blocks her jerking knee, which almost ends our foreplay for the night, and moves to tickle the sensitive skin behind her knee cap. She squirms, rubbing against my chest. The friction increases the heat rushing down my body.

"You're not helping." She pouts, kicking the foot that still has her jeans and panties tangled around it before dropping them over the edge of the sofa.

I grab her ankle and jerk the jeans free. "But it's pretty funny. I tickle her one more time and then wrap my arms around her waist. I roll her sideways so she's safely sandwiched between me and the sofa's back. "I'm living on the edge." I grin, falling into her sparkling eyes. "One false move from you and I hit the floor."

"Not happening." Her leg hooks around my waist.

I run my hand down the smooth skin of her thigh. Muscles flex beneath my hand. Her breathing quickens. Her breasts are warm against my chest. In this position, I can't give them the attention they deserve. But a warm heat presses against me within easy reach of my probing fingers. Her hips arch toward my hand when my thumb grazes her clit.

Her head falls back when I insert a finger while still rubbing her with my thumb. *She's wet.* "Oh-oh, y-yes."

I press kisses up the arch of her neck. My fingers mimic her breathing, moving faster and faster as her climax builds. Her muscles tense around my finger.

Her head lifts from my mouth. "Oh…it's coming. H-hold on."

I hear a tearing sound. She has a condom wrapper between her teeth and spits the paper onto the floor. I rock back, teetering on the edge of the sofa while her warm hands roll the latex down my shaft.

Then she guides me to her opening, and I shove inside. Her lips part with her inhale as she relaxes the muscles, then tightens them. My dick throbs. Pulsing. She quivers.

Her leg tightens around me, holding me inside her, while I roll onto my back and settle more securely on the sofa. She wiggles, drawing a groan from me, and straddles my hips.

Her fingernails dig into my chest. I cup her ass as she rocks, setting the pace. Her hips do a swivel move that almost brings me over before she's ready. But she's close.

Her muscles spasm when she comes, squeezing around me. And I let go too. The release brings us crashing together like two freight trains colliding in a cascade of sparks and fire. I think she screams. Or maybe it's me.

Chapter 25

Mala

Everything Changes

A patch of sun shines through golden brown and reddish leaves, hitting my eyes. The lemony floral aroma from a magnolia tree combines with Landry's musk. That man's pheromones cause instant arousal. I could sniff him all day long. His even breathing doesn't change when I bury my face in his chest, savoring his unique scent, but his arms tighten around my body. The gentle thumps of his heartbeats lull me, and I drift on the verge of joining him in sleep. A nap would be the perfect end to our afternoon.

The muscles in my thighs and arms throb. It's nothing to the internal discomfort, but it's a good ache compared to how I felt after leaving the doctor's office. Landry filled the hollow emptiness I felt inside. Both the physical and emotional. He took my mind off of all the pain and fear by reminding me of the future we could have together. For this one moment, I'm content to lie in his arms and not worry about all we still have to face.

We needed this time to reconnect. Too much drama had us on the verge of mental collapse. Waking up beside him in a quiet house, without kids yelling about missing socks or someone hogging the bathroom, meant morning sex and cooking breakfast naked. We made pancakes and scrambled eggs to avoid grease burns. And fed each other across the table like any other sappy couple. Even a morning running errands in town didn't have the urgency of the day before. Everything was calm. Nobody tried to kill us while we were at the market buying groceries. When we dropped by the hospital to visit Dena, I didn't get bombarded by ghosts. Even getting kicked out of her room by her nurse because we were too loud seemed…normal.

I snuggle closer to Landry, wishing the blanket I brought for our picnic had a bit more padding. A rock presses into my hip, but I can't move my upper body. He holds on to me tightly as if, even in sleep, he's afraid to let me go. I run my foot up his leg, smiling at how his hair tickles my toes.

He groans, leg jerking.

"Are you awake?" I whisper.

"I am now." His eye cracks open to show the variegated shades of gray. Seeing me staring, his lips tip in a smile. "What are you thinking about?"

I tilt my head back. "How happy I am."

"Enjoying it while it lasts?" His hand trails up to brush the hair off my cheek.

"Don't ruin my happy fantasy with lopsided pessimism, Frog Prince." I lightly bite the fingertip he runs across my lips. "My new motto is: Enjoy the moment." *The future is already predestined.* I don't say the last part out loud, but he knows. I learned that truth when I couldn't save Mama. Nothing I did changed the outcome of her death vision. Part of me will always wonder if trying to change the future only makes the situation worse. Landry and I will either have a long, happy life together or we won't. I choose to believe that we will.

I pick a twig from his hair and twirl it between my fingers. The shadow falls across his high cheekbone. "I love this spot. I'm glad we decided to stop for a while."

His chest shakes from his chuckle. "Ironically, this is also Sophia's favorite spot."

"How so?"

He whispers in my ear. "She lost her virginity to Gaston here."

"Ew, seriously?" I look around with new eyes. Shade from the oak, the scent of wildflowers, and the coolness of the pond equal a magical place. I laugh. "I can't say that I blame them. I wonder how many of my ancestors made love in this very spot. Bet this clearing is stuffed full of sexual energy. That's probably why the area is still so green in fall."

"Except over there." Landry points toward the far side of the pond. The pond's the size of a football field in width and length. Not that I went to any games for comparison. But I imagine it's pretty large. When I fish, I tend to stick to the middle, never going past a certain point where I can't swim to shore if my boat springs a leak. I never paid much attention to the far bank.

"Wow, it's really dead over there." I follow his stare. The waist-high grass in the field is brown. Even the few trees appear skeletal, as if devoid of nutrients.

I pull myself from Landry's arms and sit up, squinting at the gleam of white in the grass. My heart thuds in recognition. I need to get closer to verify my suspicions, but…"Mother Mary, I think I found the second murder spot."

"Are you shitting me?" Landry sits up to stare across the water. "That dried-up piece of land is the place from your dream?"

"I remember at the time thinking it seemed familiar, but I didn't know why. It looks exactly like it did in the dream."

I push down the blanket and grab my hooded sweatshirt, shivering at the nip in the air as I pull it over my head, then grab my panties and jeans. "Okay, maybe not exactly, since the sky doesn't look like it's bleeding. Also there aren't any…"…*butterflies.*

My throat tickles, like wings brushing my trachea. I cover my mouth and cough. *Holy psychosomatic symptom.* Every time I think of those butterflies it feels like I'm about to cough up a hairball. I'm turning into a hypochondriac.

I clear my raw throat.

Landry stands with a groan, and I pause to appreciate the rippling muscles of his pecs and washboard abs as he stretches the kinks out of his lower back. He catches me drooling and gives me a wicked grin. "So, do you want me to play Watson to your Sherlock?"

My mouth snaps shut, and I shrug. Usually, I'd be all over this clue. But not today. *My perfect day.* "No, let's call in the sheriff's office to check it out."

He gives me an exaggerated double-take. "Who are you and what did you do with my girlfriend? Are you serious? We're out here already. Let's just row over there and confirm first so we don't look like idiots when they don't find your conveniently located crime scene."

"Hey, I said I *think* it's the crime scene."

"Relax, babe. Crazy shit happens in your world. It's not a question of would someone plant a bunch of murdered kids on your land, but why?" He pulls on his jeans and sweatshirt so fast that I don't have enough time to interpret the strange reluctance curling my toes in the dirt. He tugs on my hand. "Let's go."

I don't want to. "I have a bad feeling…" A cough doubles me over. Landry gives two hard thumps between my shoulder blades. I flinch away, waving my hand. "I'm okay. It's just allergies."

"Did you forget to take your medicine? I saw it in the kitchen cabinet by the sink."

No, I didn't. "I probably need to buy the nasal spray. The pills aren't cutting it anymore."

Landry plucks a purple lilac and waves it in my direction. "At least you can't complain to Maggie and Dee that I never give you flowers. I would if I could."

I sniff, slapping it away. "Flowers are synonymous with death. No thanks."

"Actually blasted earth is the symbol of death." He squints again at the brown grass across the pond, then shakes his head. He reaches *Daisy* first and unties the boat from the stump.

I drag my feet until I reach his side. At the water's edge, I still can't see anything definitive. I flick off a curl of dried paint from the bow, noting that *Daisy* needs a new paint job.

"Aren't you getting in?" Landry asks, holding out his hand.

I can't believe the role reversal going on here. Landry's pushing me to investigate. And I'm the one second-guessing the situation. I just can't shake the fear that something bad is about to happen. Maybe I'm finally growing up. I don't know if personally solving this mystery is worth any more pain or loss.

My toes curl in the dirt. "I left my shoes on the blanket. I should go get them."

Landry grabs my arm. "Let's get this over with. Didn't George say he was dropping Pepper off with Dad half an hour ago?"

"Yeah, she's pretty upset. Hopefully your dad will help her through the grieving process." I dig my heels into the mud, resisting his nudge toward the boat.

"I still can't believe Judd's dead." He squints at the sky, trying to look all innocent with his thick eyelashes, but I'm onto his manipulative tactics. "Did he seriously have a stroke?"

My chest tightens, and I grit my teeth against the swelling sympathy I feel every time I think about Judd. "George said he died the same way Madame Ruby did—a brain hemorrhage within twenty-four hours of possession. His doctor thinks the cause of death was a preexisting condition that triggered his psychotic behavior. It's not like an autopsy will reveal the truth—ghost-fried brain."

My sigh chokes off, and I clear my throat. "Now I feel sorry for him. He's really as much a victim as the boy in his trunk. He'll probably end up catching the blame for all of the murdered kids. He'll get written up in the history books alongside Dahmer, Bundy, and Rader, the BK killer."

Landry deals the next card with no shame. "And we both know the real murderer is still free."

I can't let him get away with killing a bunch of innocent kids. My throat closes, and I wheeze. Flutters tickle my throat, rising upward. I beat on my chest, trying to clear my airway of whatever feels lodged in it. I sway, dizzy from lack of air.

Landry doesn't slap my back this time, and I remember what he always says: If you're coughing, you're breathing. *Wrong.* Black spots dance in front of my eyes. The tickle moves across my tongue. Flutters, like wings brushing against the roof of my mouth, make my nose tingle. He wraps his arm around my waist, supporting me as I double over with my mouth hanging open and hack up a blue-black blob.

It plops onto the ground, and I gulp in air, blinking the tears from my eyes. My blurry vision clears, but I still can't believe what I coughed up. Not a major hunk of phlegm, but a…a fucking butterfly.

Blue wings, almost purple, open and close, drying in the breeze. I poke it with a finger while yanking on Landry's leg. "Oh my God, do you see it?"

"The fact that you puked up a live butterfly? Yeah, kind of hard to miss."

"I didn't puke…" The butterfly spreads its wings and lifts into the air. I swing my cupped hands to catch it, but I miss. It zigzags out over the water. *It's getting away.* "Follow that butterfly," I cry, afraid we'll lose sight of it. We can't. "It's a clue. Just like Sophia said."

Landry and I push *Daisy* off the bank and wade into the water. He grabs me by the waist and lifts me aboard, giving my ass a farewell pat, then climbs in. He grabs the oars while I pull my bird-watching binoculars from the storage compartment and I drop onto the bench at the back of the boat.

"Hurry, Landry." I use the binoculars to scan the area. It takes a bit to find the butterfly, mainly because I expected it to be halfway across the pond, not flying in lazy circles above the boat as if waiting for us to get in gear.

"Let's play it smart this time," he says. "We only get close enough to the bank to verify it's the murder scene. With Gaston God-knows-where and Sophia and Ferdinand squarely on Team Evil, we're screwed if we get stuck in another trap. We're not strong enough to break free on our own."

"We'll just get close enough to see if those white sticks are really the bones I saw in my dream." The butterfly still flutters through the air, buffeted by the breeze.

"Deal." Landry puts his back into his rowing, and it feels like *Daisy* skims across the water. All his muscles make him almost as good as having an engine.

I stare without blinking at the far bank. "This is our first real clue to find out what Magnolia is up to now that she's disappeared."

"You're preaching to the choir, babe. I'm with you on that." He lets out a puff of air, and I glance back to check on him. Sweat plasters his hair to his forehead and runs into his eye. "I blame her as much as Magnolia for losing the baby," he says, voice huskier with bitterness.

I bite my lip, still not convinced I was ever pregnant. But he is. If I'm wrong and I was pregnant then… "We can get her back."

The slight roll of his eye tells me he thinks I'm spouting crazy-talk.

I don't look away. "I've been thinking that if our baby's soul still exists on the other side, then she just needs us to make her another body to inhabit."

Landry sets his jaw, and the muscle flexes as he grinds his teeth. I shut up, since he's obviously not ready to hear my theory with an open mind. His grief's too raw. I'll just sound like I took the cuckoo-ca-choo train and succumbed to the insanity that plagues my matrilineal line. Besides, to be honest, I *really* don't want a baby right now. Someday, I will. As long as she's safe on the other side, in heaven with Lainey or whishing about wherever baby souls are kept, I can wait to meet her. Can't she cross over from the other side after we get married and are ready to start a family? Do we lose out on this particular soul if we don't get pregnant right now?

We've reached the middle of the pond. The hairs on my arms rise, and I rub the goose bumps that aren't from the cool air. "I think this is as far as we can go without crossing the spell."

Landry pulls the oars from the water. "I feel it too. Do you hear the hum in the air? It's like we're next to a live wire."

I put the binoculars to my eyes and focus on what is indeed a thigh bone sticking out of the dirt, glinting in the sunlight with the myriad blue and black wings of the butterflies crawling on it. Our own butterfly crosses the barrier with a bright spark of light to join its brethren.

I drop down on the bench, and the binoculars fall into a puddle of water at my feet. It takes a few seconds to pull myself together and tell Landry what I saw, following up with my impression of the barrier we don't dare cross. "It's like the spell caster somehow brought the otherworld and this world together," I say, staring at the shimmery blur in the air. "It reminds me of the Bad Place, where the ancestor spirits gather."

Landry nods. "Ferdinand explained that the veil is thinner in that spot so the spirits cross over with ease. It must be the same here. Of course you'd know all of this if you ever bothered to attend our training sessions."

Kind of wish I'd gone too. Maybe I would've figured out what's happening a long time ago. "What about entities trapped on the other side?"

His head tilts. "What are you thinking?"

"For things like ghosts, they're already part of both worlds, like Dena was and the girl I raised with Magnolia. Their spirits are tied to their physical bodies. But what about other entities…creatures like what's his name? It can't walk this earth without a physical host. It needed you."

"I died."

"Right. Unlike Judd and Ruby, who couldn't handle the pressure of having two souls inside their bodies, you crossed over to the other side. Somehow that allowed you to gain a passenger without your brain exploding when you came back."

I bite on my lip, working through all the things I've learned. "What if our earlier suspicions were right and Magnolia fixed a spell to trick my body into simulating a false pregnancy? She used my body to open a door to the other side for a new soul to cross over and enter me. But rather than a human soul finding a fetal host, what if the plan was for something else to enter me instead?"

Whoa, as crazy as that sounds, it feels right.

"Did I really just figure out Magnolia's nefarious plan simply by watching a soul-eating butterfly?"

From the expression on Landry's face, I think so.

He thumps the flat of the oar on the surface of the water, and I flinch at the loud *thwack*. "Everything that's happened has been a calculated plan stretching back who knows how long—at least as long ago as the hotel. Maybe even from the night when Magnolia spared my life and Dad's after Ms. Jasmine died."

Oh shit! I should've kept my mouth shut. He was already broken up about the false pregnancy. This makes the situation ten times worse. "I don't know how she did it, but yes, I think so."

Tension radiates from him in waves. "Your mother's death... Lainey?"

"I don't know. We need more answers. If we could just find Sophia."

Silence grows thick. He's gonna blow a gasket. Go on the warpath. Put himself in danger. I don't even think I can hold him back since I plan on being right by his side, kicking some old witch ass. "You stopped her at the hospital."

"Did I? We don't know that for sure. And what about next time?"

"When I get my hands on Magnolia..."

"You'll die," Landry says flatly, and I realize I muttered the last bit. "She's too powerful. We can't come straight at her. We'll have to blindside her."

I let Landry rest his arms by rowing back to shore. Instead of calling dispatch about what we've found, I call Bessie with our suspicions. She says she'll send out Andy and Rex to investigate based on an anonymous tip. That works. I'm glad I called her until she asks if I'm going to Aunt March's party. Like that's important.

Except she sounds excited and giddy when she says, "I have a date tonight, *cher*. The first since my husband died. It's time, right?"

"That's awesome, Bessie. I can't wait to meet him." I hang up, knowing I can't do anything but be there for her and cheer her on.

The walk from the pond to the Acker's place takes on a new urgency. George promised to drop off the contents of Sophia's suitcase when he brought Pepper home. If we're lucky, we'll have enough time to search for more answers to our questions before heading to the party.

I push through the trees, skirting the fence surrounding the Savoie cemetery. The shield around my thoughts dings, like someone's pressing their finger repeatedly against a doorbell, as the ghosts in this area pound against it, wanting me to let them in.

"Damn, they're acting crazy today," Landry says.

"I know." They're determined to break in. "I wonder why they're so agitated?"

"Do you want me to drop the wall to find out?"

"No! Don't." There are too many. He would be overwhelmed. I focus on him, blocking out the subliminal calls of the spirits. "Did the demon come back? Have you been able to tell it what happened?"

Landry brushes his fingers against the bark of a nearby tree, peeling off a strip and tossing it on the ground. "It's like when I first came back..." I finish his unsaid sentence: *From the dead*. "My muscles ache, as if it's stretching my skin. I feel it inside me, but quiet, gathering its energy."

"That sounds ominous."

He shrugs. "It warned me that we could both be swept across to the other side when you went to rescue Dena. When I heard you screaming, I didn't care what happened to me." His Adam's apple bobs as his swallows. I tense up, sensing he's working toward admitting something he doesn't think I'll want to hear.

He turns in my direction, arms crossing. A slight shiver causes him to hunch slightly. He avoids my gaze, staring in the vicinity of the tip of my nose. "Being on the other side was...hard. On both the creature and me. The whole time I fought the tug trying to draw me through that doorway, but when Lainey went through..." His eye flicks up, then drops again. "I almost went with her."

"What?" My feet tangle up, and I stumble on the step I take toward him. He grabs my arm, keeping me from falling, but I jerk away. Shock numbs my body as I process his words. Each one hits harder than the last. I can't believe what I'm hearing. It doesn't make sense. "Are you serious? You almost left me?" I close my eyes so I don't see the shame on his face. But even that's not enough because I still feel his eye burning a hole in my forehead. "No. Don't answer."

"Mala, I—"

"Shut up! Don't say another word." *He almost gave up on us.*

"But I didn't," his voice whispers in my mind.

"Give me a minute...I—" I'm still too shaken to look him in the eye. His words sent a chill deep into the pit of my stomach. I turn my back to him. *I need to process... This sucks. Hurts.* But I understand how he felt. I wish I didn't, which makes it even more frightening. Even I felt the call of the other side. If he hadn't come when he did, Dena and I would've been swept through that black-hole thing, like Magnolia had planned. With my soul sucked from my body, what would've taken its place? The darkness that lives under her skin?

Now that her plan has failed, what does she intend to do next? Because like Landry said earlier, she's playing a long game. Always one step ahead. And even though I think I've figured out plan A, she's got a plan B, C, and D ready to put in play.

Chapter 26

Landry

Battle Prep

I hate that Mala's thoughts come so randomly. I don't get the whole picture. I'm not even sure she's aware that I'm reading her mind. She never comments on it. Not that this new ability to connect telepathically with each other matters so much in the here and now. Her shoulders tremble. A rush of heat floods through my body. My feet move without conscious direction, crossing the distance between us.

My arms wrap around her waist from behind. She gasps, stiffening. I hug her to me, afraid if I let go she'll storm off without hearing everything I need to stay. I need her to understand what happened. What might happen again if I'm faced with a similar situation? The force almost got me. Only Lainey's intervention and my love for Mala and the baby kept me from being swept away.

Mala doesn't struggle. All the tension rushes from her body, and she wilts against my chest. Her head tilts back, and I press my cheek against hers. Her shaking hand reaches up to cup my face. "I know you wouldn't leave me on purpose," she whispers.

I release the breath I've been holding since I confessed, but my fear doesn't drain away. "Do you? Because I don't." My arms tighten. "If it means keeping you safe, I'll sacrifice almost anything. Including my life."

Mala's breath rushes out. "And I'd do the same for you." She twists in my arms and slaps her palms on my chest for emphasis, like I don't get how serious she is from the growl in her voice. "So in the future, don't go trying to play the martyr. If you do, we both die. Magnolia will win. And our ghosts will feel stupid for falling into her trap. The goal is survival. No matter what happens next. We draw on our love for one another and use it to fling back anything she throws at us."

I chuckle and press a kiss on the tip of her flaring nose. "Fierce words."

"It took me a long time to accept the fact that you love me. Even longer to figure out how I feel about you. You know how afraid I was of opening my heart. I don't think I could do it again if something happened to you." She lays her head on my chest. "I know it's cheesy, but you're my soul mate. Our fates are linked, Frog Prince. You're the person destined to be by my side in this life and the next. And no matter where you go, I promise I'll find you. Even if I have to cross over to the other side and drag you back."

The image of her wearing a holster of knives, a skimpy shirt, and cutoff jeans like Lara Croft pops into my head. Her juicy ass marches up to the gates of heaven and kicks them in like they're made of matchsticks.

A grin stretches my lips. "Holy shit, you'd do it too. You'd take out those chubby cherubs with their own harps."

A tiny frown creases her brow and her nose wrinkles. She cracks her knuckles against my chest. "I'll take out anyone and anything that gets in my way."

Love this girl. My laugh erupts so hard the muscles in my abdomen cramp. I release her to double over, rubbing my side. It would help ease the pain if I could stop laughing, but I can't contain the snorts and gasps for air. Tears run from my eye, and I wipe them on my sleeve.

A glance upward shows her lips twitching as she tries to fake a pout. Soon she gives up and smiles, saying, "You'd do the same for me."

"Of course," I say indignantly. "Think I've spent years pining for you to allow you to get away now? Not likely. Anyway, enough. I can't take any more of this destiny shit. I say from now on, we make our own."

"Yep, we're makin' our own rules."

I roll my eye and slap her pert little ass as she strides down the path. She squeaks and hops forward, rubbing the spot. If we had a bit more time to hide out from the real world, I'd take her against that tree. Well, maybe not that exact tree, since it's covered in poison ivy.

Before I can find another spot, the bushes up ahead rustle. Carl steps out from behind a tree, zipping his pants, and does a double take. His face flushes, but he rushes over, talking fast, "Hey, it's about time you got here. I've been waiting for an hour. My mom's at the house with George and Reverend Prince. She keeps crying, but I can't tell if she's happy or sad. She said Judd's dead, which sucks for her. I say he brought it on himself by being a prick."

Mala's dark eyes tilt down at the corners. "Carl, he was a human being."

He runs his fingers through his mop of blond hair. "Was he? He almost killed mom and he shot at you and Landry. Axle could've caught a stray bullet and been killed just like the dead kid George found in his trunk."

Now I'm scowling. "You're right. All of that happened."

Mala puts her hand on Carl's arm. "The doctor thinks Judd's behavior was caused by bleeding in his brain. That's what caused him to go crazy and ended up killing him."

"That's the official story," I say. "You should know the truth. Judd wasn't a bad person. He was possessed by a spirit. And it ended up killing him in the end."

Carl stares from Mala to me. "Then he didn't do all those things?"

"He did, but not of his own free will. I don't think," I say. "The problem is that just because Judd's dead doesn't mean there's no longer any danger. Whatever possessed him is still out there. So stay on guard. Protect your brothers."

Carl nods. His shoulders slump and then straighten as the weight of responsibility settles on them. "George is waiting for you at the house. Said to tell you he brought the stuff you asked for so hurry up. Seems the SO got an anonymous tip about there being another murder site on your land. They plan to search your property."

Mala and I quicken our pace to match Carl's. He doesn't comment on our silence in the face of his breaking news, too wrapped up in his own worries to care about ours.

"Mom said Dena woke up yesterday." His eyes cut toward Mala with a mingling of fear and awe. "Did you do it? Wake her up?" At her nod, he shakes his head. "What about Red?"

"He passed."

"You really killed him?"

The color drains from Mala's face.

I grab the kid by the arm. "She didn't kill him. He passed over to the other side. It was him or your sister."

Carl jerks his arm free. "I know. Don't get all pissy. I just wanted to be sure he wouldn't wake up and come after her again. I know he was torturing her."

"How do you know all that?" I ask.

His cheeks turn red. "I-I felt her…Dee. Maybe I stayed connected to both of you after I helped break Mala free from the spirit trap. When you and Mala went inside Dee's head, I was sucked in too. Not all the way. I still saw the real world. But I also watched your fight with Red, like I was watching a movie in my head."

He nods toward me. "I saw you holding onto Mala and Dena. And your sister grabbed Red and jumped through the sparkly hole. It seemed real, but I thought it couldn't be until I heard Dena woke up."

Mala presses her fingers against the bridge of her nose. "Shit, Landry. What have we done to him?"

"I'm a descendant of Gerard Savoie too." Carl throws his shoulders back with pride. "Magic runs in our blood."

"Ha. It's my LaCroix blood that's magic."

Carl steps up until they're nose-to-nose. "Obviously it's not. I saw what I saw."

Her voice rises. "You're another piece of collateral damage. We broke you."

"Stop treating me like a kid. I'm fifteen. A hundred years ago I'd be married with kids by now. Give me some credit for once. I kept your secret."

I shove in between them. "Enough. Stop arguing over something so stupid."

"She started it."

"Did not." Mala huffs and crosses her arms. "I'm just saying the magic comes from the matrilineal line of the family."

"Stop talking all smart."

Mala shakes her finger under his nose. "Well if you went to school, you'd—"

"I said enough!" I yell. Okay, they've reverted to five-year-olds. So much for giving Carl credit. "You're both right. My guess is that magic calls to magic. Just like Mala and I found each other, Mala's ancestor and Gerard Savoie were drawn together. He survived long enough to have kids. My guess is the only man who can survive a LaCroix woman has to have his own brand of magic. And patience. Lots and lots of it," I finish in a mutter that earns me dirty looks from both of them. They bicker all the way to the house. I give up on stopping them. They're having too much fun.

George meets us at the top of the staircase. He looks grumpy. "Lord, I could hear you fighting from inside. Keep your voices down. The rev just got Pepper to fall asleep." He points to Sophia's suitcase sitting at his feet. "Here's the stuff you asked for. I couldn't open the lock, so…" He runs his fingers through his hair, then, catching himself, crosses his arms. "There'd better be something in there to help us. Otherwise I'll lose my job when Bessie figures out that I 'borrowed' this from evidence. She's been on high alert since the knife was stolen."

"Did you ever figure out who took it?" Mala asks.

"According to the surveillance cameras and alarm code activation, the only person in the building at the time was Deputy Toussaint. What's really creepy is that, on the video, his face is blurred out, but everything else around him looks fine."

"What did Tank say?"

"That's the problem. He's MIA. His wife called the station this morning freaking out about him not coming home last night. We've put an APB out for him. Hopefully we can locate him before it's too late."

And he dies like Judd did.

None of us say this out loud, but I bet it's what we're all thinking. Tank's a good man with no earthly reason to steal the knife unless he fell victim to the same spirit that possessed Judd. Mala saw that shadow fly out of Judd's body when he hit the wall. She didn't see where it went afterward, but I bet that's when it entered Tank.

George rolls the suitcase toward Mala. She crouches at his feet and runs her fingertips over the combination lock. The locks pop open. She empties the contents of the suitcase onto the porch. Candles and glass bottles filled with strange liquids roll across the porch. A few leather sachets thump into a pile, along with several books so old I'm surprised they didn't turn to dust immediately after Mala opened the suitcase. The one I'm interested in is leather with a golden leaf on the cover.

I squat down beside her and reach for it, but Mala snatches it from my grasp. "My preciousss," she Gollum-hisses with a wicked gleam in her eyes. *Geek.*

"Is that a spell book?" I ask.

"I think so." She flips open a page. "It's handwritten. Isn't there's a word for what they call those?"

"Grimoire," George says. When we stare up at him, the tips of his ears turn red, and he shrugs. "Like I said before, I've been studying the occult ever since I learned about Mala's abilities. I thought having additional knowledge would come in handy."

"You're so cool, Georgie," Mala says with a grin. "I want to be just like my big brother when I grow up."

I won't admit it out loud, but so do I. She's right. He's smarter than us in more ways than I can count. I hope it's wisdom I'll learn with age. But I won't hold my breath. The truth is, Mala avoids anything magic-related like it's the plague. I trained with Ferdinand, but who knows whether I can believe anything he taught me. I've never cared for studying, so it didn't occur to me to research this stuff.

Carl uses our distraction to grab the book from Mala's hand. He scoots away from her wild swing and flips to a page bookmarked with a dried plant that instantly makes Mala sneeze three times in rapid succession.

"Hey, guys. It's translated into English." His freckled nose scrunches up the same way Dee's does. "Whoa, soul swapping. Is this a real thing? And what is a *loa*? Is that some kind of spirit guardian like Gaston?"

"Oh, I read about those too," George says. At our sidelong looks, he snaps, "Seriously guys, search engines are the most relevant invention of the modern age. You don't even have to go to the library to learn all kinds of useful shit. Sue me if I like to know what I'm dealing with."

His contempt for us mere mortals burns. *Whatever.* "Speak to us, O Wise One," I drawl.

George's jaw clenches at the sarcasm in my tone. "According to Wikipedia, the *loa* are intermediaries between God and mankind. Kind of like angels, only their followers worship them. And unlike angels, the *loa* answer their followers' prayers if given the proper tribute."

I whistle. "I'm impressed that you think enough of my cognitive skills to explain that with such big words. I feel smarter already for having understood all that."

If his face flames any hotter, it'll explode.

Mala tugs on my pant leg, and I back off. She takes the grimoire from Carl and points to an underlined passage. "I think this passage about the *loa* is what Sophia wanted us to see. Baron LaCroix and his twin brother, Baron Samedi, are considered to be two aspects of the God of Death. One is good. The other not so much." She taps her lips with a finger. "Do you think it's coincidental that I have the same last name as the God of Death?"

Suddenly something the creature said makes a wicked sort of sense. I tap my temple, wishing it would wake up and answer my questions. "When we were rescuing Dena, *he* said that 'the trap is set.' He also called Mala his descendant."

"Do you think he's like an ancestor spirit only more powerful?" she asks. "Like Gaston."

"Maybe if Gaston was a gazillion years old. My guess is ancestor spirits grow in power over time. He said he's a guard and his prisoner escaped. That's why he's inside my head. To trap the prisoner and bring it back."

"Well, if I escaped from prison, I'd do whatever it took not to go back," she says.

George nods. "Escaped felons are the most dangerous type for an officer to roll up on. They're desperate and paranoid because they've got nothing to lose and everything to gain. They'll take you out before you even realize they're wanted."

"Which is why we need something to counteract its plan," I say.

The dispatcher's voice comes over George's radio mike, and he steps aside to answer the call. "I've got to go. The FBI liaison should be arriving soon. Now that the feds are involved, we'll have better luck identifying the bodies."

Mala rolls a candle between her palms. "Will they keep the case open now that Judd's dead? We both know he's not the killer."

"Not unless they get new information from the bodies. The ones from the previous site were pretty burned. Plus they've got an open-and-shut case with Judd having the body in the car."

"Too convenient, right? The real killer planted the body and made sure Judd took the fall. That bastard is going to get away with this."

"But if we're lucky, he'll get one less victim," George says. "You've got a pile of spell books in front of you. I know this kind of magic isn't what you're used to. But see if there's some spell you can cast to help Tank. Please."

After he leaves, we camp out on the porch, studying the grimoire. I wish I could ask Sophia what to do. From her notes, we figure out that she had been researching two spells. The first spell allows a non-human entity, aka demon/angel/*loa* thingy, to jump from one body into another without killing the new host by removing the original host's soul—two souls occupying the same body means exploding brains. Case in point, Madame Ruby, Judd, and likely Deputy Toussaint if we don't find him before it's too late. The second spell counters the soul-swapping spell, allowing the original host to remain in its own body somehow.

Learning how to cast spells proves to be nap-inducing. B. O. R. I. N. G. Carl gives up after half an hour and goes inside to play Grand

Theft Auto with Dad. I crap out after an hour. Squinting at Sophia's dainty script has my good eye burning with pain. I want to use an ice cream scoop to remove it. Instead of research, I use my time prepping the ingredients for the spell Mala decides to be the one most likely to save Tank's life.

We move inside when we need to use the kitchen. Mala sits at the table with the spell book and sachets of herbs. She bites on the tip of her tongue as she runs her finger down the page, then meticulously mixes the ingredients from the leather bags into a bowl, using Dena's glass measuring cups.

Daryl sits across from her with twitching hands. He doesn't know exactly what she's concocting since we all agreed that none of the other kids needed to know. But the scientist in him wants to take over. "Are you sure you don't need help?" he asks for the fifth time.

Mala points to the door. "Get out."

"But—"

"I told you if you asked one more time you're out. Go before I call the rev."

"You need to steep the leaves."

"Landry," she snaps. I usher him to the door.

It's only when I'm sprinkling dried plants into the pot that I realize I've smelled this minty scent before.

"Hey, babe, I think this is that cleanse Sophia wanted you to drink."

Her nose wrinkles. "Ew, not hardly."

"You're not pregnant. There's no reason not to drink it now."

"I can't risk breaking my connection to the murderer. Not yet." She sprinkles a handful of herbs into the pot and stirs it. "This batch holds enough for two doses. You've already taken yours so you're protected. That makes one for Tank, and later, one for me."

I glance at the clock over the door. "Let's wrap this up or you won't have time to get beautified for the party."

She brushes a sweaty strand of hair off her forehead. "Damn, I knew I should've researched an invisibility spell. Or better yet, an amnesia one. Do you think this will be horribly awkward?"

"The odds are not in your favor."

"They rarely are." She sighs. "Okay, I never thought I'd ever have to do this, but I guess it's time to introduce my boyfriend to my dad. Hopefully he's not the type to pull out the shotgun."

I stir the pot, literally and figuratively. "Does that mean I should or shouldn't ask him for your hand in marriage tonight?"

Her nostrils flare. Her mouth opens, ready to blister my hide, judging by her expression, but a booming voice from behind causes her to choke on her words.

"About time the two of you decided to get hitched," Dad says. He pats Mala's shoulder, and she cringes. "Don't worry, I'll run interference if G.D. gets out of line."

Chapter 27

Mala

Party On

Colorful paper lanterns line the sidewalk leading from the driveway to the front door of Aunt March's mansion. Only a short walk will get me there. Landry even squeezes my hand, urging me forward, but my feet won't budge. The spiked heels pinch, and my toes cuss me out for the torture I'm putting them through. I order myself to step onto the sidewalk, again, using my best threatening tone. Nothing. It's now official. I'm the biggest coward this side of the Mississippi.

My sour stomach gurgles, and I press my free hand against my flattening belly. The majority of the pregnancy symptoms began to fade once the doctor said I wasn't expecting. The tender breasts, exhaustion—gone. The only things left are the stupid recurring bouts of nausea flaring up throughout the day.

Landry thinks I've stressed myself out about tonight's party, and he's probably right. The nasty herbal tea Reverend Prince ordered me to drink to settle my stomach only made the queasiness worse, so Landry left a glass of Alka-Seltzer for me on the counter, but I forgot to down it before leaving the house. That's his fault. Not mine.

He kept rushing me while I got dressed, saying if I didn't hurry we'd be late. Bull. It's not like the party would be over if we didn't get there the minute it started. I guess he figured, the longer I delayed, the more likely I'd flake on the opportunity of bonding with dear old dad and family.

My grip on Landry's hand tightens. He doesn't even complain about it being sweaty. I glance up at him. Damn, he's sexy. His steel-gray suit and black shirt compliment his thickly lashed eye and gel-tamed hair. The patch gives him a roguish air, which is only compounded by his cocky grin.

I bask in the warmth and security he brings. If he's uncomfortable, it doesn't show.

"Are you ready?" I ask.

"I am," he says. "Let's go give them hell."

My laugh bursts out. Leave it to him to know the right thing to say to unstick my feet and get me moving. We pass the lanterns bobbing in the wind. Shadows born from their light fall across the path. Landry sticks to my side, and I move my hand to the crook of his arm. The main house beckons, sending music and laughter in our direction. More lanterns hang from the rafters of the wide veranda. Citronella candles keep away any mosquitoes still lingering this time of year.

I shift my jacket across my arm and run my hand down the flowing fabric of my new dress. I saw the shimmering cobalt confection

of lushness in the window of the Garland Rose, a high-dollar bou-
tique downtown, and immediately thought, *Mine*.

I've never had the funds to do more than window shop in the
past, and the majority of my clothing came from thrift stores. Guilt
niggled at spending so much for a dress I'd probably never have the
opportunity to wear, but I broke into Mama's insurance fund cash
and bought it anyway. I'm so glad I splurged. I may not be a wanted
child, but tonight I refuse to fall into anyone's preconceived notions
that I'm poor trash.

Aunt March waits at the front door with a huge smile, and her
eyes light up with joy. Thank God I didn't flake on her. Her heart
would've been broken over something as ridiculous as being terrified
of my father's reaction at seeing me. Or rather, his wife's—George's
cheated-on mother. She has a right to be angry. But not to hate me.
It's not like I asked to be born. For George's and his mother's sake,
I hope everything goes well. I feel bad for both of them. It must
feel like the very fabric of their reality has been shredded. I can em-
pathize, since it feels the same for me.

As far as my bio-dad, well, I'm trying my best to deal with my
abandonment issues by not getting my hopes up or caring about
him. George Dubois Sr. has known about my existence since Mama
told him she was pregnant. He's had plenty of time to adjust to the
notion of his fatherhood, but he chose to ignore me. Maybe I'll just
ignore him right back.

My grip on Landry's arm tightens when we climb the stairs. Neither of us has the best balance tonight, what with his shoddy depth
perception and my infernal high heels. What the hell was I thinking? Oh, right. How sexy they look with this dress and the look of
hunger in Landry's eye when he first saw me in them. Stupid vanity.

Ms. March's hands flutter when I walk up to her. Like she doesn't know what to do with them. I take them in mine, careful not to squeeze too tight, then lean forward and press a kiss to her baby-soft, powered cheek. I inhale her scent, letting her familiarity soothe my anxiety.

"Happy birthday, Aunt March," I whisper into her ear.

With a low cry, she pulls her hands free and hugs me. The hug cuts off my oxygen supply, but I don't care. It feels good to be in her arms. "Welcome home, sweetheart."

This, right now, makes up for all the years of loneliness. *I have a family.* Hell, the thought brings tears to my eyes. I'm going to look like a drowned raccoon if I don't get ahold of myself. It took fifteen minutes to get the smoky eye shadow applied just right.

Aunt March pulls free to give me the once-over, and I see tears standing in her eyes. I guess getting overly emotional is genetic. She sniffs and manages a watery smile. "My, don't you look beautiful. I love what you've done with your hair. How long did it take to straighten it?"

A blush rises, and I fan my heated cheeks. "Oh, you're embarrassing me." I nudge Landry in the side with my elbow. "He's the one who worked the straightening iron. I wouldn't have bothered, but he wanted to see what it would look like without the curls. I don't see what all the fuss is about."

"Your niece is just pretending to be flustered, Ms. Dubois," Landry says, winking at Aunt March, who titters. "She knows she's gorgeous. And anyone who thinks otherwise is a fool." His arm wraps protectively around my waist, and he hugs me against his side. It takes a minute for me to realize his statement isn't directed to Aunt March, but to the man who has come up behind her.

George Dubois Sr., my bio-dad, stands in the doorway. His dark eyes start at the soles of my now embarrassingly high heels, then travel upward. His closed expression leaves me guessing about what he's thinking. My insecurity sends my pulse rate soaring. Thoughts pop in my head. All of them of the negative variety: *Why would he be happy to see me? He didn't want me. Never acknowledged the witch's daughter as his out of shame. He probably thinks I turned out as messed up as Mama. I never should've worn these stupid hooker heels. And this dress…it's too tight. Makes me look like I'm about to hit a corner and turn tricks.*

Stop it! Stop. I can't do this to myself. *I know who I am.*

My shoulders straighten. The warmth of Landry's body smothers the cold doubt of my father's rejection. *I'm not alone. Or unloved. I am wanted.*

The eyes of my father strike me as being familiar. I puzzle over how weird it feels to gaze into their inky depths, until it hits that they're identical to the ones I see in the mirror every day—the same almond shape with thick lashes. Once I pick out that feature, I start looking for others. I have his nose. Powerful eyebrows. Man, why couldn't I have gotten Mama's dainty brows instead? Whatever.

The silence stretches…too long. I force myself not to shift my stance. Or dry my hands on the hem of my jacket. Can't let him see I'm sweating if he's deliberately trying to intimidate me. Should I say something first? What's the protocol for officially speaking to one's father for the first time? I'm mean, we chatted at Lainey's funeral—well, he mostly grunted in my direction—but I didn't know who he was then. So it doesn't really count.

Ugh, I hate this.

Landry's arm tightens. "Mr. Dubois, it's a pleasure to see you again."

It takes a heartbeat longer for him to shift his gaze from me to Landry. He nods and thrusts out a hand for Landry to shake. Why couldn't he have done that for me instead of staring like I'm some ten-foot-tall, blue-skinned alien?

"Likewise," he says giving it a single pump, and then his gaze shifts to me again. His outstretched hand shifts in my direction. "Malaise..."

My heart races, and I feel lightheaded. Now I'm scared to touch him. My own father and I want to run. How sad is that? You'd think I would've learned to be careful what I wished for after turning Clarisse into Humpty Dumpty—bald-headed and cracked. My wishes have the same unpredictability factor as using a wish granted by a genie trapped in a bottle.

I release Landry and reach out like I'm petting a wild animal that might bite. Our fingertips brush and then slide around each other's wet palms. That's when it hits. He's as nervous as I am. Only he's better at hiding it. My lips lift. His answering smile seems as strained as mine, but they're genuine. "Good evening, Mr. Dubois."

His fingers spasm when I say his name. Did he expect me to call him Dad? Not happening. Not yet.

Reverend Prince's booming voice comes from behind. "Oh good, I'm not too late."

I jerk free of my father's grip. A flicker of what might be disappointment passes through his eyes before they look in the rev's direction. His shaky smile turns into a full grin. "I see you come bearing gifts. Bushmills?"

Landry and I shift aside when the rev thrusts a paper bag between us into my father's hands. "Of course," the rev says, completing a slick maneuver that leaves him standing between us. He drapes an arm over our shoulders, so we're enveloped by his open-armed hug. For the first time in the last five minutes, I can breathe. Then he says, "Thanks for inviting the kids to the party, G.D. It's about time the families get together. Schedule some time next week for us to sit down and hammer out their wedding details. If we leave the planning up to them, they'll sneak off to city hall and you'll never get to walk your daughter down the aisle."

Kill me now.

Like he didn't just detonate a bomb in the middle of our group, he pats me and Landry on the shoulders, then moves around us to take Aunt March's hand. "Marchie, you look radiant." He presses a kiss to the back of her hand. "How are you, my dear?"

Landry and I share a…uh, totally horrified grimace. Which only gets worse when Aunt March flushes and giggles like a school girl. When she sees me watching, she shrugs. "I have a bit of a reputation you might not know about. For half the men in town from my generation, I'm the one who got away."

"My first love," Reverend Prince says. He shakes his head. "I never had a chance. Marchie only saw me as her baby brother's friend."

Aunt March hooks her elbow through mine. "Come on, the birthday girl has been away from the festivities too long. The other guests must be wondering where I am. Have you thought about what colors you want for the wedding? Do you plan on a church or an outside ceremony?"

"Aunt March, I haven't—"

"We can always have it here. It would be beautiful in the garden."

Dazed and unable to get a word in as she prattles on, I follow her inside. I drop off my jacket with the coat checker and follow her down the long hallway to the crowded ballroom. She waves in the direction of the bartender. "G.D., Landry, why don't you go get drinks for your ladies? I'll have a rum and coke. Mala?"

"Iced tea." At my father's quirked eyebrow, I stiffen. What? Does he think I'm a booze whore like Mama? My mouth opens to tell him to fuck off, but Landry runs a hand down my back, and I catch myself, saying instead, "I'm the designated driver."

"Mala's not much of a drinker," Landry says.

My father nods. "Neither am I."

Once again, he surprises me. I need to get myself under control. All of my resentment keeps bubbling to the surface, spawning negative thoughts that multiply like gremlins in my head. I keep expecting the worst from him, but it's really me who's the problem. I don't deserve to keep beating myself up, or thinking badly of Mama. She did the best she could under the circumstances. Maybe things would've been different for us if my father had helped her.

I don't know. It's too late to find out.

The men head toward the bar, and Aunt March pats my arm. "I'm sorry to leave you alone, but I need to go have a chat with the caterer about the pecan pie. Tell G.D. I'll be right back."

Before I can say I'll go with her, I'm alone. Using my wallflower status to full advantage, I hide in a corner and scan the room. It's packed full of Aunt March's friends. Reverend Shane and his wife, Molly, who looks fabulous after losing most of her pregnancy weight, stand by the buffet table chatting with Mable Grant. My old teacher nibbles on a jumbo shrimp with a pair of false chompers. George and Isabel stand in the far corner of the room by the balcony with his mother. I plan to stay as far away from them as possible. Mrs. Dubois and Izzy are the last two women I want to run into tonight.

Food is piled on the buffet table. It's as informal a meal as Georgie said, but I'm glad I splurged on the dress. I would've been out of place if I'd come in jeans and a T-shirt. Even the business attire I dressed in while interning at the sheriff's office would look dirty-dowdy next to the fire-engine red dress worn by the beautiful woman with glowing mahogany skin and natural-styled curls halo-ing her head.

Bessie glides across the floor in my direction, and I actually forget how to breathe for the few seconds it takes to recognize her. My sur-rogate mom's glowing. I've never seen her so beautiful. And I bet it has to do with the man holding on to her arm.

Normal Ferdinand still has the ability to make my mind do the occasional wonky dance. Sir Hotness' gorgeousness in a navy suit and teal shirt almost stops my heart. No man should be so pretty. Now stick the two of them together and I feel like paparazzi should be screaming for interviews and cameras should be flashing as they stroll down a red carpet.

Bessie swoops in to pull me into a tight hug. *"Como se va?"*

"I'm doing just fine, but obviously not as good as you," I whisper into her ear.

Bessie, who rarely shows her emotions, giggles. She steps back to Ferdinand's side, and when he places a hand possessively against the middle of her back, her eyes glaze. The air tingles. Is he using a glamour spell on her? Or is it his natural charisma that has Bessie so giddy?

A cold chill rolls down my spine. "I thought you went back to

New Orleans with Aunt Magnolia. Why didn't you answer our phone calls? We needed your help."

His white teeth gleam. "I had other business to attend to. As you can see, I've returned."

Bessie lightly touches his chest. "I talked him into coming with me tonight."

The hairs on my arms rise, and I rub them.

Landry and Georgie thread around the sofa to reach us. I look for my father, but he and his son decided to exchange their chaperoning roles since he's over by the balcony handing his wife and Isabel their drinks. Landry presses my glass of iced tea into my hand, but his eye never leaves Ferdinand. Does he sense the disturbance in the Force too?

"So this is the date you've been obsessing over, Ferdi?" Landry finally blurts out, waving his hand over Bessie, and I gasp, elbowing his side to shut him up before he inserts his foot any further into his mouth.

"She is." Ferdinand's the master of infusing a lot of meaning into few words.

Basically he managed to tell Bessie, in two words, how beautiful she is and that he's proud to be with her.

"Why didn't you say so earlier?" Landry says. "If we'd known, we could've made plans to drive in together."

I close my eyes and sigh. "Obviously they wanted to spend time alone together, Landry."

His lip quirks. "Communication is key to any relationship. Disappearing without a word the way he did, I got worried that he was still pissed at the punch I threw at him. But see, not a mark on him. He's perfectly fine."

"I am."

"And how is Magnolia? Mala and I really need to speak with her about what happened yesterday."

Ferdinand's eyes glitter. "I'm sure you'll get the opportunity to, since she still has plans for you both."

I swallow hard, pinching Landry's arm. I totally get the reason for his passive-aggressive questioning, but continuing in this manner won't get the result he wants. Ferdinand's too slick. Why I didn't see it before and focus all of my ire on Sophia, I don't know.

Bessie stares between the guys, not befuddled enough to miss the underlying tension and threat in their clipped voices. "Ferdinand, how about if we go grab a plate and find someplace quiet to eat?" she says, nudging his arm.

This doesn't feel right. I need to stop her from leaving with him. But how? I need a plan, but Ferdinand isn't giving me time to come up with a plausible excuse.

He glares at Landry, then tears his gaze free. "I like that idea," he tells Bessie but his stare moves back in our direction, focusing not on Landry but me. "Don't worry, I'll take good care of Elizabeth. We have a lot in common."

Liar... His eyes narrow. *Damn mind reader. Hear this, Ferdinand. If you hurt Bessie, you're dead.*

His lips twist in a smirk. *Asshole.*

My stomach cramps, and I cry out, doubling over.

George jumps into big brother mode and grabs my arm. "Are you okay?" I'd forgotten about him. He lurks well when he wants to, like a spider hiding in a corner waiting for a fly.

Now both of my guys hold me upright. I flutter my hands. "I'm okay. I ju— Ouch—" The cramps would've dropped me to my knees if I they weren't holding me.

"Is it the baby?" George cries, totally panicked, and I want to curl into a ball and die. Why didn't we tell him about the false positive this afternoon?

Bessie's eyes widen with each word. "Oh my God, you're pregnant."

"No, I'm—"

"What!" Reverend Prince says, and I spin around to see him. Only he's not alone. My dad, his wife, Isabel, and Aunt March all stand behind us. They heard every blurted word. I've been thinking it all night, but please…someone put me out of my misery and kill me. Now.

My stomach cramps, and I breathe through the pain. "Excuse me, I need to run to the ladies' room before I ruin my new dress." *Oh merciful heavens, I just announced the fact that I'm about to poop myself.*

Landry can deal with the false-pregnancy business however the hell he wants to. I'm out. Before they have a chance to protest, I'm winding through the crowd. Is this my worst nightmare? No, not even close. But of all the things that I imagined going wrong tonight, an acute diarrhea attack, followed by George blabbing my personal business to my whole family, wasn't even on the list.

Oh God, Reverend Prince will kill Landry. And if my father has a paternal bone in his body, my boyfriend's DOA. The only thing I can hope is that the man really doesn't give a lick about me.

Chapter 28

Landry

Who Must Be Destroyed

Deputy Dawg strikes again. George chases after Mala when she races from the room, leaving me surrounded by our shocked family. If he'd stayed within punching distance, I would've laid his ass out. Stupid bastard can't keep his mouth shut. Tension flares. All everyone needs are pitchforks to stab in my direction and the image of the old-fashion peasant mob will be complete. Unfortunately, I am He Who Must Be Destroyed in this scenario.

I back up, waving my hands. "She's not pregnant!" I shout, trying to be heard, but they're all screeching like pissed-off blue jays.

Dad and Mala's father are arguing. Ms. March wears a dazed, happy expression and rocks on her heels singing "Happy birthday to me." Bessie runs a hand down her hip and comes up empty since she left her gun at home. Ferdinand just wears a smug smile like he instigated the whole thing and is enjoying the chaos. None of them are paying attention to me so I edge toward the door.

Dad grabs my shoulders, fingers gripping on like a vice, and I'm stopped short. "How did this happen?"

My mouth opens, but Ms. March elbows him. "The same way you and Theresa made your children. Don't tell me you've gotten too old to remember how pleasurable S-E-X is at that age? It's still pretty good at fifty with the right partner." She laughs at the shock on Dad's face, and then she turns to me. "Have you decided on a wedding date yet?"

"We're not getting married right now."

Mr. Dubois steps forward. "The hell you're not, if you got my daughter pregnant."

Well crap, now he decides to be a parent. "It's not that I don't want to marry your daughter; it's that she wants to wait until she's finished with college." His mouth opens like he wants to argue, but I cut him off. "Here's an unsolicited piece of advice to help you survive the father-daughter bonding process. As someone who loves your daughter, even her flaws, know this: Mala LaCroix doesn't take orders well. Neither do I," I say, addressing this last bit to Dad. Not that he's paying attention.

I love him. I respect his beliefs, but I don't share all of them. And I'm damn tired of sneaking off to the shed to be with my girl. The only good thing about this mess is that Dad's forced to admit he knows Mala and I are sexually intimate. He'll have to accept it.

"Reverend Shane, get over here," Dad yells, waving at the young preacher who took over his church. "We'll perform the wedding ceremony right now. Why wait? Obviously the kids didn't. If they want to act like adults, then they need to face the consequences as adults."

I can't handle this anymore. I leap onto the sofa and raise my hands into the air. "Quiet! Everyone listen. I have an announcement. Malaise Jean Marie LaCroix is not pregnant. I repeat. *Not.* Pregnant."

Silence follows. Damn, I should've done that ten minutes ago instead of trying to ride it out. 'Cause that didn't work. Mob mentality's no joke.

Bessie scowls. "Then why was George asking if the baby was all right? He thought she was pregnant. I don't see him lying."

My ears heat. "We had a scare. That's all. The OBGYN confirmed that we're not pregnant." I raise my hand. "Promise."

My gaze goes to Ferdinand. He doesn't seem surprised even though he was one of the first to congratulate me on the pregnancy. What did Magnolia do to us?

The lights in the crystal chandelier over the dining room table flicker. A loud *crack* shakes the walls, and sparks light up the room. I jump from the sofa, ducking. Ms. March shrieks and wilts against my side. In the silence that follows, thumps trailed by heavy footsteps come from the direction of the front door.

Ms. March pushes off my shoulder and fluffs her hair. "I'm so sorry, Landry. That startled me."

"It's okay…" I trail off. The thumps continue their slow progress. Dread grows within me with each step. The air feels heavy, steamy. It's hard to breath. The hairs on my arms and the back of my neck stand up. But it's not just body hair. The hair on everyone's head rises until the strands float in the static-laden air.

Isabel points to George's mother's hair and laughs. "This is so weird."

Ms. March runs her hand over her brother's head. "I knew I should've had balloons for the party."

Nothing about this seems funny. Dad doesn't think so either. He senses that something's off too. The pressure in the room grows another level. The steady beats pause outside the door, and a shadow falls across the threshold. The lights in the chandelier flicker again, then another bursts.

Ferdinand stares from me to Bessie. "Get down," he yells, then grabs her and drags her behind the high-backed sofa. "Earthquake. Everyone take cover."

The walls begin to shake, and the floor bows upward like a tidal wave is rolling the foundation. A heavy-framed picture crashes to the ground, almost hitting Isabel. She screams and throws her arms around Mrs. Dubois. They crouch down with their arms over their head. The crash and tinkle of breaking glass turns me around in time to see the champagne fountain spill over the side of the table in an amber waterfall. Another tremor rocks the table, but it doesn't topple. Buffet trays filled with food crash to the floor.

It's one hell of an earthquake, but it's not natural. I don't know what's going on but Ferdinand does. He called out the warning and dove for cover before the house started rocking. I grab Ms. March and Mr. Dubois by the arms and shove them down, shouting, "Get under the table."

We'll be protected from falling debris under there. Dad has George's mom and Isabel crawling in the right direction. Part of me wants to search for Mala, but the floor rocks again. I have to trust that she's found cover. If I don't and I leave the safety of the table, I'll be as big of a fool as some of the guests who are still standing around like walking targets. Maybe they can't comprehend they're in danger, but I do. It's totally natural selection in action.

A final thump from the hall. The tremor stops. And as if we're all controlled by a hive mind-set, we pause whatever it is we're doing and turn toward the door.

Magnolia LaCroix enters the room with a *bang*. All of the remaining lightbulbs in the crystal chandelier overhead explode. Those people still on their feet raise their arms over their heads and drop to avoid the falling glass and sparks. The pressure in the room shifts, the house inhales, and the windows implode. Shards of glass fly into the room.

Reverend Shane pulls his wife into his arms and turns his back to the balcony door. A spear of glass stabs him between his shoulder blades. Blood shoots from his mouth, drenching his wife's face. Molly screams, trying to hold him upright, but he's too heavy. He collapses on top of her, protecting her as more slivers of glass fall across his back. An old woman already lies on the ground. Her hand clutches her heart as she stares sightlessly at the ceiling.

Magnolia ignores the chaos. She holds onto Etienne's arm as he leads her over to a leather chair, brushes the glass off, and helps ease her into it. The old woman fits in that seat. With her silver braid wrapped around her head the way Princess Leia's was in *The Empire Strikes Back*, she appears every inch the queen.

Then she waves her cane like it's a magic staff.

Candlewicks in the sconces on the walls flicker and light, filling the blood-splattered room with a golden glow. "Someone shut that woman up before I rip out her tongue," Magnolia snaps, pointing to Molly as she keens from beneath her husband's body.

Ms. March sticks her head from beneath the table after a quick glance at the ceiling. "Who are you? Why are you in my home?"

"Ah, the birthday girl." Magnolia claps her hands. "Gift."

Etienne pulls a velvet-wrapped box from his pocket and holds it out to Ms. March, who crawls from safety, ignoring my whispered plea to stop. Her gaze shifts from the gift to the destruction all around her.

Etienne doesn't react to Ms. March's refusal of the gift. He just stands there holding it out to her. His filmy, dead-eyed gaze tracks her as she moves closer to Magnolia.

"Do I know you?" Ms. March asks.

Magnolia gives her a black-gummed smile. "I've been planning for this night for a long time. It's the perfect time for Mala's maternal side of the family to meet her father's." She cranes her long neck. "Speaking of, where is he?"

"If you're looking for me, I'm right here." I crawl from beneath the table.

Magnolia's eyes narrow. "Not you. Mala's father." Her hand sweeps out like she's swatting a mosquito. The gust of air she created picks me up and hurls me against the wall. My head cracks the plaster and I fall, bouncing off the sofa to roll onto the floor. Dazed, I lay for a minute, unable to move.

Then I hear Dad screaming, and I push up on my knees.

He lies at Magnolia's feet like he rushed her. She's got him doubled over with his knees curled into his chest. The pain in his shrieks stabs into my core. Ms. March kneels on the ground with her hands covering her ears as she rocks back and forth. Tears run down her cheeks. "This isn't happening," she chants. "It's not happening."

"Leave him alone, Magnolia." Blood drips from a cut on my forehead, rolling down my face to soak into my patch. At least the cut isn't on the other side, or I wouldn't be able to see. "Why, Magnolia? Why are you doing this?"

"Because you got in my way. I spared your life for a reason, but instead of being grateful, you interfered and ruined my spell at the hospital. Now I've run out of time and must do this the hard way. Luckily I planned ahead. Ferdinand, Etienne," she calls, "bring me Mala's father. And while you're at it, one of you go find my niece. I need her to complete the spell. I'm tired and ready to rest this weary body."

Body swapping. It's not just something out of a movie or a book. "You won't find her here. She got embarrassed and probably snuck out the back door and is halfway home by now. Isn't that right, Ferdi?"

Ferdinand jerks Bessie up from behind the sofa. She struggles in his grasp, but even with all of her muscles, she can't break free. "That's likely, given her personality."

Magnolia's eyes narrow. "You'd better hope not, or I'll have to start killing members of her family until she returns. I'll start with the least significant and work up. Etienne…"

The zombie drone reaches for Ms. March, but she slashes his hand with a piece of glass. My eye widens as she leaps to her feet, full of fire and brimstone. "How dare you come into my house and threaten my family?" she cries, slashing at Etienne when he grabs for her again. Thick black liquid like tar oozes from the gash, but he doesn't utter a sound.

On the other hand, she's sobbing. Red blood mixes with black on the tip of the glass. She's shredding her hands. She lunges for Etienne and trips. He grabs her arm, pulling her upright. Still defiant, Ms. March yells, "Mala's my niece! I'll never give her up! I don't care what you do to me."

Magnolia's head tips in a slight bow. "Bold words. I like you. Etienne, make it quick so she doesn't suffer. Snap her scrawny neck."

Chapter 29

Mala

Choices

Thank God there isn't a line for the upstairs bathroom. I go in and lock the door. My stomach rumbles, and I barely make it onto the toilet in time. After I finish, I send a generous spritz of air freshener through the room before I move to the sink to wash my hands. The face reflected in the mirror is painted with my distress. My eye makeup has migrated in dark lines down my cheeks. I look like the love child of Rudolph the Red-Nosed Reindeer and the Stay Puft Marshmallow Man, only neither of those is genetically compatible even if they did have the reproductive organs to produce me.

Ah, hell... I sniff, but the tears won't listen and stay in my swollen eyes.

I bury my face in my hands, planning my escape from the house. It'll be down the back stairs leading to the kitchen. I'll send one of the staff for Landry. I can't go back to the party. I won't.

I throw open the door and lunge forward. My face smashes into a hard chest. Pain flares from my nose up through my eye sockets. Hands grip my elbows, and I stumble back to look up through my tears into a pair of green eyes.

"What the hell, Mala?"

I blink, trying to see through my blurry vision. "Georgie? I couldn't see—"

"Are you okay?"

"I was until you humiliated me by spilling my business in front of everyone downstairs. And for the record, I'm not pregnant. The doctor confirmed it. So…you know, there's that misunderstanding to fix with our parents."

He has the good sense to look contrite. "I'm sorry."

"Thanks. That makes me feel so much better," I drawl, shoving past him and stalking toward the staircase. The rev's shout for Reverend Shane filters up from below, and I freeze. The word "ceremony" floats like a balloon before my eyes and then bursts.

I throw a panicked look at my brother. "Oh crap, George. Look what you've done. Landry and I are going to be forced into a shotgun wedding."

"Let's go," he says, grabbing my hand.

We sprint for the staircase that ends in the kitchen. The catering staff barely glances in our direction. Now that my stomach's not revolting, I'm starving. I snatch a crème puff off a tray on the way out the door. If I've got to leave, at least I won't do it on an empty stomach.

Once we reach the garden, George pulls out his keychain and flicks on a thumb-size flashlight. He points toward the path winding through the rosebush maze. "They won't find us in there."

I wish I could've told Landry what I was planning before coming outside. He'll be worried. And I left my phone in my jacket, which is in the coat closet. Yeah, bad planning all around.

I sense a spirit hovering just out of sight. The air has a strange ozone scent. Invisible fingers brush against the shield trying to get in. I've been to this house hundreds of times when I helped Aunt March with her rose garden, but I've never seen a hint of a ghost before. Granted, I've only visited twice since inheriting my powers.

"For some reason the spirits have been upset today," I say, shivering as goose bumps rise on my arms.

George takes off his jacket and wraps it around my shoulders. "Do you know why?"

"No, I haven't asked."

He flicks the flashlight up, blinding me. "What if they're trying to communicate something important to you?"

He might be right. I close my eyes and draw in a deep breath, then slowly release it. The image of the shield forms clearly in my head. The imaginary bricks are chipped, and in some areas, broken. My subconscious must've been fielding the psychic attacks, but it's obvious that I'm losing the battle. A brick wiggles free as I watch, and immediately my senses sharpen. The scent of roses fills my nose. Sweet but also decaying.

Fear rushes through my body. "They're breaking through my shield."

George steps closer, bringing with him the starchy scent of his ironing spray. A cricket chirps to my right. "Let them in, Mala. Find out what they want. Then maybe they'll leave you alone."

"It's not that simple. They're so angry." Voices whisper in my ear—too muffled to understand what the spirits are saying. Then the second brick falls. The warning comes loud and clear. *Danger.*

I need to hear more. "What danger?" I cry out. "Where?"

She's coming.

"Get away from her!" a voice shouts, and I spin to see Sophia running down the path. Her hair trails over her shoulder. She's dirty. There are ragged holes in her long, flowing, mud-stained white skirt. She doesn't stop when she reaches me, just grabs my hand as she runs past. I have no choice but to follow her through the twists and turns of the maze. "Hurry, run. It's almost too late."

"What's going on?" I yell.

She slams to a stop at the edge of garden and then whirls around, grabbing for me. But she doesn't move fast enough. It's like I run face-first into a sliding-glass window. I bounce off the invisible shield and land on my ass. The shock coursing through my body doesn't fade quickly, reminding me of the time I played with George's Taser.

And I think my nose is bleeding.

George slides to a stop in front of me. "What the hell? Are you okay?"

I nod, holding my arms out. "I got zapped. Help me up."

He lifts me to my feet, and I wobble like a bobblehead doll. I hold out my hand. Sparks shoot off my finger when they hit the shield separating the garden from the wider yard. "Is this some kind of force field, Sophia?"

"Damn it," Sophia says, looking around as if expecting someone to pop out any minute. Which sets me on high alert. "We're too late. Magnolia invoked a boundary spell around this place. It's the accumulation of months of planning."

"To keep who or what out or in?" I ask.

"To keep us in."

George reaches out, zaps himself, and pops his fingertips in his mouth. "I guess it works on everyone, not just Mala."

Sophia's eye roll reveals more terror than contempt. It's obvious that she's barely holding her panic in check. "Did you drink the potion?"

"Uh, no. I left it in my jacket." I point toward the house. The lights inside are flickering on and off.

"Why?" she cries. "You're such a fool."

"If I drank it, I wouldn't be connected to the murderer on the other side anymore. I need that connection to figure out what he's up to."

"This spell...this is what he was up to. Gathering enough innocent souls to power this boundary spell. This mansion is the nexus of four magic points where the veil between this world and the other side is thinner. You fell right into his trap."

The ground beneath us begins to shake. We all grab for one another, trying to stay on our feet. An explosion of sound comes from the house, a mixture of breaking things and high-pitched cries. Landry's in the house. Along with everyone else I love.

"Someone's screaming," I yell to be heard over the rumbling. "They need help."

George shakes his head. "It's not safe. Wait for the tremors to stop."

I can't.

Sophia grabs my shoulder when I start toward the house. Tears streak her cheeks. "Stop. Listen, before it's too late." Her fingernails dig into my bare skin as she shakes me, hard. George grabs her wrists and jabs his thumbs in a pressure point. She stumbles back, sobbing. *She's broken.*

"I'm listening to you. I swear." I try to shrug off her hand but her fingernails dig into my skin. I'm about two seconds away from losing control. "Look, Sophie, either you figure out how to walk and talk or get the hell out of my way."

She must hear the threat in my voice because she gets right to the point. "Once you get inside, find the potion and drink it immediately. Without it, possession is a death sentence. What more do I have to say or do to make you understand the danger? I showed you the butterflies—"

"Do you really value my existence so little, Sophia?" Gaston says, stepping from the trees. My heart lifts at seeing him. *He'll help me fix this.*

Sophia stiffens. "I would do anything for you."

"Would you?" He turns to me. "I think she's lying. Magnolia reminded me how much I loved Sophia. I would do anything to be with her. Anything."

"I love you too, Gaston," Sophia says. "I always have. I swear."

He hasn't looked away from me, even though Sophia stands here pleading with him to believe her. "I want to be with her forever, Mala."

"O-okay, that's fine, Gaston," I say, patting Sophia's hand. "We can talk about you and Sophia later. Right now, I need your help. Something horrible is happening."

The screaming coming from inside hasn't stopped. If anything, it's getting louder.

With my words, his appearance changes. My mouth drops when the moon shines down on his unblemished features. "Oh my God,

Uncle Gaston. If you could look like this, why did you never—"

"I didn't mean to betray you," Gaston says softly. He reaches for my face, but Sophia jerks me away. His hand curls into a fist and drops to his side. "I didn't have a choice. The *loa* possessing Magnolia is too strong to fight. And it promised that if I let it use me, I could finally be with the woman I love."

"Gaston…please." Sophia clings to my arm, sobbing. "Don't do this. It's not worth it."

"I need a body, Mala. I don't want to be alone anymore. I'm sorry. Magnolia…"

"Made you an offer you couldn't refuse." *I finally get it.* Betrayal. All the signs are clear now. He's the man I fought in my dream. The super soldier who almost killed me with the knife I stole. The knife he got back. Nothing but an ancestral spirit with all of its faculties intact was coherent enough to pull off multiple murders. If he's here needing a body, then Tank's probably dead, like Judd. "What did you do to Mama?"

"She's been contained. If you cooperate, I'll let her go."

"No! Free her now, and I won't shred you into vapor." The wind lifts my hair. I breathe in the air, sucking power from every molecule. Hot fury races through me, and I try to keep it contained. I don't want to hurt Uncle Gaston, but I will. If he leaves me no choice.

His face shifts back to his scarred mask. Because that's what it is. He's been hiding his true self this whole time. "Please, Mala. Don't make me do worse than I already have."

Sympathy flares, but I shove it down. "How many people have you entered? Kids…you killed kids."

"I *was* a kid when I died!" he screams. "I didn't ask for this. To be away from Sophia all of these years. Am I ashamed? Yes. I did what

I had to do. What my aunt asked of me. Now it's time for you to do as you're told."

He moves before I can raise a hand to defend myself, but it doesn't matter. I'm not his target.

George's back arches, and his eyes roll up in his head as Gaston enters his body. Sophia and I are screaming for him to stop, but it's too late. My brother, my first love, and best friend is gone.

Chapter 30

Landry

Nice Catch

*S*nap her scrawny neck. The words echo through the room.

A woman screams, but it's not Mala's aunt. She's dangling like a ragdoll in Etienne's large hands. He hasn't been able to grab her throat because she continues to fight, silently fending off his grasping free hand with the glass. I see a blackened nub where his right thumb used to be. She stabs repeatedly at him, drawing more of the dark blood, but it doesn't matter.

He died a long time ago. This... *thing* feels nothing. Not pain or empathy. I push up, again, but my legs won't stay underneath me. I fight them as much as the exhaustion and dizziness that blurs my vision. Mala will kill me if I don't save her favorite aunt. Why isn't anyone else helping her?

People huddle under the tables. They look shell-shocked. Dirty faces watch what's happening with dazed eyes. Almost as if they've zoned out in front of the TV.

Mala's dad meets my gaze and then his eyes drop to the top of his wife's blonde head. She presses her face into his chest, sobbing. Isabel has gone into nurse mode. She presses napkins to Molly's bleeding face. Her husband protected her from most of the glass, but not all.

My gaze travels back to Ms. March. Her swings come slower. If I didn't know better, I'd think Etienne is playing with her like a cat plays with a mouse before eating it. But that means a bit of a sadist lurks behind those dead eyes. Unless his puppet master controls him more than I thought.

Magnolia smiles at me, and I shiver from the coldness in her gaze. "The fight for life never gets old, even for one as old as I."

"Can't you just let her go, Magnolia? Please." I roll over until I'm propped against the sofa with my legs stretched in front of me. The right one has an ominous lump in the middle of the bone. The leg broke when I either smashed into the wall or when I landed. "Take me instead. I won't fight if you let everyone go."

"Oh *cher, merci*. But I've already got you. What I want is for Mala's good-for-nothing coward of a father to crawl out from under that table of his own free will. I already knew he was a pile of manure after abandoning his daughter all these years. But I'm going to give him the opportunity to redeem himself by saving his poor, dear sister." She jams a wad of chewing tobacco between her lip and gums and licks her fingertips. "'Course, I'm getting impatient with the delay, and the poor lady doesn't have a whole lot of strength left. I know I said I'd be merciful and kill her quickly, but"—she leans forward and whispers dramatically from behind her cupped hand—"I lied."

I stare at Mala's father, but he only has eyes for his sister. How he can watch what she's going through and do nothing is beyond me. My gaze moves to Dad. He hasn't moved from the position he fell in. I can't tell if he's breathing or not. I try not to worry. He survived the psycho Delahoussaye siblings. He'll survive Magnolia.

"G.D., help me," Ms. March whimpers, exhausted. Defeated. And she knows it. I can see the resignation in her eyes when she moves them from her brother to me. Her swipe at Etienne is too slow. He slaps the glass from her trembling fingers. His big hand wraps around her throat and squeezes.

I close my eye so I don't have to watch her die.

My head throbs. The gash on my temple still bleeds. Everything around me grows muffled, fading… *"Wake up, host."*

I jerk awake as another wail fills the room. "No, don't, G.D!"

"I have to. She's my sister." George Dubois Sr. finally mans up. He ignores his wife's pleas and crawls from beneath the table. Etienne drops Ms. March, and she falls boneless beside Dad.

George Sr. scrambles toward his sister, but before he can touch her, Etienne grabs him by his suit jacket and drags him across the hardwood floor. His fingernails score the wood, and he kicks out. The heel of his dress boot connects with Etienne's jaw. A tearing sound fills the room as the lower-left jaw bone rips free, only remaining attached to his face by a hanging, leathery piece of cartilage. It dangles, swinging against his shoulder when Etienne bends over.

George Sr. screams and kicks again, but misses. Etienne grabs his foot and drags him forward, sliding him through his legs, then grasps his jacket and heaves him upright. The man swings at Etienne, but damn it to hell and back, I can't even call this a fight. Ms. March went *Battle Royale* on his ass, intending to be the last one standing.

And she would've won if the fight had been against a live person. Mala's dopey dad looks like he's trying to play patty-cake with a zombie. *Pathetic.* His daughter obviously takes after the women in her family.

Magnolia laughs, meeting my gaze. "Yeah, you right about that, boy."

I forgot about her handy mind-reading skills. *Must. Not. Think.* At least not about anything important like escaping or rescuing my family. She'll know my plan before I do, and I'm not anywhere near as clever as the billionaire who owns half of New Orleans. Of course, she has an unfair advantage by not being human. What did the grim book call her? A *loa.* A spirit inhabiting the body of Mala's aunt for…My gaze goes back to her and I deliberately think, *"How long?"*

Magnolia's head tips, and her eyebrows rise. "Long enough to forget what it feels like to be young." Her fingers drum on the end of the chair as she grins. "Ever wonder why the matriarch of Mala's family chose the name LaCroix? Because for generations I've been their cross to bear. Magnolia isn't the first, and Mala won't be the last."

Etienne thrusts George Sr. in front of Magnolia and presses down on the man's shoulders until he kneels before the queen. He can barely look her in the eye when he asks, "What do you want from me?"

"Leverage," she says and spits. The tobacco juice splatters on his cheek. He rears up, but Etienne pushes him back down. "Ah, the guest of honor has arrived. Come on in, *cher.* We've been waiting for you. Say hello and good-bye to your father. You won't be seeing him again."

Mala enters the room, flanked by George. Sophia trails behind. My girl looks defeated. Broken. Not good. I was depending on her to rescue our asses. The corners of her eyes tighten as she scans the area, taking in the damage and lingering on the bodies of Dad and Ms. March. She steps in their direction, but George grabs her arm and yanks her toward Magnolia. She stumbles after him.

The fucker's hurting her. *What the hell's going on?*

"Drop your shield," the *loa* hisses from the darkness.

"Hey, asshole," I scream back, hands clenching so I don't utter the words out loud. But I'm pissed. I want to do some damage. But I can't. *"If you're going to help, then grow some balls and show yourself. Stop hiding in my head."*

I guess goading a millennia-old snake spirit to do something it doesn't want to do doesn't work. Maybe if I wave a dead chicken in its face I can at least bribe it into answering my questions, but the only chickens I see are the hot wings scattered across the floor. Instead of scrounging for leftovers, I squint at George, trying to see the unseen. A dark shadow hovers over his skin. A part of him, but not. And it's different from the silvery shine around Etienne. George isn't dead, but he's not fully alive either. Something wears his skin.

My heart thuds, and blood rushes to my ears. I grit my teeth and grab on to the edge of the sofa to lever myself upright. I don't put weight on my broken leg; it won't hold. Still, I need to face whatever happens next on my feet.

"Mala," I call out. Her head swivels in my direction, and a spark arches between us. Now she sees, knows, that all is not lost. *I'm here. We'll get through this together.* "Kick down that gate, girl."

She nods. Her shoulders straighten when she faces Magnolia again. "Don't think you've won," she says. "It's not over."

Magnolia's lips twist. "Ever the smart-ass, girl. Told you it would get you in trouble someday, and this is the day. Bring her here, Gaston."

George jerks on her arm again, and this time she struggles.

"Let me go, traitor. I can walk on my own." Her nostrils flare. "You're gonna pay for every horrible thing you've done. But for hurting Georgie, I swear you'll never know peace. Your love will turn to dust. Just ask Sophia if you don't believe me."

Ah crap! It's her uncle wearing George's skin. Gaston doesn't acknowledge her threats, but George Sr. rocks forward at her words, staring at the meat suit. "What does she mean? What happened, Junior?"

Gaston bares his teeth in a feral grin. "Nothing, Father. As you can see, I'm fine."

Magnolia slams her cane on the man's shoulder. "Worry about your daughter if you feel inclined to express fatherly affection. She's the one in danger now."

Gaston pushes Mala forward, and she trips, falling to her knees beside her father. Gaston places his hands to the side of her head. "Are you ready, Niece?"

She stiffens then relaxes. "Born ready, Uncle Gaston."

Magnolia shakes her head. She thumps her cane on the floor. "Ferdinand, Sophia, get to your places." She raises her hands as if conducting an orchestra. Sophia moves through the room. Her emerald eyes won't meet mine, but when she reaches my side, she wraps her arms around my waist, holding the weight I can't put on my injured leg.

"Tell me you have the potion," she whispers. "That at least one of you isn't stupid."

"Neither of us is as naïve as you seem to think. And although my girl's stubborn as hell, she accepts sincere apologies." I press my forehead against hers, showing her the image of the china teacup in my mind. "Dad told her it was chamomile."

A full-bodied shiver runs through Sophia's body. Her hands clench my shirt. "Don't let Magnolia see."

Hell, I'm doing my best to keep the old witch out of mind, but Magnolia's slippery like an eel. The power inhabiting her shell winds in and out of my thoughts at will, fondling me everywhere that's not protected by the power of its twin. Whatever magic the *loa* inside Magnolia used to capture us woke up the devil inside me. Its giddy anticipation races beneath my skin, enhancing my own emotions like a shot of adrenaline through the heart. I feel supercharged. And ready for a fight.

Magnolia pulls the bone knife from her pocket and scrambles from the chair. She drops to her knees. Her breath comes in heavy pants, like she's about to have an orgasm from excitement. With a deranged cackle, she slashes the knife across the side of Mala's father's neck and leans forward. She drinks from the cut, then leans back, licking her lips like a wannabe vampire.

George Sr. covers his wound with a hand and falls onto his side.

"No, Dad," Mala cries, leaning toward him, but Gaston jerks her back. He shoves her head toward Magnolia.

"I've already tasted your blood, and your mama's before she died," the old woman says, smacking her lips. She sets the knife into Mala's open hand and presses the blade to her chest. "The door to the in-between opens. I've waited so long for this. Kill me."

"What?" Mala's fingers twitch on the hilt but don't open. Nor does she remove the knife from where it presses about her aunt's heart. She also doesn't stab the old bat with it. *What the hell?*

Magnolia smiles. She grasps Mala's cheeks with both hands and slams her toothless mouth over Mala's pinched lips. Gaston shoves Mala forward at the same time. The knife slides into Magnolia's body as if she's made of soft butter. The shadow beneath Magnolia's skin expands and, like water passing through a cell membrane, flows into Mala. My girl convulses as the shadow tears free from of its old host and claims its new one.

And I can't do anything but watch. *"It took the bait."*

"Time to reel it in, host."

I really hate all of these fishing metaphors, but I roll with it. It's hard enough to compartmentalize my emotions and keep to the plan Mala and I made this afternoon. I just never thought we'd have to put it into play tonight. Neither of us expected Magnolia to attack at the party. In front of witnesses. But after reading Sophia's book, Mala said she'd have to act fast now that the second murder site has been found or she would lose all the power those deaths accumulated.

Magnolia looks like a deflating puffer fish. The shadow filled the shell completely. Without it, her body withers. The muscles and fat beneath her skin disintegrate. Her eyes bulge in their sockets. Hollows form in her cheeks, emphasizing her sharp cheekbones. Her breasts shrivel and sag, leaving the dress she wore hanging around her thin frame like a sack.

With a final squeeze of her stick-thin arms, Magnolia pulls her head back with a choked gasp. White membranes cover her sightless eyes. Her body folds in on itself—nothing but leathery skin and bones drop to the floor.

Mala's scream jerks my eye from the remains of Magnolia's body. I lurch forward, forgetting about my leg. I collapse on top of Sophia in agony. Her hands rise to cup my forehead. Flames roll across my thoughts, and I scream as I'm swept away on a wave of fire. Spikes of energy race through my body. The veil breaks with a crash.

The room spins. Then I realize it's not the room but me. I've been sucked from my body. I see myself lying on the ground, hugging Sophia against my chest. But she also stands at my side. Etienne collapsed in on himself the same way Magnolia did. I don't see his soul here on the other side. Maybe he's finally free. Ferdinand holds onto Bessie with one hand. He looks shocked. She, on the other hand, looks ready to kill and takes advantage of his distraction. She twists her arm loose and grabs a toppled lamp off the floor. He turns toward her as she swings and coldcocks the son of a bitch.

Bessie's action energizes the huddled party guests, and they realize the dynamics of the hostage situation have changed with the death of Magnolia. Isabel grabs George's mom and Molly and ushers them past the unconscious Ferdinand. Mala's father still lies beside the bodies of his daughter and son, but he manages to roll to his knees. I guess the neck wound missed his carotid artery, because he drops his hand. The wound's no longer bleeding. After a quick check of their pulse, he runs over to his sister.

All of this happens in the real world between one revolution of the shining, silvery blue spiral of energy opening behind Magnolia's chair and the next. Its inky tentacles whip at the air, still too short to reach us bodiless souls loitering within its soon-to-be grasp. It grows with each revolution, and I fight the wind drawing me toward the mouth of the vortex—toward Mala, who clings to Magnolia's cane with both hands. She bats at her uncle, but Gaston dodges her hits.

George, who must've been brought here in spirit form by Gaston, also lunges for him, but the old ghost twists aside. He shoves George into Mala, and she stumbles toward the vortex. A snapping tentacle smacks her in the back, toppling her forward, then catches her before she hits the ground. It wraps around her waist.

George grabs on to her hands and pulls against the tentacle, but they're both being dragged across the hardwood floor. They have no traction. Nothing to hold onto.

"Don't let her go, George," I yell, while taking a running leap. I slide across the floor. My hands circle Mala's wrists just as Gaston slams the cane across the back of George's head. I kick my feet toward him, but the soldier sidesteps to grab George by the back of his shirt. He shoves him toward the vortex. If Deputy Dawg's soul gets sucked in, he's gone. Gaston will have a new body, and I'm not in a position to stop it.

"Gaston, stop. You're killing him," Mala cries, then twists her face upward. Her dark eyes tilt down at the corners. "Let me go, Landry. Help my brother."

Does she actually think sad-puppy eyes will work in this situation? "Fuck no!'"

"You have to. It's the only way to stop this thing." Black ooze drips down her cheeks instead of tears. The shadow beneath her skin ripples, trying to separate itself from her soul and claim her body as its own. "Landry, please. It's trying to get free so it can take my body. I can't let it have what it wants. It'll only kill again and again." She twists her fingers in my grip. "Let me go."

"Who's the one who gave a speech about not being a martyr? Don't you *dare* let go of my hands. I had Dad give you the tea. The one you refused to drink. Well, you drank it and said, 'Mmm mmm good, give me another cup.' That's why you had the shits tonight."

God, I can't stop cussing. Is she even hearing me? If she gives up, we're both doomed. Because if she sacrifices herself to keep the Loa of Death from getting free, then I'm going with her.

Yelling comes from behind us, and I look over my shoulder.

Sophia has her arms locked around Gaston. I can't hear her words. The whirl of the wind from the vortex drowns out her words. Gaston's shaking his head, still dragging George closer to the tentacles. She stops suddenly and clasps her hands as if in prayer and then shifts her gaze to Mala, and finally to me. Her lips move. *Good-bye.*

Then she's running toward the door.

Gaston drops George's leg and dives for her. His arms wrap around her waist, and she twists in his arms until they're face to face. Her arms circle his shoulders and then cup the back of his head, drawing his mouth down to hers. A tentacle wraps around them both and jerks. They're flying backward into the vortex, but their lips never break the kiss.

"Wow. Now that's a death scene to be remembered," I say, looking down at Mala.

Black tears trail down her cheeks. The tentacle around her leg gives another tug, and she lets out a squeak. Her eyes close as she whispers, "Kiss me."

I draw her wrists up, using her weight to slide our bodies closer together. Her arms circle my neck, and her lips part, sighing out black vapor. I breathe it in, breathe her in as I claim her mouth. I fall into the kiss, losing myself. All I know is her. The taste of our souls mingling, combining, driving out the spirits of the *loas* who infect us because there is only room for the two of us. 'Cause yeah, I drank the nasty-ass tea too.

A fading rustle of scales passes through my thoughts. *"She's one whopper of a catch, host."*

"I know. Now get the fuck out of my head."

Chapter 31

Mala

Billionaires Suck

My nose twitches when I park in front of the Acker place. Smoke rises over the top of the house, bringing the smell of hickory-smoked ribs. The crawfish boil started an hour ago, and I'm starving and pissed after having two hours of my life sucked away. Two ridiculous hours that I can't get back while I, the legal heir to Magnolia LaCroix's fortune, arranged to donate the majority of my aunt's money to a variety of charitable organizations, while ignoring her attorney's constant questioning of my decision to throw away a billion dollars.

The answer was simple. 'Cause I don't want her dirty money. Nobody can guilt me into keeping all of it. Or call me a fool to my face for getting rid of it, unless they want a beat down.

Harsh words, maybe. But true.

But I didn't answer his questions. And even though I loathe Magnolia with a passion, I only told the lawyer to donate the majority of her money. I didn't say all. She hurt a lot of people in Paradise Pointe, and I aim to see they're made as whole as possible monetarily. The absences of the people who passed because of my aunt can't be fixed, but their families won't have to worry about how they'll pay their bills during their time of grief. Or ever, if they invest well.

The one good thing is that the survivors of the birthday party tragedy don't remember anything other than that a minor earthquake rocked Paradise Pointe, and the epicenter was located beneath Aunt March's house. They don't remember Magnolia's reign of terror. They do, however, remember the pregnancy debacle. And lucky me, I'm still getting asked when the baby is due even though it's been almost two months. And I'm definitely not rocking a baby bump. Or getting married in the foreseeable future.

I grab my briefcase and climb out of the new van. Cold wind nips at my cheeks, and I wrap my jacket tighter about my body. We could've held the party inside, but the birthday boy insisted on having us all out in the winter air. I think Axle's a little demented. Cute, though.

He sees me first and races across the lawn with a new graphic novel, *Dark Knight Returns*. "Mala, who do you think would win in a fight? Batman or Spider-Man?"

"Batman."

"Hey, you answered without even thinking about it."

"What's to think about?" I hold up my fingers. "He's rich, smart, and does the right thing even though he doesn't have superpowers."

His nose crinkles. "But Spider-Man's a genius who can shoot webs, throw a car, and walk on walls."

"Batman punched out Superman. Beat that."

His head tilts as he contemplates that, then he sighs. "I guess Jon-jovi's right. I need to read more."

We walk across the lawn chatting, and I tell him about Reverend Prince's secret trunk of comic books, his prized collection, which another charitable donation from the Aunt Magnolia fund saved from being auctioned off on eBay. All of the Prince family's medical bills and attorney fees are paid. With enough left over that the rev can finally get his own place. Thank you, God!

Rap music blasts from the backyard. Carl's on a new kick about becoming a DJ. Says he can work parties with his new equipment. Yes, some of Magnolia's money went to the Ackers. If any family has suffered from what she's done, it's them. Pepper doesn't have to sell the house now. Not that Dena would let her, and since her father put all of his assets in her name, Pepper doesn't have much choice but to play nice if she wants to keep her family and a roof over her head. The kids were fine without her. They'd be sad, but they'd sur-vive if she took off again. The boys and Dee now have their college educations paid for. So as long as Carl graduates, I'm cool with him having a part-time job as a DJ. But it's his mama's and Dena's busi-ness to deal with if he gets out of line.

"I'm back," I yell, throwing open the gate.

Bessie, the Acker boys, and my handsome fiancé sit around four card tables set up side by side in the yard. Heaping piles of boiled crawfish sit in the middle of each table. My family has already loaded up their plates with the side dishes: yellow corn, potato salad, dev-iled eggs. All of the kids, except for Daryl, who's watching his weight, avoided taking any of the salad, peas, or green beans. My guess is his crush on Astrid is ramping up in intensity, and he's get-ting ready to make a move. Will true love prevail? Or will he feel the soul-crushing heartache of rejection? I can't wait to find out. That's the thing. I can finally find out things set way in advance. I have time. Well, besides the two hours I can never get back.

I drop my briefcase on the ground and slide into the chair beside Landry. He leans in for a long welcome-home kiss that inspires Jon-jovi and Axle to pretend gag, ruining the party mood for everyone else at the table. Landry and I ignore them all.

Kissing saved our lives. Cliché, maybe. But true.

Landry pulls back. He wipes the barbecue sauce from my lips with his thumb, then slowly licks it off. My thighs clench, and he grins, knowing how he affects me. "I take it you didn't kill the lawyer," he says with a smirk.

"I can't tell if that's a question or a statement."

Bessie sucks the juice out of a crawfish head and drops it onto the pile of discarded shells. "I didn't get dispatched to a call, so I guess everything went fine. Unless she hid the body."

"Ha, ha, very funny," I say. Only I'm not sure if she's joking. Ferdinand fucked her over. After all those years of not being able to get past her husband's death, she finally allows herself to let a man in, and it turns out he's in cahoots with an ancient ancestral spirit. How's a decent woman supposed to get past that and trust again? My biggest regret is that he got away with everything because nobody else at the party but us remembers what he did.

"I think Bessie's hilarious," Dena says, dropping a plate in front of me. She winks, then hustles away from my swat. She and her mom are running the second grill with the boiling pot of crawfish, while Reverend Prince and George take care of the meat. My eyes linger on my brother for a bit. Landry catches me staring, and he scowls.

"He's fine. And you're hovering again."

"I'm not hovering. I'm sitting in my chair." He raises an eyebrow, then lowers his head to gnaw off a huge hunk of meat from the bone. Not passive aggressive at all. "Fine, I'll try to stop. It's hard. Every time I see him I think 'what if?'"

What if Sophia hadn't stopped Gaston from throwing George into the vortex? What if we hadn't gotten him to the hospital before the ticking time bomb in his head went off? I hope wherever Sophia landed, she is happy.

Landry grabs my fingers and brings the back of my hand to his lips. "The autopsies on Judd and Tank were able to pinpoint the location affected by the possession, and the neurosurgeon caught the problem in George and fixed it. Plus, he drank the magic tea. So again, he's fine. Besides, I don't see you freaking out every time I sneeze."

He sounds grumpy about that. "That's because you've already died and come back. I don't want that to happen to George. The dying part. But if he did die, yes, I'd want him to come back too."

Landry stuffs a corncob between my teeth. "You're rambling. Eat."

So I do. And I ignore the dead woman staring at the steaks on the barbecue. Mama sees the trespassing ghost and runs over. I'm surprised when she doesn't go into her grumpy "get off my lawn" spiel and kick her off the property. Something must be wrong, because heaven forbid that the crazy spirit world I half live in will hold off on falling apart until later.

Oh well, even when things unexpectedly go sideways, I won't have to deal with the chaos alone. It's funny, but not. See, I once wondered whether my ancestors always had an affinity for the dead or if some ancestor asked the Loa of Death to grant her his power.

Now I know the answer. Generations of LaCroix women were possessed by that spirit, but I broke the family curse.

My future children and grandchildren are safe. They're free to love and live their lives in harmony with our gifts. As for myself, I intend to live a long, happy life with this man that I love, and when we die, Landry and I will be buried together and eventually our children and their families will be buried around us. But for right now, I'm alive. Loved. Accepted. Safe.

So yeah, ghost lady can wait until I finish my ribs.

Did you miss the beginning of Mala and Landry's love story?

Please see the next page for an excerpt from *Dark Paradise*.

Chapter 1

Mala

Floater

Black mud oozes between my toes as I shift my weight and jerk on the rope, sending up a cloud of midges and the rotten-egg stench of stagnant swamp water. The edge of the damn crawfish trap lifts out of the water—like it's sticking its mesh tongue out at me—and refuses to tear loose from the twisted roots of the cypress tree. It's the same fight each and every time, only now the frayed rope will snap if I pull on it any harder. I have to decide whether to abandon what amounts to two days' worth of suppers crawling along the bottom of that trap or wade deeper into the bayou and stick my hand in the dark, underwater crevice to pry it free.

Gators eat fingers. A cold chill runs down my spine at the thought, and I shiver, rubbing my arms. I search the algae-coated surface for ripples. The stagnant water appears calm. I didn't have a problem wading into the bayou to set the trap. I've trapped and hunted in this bayou my entire life. Sure it's smart to pay attention to my instincts, doing so has saved my life more times than I can count, but this soul-sucking fear is ridiculous.

I take a deep breath and pat the sheathed fillet knife attached to my belt. My motto is: Eat or do the eating. I personally like the last part. A growling belly tends to make me take all kinds of stupid risks, but this isn't one. If I'm careful, a gator will find my bite cuts deeper than teeth if it tries to make me into a four-course meal. Grandmère Cora tried to teach her daughter that the way to a man's heart was through his stomach. Since Mama would rather fuck 'em than feed 'em, I inherited all the LaCroix family recipes, including a killer gator gumbo.

Sick of second-guessing myself, I slog deeper into the waist-high water. Halfway to the trap, warm mud wraps around my right ankle. My foot sticks deep, devoured. I can't catch my balance. *Crud, I'm sinking.*

Ripples undulate across the surface of the water, spreading in my direction. My breath catches, and I fumble for the knife. Those aren't natural waves. Something's beneath the surface. *Something big.* I jerk on my leg, panting. With each heave, I sink deeper, unable to break the suction holding me prisoner. Gator equals death...But I'm still alive. *So what is it? Why hasn't it attacked?*

A flash of white hits the corner of my eye—

Shit! I twist, waving the knife in front of me. My heart thuds. Sparkly lights fill my vision. Blinking rapidly, I shake my head. My mind shuts down. At first I can't process what I'm seeing. It's too awful. Too sickening. Then reality hits—hard. The scream explodes from my chest, and I fling myself backward. The mud releases my leg with a *slurp.* Brackish water smacks my face, pouring into my open mouth as I go under. Mud and decayed plants reduce visibility below the surface.

Wrinkled, outstretched fingers wave at me in the current. The tip of a ragged fingernail brushes across my cheek. It snags in my hair. I bat at the hand, but I can't free my hair from the girl's grip. She's holding me under. Trying to drown me. I can't lift my head above the surface. *She won't let me go!*

My legs flail, kicking the girl in the chest. She floats. I sit up, choking. I can't breathe and scream at the same time. I'm panting, but I concentrate. *Breathe in. Out. In.* The girl drifts within touching distance. Floating. Not swimming. Why doesn't she move? Is it stupid to pray for some sign of life—the rise of her chest, a kick from her leg—when I already know the truth?

Water laps at my chin. I wrap my arms around my legs. Shivers shake my body despite the warmth of the bayou, and my vision's fuzzy around the edges. I'm hyperventilating. If I try to stand I'll pass out. Or throw up. Probably both 'cause I'm queasy. I close my eyes, unable to look at the body any more. Which is so wrong. I've studied what to do in this sort of situation. Didn't I spend a month memorizing the crime scene book I borrowed from Sheriff Keyes? *Come on, Mala. Pull it together.* A cop—even a future one—doesn't get squeamish over seeing a corpse. If I can't do something as simple as reporting the crime scene, well, then why not drop out of college, get hitched, and push out a dozen babies before I hit twenty-five, like everyone else in this damn town?

I lift my hands to scrub my face. Strands of algae lace my fingers. I pick them off. My legs tremble as I rise, which keeps me from running away. I have to describe the crime scene when I call the Sheriff's Office, and I imagine myself peering through the lens of a giant magnifying glass like Sherlock Holmes—searching her body for clues. Each detail becomes crystal clear.

Her lips are slightly parted, and a beetle crawls across her teeth, which are straight and pearly white, not a tooth missing. She's definitely a townie. A swamp girl her age would have a couple of missing teeth, given she appears to be a few years older than me. Her expensive-looking sundress has ridden up round her waist. Poor thing got all gussied up before she killed herself.

The deep vertical cuts still pinking the water on both of the girl's wrists makes my stomach flip inside out. I double over, trying not to vomit. It takes several deep breaths to settle my gut before I can force myself to continue studying the body.

Long hair fans out like black licorice around her head, and her glazed blue eyes stare sightlessly at the heavens. Faint sunlight glistens on the flecks of water dotting her porcelain skin. I've never seen such a serene expression on anyone's face, let alone someone dead, like she's seen the face of God and has found peace.

After seeing her up close and personal, I can't stomach leaving her floating in the foul water. Flies crawl in her wounds, and midges land on her eyes. Slimy strands of algae twine through her hair. Soon the fish will be nibbling at her. Unable to bring myself to touch her clammy-looking skin, I take a firm grip on her dress and drag her onto the bank—high enough above the waterline that she'll be safe from predators while I get help.

I'm halfway across the stretch of land between the bayou and my house when a shiver of foreboding races through my body, and I slow my pace. *Shit! I took the wrong path.* Usually I avoid traveling through the Black Hole. It's treacherous with pockets of quicksand. Cottonmouths like to hide in the thick grass, beneath lichen-smothered fallen trees. Those natural obstacles are pretty easy to navigate if you're alert. What makes the hairs on the back of my neck prickle is the miasma that permeates every rock and rotten tree in the clearing I cross to get home. A filmy layer of ick coats my skin and seeps in through my pores until it infects my whole body with each step. I feel...*unclean*. I'm not big on believing in the whole concept of evil, but if there's any place I'd consider to be tainted ground, I'm walking across it.

Instinct screams that I'm not alone. I'd be a fool to ignore the warning signs twice. If I listened to my instincts earlier, I never would've found the body. I stretch out my senses like tentacles waving in the wind. Nothing moves...chirps, or croaks. A strange, pungent odor floats on the light breeze, but I can't identify it. My darting gaze trips and reverses to focus on the *Bad Place*. I swallow hard and yank my gaze from the dark stain on the rock in the middle of the circle. Mama said our slave ancestors used this area for their hoodoo rituals because the veil between the living and dead is thinner here.

It's always sounded like a whole lot of bullshit to me until I stumbled across the blood-stained altar and shards of burnt bone scattered across earth devoid of grass or weeds—salted earth, where nothing grows. Mother Mary, it creeps me out.

'Cause what if I'm really not alone? What if something stands on the other side of the veil, close enough to touch, but invisible? Watching me.

Whatever's out here can go to the devil 'cause I'm not waiting to greet it.

By the time I burst out of the woods that border our yard, the sun has started its downward slope in the sky behind me. I double over, hands on my knees, to catch my breath after my half-mad run. Our squat wooden house perches on cinder-block stilts like an old buzzard on top of the hill. The peeling paint turns the rotting boards an icky gray in the waning light, but it's sure a welcome sight for sore eyes.

With a final glance over my shoulder to be sure I wasn't followed, I dash beneath the Spanish moss–draped branches of the large oak that shades our house, dodging the darn rooster running for me with tail feathers spread. I brush it aside with my foot, avoiding the beak pecking at my ankle.

"Mama!" My voice trembles. I really wish my mother had come home early. But the dark windows and empty driveway tell me otherwise. I track muddy footprints across the cracked linoleum in the kitchen to get to the phone.

Ms. Dixie Fontaine answers on the first ring. "Sheriff's Office, what's your emergency?" The 9-1-1 dispatcher's lazy drawl barely speeds up after I tell her about the dead girl. "All right, honey. I'll get George on over. You be waiting for him and don't go touching the body, you hear?" She pops her gum in my ear.

A flash of resentment fills me, but I'm careful to keep my tone even. "Don't worry, I know better, Ms. Dixie. I only touched her dress—to drag her from the water."

"That's fine, Malaise, quick thinking on your part. Bye now."

"Bye," I mutter, slamming the phone in the cradle. I breathe out a puff of air, trying to calm down. I'm antsy enough without having to deal with Ms. Dixie's inability to see me as anything but a naive kid. I'm not an idiot. How can she think I'd make a rookie mistake like contaminating the crime scene? I've been working with her now for what? Nine…no, ten months. Hell! What does it take to prove myself to her? To the rest of the veterans at the sheriff's office who remember every mistake I've ever made and throw them in my face every chance they get?

Disaster. That should've been my name. Instead, I've been saddled with Malaise. Well, whatever. I stomp into the bathroom, slip off my muddy T-shirt and cut-off jean shorts, and take a scalding shower. I scrub hard to get the scummy, dead-girl film off my skin. It takes almost a whole bottle of orchid body soap to cleanse my battered soul and wash the tainted, dirty feeling down the drain with the muck.

The whole time, three words echo in my head. *Deputy George Dubois.* My heart hasn't stopped thudding since Ms. Dixie mentioned his name. The towel I wrap around my heaving chest constricts my rapid breaths like a tightened corset. Hopefully, I won't do an old-fashioned swoon like those heroines from historical novels when I see him.

It's a silly reaction, but George comes in third on my list of People I Want to Impress the Most. It's not that his six feet of muscled, uniformed hotness tempts me to turn to a life of crime just so he'll frisk me and throw me in the back of his patrol car. Nope, that pathetic one-sided schoolgirl crush passed after we graduated and started working together. I'd be as cold as the dead girl if I couldn't appreciate his yummy goodness, but the last thing either of us need is for a romantic entanglement to screw up our professional relationship.

George epitomizes everything I want to become when I "grow up." He graduated from Paradise High School my freshman year and went to the police academy at the junior college. Once he turned twenty, he got a job at the Bertrand Parish Sheriff's Office.

When news of a part-time clerical position floated around town, guess who stood first in line for the job assisting Ms. Dixie with the data entry of the old, hardcopy crime reports into the new computer system. It's not always what you know at BPSO, but *whose* ass you kiss to get hired as a deputy. The recession left few open positions, forcing rookies to compete against seasoned officers who were laid off at other agencies. I don't have family to pull strings for me, but I've made job connections with people in positions of authority while obtaining practical experience working for the Sheriff's Office. I refuse to leave my future to the fickle whims of fate.

My last year at Bertrand Junior College begins in two months. I'll graduate with an Associate of Arts degree in Criminal Justice. I haven't decided whether to transfer to a larger university for a BA, but if not, I will definitely enroll in the police academy next summer. One year. I just have to survive one more boring year, and I'll finally get to start living out my dream of becoming a detective.

Calm down, Mala. I fuss with my thick, russet curls for a few minutes in the bathroom mirror then give up and pull it back in a high ponytail. My hair's a lost cause with the darn humidity frizzing it up. I finish dressing in my best jeans and a lavender T-shirt. Rocks pop beneath tires traveling down the gravel driveway. Instead of remaining barefoot, I slip on my rain boots, not wanting to look like a complete heathen or worse, reminding the higher-ups at the crime scene of my true identity—the prostitute's bastard.

Rumors about Mama's choice of occupation have been whispered about since before my birth. You'd think being the daughter of the town whore would be humiliating enough to hang my head in shame. Then add in the fact that most folk also think she's a broom-riding witch. The kids in school were brutal, repeating as gospel the stupid rumors they overheard from their parents, who should've known better. It boggles the mind that people in this day and age can believe ignorant stuff like Mama can hex a man's privates into shriveling if he crosses her. The only good thing about being the witch's daughter is it keeps most boys from straying too close. I don't have to deal with a bunch of assholes who think I'll blow them for a couple of twenties and an open bar tab like Mama.

With one last rueful glance at my face in the mirror, I shrug. This is as good as it's gonna get. I run onto the front porch and freeze halfway down the steps. The patrol car I expect to see in the drive turns instead into a good view of Mama on hands and knees beside her truck with a flowerpot stuck under her chin as she pukes in the geraniums. *Crud! Georgie will be here any minute.* I've got to hide her in the house. She can spend the night heaving up what's left of her guts in the toilet without me babysitting her.

Mama senses me hovering. She rolls onto her backside and holds out her hands.

"Don't just stand there gawkin' like an idiot, help your mama up," she says.

With a heavy sigh, I trudge to her side. I grit my teeth and lift her to her feet while she flops like roadkill. Upright, she lists sideways. A strong wind would blow her over. The vomit-and-stale-beer stench of her breath makes my nose crinkle when she throws her skinny arm around my shoulders.

"What you been up to today?" She tries to trail her fingers through my ponytail, but they snag on a knot I missed. She jerks her hand free, uncaring that it causes me pain since she's purposely deadened her own feelings with booze. Mama can't cope with her life without a bottle of liquor in one hand. It's like the chicken-and-the-egg question. Which came first? Was her life shitty before she became an alcoholic, or had booze made it worse? I can't see how it could be better, but maybe I'm naive, or as stupid as she always calls me.

I rub at the sting on my scalp. "Why are you home so early?"

She sways. "Can't I miss my baby girl?"

"Missing me never slowed you down before. What makes tonight any different?"

"Why you so squirrelly? You act like you don't want me here." She pulls back far enough to look me over. "Expectin' someone or you all dressed up with nowhere to go?" She cackles, slapping her leg like she's told the funniest joke ever.

"Georgie Dubois's coming out."

"Why? I know the deputy's not comin' to see you."

I grit my teeth on the snappy comment that hovers on the tip of my tongue. "Found a dead girl floating in the bayou."

Mama pulls her arm back and strikes cottonmouth quick.

I end up flat on my back with stars dancing before my eyes. My cheek burns. I blink several times, trying to clear my head, then focus in on the shadow hovering over me with clenched fists. "God damn it! Are you crazy?" I roll over and stagger to my feet. She steps forward again, fist raised.

"Don't you dare, Mama!"

"Don't take the Lord's name in vain. Or threaten me."

"I haven't threatened, *yet*. But I swear, you hit me again, I'm out of this rat hole you call a house. I've earned enough scholarship money to move into an apartment."

"Why you sayin' such things, Malaise?" Tears fill her eyes.

Money. The only thing that still touches Mama's fickle heart.

"You just backhanded me, Mama! What? Do you expect me to

keep turning the other cheek until you break it? Or accidentally kill me like that girl I found…"

Mama's mocha skin drops a shade, and she sucks in a breath. I don't think it has to do with any feelings of regret. No, it has to do with the girl. She hit me after she heard about George coming out for the body.

"Why do you look so scared?" Suspicion makes my voice sharp. "What did you do?"

Mama staggers toward the house.

"Don't walk away from me," I yell. "What's going on? Georgie will be here any minute. If I've got to cover for you, then I need to know why or I might let something slip on accident."

Mama makes it to the stairs and collapses onto the bottom step. She buries her face in her palms. Shudders wrack her body. "I need a drink, Mala. There's a bottle in my bottom drawer. Bring it out to me."

"That's not a good idea…"

She lifts her head. Her dark brown eyes droop at the corners, and I see the faint trace of fine lines. Strangest of all, her eyes have lost the glazed, shiny appearance they held a few minutes earlier. *The news shocked her sober.*

"I'm not askin' again, Malaise. Get in there if you want to hear the story."

Chapter 2

Mala

Trigger Happy

I scramble up the stairs. It doesn't take but a minute to find the bottle hidden under her nightgowns in the dresser drawer. The seal on the bottle of Johnnie Walker Red remains intact. She must've been saving it for a special occasion. That doesn't bode well for the direction of the conversation we'll be having in a moment. I don't bother with a glass. Mama always says, "Don't need one for beer. Don't want one for liquor." I ease down the staircase. She doesn't even look up, just holds out a shaking hand.

"Want a swig?" she asks, opening the bottle with a deft twist. A slight smile dances on her lips. "No? My, my, such a good girl I got. Funny thing is, girl, I was just like you at your age. Thought I was better than my mama. Thought she was trash."

Silence fills the space between us, but I twitch first. "That's not how I feel—"

"Don't lie. I see it in your eyes. You'll learn different when your time comes." Her chapped lips purse. She takes a long drink and sighs. "Come on over here. Sit by me, *cher*."

I shuffle forward then stop.

She stretches out the arm not holding the bottle. "Come on, I won't bite."

When I sit down beside her, she pulls me close, and I lay my head on her shoulder. For a long minute, we sit in silence, staring out toward the woods. The sun has almost reached the tips of the moss-draped trees, and the clouds have turned crimson and gold. Day and night. Love and hate. One can't exist in the world without the other. They come together at twilight—the perfect symbol for my chaotic feelings for Mama because, as much as I hate how she treats me when she's drunk, I still love her.

"Mama, I'm sorry I cursed you," I whisper, head tilting to stare into her pensive face.

She squeezes my shoulders. "Don't worry, *cher*. I won't be around to hurt you much longer."

"What does that mean?"

"Means I had my death vision and I'm gonna die. Soon. I'd hoped to keep the news from you for a while yet, but I need to set my affairs in order before I pass."

I snort and pull free of her embrace. "That's silly, a death vision." The wellspring of anger reserved just for her crazy shit has been tapped, and it bubbles up again. "The drink has you hallucinating."

"Wish that was the case, Malaise. The day's comin'. I'm not sure exactly how or when, but it's tied to that girl you found. I dreamed about her." She takes another drink then burps. "S'cuse me."

I shake my head. Mama, the epitome of a southern lady.

"I don't believe in dreams that foretell the future." My arms fold across my chest with a chill that caresses my spine like an accordion being played by a zydeco master. "You're just *crazy*—"

She rolls her eyes at me then shakes her head. "Sure, I'm crazy. I know I am, but it's those dreams that done drove me nuttier than Ida Jean's fruitcake, not the other way around. After I die, the visions will pass on to you like mine came from my mama and hers from her mama, and so on, all the way back to mother Africa. Then you'll sit on my grave and beg my spirit to teach you how to control the horrors you see." She takes another drink. "Maybe I'll have forgiven you by then and will help you out."

"I'm not sitting on your tomb. That's creepy. And I'm the one who should be forgiving you," I say, voice rising. "Why you always got to turn things around and make yourself the victim?"

"Talk to my bones and find a bottle of whisky. Both'll be your best friends. Helps ease the pain of dreaming of deaths you can't change."

I roll my eyes, careful not to let her see. No use arguing when she refuses to listen. "Tell me about the girl."

"Long black hair? Blue eyes to match her fancy sundress?" Mama sits the bottle between her legs. "A spoiled, rich brat from town."

"Yeah, I guess. You met her before?"

Red and blue flashing lights and a siren drift from the end of the long driveway leading to the house. The patrol car's wheels had rolled over rain-filled puddles that splattered the sides with mud during its close to thirty-minute journey through unpaved wood-land.

Mama reaches for the railing and uses it to pull herself to her feet. "I'm going to bed. You tell little Georgie Porgie to tell his daddy hello for me. We go way back, me and Dubois senior. He'll remember me."

Does that mean Georgie's dad and Mama did the nasty back in the good ol' days? *Eww.* "Yeah, sure," I drawl. *Thanks, Mama. Scarred for life with that image.*

I squeeze my eyes shut and shove the thought of Mama dying into the farthest recesses of my mind. As much as she drives me crazy, I love her. The idea that she won't be around forever terrifies me.

George parks his patrol car and steps out with a scowl. My gaze travels over his body. I compare the change in his appearance. It's been a month since he went to the graveyard shift, and the beginning of a Dunkin' Donuts belly stretches his starched, tan uniform shirt, but he still looks mighty tasty.

He catches me staring. A smile lights up his face. "Hey, Mala Jean." He waves me over. "Dixie said you found a body?"

"Uh yeah, down in the bayou." My feet tangle together. I must look as drunk as Mama when I stumble over to him on wobbly legs. *Stupid feet.* "Just you coming for her?" I ask, glad my voice doesn't shake too. I wipe sweaty palms on my jeans. *I am a professional.*

George blushes, a light dusting of freckles standing out against his pale skin. The setting sun brings out the fire in his reddish-gold hair. "Sheriff Keyes, Andy, and Bessie are out on Route Seven. A bunch of buffalo broke free of McCaffrey's pasture and ran out into the road. It caused a major pile-up."

"Merciful heavens, anyone dead?"

"Four buffalo got killed. No human fatalities, but some pretty serious injuries. A little boy needed to be flown over to Lafayette. The sheriff's ETA is in an hour with the coroner." He remembers to take a breath before continuing, "So, where is my crime scene?"

"About half a mile away. Got a flashlight? It'll be dark by the time we get there."

George climbs back into his car and comes out with a long-handled flashlight and his shotgun. He pulls a mini-flashlight from his duty belt and hands it over.

"Okay, let's go," I say, leading him into the woods.

He walks with the shotgun pointed skyward, alert for trouble. His eyes scan the dense foliage completely oblivious to my desperate attempts to keep the conversation going so I don't have to think about our destination. How can silence be so deafening? *Say something. Anything.*

George clears his throat. "How's your ma? She been staying out of trouble? I haven't seen her at the station for a few days."

Heat floods my cheeks, and my steps quicken. I swallow hard around the lump in my throat. "Mama's doing just fine, Georgie." Somehow I manage to answer without my voice betraying the immense humiliation I feel. Why did he have to go and irritate me by bringing up Mama? "I'm sure she'll be real grateful for your concern over not seeing her in the drunk tank."

God love him, but it takes a few seconds for the sarcasm to sink in.

"Oh, Mala, you know I didn't mean anything bad by that. I hadn't seen her is all, and I usually see her every weekend…uh, this isn't going too good for me, is it? Might be better if I shut up, huh?"

My eyes roll at George's horrified tone. He has a good soul, not a mean bone in his body, and the faux pas leaves him flustered. Wanting to put him out of his misery, I look over my shoulder with a forced grin that I hope doesn't scare him. "Don't worry. You mess with me, I mess with you."

"Still, I'm sorry. I wasn't thinking. Truth be told, I'm a little nervous." He gives me a sideways glance. "I wouldn't say this to anyone but you 'cause…"

"'Cause you know I'll have your back?" I arch an eyebrow and echo his relieved smile. "Stop avoiding the subject by buttering me up with compliments. What's wrong?"

His hand tightens around the shotgun. "Fine, but don't laugh. Swear."

I cross my heart.

"I've never seen a corpse before, and Sheriff Keyes expects me to work the crime scene alone until he arrives with the coroner." He pauses, and I give him a blank face—the expression I hide behind whenever someone says something hurtful. Or in this case, to keep from laughing my head off over seeing big, bad, ex–football player, super-cop Georgie shaken. It makes him a little less superhero-like and more human.

He gives me a relieved smile. "I don't want to make a fool out of myself."

"Don't worry, I won't let you do anything stupid, like vomit on the body," I tease. A slight chill in the air makes me shiver, and I wrap my arms around myself for comfort. I smell the sulfur stench of the water before I see the girl's body lying on the muddy bank. "There she is."

George plays the flashlight across the corpse. "Oh Jesus, damn it," he whispers, voice choked up. "It's Lainey—Elaine Prince."

"*Lainey.*" I sigh the nickname. Knowing it makes her feel real. She didn't before, not totally. I turn to George, unable to face her glazed stare. "She's exactly how I left her."

"O-oh, well, that's good."

We stand side by side over her body, coming to grips with the harsh reality of her death in our own ways. Seeing her again stirs up volatile emotions I refuse to contemplate too closely. I can't afford to look weak, and breaking down in front of George is not an option. Finally, I can't take the silence and ask, "You gonna pass out?"

"Nah, I'll be fine. I knew Lainey." George clears his throat. "She's…she was a couple of years ahead of me in school. I had a huge crush on her in ninth grade."

He squats down beside Lainey and pulls her dress down over her legs. I almost remind him to put on gloves, but it doesn't matter. Any evidence probably washed away in the swamp.

"Lainey comes from a good family," he says. "Her father's a well-respected preacher. Her mama's always donating time. You know, doing good deeds like feeding and clothing the poor. They'll be crushed."

My rubber boots squelch in the muck as I hunker down next to him. "Prince, huh?"

The name sends tendrils of unease down my spine. The image of Landry Prince's gray eyes form in my mind. His heavy stare followed me whenever I walked past him at school. I memorized his schedule last semester to avoid going to the places where he hung out with his friends. I'd shaken him until a few weeks ago when he started coming into Munchies on the weekends when I work a second job—not sure why he finds my waiting tables so fascinating. The irritating thing is he never speaks to me. Hell, he doesn't even come in alone. He has a different bobble-headed girl clinging to his arm each time, but do his dates keep his attention from turning to me like a needle drawn to a lodestone? Nope!

George glances over at me. The shadows make it difficult to read his expression, which means he can't see how freaked out I am either. "Her younger brother, Landry, went to your school."

My chest tightens. I can't breathe. I close my eyes and focus on drawing in air.

Crap, she is related to him. My juju's the worst today.

"Mala, are you okay?"

I twitch, blinking in George's direction. I wipe my sweaty palms on my jeans. "Oh, yeah, Landry got accepted to play football at the JC. I've seen him on campus."

I try to picture Landry's face, but I've always avoided studying him too closely because he makes my stomach squiggly. The only image that forms clearly is of eyes like the sky before a hurricane. The rest of his features blur and morph into his sister's bloated face and dead-eyed stare. My stomach sours like I ate a tainted batch of crawfish, and I swallow hard. Desperate for a distraction from how queasy I feel, I walk over to a downed log and sit down. "He's never said two words to me, but he struts around campus like he's the king and we're subjects who must bow down before him. He's an arrogant jerk."

Landry watches me, Georgie, like I'm a deer he's tracking. I shiver, rubbing my arms. I've had boys interested in me before. Some hate me. Others are scared or curious because of the witchy rumors. But Landry…he creeps me out but also strangely fascinates me. I can't tell what he's thinking, and the touch of his eyes on my skin feels…electric, like when thunder rumbles overhead just before lightning strikes. I hate it.

George follows and sits beside me. His arm brushes mine. "Sounds about right from what I know of Landry, but Lainey was a good person." I can't see his eyes, but I feel his gaze fall on me. "You know, Mala, you've never gone out of your way to try to get to know folks. Not everyone has it out for you."

I tense up. Of all people, he knows better than anyone the sort of special hell my life has been. "Maybe if I hadn't been bullied all through high school, I'd be more social, Georgie. I can't help that I didn't always have clean clothes, let alone name brands..." I trail off, feeling hot and sticky. *Hellfire! Arguing over the body of a dead girl. How low could I get?* "Look, I have my reasons for not liking Landry, but this is his sister, and I don't mean to disrespect the dead."

George blows out a breath, running a shaky hand through his hair. "No, it's my fault. I shouldn't have said anything. It's not the time or place."

"But you *did* say it."

"Yeah, I did. 'Cause it's true. And life's kind of short to leave things unsaid, don't you think?"

No, I've never thought that. I draw in a deep breath. His fresh, clean scent washes away the scent of decay. George bumps his shoulder into mine, and I almost tumble off the log.

"Damn it, Georgie." I jab my elbow into his side. "How about if we agree to disagree on this issue and call it even?"

George's mouth opens. I can tell by the set look on his face that he has an argument prepared and ready to launch. Then his eyes follow mine. When his gaze lands on Lainey, he shudders. The radio connected to his belt crackles. He speaks quietly into the microphone attached to his lapel and then turns to me.

"We'll finish this discussion later. Sheriff Keyes, Detective Caine, and Coroner Rathbone are at your house with the crime scene techs. You okay to get them alone?"

"Sure, if you aren't too scared to stay here by yourself. I think you'll be fine. Just march around and make a lot of noise to scare off any critters. Don't get trigger happy when we return and shoot us on accident," I tease with a flashlight-enhanced grin, then shut off the light to fade ghostlike into the brush.

* * *

The moon lets in faint light through the treetops. I allow my eyes to adjust, then lead my group toward the crime scene. Sheriff Keyes, the parish coroner Dr. James Rathbone, Detective Bessie Caine, and two crime scene technicians with their large flashlights and bags of equipment follow like the pack of stampeding buffalo that caused the traffic accident.

Damn. I'm sick of this crawling, choking feeling of dread. It smothers me with each step. My breaths quicken. I desperately try to take my mind off of seeing Lainey again. I really, really don't want to go back. But I owe it to George to suck it up. Only a selfish loser would abandon him when he's waiting for me. Plus it's part of the job description.

Sheriff Keyes pats my shoulder, and I flinch. "Are you doing okay?" he asks.

My voice cracks, but I manage a shaky smile as I say, "Well, sir, stumbling across that girl's body tonight certainly put some gray hairs on my head. I'll look as stately as you soon enough, if I'm not careful."

He runs his fingers through his silver hair. "I've seen a lot of untimely deaths in my life, and it's never easy or kind on the living."

My head drops as I sigh. "No, it's not."

"All things considered, you handled a difficult situation like a professional."

Joy rushes through me. I squeeze my hands together and hold in my squeal. It won't do to act like a dippy-brained teenager after getting such a high compliment from my hero. The sheriff doesn't know it, but he's the closest thing I have to a father figure. I've idolized him ever since I was a little tot, hanging onto Mama's skirt and trying not to cry as she was carted off to jail. He teases me to make me feel normal. And I tease him back to feel strong. He'll never admit it to me, but he likes my spunk. I overheard him tell Bessie so.

Keep it cool, Mala. "I hope you'll remember you said that when I apply for deputy next year and not all the silly things I've done since you've known me, Sheriff."

He gives me a weary smile. "I don't think that will be a problem. Ah, Bessie's coming. I'll let the two of you take point."

"Yes, sir."

When the chief detective reaches me, I wrap my arm around her waist. "Hey, Bessie, *konmen to yê?*"

"*Çé bon, mèsi,*" Detective Bessie Caine says, squeezing me so tight that I almost trip. When she loosens her grip enough for me to step aside, I see her solemn expression, but I also detect a bit of a twinkle in her dark eyes. She's always been nice to me. Hell, to be honest, she raised me. At least once a week, when Mama got too drunk to drive home, Bessie dragged her out of the bar and dropped her off at the house. She even stayed a bit to make sure I had something to eat since Mama tended to forget that a growing girl needed food.

Bessie sighs. "So, tell me what happened."

I shrug and pull from the safety of her arms. "Pretty much what

I told Ms. Dixie. I found the girl—Lainey Prince—floating in the bayou…"

Bessie places her hand on my shoulder and squeezes. "You didn't mention a name when you called, Malaise. How do you know her?"

"I don't. Georgie recognized her. Speaking of, maybe we can move a little faster 'cause he's all alone and kind of freaked about the gators."

Sheriff Keyes chuckles from behind. "Oh, is he?"

Instant regret stabs a hole in my chest. I didn't realize he'd be able to overhear our conversation. Why did I open my big mouth? Not wanting to make George look bad, I say, "George secured the crime scene, and he's protecting it from gators. I also saw tracks this morning for Mamalama. She's the biggest razorback we've got in these parts. It's lucky I found Lainey before that old boar came for water and smelled her, or the boar might've eaten her."

Sheriff Keyes points the flashlight directly at my face. "That's a gory thought."

Blinking, I shrug and pick up my pace. "I like to watch mob movies. Pigs eat anything. I've heard the best way to dispose of a body is to throw it in a pigpen. Not that I've been researching body disposal for a specific reason or anything." *Oh God, Mala shut up.*

Bessie's shoulders twitch, her version of a knee-slapping guffaw.

I blush and duck my head, wishing I could rewind the last few minutes. Great. I protected George's reputation by making myself look like a blithering idiot.

The report of a gunshot fills the air and, with it, a shout.

"Georgie!" I yell, and lurch forward. *I never should've left him alone.*

Acknowledgments

To the readers of the *Dark Paradise Series*, thank you. If these novels allowed you to escape for a single second from the troubles of your daily life, then I truly have attained my dream.

This series was a labor of love, and I am grateful to the many people who have helped me along the way. Without your support, I would not be seeing a lifelong dream come true. My love and gratitude goes to my family, whose unwavering support inspired me. Nate, my soul mate, thank you for talking me off of the ledge whenever I wanted to quit and for keeping me supplied with chocolate and peach tea. Kierstan and Maxwell, Mama could not have done this without your patience and love. You inspire me every day. Dreams are attainable when your loved ones believe in you. Never give up. To my parents and, later, my in-laws, you cultivated a love of reading and writing in your children and grandchildren. Thank you for that gift. To my supportive siblings, I love you.

To my amazing agent, Kathleen Rushall, you are my champion, a friend, and the Ned Stark of my heart. You never gave up hope and found us the perfect home in Grand Central Publishing. To my amazing editors, Alex Logan, Debra Manette, and Chris Gage, I appreciate the opportunity that you have given me. You amaze me with your questions, your insight, and your willingness to push me to be the best that I can be. My gratitude to Madeleine Colavita and the extraordinary Grand Central team, who work so hard behind the scenes to make their authors feel special and wonderful. To J.A. Redmerski, thank you for your wonderful words. I'm thrilled and encouraged every time I read your blurb.

A special shout-out goes to the amazing folks at AQC, especially the Speculative Fiction group. I found you when I needed you the most. Thank you to my amazing critique partners. Kate Evangelista, you were the first person other than family to read my work. Thank you for letting me know that I didn't completely suck at writing and for being a mentor, a friend, and a psychic twin. You taught me how to grow in my craft, supported me when I thought all was lost, and cheered me on when things went well. Carla Rehse and Sarah Gagnon, my writing sisters, the two of you mean the world to me. We've been through the thick of it, and we've come out stronger. Thanks for reading my rough first chapters and making them shine. Donald McFatridge, King of Echoes, thanks for getting my twisted sense of humor by being even more twisted. You're the funniest man I know. Michelle Hauck, Queen of Plotholes, thank you for catching my dangling threads. Without you nothing in this story would make a lick of sense.

Thank you to my awesome betas, Joyce Alton, Jennifer Troemner, Diana Robicheaux, Debra Kopfer, Jordan Adams, Jason Peridon, Kierstan Sandro, Bessie Slaton, Jonathan Allen, Christine Berman, and Margaret Fortune. You all rock! I couldn't have done this without you and so many others from AQC.

To my wonderful friends and coworkers at BCP, thank you for listening to my crazy ideas. You supported me when I only thought of this as an unattainable dream. I appreciate each and every one of you.

About the Author

Angie Sandro was born at Whiteman Air Force Base in Missouri. Within six weeks, she began the first of eleven relocations throughout the United States, Spain, and Guam before the age of eighteen.

Friends were left behind. The only constants in her life were her family and the books she shipped wherever she went. Traveling the world inspired her imagination and allowed her to create her own imaginary friends. Visits to her father's family in Louisiana inspired this story.

Angie now lives in Northern California with her husband, two children, and an overweight Labrador.

Author Web site: http://anjeasandro.blogspot.com/

Twitter: @AngieSandro

Facebook: http://facebook.com/pages/Angie-Sandro/253044268078356